A CHRISTMAS CAROL MURDER

The Dickens of a Crime Mystery Series
by Heather Redmond

A Tale of Two Murders

Grave Expectations

A Christmas Carol Murder

The Pickwick (coming in November 2021!)

A CHRISTMAS CAROL MURDER

HEATHER REDMOND

KENSINGTON
PUBLISHING CORP.

www.kensingtonbooks.com

KENSINGTON BOOKS are published by
Kensington Publishing Corp.
119 West 40th Street
New York, NY 10018

First Kensington Hardcover Printing: October 2020

ISBN-13: 978-1-4967-1720-7 (ebook)

ISBN-13: 978-1-4967-2049-8
First Kensington Trade Paperback Printing: October 2021

10 9 8 7 6 5 4 3

Printed in the United States of America

For Peggy Bird, who is missed. You are welcome to haunt us anytime.

Cast of Characters

Charles Dickens*	23	Our sleuth
Kate Hogarth*	20	His fiancée
George Hogarth*	52	Kate's father, music critic, newspaper editor
Georgina Hogarth*	42	Kate's mother
Frederick Dickens*	15	Charles's brother and boarder
Mary Hogarth*	16	Kate's sister
William Aga	28	Charles's fellow journalist
Mrs. Julie Aga	17	An underemployed actress
Emmanuel Screws	67	A countinghouse owner
Jacob Harley	67	A business owner
Primus Harley	30	A member of the Harley family
Edward Pettingill	28	A member of the Screws family
Betsy Pettingill	22	Edward's wife
Powhatan Fletcher	32	A countinghouse employee
Amelia Osborne	25	Mr. Fletcher's fiancée
Mrs. Dorset	58	Mr. Screws's housekeeper
Johnny Dorset	23	Mrs. Dorset's son

Hugh Appleton	45	A chain manufacturer
Sir Silas Laurie	37	A coroner
Breese Gadfly	23	A songwriter
Aaron Vail*	39	An American ambassador
Lucy Fair	13	Leader of the Blackfriars Bridge mudlarks
Timothy "Dickens"	0	An infant

*Real historical figures

"Marley was dead, to begin with. There is no doubt whatever about that."

—Charles Dickens, *A Christmas Carol*

"It was only a change in the wind, towards dawn, that enabled the firemen to get the blaze under control . . ."

—Michael Slater, *Dent Uniform Edition of Dickens' Journalism*

"Now I know what a ghost is. Unfinished business, that's what."

—Salman Rushdie, *The Satanic Verses*

Chapter 1

Hatfield, Hertfordshire, England, December 1, 1835

They hadn't found the body yet. Old Sal was surely dead. Feathers had caught on candles, igniting the blaze. Maybe a yipping dog had some part in the fiery disaster. The marchioness's advanced age had surely contributed to the fatal misadventure. The marquess, her son, had nearly killed himself in a futile attempt to rescue her.

Charles Dickens's cough forced him to set down his pen. Ink dribbled from it, obscuring his last few words. He found it hard to stay seated, so he pushed his hands through his unruly dark hair, as if pressing on his sooty scalp would keep him on the pub bench. Only three hours of sleep before being dragged from his bed to make the twenty-three-mile journey from his rooms at Furnival's Inn in London that morning. Nervous energy alone kept his pen moving.

He rubbed his eyes, gritty with grime and fumes from the fire, both the massive one that had destroyed the still-smoking ruins of Hatfield House's west wing, and the much smaller one here in the taproom at Eight Bells Pub. Some light came in from out of doors, courtesy of a quarter-full moon, but the windows were small.

He called for a candle and kept working.

Putting the messy slip of paper aside, he dipped his pen in his inkwell. Starting again, he recalled the devastation of the scene, the remains of once noble apartments now reduced to rubble and ash. He filled one slip after another, describing the scene, the architecture, the theories.

When he ran out of words, he let his memories of massive oaken Tudor beams, half-burned; heaps of bricks; lumps of metal; buckets of water; black-faced people; and unending, catch-in-your-throat soot—all that remained of forty-five rooms of storied, aristocratic things—fade away.

The ringing of St. Ethelreda's venerable church bells returned him to the moment. Had it gone eight p.m. already? Hooves and the wheels of a cart sounded in the narrow street outside. A couple of men passed by, discussing the fire. The door of the pub opened and closed, allowing the flash from a lantern to illuminate the dark room.

Charles noted the attempts to make the room festive. Greenery had been tacked to the blackened beams and draped around the mantelpiece. He thought he saw mistletoe mischievously strung up in that recess to the left of the great fireplace.

Next to it, a man slumped in a chair. He wore a tired, stained old surtout and plaid trousers with a mended tear in the knee. Next to him waited an empty stool, ready for an adoring wife or small child to sit there.

Charles stacked his completed slips of paper on the weathered table and took a fresh one from his pile, the pathos of that empty seat tugging at him. He began to write something new, imagining that last year at this time, a sweet little girl sat on the stool, looking up at the old, beaten man. How different his demeanor would have been then!

Charles drew a line between his musings and the lower blank

part of the page. His pen flew again, as he made the note. *Add a bit of melancholy to my Christmas festivities sketch.*

Unbidden, the serving maid delivered another glass of hot rum and water. The maid, maybe fourteen, with wide, apple-colored cheeks and a weak chin, gave him a sideways glance full of suspicion.

He grinned at her and pointed to his face. "Soot from the fire. I'm sending a report back to London." His hand brushed against his shoulder, puffing soot from his black tailcoat into his eyes.

She pressed her lips together and marched away, her little body taut with indignation. Well, she didn't understand he had to send his report by the next mail coach. Not much time for sentiment or bathing just yet.

By the time he finished his notes, the drinks hadn't done their job of settling his cough. He knew it would worsen if he lay down so he opened his writing desk to pull out a piece of notepaper.

Dearest Fanny, he wrote to his sister. *Where to begin? I wrote to my betrothed this morning so I thought I should send my news to someone else. Was ever a man so busy? I am editing my upcoming book. Did I tell you it will be called* Sketches by Boz? *I have to turn in the revisions for volumes one and two by the end of the year, in advance of the first volume releasing February eighth. I am also working on an operetta, thanks to that conversation with your friend John Hullah, in my head, at least. I hope to actually commence writing it as soon as my revisions are done.*

I remember all the happy Christmas memories of our earliest childhood, the games and songs and ghost stories when we lived in Portsmouth, and hope to re-create them in my own sweet home next year. How merry it will be to share Christmas with the Hogarths! To think that you, Leticia, and I will all be settled soon with our life's companions. Soon we will know the sounds of happy children at our hearths and celebrate all the joys that the season should contain in our private chambers.

He set down his pen without signing the letter. It might be that he would have more to add before returning to London. He had no idea how long it would be before they recovered the Marchioness of Salisbury's body, if indeed, anything was left. Restacking his papers, he considered the question of her jewels. Had they burned? At least the priceless volumes in the library all had survived, despite the walls being damaged.

His brain kept churning, so he pulled out his copy of *Sketches by Boz*. He would edit for a while before retiring to his room at the Salisbury Arms. No time for sleep when work had to be done.

Pounding on the chamber door woke him. Daylight scarcely streamed around the tattered edges of the inn's curtain. Charles coughed. He still tasted acrid soot at the back of his throat. Indeed, it coated his tongue.

The pounding came again as he scratched his unshaven chin. Had the *Morning Chronicle* sent someone after him? He'd put his first dispatch from the fire on the mail coach. Pulling his frock coat over his stained shirt, he hopped across the floor while he tugged on his dirty trousers. Soot puffed into the air with each bounce.

"Coming, coming," he called.

The hinges squeaked horribly when he opened the door. On the other side stood a white-capped maid. She wore a dark cloak over her dress. A bundle nestled between her joined arms. Had she been kicking the door?

"Can I help you?" Charles asked, politely enough for the hour. To his right, his boots were gone. He had left them to be polished.

The girl lifted her bundle. The lump of clothes moved.

He frowned, then leaned over the lump. A plump face

topped by a thatch of black hair stared back. A baby. Was she hoping for alms? "What's your name, girl?"

"Madge, sir. Madge Porter."

"Well, Madge Porter, I can spare you a few coins for the babe if you'll wait for a moment. Having hard times?"

She stared hard at him. He realized the cloaked figure was the tiny serving maid from the Eight Bells. "He's my sister's child."

"I see. Is she at work?" He laugh-choked. "She's not in here with me, if that's what you're thinking."

Her mouth hung open for a moment. "No, sir, I don't think that."

"What, then?" He glanced around for his overcoat, which had a few coins in a pocket. "What is the babe's name?"

"Timothy, sir." She tightened her weak chin until her pale skin folded in on itself. "Timothy Dickens?" she warbled.

"Dickens?" He took another glance at the babe. Cherry red, pursed lips, and a squashed button of a nose. He didn't see any resemblance to his relatives. His voice sharpened. "Goodness, Madge, what a coincidence."

Her voice strengthened. "I don't think so, sir."

He frowned. The serving maid did not seem to understand his sarcasm. "I've never been to Hatfield before. My family is from Portsmouth. I don't know if your Timothy Dickens is a distant relative of mine or not. Who is his father?"

"She died in the fire."

He tilted his head at the non sequitur. "Who?"

"My sister. She died in the fire. She was in service to old Sarey."

Charles coughed, holding the doorjamb to keep himself upright. This was fresh news. "How tragic. I didn't hear that a maid died."

"They haven't found the bodies."

"That I know. I'm reporting on the fire, but then, I told you that. Thank you for the information. I'll pay you for it if you wait a moment for me to find my purse."

She thrust the bundle toward him. "Timothy is yer son, sir. You need to take him."

Charles took a step back, waving his hands. "No he isn't."

"He's four months old. It would have been last year, around All Hallow's Eve. Do you remember the bonfire? She's prettier than me, my Lizzie. Her hair is lighter, not like yers or mine."

"Truly, I've never been in Hatfield before now," he said gently. "I work mostly in London."

She huffed out a little sob. He sensed she was coming to a crescendo, rather like a dramatic piece of music that seemed pastoral at first, then exploded. "I know yer his daddy, sir. I can't take him. My parents are dead."

He coughed again. Blasted soot. "I'm sorry. It's a terrible tragedy. You're young to be all alone with a baby."

Her entire being seemed to shudder, then, like the strike of a cobra, she shoved the wriggling bundle into his arms and dashed down the passage.

His arms fluttered like jelly for a moment, as if his bones had fled with the horror of the orphaned child's appearance, until the baby opened its tiny maw and Charles found his strength.

Then he realized the blankets were damp. Little fatherless, motherless Timothy whoever-he-was had soiled himself. The baby wailed indignantly but his aunt did not return.

Charles completed his reporting duties with one hand while cradling the infant, now dressed in Charles's cleanest handkerchief and spare shirt, in the other arm. Infant swaddling dried in front of the fire. When Charles had had his body and soul together well enough to chase after little Madge Porter, the proprietor of the Eight Bells had told him she wasn't due there until the evening.

He'd begged the man for names of any Porter relatives, but

the proprietor had been unhelpful. Charles had tripped over to St. Ethelreda's, still smelling smoke through a nose dripping from the cold. The canon had been of no use and in fact smelled of Hollands, rather than incense. He went to a barbershop, holding the baby while he was shaved, but the attendant refused to offer information.

When the babe began to cry again, he took him to a stable yard and inquired if they had a cow. A stoic stableman took pity on him and sent him to his quiet wife, a new mother herself. She agreed to nurse the child while Charles went to Hatfield House to see if the marchioness had been found yet.

He attempted to gain access to the marquess, still directing the recovery efforts. While waiting, he offered the opinion that they should pull down the remaining walls, which looked likely to kill the intended rescuers more assuredly than anything else in the vast acreage of destruction. Everyone coughed, exhausted, working by rote rather than by intelligence.

After a while, he gave up on the marquess. He interviewed those working in the ruins to get an update for the *Chronicle*, then went to the still-standing east wing of the house to see the housekeeper. She allowed him into her parlor for half a crown. The room's walls were freshly painted, showing evidence of care taken even with the servant's quarters. A large plain cross decorated the free space on the wall, in between storage cupboards.

The housekeeper had a tall tower of graying hair, stiffened by some sort of grease into a peak over her forehead. Her black gown and white apron looked untouched by the fire. When she spoke, however, he sensed the fatigue and the sadness.

"I have served this family for thirty-seven years," she moaned. "Such a tragedy."

He took some time with her recital of the many treasures of the house, storing up a collection of things he could report on, then let her share some of her favorite history of the house. But he knew he needed to return to gather the baby from the stableman's wife soon.

"Do you have a Lizzie Porter employed here?"

"Yes, sir." The housekeeper gave a little sob and covered her mouth. "In the west wing, sir. I haven't seen her since the fire."

His fingers tingled. "Do you think she died?"

"I don't know, sir. Not a flighty girl. I doubt she'd have run off if she lived."

"Not a flighty girl?" He frowned. "But she has a babe." He was surprised to know she had kept her employment.

The housekeeper shook her head. "She's an eater, sir, but there never was a babe in her belly."

The story became steadily more curious. "Did she take any leave, about four months ago? In July or August?"

The housekeeper picked up her teacup and stared at the leaves remaining at the bottom. "An ague went around the staff in the summer. Some kind of sweating sickness. She had it like all the rest. Went to recuperate with her sister."

"Madge?"

She nodded absently. "Yes, that Madge. Just a slip of a girl. Hasn't come to work here but stayed in the village."

"I've met her. How long was Lizzie with her?"

"Oh, for weeks. She came back pale and thin, but so did a couple of other girls. It killed one of the cook's helpers. Terrible." The housekeeper fingered a thin chain around her neck.

It didn't sound like a group of girls made up the illness to help Lizzie hide her expectations, but the ague had been timed perfectly for her to hide wee Timothy's birth. Who had been the babe's wet nurse?

"Do you know where Madge lives?"

"Above the Eight Bells, sir. Servants' quarters." The housekeeper set down her cup and rose, indicating the interview had ended.

Charles checked around the pub again when he returned to

town, just a short walk from the grand, if sadly diminished, house. The quarters for servants were empty. Madge seemed to have gone into hiding. How she could abandon her nephew so carelessly, he did not know, but perhaps she was too devastated by her sister's death to think clearly.

A day later, Charles and the baby were both sunk into exhaustion by the long journey to London. Charles's carriage, the final step of the trip, pulled up in front of a stone building. Across from Mary-le-Bow Church in Cheapside, it had shop space, three floors of apartments, and a half attic on top. He'd had to hire a carriage from the posting inn where the coach had left them on the outskirts of town. While he had no trouble walking many miles, carrying both a valise and an infant was more than he could manage. At least they'd kept each other warm.

He made his awkward way out of the vehicle, coughing as the smoky city air hit his tortured lungs. In his arms, the babe slept peacefully, though he had cried with hunger for part of the long coach journey.

Charles's friends, William and Julie Aga, had taken rooms here, above a chophouse. The building exuded the scent of roasting meats. His stomach grumbled as he went up the stairs to his friends' chambers. William was a reporter, like Charles, though more focused on crime than government.

Charles doubled over, coughing, as he reached the top of the steps. He suspected if he'd had a hand free to apply his handkerchief, it would come away black again.

The door to the Agas' rooms opened before he had the chance to knock.

"Charles!" William exploded. "Good God, man, what a sound to torture my ears."

Charles unbent himself and managed a nod at his friend. William had the air of a successful, fashionable man-about-town, even at his rooms on a Thursday evening. He wore a paisley waistcoat under an old black tailcoat, which fit him like it had been sewn directly on his broad-shouldered body. They both prided themselves on dressing well. His summer-golden hair had darkened due to the lack of sun. He had the look of a great horseman, though Charles knew that William, like he, spent most of his time hunched over a paper and quill.

"I like that fabric," Charles said. "Did Julie make you that waistcoat?"

"Charles." William waved his arms. "Whatever are you carrying in your arms?"

Charles dropped his valise to the ground. It grazed his foot. He let out a yelp and hopped. "Blast it! My toe."

William leaned forward and snatched the bundle from Charles's arm. The cloth over little Timothy's face slid away, exposing the sleeping child. "No room in the inn?"

"Very funny," Charles snarled. He rubbed his foot against the back of his calf. "That smarted."

"Whose baby?"

"A dead serving maid's. I remember you said that a woman across the hall from you had a screaming infant. Do you think she might be persuaded to feed this one? He's about four months old."

William rubbed his tongue over his gums as he glanced from Timothy to Charles, then back again.

"He needs to eat. I don't want to starve him. Also, I think he's a little too warm." Charles gave Timothy an anxious glance.

"Let's hope he isn't coming down with something." William stepped into the passage and gave a long-suffering sigh. Then, he crossed to the other side and used his elbow to bang on the door across from his. "Mrs. Herring?"

Charles heard a loud cry in the room beyond, a muttered imprecation, and a child's piping voice, then the door opened. A girl about the age of his youngest brother, Boz, opened the door.

"Wot?" she said indistinctly, as she was missing several teeth.

"I need your mother," William said, smiling at the girl.

The girl turned her head partway and shrieked for her mother. A couple of minutes later the lady of the house arrived, a fat babe burping on her shoulder. She appeared as well fed as the infant, with rounded wrists tapering into fat fingers peering out from her cotton dress sleeves.

"Mr. Aga!" she said with a smile.

Charles instantly trusted Mrs. Herring's sweet smile. Her hand had gone to the top of her daughter's head for a caress, the sort of woman who genuinely enjoyed her children.

"Good lady," Charles began. "I've been given the custody of this orphaned child due to a rather dramatic situation. Might you be able to take him in to nurse?"

Mrs. Herring stepped toward William. She took one look at the sleeping Timothy and exclaimed, "Lor bless me!" She handed her larger infant over to her daughter, then reached out her hands to William. He promptly placed the bundle into the mother's arms.

Charles saw Timothy stir. He began to root around. "Hungry. Hasn't been nourished since this morning."

"Poor mite," Mrs. Herring cooed. "How could you have let this happen? They must be fed regularly."

"I don't know how to care for a baby," Charles admitted. "But I remembered my friends had you as a neighbor. Can you help him?"

"We've no room for the tiny lad," Mrs. Herring said sternly. She coaxed her daughter back inside.

"I can pay for his board," Charles responded.

Mrs. Herring didn't speak but her eyebrows lifted.

"Just for tonight at first," William suggested with an easy smile. "You can see the situation is desperate."

Charles reached into his pocket and pulled out a shilling. "I'm good for it. Truly. This would pay for days of his care if I hire a wet nurse. He has an aunt but she disappeared. I couldn't find her before I had to return to London."

"We'll talk to you again in the morning," William said. "I won't leave the building until we've spoken."

"Where am I to put him?" she asked, staring rather fixedly at the shilling. "The bed is full and we don't have a cradle."

William nodded wisely, as if he'd thought of this already. "Mr. Dickens and I will consult with my wife and bring something suitable. If you can feed him while we wait?"

Mrs. Herring reached out her free hand. Charles noted she had clean nails. She seemed a good choice for wet nurse. He placed the shilling in her palm and prayed they could make longer-term arrangements for a reasonable price.

Timothy let out a thin wail.

"He sounds weak," Charles said, guilt coloring his words.

"I'll do what I can." Mrs. Herring glanced at the babe in her arms, then shut the door.

Chapter 2

Charles followed William across the chilly passage to his chambers, happy to have the emergency of baby Timothy's hunger dealt with for now. He couldn't let Timothy die on his watch. What would it say about his future skills as a father? Yes, children might die of illness and from accidents, but not from hunger, not if he could help it.

"You came to the right place," William said in a resigned tone, leading him directly to the fireplace. He gestured Charles to a pair of giltwood chairs with arms in the shape of lions' paws. Charles recognized them as having come from the library of Lugoson House, owned by Julie Aga's baroness aunt. "I can't believe you remembered my neighbors."

"I have an excellent sense of recall. Lady Lugoson offering you her castoffs?" Charles asked, proving his point.

"She's redecorating her library," William said. "Wanted to remove anything her late husband liked from the room."

"Understandable. Dreadful man from all accounts," Charles said. He glanced around the room. The Agas had moved in only recently, but they'd finished decorating. A games table complete with black and white pattern painted across the top waited next to a long decorative bench and a deal table pressed against the wall opposite to the fireplace. Three inexpert watercolors were framed on the walls and the coal hod was new and decorative. The mantelpiece held two enameled candlesticks and a framed duo of silhouettes that someone had cut of William and Julie. "Now, as to the matter at hand. Do you think you can talk Mrs. Herring into keeping Timothy?"

"No," William said. "Her husband makes a decent wage and their rooms are crawling with children as it is."

"That is bad." Charles sighed. He held his hands out to the fire, attempting to warm them. "I am half dead and about as hungry as the babe. I can't think of where else to take an infant who still needs to be nursed."

"Someone might be able to bring him up by hand. He is old enough," William opined while Charles's stomach rumbled.

"I'll feed you, Charles." Julie Aga came into the room, wiping her hands on her apron. Just seventeen and a fiery redhead, she was young to be a wife of eight months, but her unconventional upbringing and time treading the boards as an actress had made her grow up quickly. "We ate hours ago, but I have the remains of a roast and a couple of slices of potato."

"If you can add a cup of tea, I'll take it." He smiled at her. "Thank you."

After she departed, William opened a chest hidden behind the coal hod and pulled out a bottle of rum and two glasses. He poured, then added hot water from the kettle over the fire into it.

"Many thanks," Charles said, taking his share. "Though it may put me to sleep."

"What are you going to do with the baby?" William asked. "You'll have no problem finding someone to take it for your shillings. The problem is, will they keep it alive?"

"I know it's hard to find a place with trustworthy, clean wet nurses who won't dose the babies with laudanum. Your Mrs. Herring is ideal."

"I know," William muttered. "I should go and pull out a drawer from the bedroom chest so he has something to sleep in for tonight."

"Do you have an old towel or blanket for it?"

William nodded. "The problem is really what to do with Timothy tomorrow."

"Who is Timothy?" Julie asked, coming back in with a tray. On it was a plate with meat, potatoes, and bread. Next to that rattled a small teapot and a china cup.

William stood and pulled the game table over to Charles. Julie set down her tray, then busied herself with pouring water over the tea leaves. Charles stared at the elaborate and messy braid coiled around the back of her head. His fiancée, Kate Hogarth, could never manage such a hairstyle with her fine blondish brown locks. Nor did she have the time to fiddle with her hair, with abundant younger siblings needing her attention.

Looking away, he drained his rum and water with one long gulp. "Timothy is the baby I brought with me from Hatfield. His mother died in the fire and his aunt seemed convinced I was his father."

Julie sloshed hot water over the tray. She lifted the kettle away and placed it back on its nail, then tore off her apron and blotted up the boiling water before it buckled the tray's painted surface.

"You don't say," William exclaimed, replacing the lid. "A father? You?"

"Kate will be devastated," Julie said in a similar tone of surprise. "I hope it isn't true."

"You know it isn't true," Charles rejoined. "I'd never been in Hatfield before this month."

William winced and poured more rum into his glass, motioning to Julie to pour water over it. "Why did she think you were the father?"

"I don't know. She disappeared after that. Quite young for the responsibility of a child and distraught over her dead sister."

"The kettle is empty," Julie said. "Stop talking for a minute so I can refill it."

Julie went for her water can while Charles stared blankly at the brown glazed teapot, not much bigger than a child's plaything.

"She must be getting along with Lady Lugoson and her son, for you to have received all this largesse," Charles said.

"Lady Lugoson asked Julie to take watercolor lessons with her," William explained. "They started in October."

"Oh, they are spending time together." Charles nodded wisely. "That makes sense. Lord Lugoson is at school?"

"Yes, her son is at Harrow. Not too far from my father's school."

"That would give the lady more leisure time," Charles said. "I saw her at the theater last month."

Julie bustled back into the room and put the teakettle over the fire. She tossed the wet apron on the bench, then came to perch on the corner of her husband's chair. "Now, do tell everything, Charles. Let's have some excitement."

"You'd have rather a lot with a four-month-old infant in your rooms," Charles suggested.

Julie and William glanced at each other, then back at him.

Charles knew Julie had lost a baby earlier in the year. He'd seen no signs of her increasing since. He cleared his throat awkwardly, hoping he hadn't caused her pain. "Excellent training for when you have your own children. He'll be across the hall with Mrs. Herring tonight. William, do you think she would nurse the child as long as he lived in your rooms?" he asked, as if the thought had only just occurred to him.

"Why would I want him to do that?" William asked.

"Practice," Charles said patiently. "When I have time, I'll go back to Hatfield and track down the aunt."

"You can't do it tomorrow," Julie reminded him. "We have our caroling party in the evening."

"Yes. My Kate is looking forward to it," Charles assured her. "But you can see I'm left with no options for the poor babe. Can you take him?"

Julie's gaze moved from one end of the room to the other. She seemed in a considering mood, rather than a sorrowful one. "I suppose I could try."

"Only until you have time to return to Hatfield, Charles," William cautioned. "There will be an inquest on the fire?"

"Once all the bodies are found." Charles shook his head. "As I was leaving town, I heard they were finding bones."

"Good," William said. "I suppose we can keep the baby for a week or so, if Mrs. Herring will agree to be his wet nurse."

Julie nodded. "We won't have him all the time, then. I'll be able to leave him with her and do the marketing."

"Yes, and Charles will pay for everything," William said with a smile.

"No Kate?" Julie Aga asked from one of the giltwood chairs the next night when William and Charles walked into the Agas' chambers after their walk home from the *Morning Chronicle's* offices.

William immediately went to his wife and looked down at the bundle in her arms.

"She'll be along with her sister Mary," Charles assured her, smiling at the rosy-cheeked babe. "My brother Fred has started working in a law office in Birchin Lane, so he should be here soon."

"That's so convenient to hear." Julie handed Timothy to William. "You should think about moving to this building. The

Herrings cannot last much longer. They are fit to bursting out of their chambers with all of those children."

"Kate has agreed to Furnival's Inn," Charles said stiffly. It had been a topic of much discussion and he did not wish to revisit it. He'd made a disastrous attempt to live in Brompton near the Hogarths' home over the summer that was best forgotten.

Here in town, the young literary lions of London had been seeking him out of late, like his mentor and friend William Ainsworth, who had introduced Charles to his new publisher. They knew to find him in his current rooms.

"I'll take Timothy to Mrs. Herring in a minute," Julie told them. "She's agreed to have him overnight, so that she can feed him just before they sleep and right when he wakes up. During the day I'm supposed to try to give him porridge."

"Well done," Charles praised.

"That sounds like a lot of work." William pulled off his damp coat and hat and spread them over the fire screen to dry out a bit. Charles followed suit.

"Most new mothers can't sleep much, because of the baby needing to be fed." Julie bent over the sleeping baby and kissed its forehead. "This is good, easy practice for me. If he won't take enough porridge then I have to give him back to Mrs. Herring to be fed."

"I did send a letter to place an advertisement about the baby in the newspaper that serves the Hatfield area," Charles said.

His words seemed to fall on deaf ears, with both Agas cooing over the baby. After Julie gave him a final kiss, William tucked Timothy up against his shoulder and went to give him to Mrs. Herring.

Charles sat and pointed his toes at the fire. It had sleeted during the first part of their walk from the *Chronicle's* offices at 332 Strand, though the skies were dry again by the time they arrived.

Julie dropped into the matching armchair. "Can I speak to you about something serious before everyone arrives?" She cleared her throat. "I couldn't sleep two nights ago. I went for a walk, like I used to."

"You used to run errands for Percy Chalke all hours of the night," Charles said, remembering the actor-manager who had employed her. "I assumed you'd ceased such tomfoolery."

"I couldn't sleep," she repeated. "I ended up on the foreshore by Blackfriars Bridge, where our mudlark friends sleep."

Charles shook his head at her. He and William had started a charity to help a small band of young people who made their living from scrounging by the river, but that didn't mean they were tame. "It's not safe for you to be down there alone."

"I'm good at blending in. I'm an actress, remember? It's only the upper classes who are afraid on the streets at night."

"You are the upper classes now," Charles cautioned.

"Not really." She shook her head abruptly, as if to banish a memory. "Charles, I saw something that disturbed me, and I'm worried about Lucy Fair."

"She's turning into a young lady," Charles said, remembering how he'd thought the mudlark gang leader was filling out when he'd seen her in the summer. Now, with winter weather, she was bundled up again, hiding her curves.

"New mudlarks are encroaching on Lucy's territory," Julie explained. "Older boys. And older boys could mean trouble to a girl that age."

"It would be hard for her gang of younger boys to protect her," Charles agreed.

"Plus the lot of them might be oblivious to the danger." Julie's brow creased. "Could you wander down there sometime soon and judge the situation for yourself?"

He moved his feet to change the angle of the drying. "Have you told William?"

Julie nodded. "Yes, but he has had so many busy evenings."

Charles closed his eyes. "I'll manage it. Could you please put the kettle on? I don't want the Hogarths to take a chill."

After a moment, he heard her skirts rustle. With a sigh, he

grabbed today's *Morning Chronicle* from the deal table and applied himself to the theater notices.

Julie had not yet reappeared when he heard a knock on the door. He went and opened it, expecting William's return, but instead it was his brother, accompanied by the Hogarth sisters. Clapping his hands together, he kissed his fiancée, Kate Hogarth, on the cheek.

"We met in the street," Kate explained. She looked very merry, with pink cheeks and rosy lips. Her dark blond hair curled around her jaw under her green velvet bonnet. She wore an expensive white velvet cape edged in black that she'd inherited from Christiana Lugoson. He could see her pale yellow and blue tartan dress hem underneath.

"How ever did you manage to keep that clean?" he asked, stroking her arm.

Mary grinned at him. "She made me walk in front of her to catch all the mud."

He chucked Mary under the chin. "I well believe it. What do you think of my hardworking brother?"

Mary glanced at Fred, then rolled her eyes as she turned back. "I hope he is applying himself."

Fred's merry expression went mulish. He had a round face, but a growth spurt had thinned his body for now and his breeches were just short enough to need replacing.

Julie reappeared with the kettle and set it on its hook over the fire before greeting everyone.

"Are you well?" Kate asked, clasping Julie's bare hands with her gloved ones.

"I'm very well." Julie opened her mouth again, and Charles, worried that she might say something about the baby, shook his head sharply. Julie's head lifted proudly. "Just a bit flustered. Would you like tea?"

"We're fine," Kate said. "We didn't walk here all the way from Brompton."

William ducked into the room. "Are we ready? I'll just put my things back on so we can go."

"Where are we going to carol?" Kate asked.

"On the street right here, I should think. A main thoroughfare like Cheapside?"

"Do we have an order of songs?" Fred asked. "Are there any friends you want us to particularly visit?"

"I hope this is a good way to meet the neighbors," William explained.

"We must collect funds for your Charity for Dressing the Mudlark Children of Blackfriars Bridge," Kate added.

"William croaks like a frog," Julie announced. "He will stand in the back and pretend to sing."

Charles shook his finger in William's direction, but his friend smiled angelically and handed Charles his coat and hat. "Let's start with 'God Rest Ye Merry Gentlemen.' You can croak through that."

Julie pulled a black velvet cape with a matching bonnet and muff from a stand by the door while Charles redressed, and then led the party into the hall.

"Should we all make sure we start on the same note?" Kate asked in the passage.

Charles grinned at her. "Part of the fun of caroling is the surprise of the beginning."

"Ha," William said. "What are we going to use to collect the money?"

Julie muttered something, then vanished back into her chambers. A moment later, she flourished an old top hat. "Your second best, Mr. Aga."

Charles pulled out a pencil and slip of paper from his pocket and wrote *Charity for Dressing the Mudlark Children of Blackfriars Bridge* on it in the darkest letters he could manage, then stuck it upside down under the hatband. "All sorted."

"God," Mary tried to sing tentatively.

"God rest," Kate joined in.

Charles listened as the musical sisters melded their voices together. It wasn't for nothing that their father was a musical genius.

After they sang "remember," Julie, a born performer, joined in, followed by the men. They walked down the hallway and through the second story of the building, then down to the first, where they had their first door open. An elderly gentleman, neatly dressed in cream trousers and a navy jacket, offered them a penny for their troubles. By the time they reached the ground level and the back of the chophouse, Charles was feeling parched, his throat still irritated from the Hatfield fire. They finished their first song outside, in front of the chophouse windows. At the end, a couple of happy, drunken fellows tripped out of the door and gave them a handful of small change.

"Well done," Charles exclaimed. "If this keeps up, we'll have the mudlarks in blankets and shoes all winter."

Fred began, "I saw three ships . . ."

"Come sailing in," William bleated, and then the rest joined in.

They stayed on their side of the street, heading toward St. Paul's. The thoroughfare was lined with buildings similar to the Agas', with shops downstairs and residences upstairs. People were busy about their business, red cheeked and merry when they heard the carolers. They finished that song and started "The Twelve Days of Christmas."

A stop in front of a public house netted them a few shared glasses of hot buttered rum, and they collected pennies from passersby. Eventually, as they sang "The Ditchling Carol" with its exhortation to give to the poor, they found themselves in Finsbury Circus. Its stone-faced terraced houses, home to merchants and gentlemen, circled around a garden. The area was fairly new and quite smart. The clouds parted as they reached a house, creating a nimbus of gray around the nearly full moon.

"Nature's spotlight," breathed Charles.

Kate smiled at him and tucked her hand under his arm as he stared up into the sky.

"The holly and the ivy," sang Julie, beginning another song.

"When they are both full grown," everyone joined in.

They finished three verses of the song before their memories faltered.

"You know, the lights aren't on here," Julie said.

"No audience," Charles agreed. He'd been distracted by the moonlight. "We won't earn any money playing to an empty stage."

"A lot of lights over there," Fred said, pointing to a house a few doors down, stone faced like all the others. "Every window is lit except in the attics. They must be having a party."

"That's perfect." Julie pulled at her husband. The rest of them followed her down the street.

They stopped in front of the steps. A couple of the houses had railings twined with greenery or a wreath on the door. This one had nothing, but every window had a candle in it.

"Christmas should be merrier than this," Charles said, squeezing Kate's arm. He stared up at the door. Something about it seemed vaguely familiar to him.

"I'll decorate our home every year," she promised. "Holly, ivy, evergreens, and mistletoe."

William winked at Charles. He couldn't help but imagine the delight of soft lips under the mistletoe in his own home.

"I'll start." He pulled Kate to the base of the steps. William, Julie, Fred, and Mary crowded in behind him. "Hark! The herald angels sing, Glory to the newborn King; Peace on earth . . ."

As he sang the words, a window on the second story opened, directly over the door. Charles threw back his head and continued to sing lustily, happy to have an audience. "And mercy mild . . ."

Fred boomed out the last phrase in bass counterpoint, "God and sinners reconciled!"

A mass came from the window, heading in their direction. A

thick mass, not a handful of coins. Kate screamed, pulling Charles back as it came at them.

"We didn't sing that badly—" Charles started; then his mouth fell open.

"Holy Mother of God," Mary cried.

The man, for it was a man, dressed in pale trousers and a black tailcoat, snapped up into the air, in a puppet dance far more grotesque than anything ever seen in a theater, then fell again as a loud crack resounded in the winter sky. In an instant, he had crashed onto the front steps of the lit-up house, then rolled down them until he landed faceup on the pavement. The moon highlighted the blood puddling under his shattered body, coloring his gray hair.

Chapter 3

"No!" Kate sobbed, her voice full of emotion.

Charles wrapped his arm around Kate, pulling her head against his shoulder, attempting to prevent her from seeing more of the gruesome sight at the foot of the stone steps. She relaxed into his coat.

William stepped forward, going to one knee next to the body. "Chains," he reported. "He's wearing wrought iron chains around his neck."

"That's why he seemed to bounce," Charles suggested. "He was caught in them."

Mary clutched at Kate's arm. "What a horrible accident."

Kate lifted her head from Charles's chest when Mary's voice caught. She wrapped her arms around her younger sister.

"Fred?" Charles turned to see his brother, his face stiff with shock. The coin-collection hat dangled from one hand. "Tut tut," he said. "Come and comfort the women."

Fred blinked, but Julie went to him and picked up his free hand. They clutched at each other and bent their heads together, facing away from the body.

Charles patted her arm, then went to join William. His fellow reporter had crouched a couple of feet away from the body. "Elderly," Charles said, trying to keep an objective reporter's eye as he stared at the sunken, yellowed cheeks of the corpse. "Male. Taller than average, and exceedingly well fed. Fell out of a second-story window."

"What else?" William asked, crab-walking a few inches to the left.

"Signs of jaundice, and broken veins on his nose and cheeks."

"Unwell," William agreed. "Could he have fainted and fallen? What a notion, given these chains."

"Suicide, perhaps? I heard the chains break." Charles glanced at the door. No one had responded to the commotion and come outside yet.

"I heard that, too." William pointed a gloved finger at the chains. "Good quality. Made for a ship or something like that."

"He was anchored by them," Charles suggested. "What a way to die. And in December, which should be merry."

William ignored his words. "Anchored to something on the house? I agree suicide is a possibility."

Charles glanced up at the window. The candle that had been in it had gone out. It might be found under the man's body. He hoped it didn't catch the man's clothing on fire. He shuddered, remembering Hatfield. No smoke, at least. "He opened the window, wrapped chains around his neck, and jumped?"

William frowned. Before Charles could say more, he heard a low "oh."

He turned quickly and saw Julie slump. Fred caught her, his eyes wide. The top hat dropped from his hand, spilling coins across the pavement. The Hogarth girls rushed to her.

"My poor friend," Kate crooned, helping to support her.

William leapt up and tore off his coat. He spread it on the pavement so Fred could set Julie down.

Julie's head lolled to one side.

"We need to get her out of this cold," Kate said, tucking unconscious Julie's cloak around her skirts.

"We can't leave. We just witnessed a death. I need to fetch a constable," Charles protested.

"What do you think happened? Did she recognize the man who fell?" Mary asked.

"Ahoy there!" Charles called, seeing a hired coach pull onto the circus road. He ran down the street as a gentleman, dressed in a tall hat and a fur-lined overcoat, exited the passenger compartment to the pavement. "I need your carriage, sir," he said to the man. "If you would be so kind as to fetch the constable on the beat, I would be much obliged."

"Whatever for?" The man glanced at the house behind them, probably eager to open his door, then pointed his cane at Charles.

"A man has died, and a lady has collapsed," he explained. He looked up to the coachman's seat. "You, driver, please take yourself to my friends down the street. A lady has fainted."

"I-I believe the constable is most often found to the west," the gentleman stammered. The coachman snapped his whip and his horses moved up the street toward the tragic scene. The gentleman's walking stick clinked against the pavement as he trotted away. "You want me to fetch him?"

"Please, sir." The wind caught at Charles's hat. He grabbed for it, pulling it against his temples. Should he go in search of a constable as well? He glanced up the street and saw Kate bent over the corpse. Mary was next to Julie now.

No, no, he couldn't have that. Kate had much too much eagerness when it came to murder. While he had no trouble with her puzzling out a mystery, staring at dead men could not be a suitable pastime for a gently reared female. He dashed up the street as the carriage drove toward them, then took her by the arm.

"You should go with Julie," he told her. "Take Mary and my brother with you."

William lifted his wife and carried her into the carriage. The coachman fought to keep his mismatched pair of horses steady.

"William insisted on leaving with her," Kate said at Charles's side.

He rapped on the window as the carriage rocked. William pushed it down and peered out.

"How is Julie?" Charles asked.

"Not well."

Charles dug some coins out of his pocket. "Could you take the children with you? When you can, send my brother on his way and have the hackney take Mary home."

"That's much too far for her to go alone," William demurred.

"I can escort her," Fred said, appearing at Charles's shoulder. "We are practically family. Are you coming, Kate?"

"Oh, I'm not leaving," Kate said in the calmest of voices. She waved her muff. "The Agas need to return home right away for Julie's health. No more dillydallying."

Charles knew better. From the pink in her cheeks and the sparkle in her eyes, his fiancée was in the throes of mystery heaven. He handed Mary into the hackney. Fred slid in behind her. "Head toward St. Mary-le-Bow," he instructed the driver. "Then out to Brompton, toward St. Luke's."

The driver sighed visibly. "Better than waitin' with a corpse, upon my soul." He sent the horses coursing forward, circling around the private park.

Charles turned back to Kate. "We should pick up our coins before anyone comes. I wouldn't worry, except they are meant for the mudlarks."

"I'll stand watch," Kate said. "You may scrabble around on the pavement."

He bowed and bent to pick up the coins. "Madam, as you wish."

"Our caroling party ended memorably, but not well." Kate

hesitated, but before she could say more, the front door of the undecorated house opened.

A thin, elderly man in evening dress stood in the doorway above them. The stone staircase distanced him from the body on the pavement below, shrouded in darkness. "What is all this commotion, sir?" he cried, waving a cane in Charles's general direction.

"Do you own this house?" Charles called, grabbing the last of the pennies and dropping them into the hat.

"I have that honor," the man said, in a voice high and cracked with old age.

"Must be deaf and half blind," Charles said in a low voice to Kate. She took his arm and they walked to the side of the iron railing on the sides of the stairs. Up close, Charles could see scrollwork that tugged at his memory, like something he'd peered through as a child. Seven steps led up to the old man and his front door, but they could not traverse them without stepping over the corpse. Also, blood splattered and pooled on the pavement, though the wind kept the worst of the smell from them. "What is your name, sir?"

"Emmanuel Screws, stripling," he replied. "Why have you been making so much noise in front of my house? Humbug, I tell you, on all that caterwauling. I don't hold with carols, sir— they irritate my ears."

"We were collecting for charity, sir." Charles frowned. First the house looked familiar, and now this elderly man. But he'd never been here before. Had he?

"I don't want none and I offer none," was the old man's prompt reply, belying Charles's theory of deafness.

"That is well enough," Charles rejoined, "but did you know you have an upstairs window open?"

"I do?" The old man glanced up instinctively, then back at Charles.

"I can see you, because of the light in your doorway, but can you see down to the base of your front steps?" Charles asked.

"Why?" the man asked suspiciously. "You had better not be leaving me some infant mouser. I won't hold with it, sir. I don't want your cats."

"A man is dead," Kate said gently. "He fell from your window."

The old man's eyes bulged in their wrinkled sockets. "A man? Dead?"

Kate pointed to the base of the steps.

"Who is in your house tonight, sir?" Charles asked.

The man stepped onto his doorstep and peered down. "Is there no lantern?"

Down the street, just within the puddles cast by a streetlight on the corner, Charles did see a lantern swinging, and the shapes of two men. "That will be the constable with your neighbor."

"Which one?" Mr. Screws demanded suspiciously.

"A couple of doors down. Maybe fifty?" Charles asked. "Carries a hooked cane with a silver overlay. Wears a fur coat?"

"Solicitor," Mr. Screws sneered. "Does he think this is Scandinavia? Such extravagance."

The constable arrived with the solicitor, stopping next to Kate. His reinforced top hat sat uneasily at the apex of his sloping forehead. He appeared squat next to the thin but bundled body of the solicitor. "Wot's this now?"

Mr. Screws came down one step as the constable's lantern swung out over the gruesome sight. He gasped and swayed as light illuminated the corpse for a moment, catching at his iron railing with clawed fingers.

Kate reached out a hand as if to catch or console the old gentleman, but he was too far up the stairs.

"Watch yourself," Charles called, reaching a hand through the railing. He only brushed Mr. Screws's trousers before he returned to his doorway.

"Halt," the constable commanded. " 'Oo does this 'ere body belong to?"

Emmanuel Screws froze. After a moment's pause, his shoulders went back and he sneered, an expression that seemed habitual on his worn face. "Jacob Harley, constable. My business partner."

Charles could well believe that both men were the same age. While the living man seemed familiar to him, the dead one caused no pang of memory.

The constable pulled his single-bladed oak rattle from its particular uniform pocket. He moved into the street, lifted it skyward, and spun it to summon other peelers nearby.

At the sound of the whirring clicks of the rattle, the warmly clad solicitor slunk backward down the pavement toward his home. Charles didn't call attention to the man since he had been unlikely to be involved.

"Can I tell you what we saw?" he asked the constable. "I'm Charles Dickens of the *Morning Chronicle* and my fiancée is very chilled."

"I'm fine," Kate insisted. Indeed, her body vibrated with excitement under her cloak. Her love of mystery had reared its head. She stared up at Mr. Screws, hovering on his front step. "Was anyone in the house other than your business partner? Mr. Screws? Do you have a cook? A valet? A maid? Dinner guests?"

The constable put up his hand. "Why don't you go into the house, miss? You don't need to see down 'ere."

"We aren't guests of Mr. Screws," Charles interjected. He displayed the worn top hat in his hand. "We were caroling outside his front door, collecting for charity."

"We were singing 'Hark! The Herald Angels Sing' when the man fell out of the window," Kate added helpfully.

"Just the pair of you?" the constable asked, his eyes narrowing.

"No, we were in a party of six, but one lady fainted. Her

husband took her home, along with our younger siblings. I can tell you how to contact them," Charles said.

The constable sighed. "Give me the names and addresses of all the carolers, sir."

Charles offered the information. In the doorway at the top of the steps, a woman appeared, dressed in a sober black dress, and helped Mr. Screws wrap a shawl around his thin shoulders before disappearing out of sight again.

"Had you ever seen the deceased before?" the constable asked Charles.

"No," he said. "We don't know him."

"You must let the poor man go inside," Kate protested. "He's shivering up there."

"I can't leave the body," the constable said, rather helplessly.

"We'll watch it for you," Charles promised. "You go inside. We were here before and didn't touch anything."

"I only have your word for what you saw."

"Not so. Is it not obvious to you that the man fell to his death from a height?" Charles pointed at the blood congealing on the pavement.

"What about the chains?" the constable asked.

"We haven't touched them," Kate said. "They were around his neck when he fell."

"Did you have the chains in the house?" the constable called to Mr. Screws.

"Yes, but I hadn't noticed them for a couple of days," he said through chattering teeth.

"Why would you have such chains in your house?" Charles asked.

"Business," was Mr. Screws's one-word answer.

Charles heard boots coming up the street. "I hope that's another policeman."

"Me too," muttered the constable. "Look 'ere, did you see anyone else around the property?"

"Only Mr. Screws, and only after the man fell," Charles said. "Our caroling didn't bring anyone out of the houses on this street."

"Very well then," the constable said grudgingly. "The old gentleman can go inside for now."

Mr. Screws stepped inside without another word, and shut the door.

"All the windows had candles here," Kate reminded Charles.

He lifted his hands. "We didn't see anyone in the windows."

"There must be someone else in there," Kate insisted. "Mr. Screws is too frail to have pushed a large man out of a window."

"Then who did it?" the constable asked.

"He could have fallen alone," Charles said, "tangled in those chains somehow."

"Seems unlikely," Kate said. "The butler must have done it."

"There's a butler?" the constable asked.

"A poor jest," Kate said quickly. "Truly, we saw no one else until that woman came into view just now."

The constable narrowed his eyes at her. "You're sure you didn't go inside?"

"We haven't even been on the stairs." Charles rattled the old top hat with the coins. "This is all we were doing, trying to collect for our Charity for Dressing the Mudlark Children of Blackfriars Bridge."

"We've been working with the mudlarks since last winter," Kate added. "We even sent one to school."

"I'm sure you're doing the Lord's work," the constable said.

"What's 'appening 'ere?" said another constable, older, taller, and rougher than the first, as he reached them.

"Suspicious death," the first explained. "Come closer."

The constable lifted his lantern and walked around Charles, then made a Papist gesture when he saw the body. "Fell, I expect."

"From that window," Charles said, pointing up. "There had been a candle in it. Might be underneath the body."

Charles and Kate explained who they were to the second constable. The second constable, an Irishman by the name of Boyd, sent the first constable to the nearest station for additional help.

"You won't be able to leave him here until the coroner's inquiry," Charles said.

"No, but you'll need to attend," Boyd warned.

They nodded their assent. "We will be there," Charles said. "You have our information. Now, can I please take Miss Hogarth home?"

The constable was still distracted by the body. He waved them off. Charles took Kate's arm without further delay and tugged her down the street, moving rapidly through increasing chilly drizzle until they found a free hackney on London Wall.

Once they had settled themselves inside, Charles distracted himself by puzzling over the mysterious death. Even more so, he found himself distracted by that wisp of memory. Why had the house, and the man Screws, seemed so familiar to him?

The next morning, Charles made the excuse of walking to a bakery in Brompton to fetch special treats for the Hogarths as a thank-you for allowing him to sleep in front of their fire. He ducked into a news agent's stand to find the newspaper for Hertfordshire. He wanted to make sure his advertisement about Timothy was running since there had been no responses yet. How long would the Agas and Mrs. Herring remain tolerant of the orphaned babe? He found the ad in the newspaper and hoped letters would be waiting for him when he arrived at Furnival's Inn.

In a sleet of rain mixed with icy shards, he returned to the Hogarths with an assortment of cream-filled buns. A feeling of nostalgia for last summer rushed over him as he ventured past

the Hebrew burying ground where he and his friend Breese
Gadfly had worked on their first song together some six
months before. The memory of the murder then brought his
thoughts back to this new death he had witnessed. What had
the police decided to do with Jacob Harley's body? It had to be
available for the inquest and they wouldn't have left it on the
street.

The man had probably been prosperous enough for a funeral
furnisher. They'd have at least called an undertaker to put the
body in a coffin, even if it had to stay in Mr. Screws's house.

He opened the Hogarths' garden gate, holding his bundle
carefully so the cream wouldn't break free from the buns. Inside the dining room, the youngest Hogarths, twins Helen and
Edward, were running around, chased by older brothers James
and William. All nine of the Hogarth offspring were in the
room, lounging at the piano or sitting at the table if they
weren't on their feet.

Charles set his purchases on the table and Mary came running over to see what he'd brought.

"Just in time," Mrs. Hogarth exclaimed, coming in with a
pot of what smelled like kedgeree. A crock of oatmeal already
waited on the table along with the massive teapot and a jug of
milk.

Mr. Hogarth walked in from down the hall, pulling off fingerless gloves. One of them fell to the floor as he absently attempted to push it into a pocket.

"Cream buns!" cried Mary with an expression of heaven-
sent delight. "For breakfast!"

Georgina rushed for the buns. Despite her trio of slightly
older brothers, she had a greater hunger than all of them. Her
mother set her pot on the table, then slapped Georgina's hand.

"Away wi' ye, troublesome," Mrs. Hogarth said. "Until we
make sure there is enough for all."

Charles counted in his head. "I bought a dozen."

"Such a waste of money," Kate's mother scolded him, in much the same tone she'd used for Georgina. "As if the twins need an entire bun at their age."

"And you with a house to furnish and a wife to pay for," Kate said, coming up beside him with a shy smile. She wore her gray wool, with its faint, faded tartan pattern and fresh white cuffs and collar. A blue ribbon that matched her eyes was stitched around the edge of the collar and she'd reinforced her hem with black that would hide some of the mud in the streets. She had her father's stray glove in her hand.

Charles winked at her and wished he dared steal a kiss. How much longer would they have to wait to be in their own snug space? He had set his hopes on the Agas' rooms in Furnival's Inn when they moved out, but they'd already been promised. For now, he'd made inventory of everyone in the front-facing chambers with the best light, and anxiously awaited word of who would move next.

He'd also convinced Reuben Solomon, a dealer in old clothes, to keep watch on the secondhand furniture shops near his location for complete suites of good furniture. He liked the history in old things and the elderly Jewish man had an even better eye than he did.

"Are you dressed to go out?" Charles asked. "Do you need to go over to St. Luke's or pay a call?"

"We need to call on Mr. Screws," Kate said, handing the glove to her father. "We should make sure he is well, poor man."

"Whatever for?" Mr. Hogarth asked. Smoke trailed from the pipe in his hands as he seated himself at the head of the table. On his right, the fire crackled in the hearth. Mr. Hogarth scooped up little Edward from the rug and deposited him in a chair, then did the same with Helen. "Come and sit."

Charles agreed with Mr. Hogarth. He had no particular interest in paying a call on a cold, old man, gentleman or not. Surely he had been the one to push the other old man out of the window. He sincerely hoped he had never met such an unpleasant person, no matter what his memory told him.

The twins picked up their spoons as the rest of the family piled into their mismatched chairs. Mr. Hogarth said a prayer and the food was passed around.

"Do ye want yer mother to come with ye?" Mr. Hogarth asked, when Kate explained her plan for the day.

"No," she said. "I don't think there is a lady of the house."

"We did see a woman," Charles reminded her.

"Definitely a servant, not a wife," Kate said. "Her clothing made that obvious."

"I don't think we need to pay a call on a murderer," Charles opined.

Mrs. Hogarth gasped but Kate shook her head. "He's not, much too tottering and weak to have done it."

Charles grimaced comically at Mary. As she giggled he said, "Then you think Mr. Harley did himself in?"

"Not at the table please," Mrs. Hogarth insisted. "Children are present."

Charles nodded and applied himself to helpings of kedgeree and porridge, then ate his cream bun with relish. He could walk all the way to Finsbury Circus in the sleet with his belly that satisfied and warm, but Kate would not be pleased. After he was finished eating, he sent George to collect a hackney and escorted his fiancée out of the house as soon as her brother returned.

They spent the long drive holding hands and discussing different woods, settling on mahogany as their preferred choice. Kate blushed so furiously when Charles mentioned bedroom suite possibilities that he dropped the subject, grinning to himself.

As they drove down the street of terraced houses, Charles again noticed the Screws mansion was the only one without a simple wreath of greenery on the door. The man had shown little evidence of holiday spirit, or maybe he kept to the old ways of focusing all celebration on Twelfth Night, instead of earlier in the season.

They went up the steps. Charles paused on the landing, confused.

"What is it?" Kate asked.

Charles lifted his chin at the knocker. He'd seen this before, and not in the night, when it had been too dark to see anything in detail. The iron ring of the knocker hung from the nose of a man's face with closed eyes, appearing something like a death mask. When they tapped the knocker with the ring, Mr. Screws's door was opened by the same woman they'd seen the night before.

"Good morning, Mrs.—" Charles said suggestively.

"I am the housekeeper, Mrs. Dorset," the woman said in a forbidding manner.

"We saw you last night," Kate said helpfully. "With Mr. Screws. Is he at home?"

"He is normally at his office today, but under the circumstances he has not left the house," the housekeeper said, stepping aside. "I will see if he will receive you."

"Are you the sole domestic support of such a large house?" Charles asked.

"No, sir," she said, holding out her hands for Kate's cloak and Charles's hat. "There is an appropriate complement of staff for Mr. Screws's position in life."

"It seems a rather lonely place," Charles mused. A gleaming brass umbrella stand stood next to a boot bench, but nothing else cluttered up the austere front hall. The lushly wallpapered walls were sufficient decoration, with two candle-filled sconces throwing light across the spindly green fern print.

The housekeeper frowned but said nothing. She led them into a cheerless parlor, then left the room without further speech.

"No ornaments," Kate said, staring at the unlit fireplace, the empty mantelpiece.

Charles glanced at the wall opposite the windows. A trio of engravings were indifferently framed on more green-wallpapered walls. They seemed to be political cartoons from a generation before and he could not discern the significance of them. Instead of ferns the wallpaper featured leafy trees.

Both of them, having avoided the matter thus far, turned to the bowed front window, in which space rested an open coffin on a temporary dais. Charles knew what was inside: the flattened remains of Jacob Harley. Had the police removed his chains? Charles leaned forward, forcing himself to look inside.

Chapter 4

Charles glanced at the coffin's contents. Jacob Harley's features had set bloodlessly into a puffy mass of gray. A length of white cloth had been tied around his head to keep the jaw in place. Someone had wrapped a black cravat around his neck, with an extravagant knot straight out of Beau Brummel's time. Charles expected it hid extensive bruising from the chains.

He couldn't recall exactly what Mr. Harley had worn the night before. It had been too dark for clarity, but now, he saw a dark coat, a wine-colored velvet waistcoat, and a white shirt on the corpse. He didn't see any blood so most likely the body had been cleaned and redressed, despite the suspicious death. The bottom half of the coffin was hidden from view by drapery.

Kate sighed and leaned her arm against Charles's. "I'd rather stare at a fire."

"It's best to let the room stay cold," Charles said, remembering the summer before, when he and Kate had discovered a decomposing body.

"Indeed," she said with a shudder. "Do you think they sketched the body before they moved it?"

"I have no idea," Charles admitted. "But they'll have our testimony. I have tried to set it firmly in my mind, but I realize now how inadequate my memory is."

"You are so good with details," Kate said. "For myself, I prefer a fresh corpse to an aging one."

"A lot was happening." Charles set his cheek against her bonnet. "Julie fainting, your sister and Fred wandering about."

"The main event happened upstairs, whatever that was," Kate said. "I'd love to get a look into the room he fell from. And what happened to the candle?"

"Here to pay your respects?" asked Mr. Screws from behind them.

Charles turned around, taking Kate toward the opposite end of the small parlor, so they did not have to converse with the house's resident next to the coffin. "Yes, Mr. Screws."

Kate rushed to the old man and took his hand in hers, a sweet gesture. "Of course, Mr. Screws. Last night was such a muddle. Are you well?"

"As well as I might be, despite my tribulations. But I do not complain," Mr. Screws said with an air of pride. "Who are you? We were not introduced before."

"I am Charles Dickens and this is Catherine Hogarth," Charles said. "I am a parliamentary reporter for the *Morning Chronicle* and Miss Hogarth is my fiancée."

"I met a Dickens once," Mr. Screws said, fixing a stern eye on Charles. "A John Dickens, fancied himself a gentleman. Wanted money for a school, I believe. I didn't give it to him."

Charles felt his eyes go wide at the casually cutting remark. His mother had rented a large house for a school when he was eleven but no one had come to be educated. It had made his family's debt even worse, eventually leading to his father being taken to debtor's prison the next year. "My father is John Dickens. I must have come to a meeting here with him. I thought the front of the house looked familiar, though Mr. Harley did not."

"We are too blessed with business to see everyone together," said the old man.

"Do you remember why you rejected the loan?" Charles asked, remembering hungry days as the school failed. "Out of curiosity."

"I never forget these things. House too expensive for a school. Principals too unqualified. Smelled wine on the man," Mr. Screws said, his nose pinching as if from an unpleasant odor remembered. "I must not have found you impressive, either, for I don't even remember he brought a boy along."

Charles stiffened. He would prove himself worthy of notice, hopefully by having the man arrested for murder.

Kate took Charles's arm as he asked, "Was Mr. Harley your friend as well as business partner?"

The man shuddered. "I cannot stay in this room. Come."

Kate gave Charles a warning glance as Mr. Screws led them out of the street-facing parlor and back into the passage. They walked behind the front staircase and to the opposite side of the house. This room had the appearance of a mixed study and library. One bookshelf held a series of bound almanacs. Another held books Charles recognized from his childhood, like *Tom Jones* and dear *Robinson Crusoe*. The bottom shelf looked like it contained privately bound books of sermons, for all that Mr. Screws seemed to have no kindness in his soul.

"Sit." Their host pointed to a chair with a flattened and faded cushion on the seat.

Kate took it and Charles perched on a bench.

"What can I do for you?" the old man asked as he sat in an ancient brown armchair by the fire, which at least was lit in this room.

"It's what we can do for you, sir," Kate said. "Do you have any idea what happened last night?"

Charles kept his thoughts to himself, given that they involved a cell and Newgate Prison as the ultimate reward for the previous night's activity.

"Not at all," the man responded. "Jacob excused himself from the dinner table. He was gone so long that the party broke up. I came in here to have a cigar and had smoked most of it before Mrs. Dorset came to notify me of the caroling."

"You didn't come outside to listen," Charles pointed out.

"Not a music lover," was his response.

"Have you looked at the window upstairs?" Kate asked. "Was a latch broken?"

"The police checked all that. I'm sure we will hear the details at the inquest."

"You must have a theory?" Charles demanded.

Mr. Screws's age-spotted hands fluttered on his thighs. "He was never still. I expect he was examining the chains. They were a product we had invested in."

"I see," Charles said. The business partner had gone upstairs to fondle some portable property.

Mr. Screws continued. "Perhaps the window latch did break. He could have caught his coattails on fire with the candle. My housekeeper, Mrs. Dorset, will insist on wasting money by lighting the house. She found the candle on the floor inside the window after. We were lucky it didn't burn the house down."

"Mr. Dickens is an excellent observer," Kate said proudly. "If you show him the room, I'm certain he will have some opinions to offer."

"Do I need his opinions? Or want them?" rejoined Screws. "My business partner is dead, a man I have known since our school days. It does not matter why."

"The coroner will want to know," Charles explained. For himself, he wouldn't mind proving the old man's guilt. He had the Dickens family honor to uphold. "Your own neck could be at risk. What if it is decided that you killed him?"

"Humbug," said Screws. "I don't need your help."

Kate glanced between the two men. "I understand you must not have slept well and are sick with grief, sir. But Mr. Dickens can help you clear your name if it becomes necessary."

Charles winced at that. Mr. Screws had not helped his family a dozen years ago. Why should a Dickens help a Screws now? And yet, if he proved he had a first-class mind and solved the crime either way, it would prove the old man wrong about his family.

He focused on his fiancée. Why did Kate think Mr. Screws was not involved? They only had his word for his actions. "Can you tell us who else was at dinner that night?"

The man grew quite red in the face. "I do not know you, and my private guests are none of your concern."

Charles did not want to goad him into some sort of bilious attack in front of Kate. There were other avenues of research. "We will leave you to your rest."

"I do not need your permission," the old man said with dignity. "You did not know Jacob and I will not allow him to be the subject of your prurient interest. Please leave."

Five minutes later, they were back in the street. Charles steamed at the insult of their departure. Mrs. Dorset had handed them their garments with a complacent air and opened the door. While she didn't slam it behind him, Charles had heard a definite click.

Kate tightened her bonnet strings. "They don't seem very concerned."

"That's because Mr. Screws killed his business partner." Charles wrapped his muffler to keep any drafts at bay.

"We saw him soon after Mr. Harley's fall. He didn't seem to be out of breath or have any notion of what had happened."

Charles led her back around the street so they could leave Finsbury Circus. On a late Saturday morning, the area was quiet. Any tradesmen had come and gone. The steps had been swept. "He could be a good actor. The murder might not have winded him. The way he dismissed my father shows he is a coldhearted old man."

"No," Kate insisted. "Though I am sorry he did not help your father start a school, Mr. Screws is too frail to have pushed the old man out of the window. Don't forget he would have had to go up and down steps to the room Mr. Harley fell from."

"A few steps," Charles said, taking her arm to lead her around horse muck. "He is used to them."

"He has such a strong character that he seems more than he is, physically. Did you notice his tremor?"

His breath puffed white, mingling with Kate's. "That's what I'm saying. The fall may have been accidental, but he'd have been dead from the chains. It's possible that would have killed him without too much strength being exerted."

"Mr. Harley had a thick neck," Kate observed. "Or so it seemed from what we saw today."

"Inflammation?" Charles suggested. "His face was a mess."

Kate's lips flattened. "I tried not to look too closely."

"Let us find a hackney," Charles suggested as they reached the main road. "I want to call on the Agas. William will want to hear about our interview with Mr. Screws."

"I'll join you to check on Julie," Kate said.

"No, your mother wants you home," Charles said quickly, remembering the baby. "I noticed the twins had runny noses. She'll need your help."

Charles reached Cheapside under leaden skies, grateful that Kate had agreed to return home without visiting the Agas. Their happiness might be spoiled at any moment if she thought he'd been sporting with maids shortly before meeting her. How could she trust that he would care for their children together if he had fathered a child all unknowing, and done nothing for its care? He needed to find a home for baby Timothy, and discover his real father.

He bounded up the stairs to the Agas' rooms. The close air

of the passage smelled of fried fish and potatoes. His stomach rumbled in expectation. Julie often fed him, a habit established during those brief days when she'd worked as his maid.

He knocked, but no one answered. Were the Agas out? If so, the smell of cooking food wasn't coming from their door. He turned in one direction, then another, thinking he might go to the chophouse downstairs and have a meal. If he sat in the windows, he could see his friends returning.

Just as he'd decided to leave, the door opened. Julie's red hair, though pinned back, surrounded her face in a frizzled halo. She held the baby in her arms. Timothy squealed and waved his thin arms. His fingers latched onto a beaded necklace Julie wore, dragging her head forward.

Charles untangled the baby's fingers while Julie spoke. "Mrs. Herring said he should be able to sleep most of the night through by now, but he isn't, so she gave him back to us after his late feeding."

Charles noticed she had purple shadows under her eyes. "That means you each had him for just one night. Why do you look so tired?"

Julie's mouth tightened. "How well did you sleep last night, Charles, after seeing a man fall to his death?"

"I'm sorry," he said. "I forget you missed most of the actual corpses we've been unfortunate enough to discover."

She worked her jaw and shuddered. "It was as if the moon highlighted all the blood."

"Is that why you fainted? The sight of blood takes people that way sometimes."

Timothy gave a shrill cry and pushed his fist into his mouth. Julie stared down at him in dismay. "Is he teething?"

"It's early," Charles said. "But we only have the aunt's word for his real age."

"Mrs. Herring seemed quite certain that four months was correct. She said he ought to be able to sleep at least seven hours straight, plus two long naps."

Charles touched the infant's forehead. "Ill?"

"Just malnourished, I think. He isn't warm. But he is too thin, don't you think?" Julie asked anxiously.

He gestured her to back through her door, then followed her in and closed it. "Yes, I do think he is too thin. Every child is different but his arms are like little sticks."

"What should we do?" She went to the boot bench just inside and sat.

"More thin oatmeal gruel," Charles said with assurance, remembering his brother Boz's infancy. "I can get you some milk biscuits, too, to soak and feed him. If Mrs. Herring becomes unwilling, we shall have to search for another wet nurse as well."

"It's only been two days," Julie said. "I know that, but he's such a little dear. I don't want him to die."

"I don't either."

She gave him a look of great seriousness. "You are certain he isn't your child, Charles? I wouldn't mind if it was, you know. I'm not a proper sort of lady."

Charles stiffened. "I assure you he is not. I had never been to Hatfield."

"Timothy's mother might have come into London."

"With the dowager marchioness? She was employed by the old woman. I hardly think so," Charles said. "That is not the picture I have of the situation at all. No, the little barmaid seemed to think she knew me. I suspect the father is in Hatfield or nearby, and resembles me."

The door opened behind Charles, almost swatting him on the backside before he leapt out of the way.

William strode into the entryway and leaned over Julie, giving her a smacking kiss on the forehead, then put his forefinger in Timothy's palm so the baby could clutch at it.

"What are we going to do with him?" William asked.

"Keep him," Julie said promptly. "I can't imagine sending

him to die in a workhouse or farming him out to some baby mill." She smiled tenderly at the child.

William shuddered. "Baby mills are slaughterhouses, with their poor care and drugging of infants. We are not so desperate as that."

"Someone needs to find the father," Charles said. "My advertisement might bear fruit yet, but if you went, William, and found the aunt, you might be able to find out who the father is once and for all. If I go, little Madge will simply hide again."

"Then what?" William asked.

"If you want to keep the child, then nothing. The worst thing would be to fall in love with him and then have someone come to take him away."

"Someone dreadful, like my mother, might get him," Julie said in a tremulous voice.

"We know Timothy's mother is dead, burned up in the fire," Charles said. "And no father would keep an infant. He'd give him to a relative to raise, or something worse."

"We just need to know," William agreed, patting his wife on the shoulder. "Instead of taking the word of one young, upset girl who had just lost her sister."

"Exactly." Charles reached for the baby and Julie transferred him from her arms to his.

"I should make the tea," she said, rising. "William, did you purchase the sausages?"

He pulled a packet from his pocket and handed it to her.

"I'll grind some oatmeal very fine for that gruel," Julie said. "I'm going to need help if I have to do a lot of hand-feeding and William is traveling."

"Should I really go north?" William asked.

Julie nodded. "I need to know if we must keep him or if another safe place exists for him."

William sighed. "Very well. How fast do you think we can hire a nursemaid?"

Charles connected that thought with a past conversation. "What about Lucy Fair? You mentioned your concerns about her well-being. She's the right age for the job and we know she's good with children."

"I like her," Julie said, tossing the sausages from hand to hand.

Charles could smell spices rising from the packet. His stomach rumbled again. "I'll go to Blackfriars Bridge after you feed me and see if I can persuade her to help you."

"You can have my sausages, Charles." William grabbed a carpetbag that was packed and by the door. "I have to attend a meeting near Harrow tomorrow morning so I might as well head to Hatfield now."

"What about the inquest?" Charles asked. He started to tell the Agas about the Dickens family history with Mr. Screws, but then the baby gave a thin wail. Julie dumped the sausages into her waiting pan on the hob, then went to her pantry to grind oatmeal.

"I haven't yet been called," William said. "Have you?"

"No, but I haven't been back to Furnival's Inn."

William gave him the old, open grin. "Not much they can do if I'm not at home for the summons. Besides, I don't know anything you do not." He clapped Charles on the shoulder and walked out.

Charles sighed and smiled down at the baby. He had been so distracted by all of his projects of late, and his new, exciting literary friends, that he had neglected William. Yet here his friend was, willing to take on this baby on nothing more than Charles's word.

After Julie had fed herself and Charles, and they had spooned enough gruel into Timothy that he had fallen asleep, he walked to his chambers for the first time since well before Jacob Harley had fallen to his death. At home at Furnival's Inn, he found his brother munching on a mincemeat pie. Fred handed him a written summons that ordered Charles to appear at the inquest in a tavern near Finsbury Circus.

"I suppose you're hungry," Fred said with a mournful look at his pie, two-thirds consumed and glistening with currants.

"Julie fed me."

Fred brightened. "Why did you go back to Cheapside?"

"Left some things there," Charles said carelessly. If he told Fred about Timothy, word would get to Kate. Fred had not yet learned to keep a secret. "Do you remember if we have any relatives in Hatfield?"

"I don't think so," Fred said, then quickly filled his mouth with pie before Charles could change his mind.

Charles uncoiled his comforter from his neck. Kate had knitted it for him in alternating blue and white stripes, but it was so long he had to wind himself into it until he looked like a turtle. "I'm going to edit a couple of the stories for my book; then I have to go out again."

"Are you reviewing a play? I could go with you," Fred said.

"No." Charles poured hot water from the kettle into a cup and added a tot of rum. "Just an excursion. Nothing worth you catching a chill for."

Fred swallowed. "Are you investigating that man's death?"

"Kate offered my services to Mr. Screws," Charles admitted. "But I'm of the belief that he pushed the old man out of the window himself."

"She doesn't agree?"

"No, but she's being sentimental. She sees the frail body and forgets that a wicked heart can hide underneath. Besides, I realized I had met him before. He'd turned Father down for a loan when he was trying to open that school."

"You can't blame him for that," Fred protested. "Father isn't good with money."

"He didn't remember me," Charles said plaintively.

Fred lifted his eyebrows. "You might be of consequence now, but back then?"

Charles lifted his fists in mock defiance and Fred went into battle stance. They sparred, laughing, until Charles remembered. "We promised Mother we'd come for church and a family dinner tomorrow."

"I remember," Fred said. "Best not tell Father you've run across this Mr. Screws again. He'll go on a rant."

"Best not to," Charles agreed, then fetched his writing box. "At least, not until I have him arrested for murder."

Charles set down his pen as church bells tolled eleven times. He bundled up warmly, eager to clear his head after hours of revising his old stories. While he pulled on his gloves, he imagined walking past a bookshop and seeing his book in the store. What a moment of pride for that boy who'd been robbed of his education by his father's unending money woes.

Outside, fog swirled around the streets, blotting out light with a thick coat of brown sludge. He kept his lantern close, but after so many visits, he knew the scant half mile to Blackfriars Bridge well. As he walked down to Fleet Street, Temple Bar was off to his right, not creating a traffic problem at this time of night. Then he kept south, cutting through the Temple area, including gardens with ghostly trees branching into the fog, then into the maze of streets that led to the Thames foreshore and the bridge.

A pair of lanterns bobbed down by the water. Mudlarks were at work, hunting for what the mighty Thames had cast up that day. It might be lumps of coal, or the remains of lost jewelry, or coins, or pipes, or even bones. They'd found manacles last summer, cast in by an escaped convict from Coldbath Fields.

He walked down, scanning for Lucy Fair's slim figure, usually surrounded by younger children. Two male forms straightened, looking taller than his group of young friends. He dropped the pair of new secondhand blankets he carried over his shoulder onto a waiting rock and held the lantern close to his face.

It didn't stop the figures from approaching, their arms held menacingly away from the body.

"'Oo's this?" called one of them.

"Dickens," Charles called. "From the Charity for Dressing the Mudlark Children of Blackfriars Bridge."

"Oo, don't say," sneered the voice.

Charles identified it as belonging to a youth, with a half-broken voice that put him at fourteen, or so. Nothing he couldn't defend himself from, though two together seemed more daunting. "Where's Lucy Fair? My business is with her."

"She your girl?" the voice sneered.

Charles moved his lantern, flashing over the two faces. Both too young for facial hair, and a likely pair of villains. One had a turned-in eye, and the other seemed to be missing a good number of his top teeth. "Your clothing is little better than rags," he observed. "At least take the blankets. You can use them as shawls."

"We don't want 'em," said the first boy again. "Or you."

"Lucy Fair!" Charles yelled into the night.

"We'll care for 'er now," said the boy. "Right pretty bird, that un."

Charles's hand shook. The lantern wavered over the threatening faces. He resolved not to leave until he saw the girl. They'd known her for close to a year now. He wouldn't leave her to be raped by a couple of ruffians who could never take care of any babe they got on her. His hand stiffened on the handle and he stepped backward toward the blankets, thinking he could kick them at the villains somehow, and tangle their feet in them if it came to an attack.

"Mr. Dickens?"

He heard the sought-for female voice with relief. "I'm here, Lucy. We took up a new collection and I have more blankets."

A shawl-wrapped girl peeled away from the murk of the water's edge, where she had blended in with the night. She walked toward him, swinging her collection bucket at her side.

When she reached him, the first boy grabbed for her bucket. "What oo found, girl?"

She tore it away from the young ruffian. "None of your business, Lack."

The boy's bad eye rolled in its socket as she stepped closer to Charles. He also noticed that Lucy Fair stood taller than the lad, though he suspected she was younger. But every time he saw her, she had filled out more, looked less of a girl. No, she couldn't stay here anymore.

He pulled a packet of sausages and fried potato slices from his pocket, cold now, though it had been toasty warm when Julie had wrapped it for him, and handed it to the girl.

"Poor John!" she called. "Brother Second! Cousin Arthur!"

Her little band turned from where they had been picking through rocks almost out of sight up the river. The trio all had more robust appearances than the newer, older boys. The youngest two, in fact, were quite stocky. They were cousins.

He let Lucy parcel out the food. Lack growled something nasty under his breath and stalked away.

"Blanket?" Charles called pleasantly, to make the point that they could be involved if they cared to behave, but the boy's shoulders merely hunched.

"New blankets?" Poor John asked.

Charles leaned closer to the boy, at the cusp of leaving boy-hood, and saw he had a new bruise on his cheek and a long cut leading from the side of his mouth. "I thought you sounded strange. What happened?"

Cousin Arthur lifted his grimy hands, shoved his half of a sausage into his mouth, and began to punch the air with his fists. "Lack, 'e did this! 'n that!" He swung his fists in the air while his cousin laughed.

"Poor John had a big hole in his blanket," Lucy Fair exclaimed. "So he had it over his head, and Lack wanted it."

"He does want blankets then?" Charles asked.

"Sure, if 'e can steal 'em," Lucy Fair said with a curl of her lip. "'e's evil, that one. Sells everything."

"I don't like the look of him," Charles said. "Even less, his companion."

"'e's got a good eye," Brother Second insisted, tucking food into his cheek. "Finds more coal than anyone. Nice fire."

"But no teeth," Charles muttered. "Well, my dear mudlarks, the time has come for a change, and not a moment too soon, given the fetid fogs we've been having."

"What?" Lucy Fair asked.

"Our friend William has taken in a foundling," Charles told her. "An infant who is poorly. I promised his wife, Julie, that you would come and help her. A proper job as nursemaid."

Lucy Fair's eyes grew wide. "Nursemaids have to be clean."

"We can get you clean," Charles said. "The important thing is to know how to care for children, and you do that." He cuffed Cousin Arthur gently on the side of the head. The boy plopped down on the rocky sand, pretending to be knocked out, then jumped up and plied his small fists around Charles's midsection.

"What about us?" Poor John asked. "I don't want to be the leader of our gang."

"I'll put all of you on the stage to Harrow," Charles said. "You can join your old friend Ollie at school."

"At school?!" Brother Second yelled, outraged.

"Ollie lost 'is 'and," Cousin Arthur said. "'e can go to school. Not me."

Brother Second nodded. "The lads are keeping us warm."

Charles sighed. "I'm glad they can find coal, but I bring you the blankets and buckets and food."

Brother Second shrugged. "Keep doin' that." He grabbed his cousin's hand and they ran down the shore toward the little fire that Lack and his toothless henchman had built near the bridge.

Charles glanced between the two older children. "You know it's for the best," he said to Lucy.

"I don't like my chances with that Lack," she said with a shudder. "I wanted to move our camp, but then them two's families couldn't find them."

Only Arthur still had a parent living, Brother Second's uncle, and he was a drunkard. "Do you think the younger boys will be safe enough?"

Poor John puffed up his skinny chest. "I'll get an education and come get 'em," he said. "They'll see the right of it. Little Ollie must be a proper gentleman by now."

"We can hope," Charles said. "Collect your things and we'll be off."

Lucy Fair stared at her bucket, then held out her hand for Poor John's. "Can you get our blankets?" she asked him.

Charles wanted to tell her to leave the filthy things, along with anything else they'd collected, but what else did they have to hold on to?

He waited, then helped the children climb up the ladders to the road, between a dilapidated house and a slightly more structurally sound tavern. They walked through the fog to Cheapside, where Charles left Lucy Fair with Julie, and then he and Poor John headed toward a coaching inn.

In the taproom, Charles called for paper and ink, then wrote a letter to Mr. Aga, the master of the school and William's father, to take in Poor John. Then he left the boy, snoozing by the fire under his blanket, and went to make arrangements for the next coach to Harrow.

* * *

As he made his weary way home after being up most of the last twenty-four hours, he thought that he'd done a good night's work. He could only hope that the two youngest mudlarks had not been lost to them. How long would Lucy Fair stay with the Agas when her two youngest gang members were keeping such villainous company?

Chapter 5

Charles entered The Cooked Goose public house on Monday morning after the church bells rung eleven. He'd had to find the door by touch. The night's brown fog had yet to lift and the only way to see through the streets was with whatever light the street lamps had to offer. The building's interior wasn't much more visible due to heavy smokers creating a localized fog in the taproom.

The barman pointed him upstairs. "The inquest is under way. The jury members were sworn in and already saw the body."

"At Mr. Screws's house?"

The man rubbed his hands down his apron. "No, sir. They took the coffin upstairs. It's going to be buried straight after."

Charles was very glad he'd finished his morning porridge hours ago. At least Mr. Harley had only been dead two days. He'd been around worse. "Who is the coroner?"

"Sir Silas Laurie."

Charles recognized the name. He'd even been to the baronet's house. In his late thirties, Sir Silas had a keen, intelligent, rather disappointed face. But other than being a man of wealth and taste, Charles knew little about him. "Thank you."

He went upstairs. Outside of a wall with a door inset in the passageway, Mr. Screws's housekeeper, Mrs. Dorset sat, sandwiched in between a flashy young man and the most extraordinary looking bear of a derelict on a long bench.

A constable, whose fingers kept going to his leather stock and tugging at it, directed him to the opposite bench.

"Another witness?" asked the young man. He wore a brown coat and a pink silk waistcoat with dark trousers and black shoes. His top hat had a pink silk flower attached in a jaunty fashion. Not really a London wardrobe, so Charles wasn't surprised to hear another land in his voice.

"Yes, I'm Charles Dickens," he said.

"Powhatan Fletcher at your service, sir," said the man, tapping the brim of his hat. "I worked for Mr. Harley and Mr. Screws."

Charles regarded the brash, well, not youth exactly. He put off an air of vigor but his short brown hair, visible now, receded at the temples. There might have been a hint of silver above his ears. "Do I detect American in your accent?"

Mr. Fletcher righted his hat. "Oh, yes. Virginia born, you see. Related to the Lees, who are of course related to the Catons. One of them is married to the Marquess Wellesley. Out of power for now, but you never know what is going to happen next in politics."

"Unusual name you have," Charles commented.

"Descended from some native king," Mr. Fletcher said carelessly. "We're proud of that sort of thing where I come from."

Charles looked at the man's ruddy skin and saw no sign of regal savage in him. "I dare say. I am a parliamentary reporter by trade."

"How very strange," Mr. Fletcher exclaimed. "What brings you to a murder inquest?"

"I saw your Mr. Harley fall to his death. I'm very sorry it

happened." He nodded soberly at the man in case he had liked
the deceased.

Mr. Fletcher glanced at the housekeeper, then leaned forward. "I heard the carolers that night, but we were enjoying
Mrs. Dorset's lovely beef and didn't want to leave the table."

"Mr. Harley did," Charles pointed out. So, this man had
been a dinner guest that night.

"That's best left for the inquest, I think," Mr. Fletcher said.

Charles persisted. "Was it just the three of you at dinner?"

"No, my fiancée was with us. Miss Osborne. And Mr. Harley's son."

Mr. Screws might not have been willing to share the information, but this gentleman had a much more open character. "Oh,
is she American?"

"No. I met her in America, though, and she persuaded me to
come here for a time. I'm a sort of apprentice to Harley and
Screws, learning the business." His voice had slowly lowered as
if his natural good humor was being overlaid by the realization
that those days were lost.

"Did your fiancée like Mr. Harley?"

"She didn't know him well. He was often ill. No, the burden
of running the business often fell on Mr. Screws. I do my best
to help him shoulder his responsibilities."

"Had Mr. Harley become ill that night?"

Mr. Fletcher spread his hands. "Precisely so, Mr. Dickens.
You are astute."

Charles warmed at the praise. "Who are you?" he asked the
large young man on the other side of the housekeeper.

He looked to be about the same age as Charles, but wore
rough clothing, some sort of nubby gray wool. Maybe his best
trousers and coat, but uncomfortable looking. Enormous hands
rested fat fingered on his meaty thighs. If he'd been lost in Africa
the wild animals would have found him a tasty morsel. Under-

neath his cap, his black hair hung greasily around his face. His lips were as thick as his fingers but he didn't speak, his expression rather blank.

"This is my son, Johnny," Mrs. Dorset said. "He helps out around the house. I need him, you see, as we did for Mr. Harley as well."

"Oh, he actually lived at the house?" Charles asked.

"He didn't sleep there every night, but he didn't keep his own servants," Mrs. Dorset told him.

"I wonder what he was doing upstairs that night?"

"He had his own chamber," Mrs. Dorset explained. "His clothing stayed there, and he often worked from the bed because of his ill health."

"How extraordinary," Charles murmured.

"Indeed," Mr. Fletcher agreed.

The door opened. "Mr. Dickens?" a constable inquired.

Charles stood and followed the man into the main room. Immediately, his eyes went to the familiar coffin on a table along an external wall. Thankfully, it was not open. He'd seen enough of the corpse. The window was open, blowing tendrils of fog into the room, but the coal-laden air covered up any hint of decay.

In the back, in front of the clerk's desk with two candelabras on either corner, Emmanuel Screws sat on a stool and Sir Silas paced back and forth between the jurors and his witness. Mr. Screws wore old breeches and a tailcoat, with long boots. He placed his hat back on his wizened apple of a head when Sir Silas thanked and dismissed him.

The old man nodded at Charles as he passed him. Charles nodded back. Mr. Screws had best enjoy his freedom while he still had it. Newgate Prison called.

Sir Silas lifted a brow, recognizing Charles, but made no comment other than the legal ones.

"Now, Mr. Dickens, can you tell us about the events of Friday past?" Sir Silas asked after Charles was sworn in.

"We had resolved to collect for our charity by caroling on select streets of a prosperous nature," Charles explained. "Finsbury Circus seemed a likely location, but Mr. Screws's abode was the first that seemed to have people at home. We stopped in front of his steps and sang." He described what they had seen.

Sir Silas paced past him. "You say a candle was lit in that particular window?"

"In all of them, sir."

After he reached the wall, the coroner turned back. "Did you see anyone other than Mr. Harley at the window?"

"I did not. When Mr. Screws opened the front door, that was the first time I saw any inhabitant of the house."

He stopped in front of Charles. "Did you see anyone else?"

"Mrs. Dorset, who I am now acquainted with, brought him a shawl after a time. He was shaking with cold. I had no idea who else was present, or what the occasion had been."

"Did you hear raised voices coming from the house? Any sort of argument?"

"No, but then, we were singing rather loudly. The six of us can make a great deal of noise."

"Did you see any foot traffic?"

"Not until after the death." He explained the carriage and the solicitor who'd come and then gone in search of a constable.

"Do you have any connection to the Appleton Smithy?"

"I've never heard of it. A blacksmith shop?" Charles asked.

"They specialize in chains."

"I see," Charles said. "No, I shouldn't think so. Where are they located?"

"South London."

Charles shook his head. "I don't believe so."

Sir Silas asked him a few more questions and then dismissed

him. Charles went back into the passage. He sat on the bench, thinking, and when the constable called for Mr. Fletcher, he hoped he might be able to hear the testimony. It didn't filter through the wall. Disappointed, he went downstairs and ate bread, cheese, and pickle, while puzzling over some shorthand notes he needed to translate into an article for the *Morning Chronicle*.

"Still here?" said Mr. Fletcher, spotting him by the fire half an hour later.

Charles forced a smile. "I had some work with me. I need to go over to my office, but this seemed like a hospitable spot."

"Pickles good?"

"Yes indeed."

Mr. Fletcher called for a plate, then pulled out a pair of fat cigars. "Tobacco from Virginia," he said, handing one to Charles.

"Thank you." Charles inspected the cigar band, which had *Rolfe* emblazoned across it. "Your family's plantation?"

"I became attached to this particular blend. Very smooth," said the man. "I need a cigar before going back to work. I don't want to know what Mr. Screws is going to decide about poor Hugh Appleton."

"That's the blacksmith?" Charles used his knife to clip off the end of the cigar and bent over the fire to light it.

Mr. Fletcher did the same, then leaned back in his chair, his free hand tucked into his pink silk waistcoat. "He's bigger than that. Ran into debt. Borrowed money from us, of course. Mr. Harley was deciding what to do about the inventory."

Charles puffed smoke, then finished off his beer. He really needed to get to the office. "Is that why he had the chain?"

"Yes. It was a sample. He did all his work from Mr. Screws's house, you see. Rarely left it toward the end."

"Did he suffer from vertigo, or something like that? If he was ill?"

Mr. Fletcher considered. "General weakness, really. He'd have bouts of fever in the late afternoon."

"Do you think that's why he fell?" Charles asked.

The side of Mr. Fletcher's mouth tilted up. "That's for the coroner to say. It won't do for an American to mix himself up in English legal matters."

"Indeed." Charles stood and put his hat on as the barman came with Mr. Fletcher's plate. "Thank you for the cigar, but I must be on my way."

He walked past the stairs. A stretched-thin man, coming down them, crossed his path as he pushed open the door.

"Troubling matters, sir," said the man, who seemed to know who Charles was.

Charles flicked ash from his cigar into the street. "What say you?"

The man's narrow face creased into an unctuous smile. "I'm Dawes, sir, the undertaker. I met you when I cared for Horatio Durant's mortal remains."

Charles stared hard at the man, but the only thing unusual about him was a seeming absence of anything but skeleton under the skin. Still, he did remember that horrible night in January. "Ah, yes. You were with Matthew Post, the solicitor. I remember now."

He heard horrible scraping noises, then a bump, and behind them, the door opened again. As he turned around to see what was causing the commotion, two men in smocks came out, carrying the coffin. They looked strained, red faced, and perilously close to disaster.

Mr. Dawes directed them to a horse-drawn cart, where they manhandled the coffin onto a bed of straw. It rocked before settling and Charles thought uneasily of the body drifting inside.

"You need more than two men to handle a coffin and a

body," Charles protested. "The consequences of such a decision—"

"Were unavoidable," interrupted Dawes. "I beg your pardon, but there was only room for two on the steps. We tried four to move the coffin upstairs but it didn't work. They should have viewed the body at my premises or Mr. Screws's, but Sir Silas does have his own way of doing things."

"I see." Charles put his cigar to his mouth, then took it away again. "What did you mean by troubling matters, sir?"

"What?" asked the undertaker.

"You were muttering when you came down the steps."

"Yes," Mr. Dawes said. "I meant the shameful condition of the body. I knew Mr. Harley in life, you see. Harley and Screws were kind enough to offer me a loan a decade ago when I opened my premises."

"A hanging by chains is not a pretty sight," Charles agreed. "And then the fall."

"True, true," agreed Dawes. "But I meant the bruising on Mr. Harley's upper arms. An old man, pushed to his death in such a gruesome manner. Makes one want to return to the country of his youth and raise cabbages."

Charles's focus narrowed. Bruises? Under his clothing? He, William, and Kate never would have seen them. "You performed an autopsy?"

"I embalmed the body," Mr. Dawes explained. "For the sake of the inquest. Therefore, I acquainted myself most intimately with the mortal remains."

"Very wise to embalm," Charles said. "Having seen the opposite approach in the past. Anything else troubling you?"

"Thank you, Mr. Dickens, but no. May I offer you my card?"

"Please," Charles said. Useful person to know, this Mr. Dawes. "I do hope you informed the coroner of your findings. If murder was done in your opinion, he must know."

"Oh yes, he is aware." The undertaker reached into his

pocket and frowned when it came up empty. "I am very enthusiastic about your articles, sir, and my profession is much maligned. If you are interested in the likes of humble me for one of your little projects, I would be most obliged."

Charles inclined his head, pleased to be recognized as an author. "Presently I am focused on writing sketches about holiday matters, but I shall consider it for the new year."

"Excellent." The man rubbed his bony hands together, then pulled mittens from his pocket and slid them over his very thin, very white hands.

Charles did not like to think of those hands in connection with handling remains. "And do look for my sketches in book form very soon. There will be one or two new articles that you may find of particular interest given your profession."

The man looked mildly intrigued. Hopefully, he'd made an advance sale for his book.

"Very good," Mr. Dawes said.

They shook hands, and Charles went west toward his office. However, he met an old friend near the Courts from his law clerk days, and ended up having a drink with him. By the time they parted, two hours had gone, so he decided to return to where he had begun and see if anyone remained from the inquest.

As he went in the public house's door, he saw a trio of jurors bent over a table, drinking steaming punch.

"What's the word, gentlemen?" Charles asked.

One of them, a graybeard with tobacco-stained teeth, glanced up. "Sir Silas summed it all up wery fine. Our werdict vas accidental death."

"Accidental?" Charles gasped. "What about the bruising on the arms? Surely that means Mr. Harley was helped to his death."

"He was in a rough trade, money lending," said a second juror, a much younger man who had the look of a scholar, with rumpled hair, round spectacles, and a paunchy belly. "Might have been grabbed by someone who owed the firm money shortly before that fateful night."

"He'd been ill. Spent most of his time in a room in that house," Charles said. "Mind you, I have no idea who could have pushed him."

"It wasn't that elderly Mr. Screws. He had his housekeeper to tell us she'd never let him out of her sight," said the second juror.

Charles doubted the truth of that. He'd seen Mr. Screws in the doorway, and no housekeeper in sight until she'd arrived with the shawl. She had that son of hers to keep an eye on. But this hard old man had staff either too frightened or too awed by him to admit he might have killed his partner.

"He's the heir to the business," the younger juror added. "If he didn't do it, no one else would have bothered."

Charles squinted. He felt the need to clarify the motive for murder. "Mr. Screws owns the entire business now?"

"Was quite businesslike about it," the juror agreed.

"If you find there vas some other killer, you'd best tell Sir Silas," said the first man. "Vell out of it, ve are."

The trio turned their backs to him. Charles opened his mouth but thought better of arguing with the jurors. After all, he knew how to find the coroner. Setting his fancies against the hot rum and water he craved, he went back into the fog and set out for the *Chronicle*.

He heard church bells pealing three o'clock while he walked through the streets on his way to the newspaper office. It had gone full dark by the time he reached it, dodging figures in the fog. He would not have known if he passed living, breathing people or shades in the brownish muck.

Inside, he coughed in hacking Londoner fashion as he tossed his coat over his chair. William's desk, behind his, looked undisturbed. What would the news from Hatfield be?

A boy ran up to him, his fingers black with newsprint. "Mr. Hogarth wants you, sir."

Charles groaned. A full day lost. What assignments had he missed? He walked down the row of desks, his feet aching with damp, his trousers dark with mud. He might as well have been tramping on the Thames foreshore.

A cloaked, bonneted figure turned away from Mr. Hogarth's desk as he knocked and walked in. "Charles!"

"If it isn't my darling!" Charles exclaimed, kissing Kate on the cheek. "You didn't get called to the inquest, did you? Did I miss you at the public house?"

"No, but I wanted to hear the news, and Mother needed me to pick up dried sweet cicely from a Scottish apothecary for Helen's chest cold. She's developed a bad cough."

"Poor wee one," said Mr. Hogarth from behind Kate.

The boy reappeared in the doorway. Now he had ink on his nose. "Mr. Black wants you, sir. Something about tomorrow's front page?"

Kate's father stood, sticking his pipe stem into his mouth. "Duty calls." He patted Kate's shoulder as he passed by and picked up a small sheath of papers. "Work for ye, Charles."

"Thank you, sir," Charles said, taking the papers. After the editor left, he said, "I never made it here today, between one thing and another. But I did talk to a few of the jurors and one of the witnesses."

"What was the verdict?" Kate asked, unbuttoning her cloak.

Charles helped her remove it and set it over the back of a chair. It rustled with a package, probably the herbal remedy. "You won't like the result. Accidental death."

Kate nodded thoughtfully. "It could have been. We can't see murder in everything that happens."

Charles held up a finger. "Ah, but there is more."

Her lips curved and her eyes began to sparkle. "Oh?"

He grinned at her. "Oh, yes. I met Powhatan Fletcher, who

has apprenticed himself to Harley and Screws to learn the business. And I saw the housekeeper's son, the least promising sort of young man I've seen outside the rookeries."

"Oh," Kate mused. "Suspects."

With no one to see, he dared to take her soft hand and squeeze it between his own. "There does not seem to be a butler to amuse you, but an indication of force presented itself."

Kate's teeth bit into her lower lip. "You think someone pushed Mr. Harley?"

"He was admittedly unwell, so certainly could have overbalanced and fallen, but—" Charles paused.

"What?" Kate bounced on the balls of her feet.

He grinned at her. "Darling Kate, you're so bloodthirsty. What kind of children will a mother like you bring into the world?"

"Intelligent ones," she insisted, pulling her hand away. "Tell me what you've learned, Charles."

He bent over her ear and whispered into it. "There may be something to investigate since bruising on the corpse's upper arms indicates he was pushed out of the window."

"Bruising," she mused, picking up immediately on the most important word. She turned away from him and paced behind the chairs, biting on her gloved forefinger. "Who would have wanted to kill him?"

"Mr. Screws inherited the Harley share of the business," Charles said. "He might have thought Mr. Harley wasn't earning his keep, since he'd been ill. Why not hasten his end along?"

"I don't believe that," Kate griped. "Who else was there? Just the apprentice and the housekeeper's son?"

"Huge hands, he has." Charles said in a drawn-out, spooky voice. "They would leave bruises. The apprentice is American."

"We can't hang him for that," Kate said absently. "Then there's the housekeeper."

"You do like a servant for the killing, darling," Charles observed. "Why is that?"

"It's such a domestic crime. And the chains, you know. A woman could apply force with chains, the way she couldn't with smaller hands."

"Maybe they all did it together," Charles suggested. "Mrs. Dorset applies the chains, irritated by the extra washing. Harley was too cheap to pay for his own domestics. Her son causes the bruises, pushing Mr. Harley to the window, upset by the necessity of taking down an extra pot of slops each day. Finally, Mr. Screws himself goes down on his aged knees and lifts his partner's feet, tipping him out the window that Mr. Harley's son has opened."

Kate clapped. "Well done, Mr. Dickens."

Charles took a modest bow. "It's as good an explanation as anything."

The office boy dashed past the door, waving his hands. He went past Mr. Hogarth's open door, then flipped around, dancing on his boots, then came back and stuck in his ink-spattered head. "Mr. Dickens, you're wanted, sir."

Charles stared at the breathless boy. "By whom, Infant Disaster?"

The boy wiped at his cheek, depositing more ink. "I don't know, sir. Some old gentleman with wild eyes."

Charles glanced at Kate, then followed the boy back toward the front room of 332 Strand, where a secretary fended off the public. Kate followed behind.

In front of the secretary's desk, Emmanuel Screws himself paced back and forth, scarecrow-like on legs greatly thinned by age. His boots shone, evidence of his housekeeper's command of the household, though his buff breeches had a new long stain from ink or coffee. He had a general air of one ripping his hair out with his fingers, though his hands were grasping the tails of his coat.

"Mr. Dickens," the old man cried.

"Calm yourself, sir," Charles said, rushing to help him, despite his revulsion at the sight of the old sinner.

Kate came up next to him and patted the old gentleman's arms. "What is troubling you, Mr. Screws? The verdict?"

"What?" Mr. Screws said, wide eyed. "No, child, not the verdict, the body. Jacob's body has been snatched!"

Chapter 6

Charles stared at Mr. Screws, all irritation at the man's appearance gone in the excitement of a new puzzle. "You're saying that Mr. Harley's corpse has vanished?"

Behind him, the *Chronicle*'s secretary ceased scratching in his ledger. The two men who'd been accosting him, asking for a donation from the newspaper to their charity, stopped their patter. The newspaper's anteroom had gone silent.

The old man nodded. "Yes."

"Are-are you certain?" Charles stammered. "I saw Mr. Dawes myself, the undertaker. I met him early in the year and he truly is in that trade. He had two men with him. They loaded the coffin into a cart outside of the public house."

"Maybe the body was no longer inside?" Kate asked, her gaze fixed on the old gentleman.

"What would they have done with the body?" Charles asked. "Tossed him into the rubbish heap in the alley from the back window of the pub?"

"The coffin has vanished as well," Mr. Screws said heavily. He seemed to falter on one leg, as if a kneecap had suddenly disappeared.

Kate and Charles helped the elderly man to a bench by the door.

"It never arrived at your home after the inquest?" Kate asked.

"They were meant to take the coffin right to Jacob's grave," Mr. Screws said. He squeezed his knees with bony fingers, holding back emotion. "I returned home in my carriage and ate a late, cold dinner prepared by Mrs. Dorset before going to the burial site. By then Jacob was supposed to be delivered to General Cemetery of All Souls, Kensal Green. The grave was dug, but no coffin ever arrived."

"How odd," Kate said. "Might there have been a traffic accident? A horse that lost a shoe?"

"The cart looked rickety," Charles said, struck by the tears in the old man's eyes. Perhaps he had a heart after all, even if he had not employed it with the Dickens family. "I only met Mr. Dawes at a private gentleman's home. But I will find his establishment for you and sort things out."

"Let Mr. Dickens look into the matter. You should go home to bed, Mr. Screws," Kate said gently. "You don't look well."

"Thank you both," Mr. Screws said tremulously. "I am not an indecisive, fluttering sort of man, but I must say the death of my business partner has made sport with me."

"It is a terrible thing," Kate soothed. "Mr. Dickens will have your carriage return to the door if you are ready to leave."

"Yes, have John return," Mr. Screws said.

Charles nodded and stepped into the wide street. He spotted an ancient private carriage up the street. Dashing past a crossing sweeper cleaning up muck, he ran down the pavement waving until he caught the coachman's eye.

"For Mr. Screws? Are you John?" he called up.

"I am," said the gravelly voice. The coachman's face looked even older than his master's, but his hands were steady on the reins.

"You're to return," Charles said. "And take the old man home."

"Wery vell," said the coachman, and snapped his reins.

Charles watched him disappear into the fog. He'd have to find a spot to turn around. Charles reversed and almost bumped into a street seller carrying potatoes. Must have been an out-seller from someone with cooking equipment elsewhere. Thinking of the cold, he bought three hot potatoes from the Irishwoman and tucked them into his pockets, enjoying their warmth on the dash back to the *Chronicle*. Instead of tormenting Mr. Screws, he now wanted to comfort him, a strange twist of fate.

Inside, Kate sat on the bench next to the old man. The coal brazier was on the opposite side of the room and Charles thought Mr. Screws's lips looked blueish. He offered him two of the potatoes and the other to Kate.

"For warmth if not for eating," Charles said.

"Thank you. Where is my carriage?" queried the old man, taking the potatoes in shaking hands. He lowered them to his thighs.

Charles smiled at Kate as she took her potato. "Still on this side of the street, I'm afraid. He'll have to come around."

Mr. Screws made an irritated noise, put one potato into his pocket and opened the other. As he pulled back a piece of skin, steam expelled from it.

"That looks delicious," Kate admitted. "I think I will eat mine if you don't mind. Charles, do you want a bite?"

"No, I have some badly cured pickles sitting uneasily in my stomach," he said. "Go ahead."

"Have you gone to the police, sir?" Kate asked. "Are they looking for the coffin?"

"I tried them first," Mr. Screws said wearily. "But the station was full to bursting with malodorous fishmongers who had been fighting. The constables were thoroughly engaged in the mess. I did not have the strength to wait them out, so I came here instead." He considered his potato.

Charles stood against the wall while his charges ate. "Why would anyone steal Mr. Harley's body?" he asked aloud without meaning to. Street accidents were common so it seemed likely that something had happened to Mr. Dawes's wagon along the way to the cemetery.

"Body snatchers, sir," Mr. Screws said. "Perhaps you are too young to recall the considerable reports of them at the start of this decade."

"The laws have changed since then," Charles pointed out.

"Maybe something about Jacob's body made him worth the risk. But I made sure nothing valuable was on his person," Mr. Screws rejoined.

"Maybe the value was in his remains," Kate said gently. "Evidence of his murderer."

"The coroner thought differently," Mr. Screws said.

"Sir Silas is an intelligent man," Charles told him. "The fact that the corpse is now missing may change things."

After a long wait, the plain black carriage arrived in front of the *Chronicle* and Mr. Screws tottered off into his coachman's care. After he had left, Charles and Kate stared at each other.

"I know it makes no sense," Kate said to him, "but I like Mr. Screws, even though he is obviously a hardened businessman."

"I cannot deny that he is unwell, or that he is obviously distraught over what happened to the corpse," Charles admitted. "I wonder if he and Mr. Harley were generally ill due to old age, or if something more insidious is going on? That housekeeper and her son concern me. He has an air of oversized danger about him."

Mr. Hogarth walked into the front room, thrusting his hands into his unwieldy greatcoat. Little Georgina had knitted him a new comforter with tight, uneven purls that looked like they'd scratch the skin. But her father had gamely tucked it under his collar, where it rubbed only against his chin.

The office boy dashed around him and ran out the door.

"He'll call a hackney," Mr. Hogarth told them. "Charles, do ye want to come to dinner tonight?"

"Thank you, sir. I want to track down William. I know he had to go out of town for a speech, but he should be back by now."

"Charles has to find Mr. Harley's body. It's missing," Kate told her father. "He promised Mr. Screws."

"I think you did that." Charles winked at Mr. Hogarth. He didn't want the Hogarths asking questions about why he'd want to see William, though he was all agitation, wondering if he had learned anything about Timothy's father. "Yes, I need to find that undertaker. I thought William could help."

"Ye've lost a body?"

"Disappeared on the way to Kensal Green. I saw the coffin on the undertaker's cart," Charles verified.

"Why don't ye ask Thomas Pillar for advice?" Mr. Hogarth suggested. "He has a bonny mind for details about tradesmen."

"Thank you," Charles said. "I will run along and do just that." He squeezed Kate's little hand in his and went back into the offices.

"Good luck," she called after him. "Write me with an update."

Thomas, the *Chronicle*'s under-editor, told Charles that Mr. Dawes, cabinetmaker and undertaker, had his enterprise in Spitalfields on Commercial Street. Charles bundled up and walked through the busy end-of-day, darkened streets to that destination, but found the three-story house entirely shut up, not even a wife and children at home. Any corpses moldering inside would not be able to speak to him.

Chilled by his windy walk, he trod quickly past a cluster of street hawkers around Old Castle Street. He regretted it when he considered his empty stomach and turned back to buy two pounds of oysters from one of them. After that, he followed behind a hulking laborer who left a trail of plaster bits in his wake, but kept the wind out of Charles's face. When he turned off onto a rancid court, Charles stopped to buy a cup of pea soup from a dark-skinned, ragged girl with a tureen over a fire. That kept him warm enough to continue without his wind block.

Never had he been so happy to hear the Bow bells when he had Cheapside in sight. He hadn't been walking long, just fifteen or twenty minutes, but his fingers felt like thin blocks of ice despite his pockets and gloves.

Julie let him into her rooms without a word, then closed the door behind him and spoke in a low voice. "Warm yourself in front of the fire, Charles. Your lips are blue."

"I'm sure they are not," he rejoined. "Or I would have lost the ability to speak." Even so, he stripped off his damp comforter with alacrity and leaned his head over the hob, since nothing was on it to pop grease into his face. "How is Lucy Fair settling in?"

"We spent a lot of time hauling cans and heating water to give her a proper bath," Julie said, tugging at his arm to pull him closer to the fireplace. "I had to take her to Petticoat Lane to see your friend Mr. Solomon. He found her some clothes for a reasonable price."

"Where is she now?" Charles took off his hat and set it on the table. Even his hair felt heavy with moisture, falling into his eyes.

She put her finger to her lips. "Keep your voice down, please. Across the way with Mrs. Herring. Did you know Lucy has blond hair? That's why she's called Fair. I had no idea."

He tucked strands of his black hair behind his ears with leaden fingers. "It's nearly always been dark when I've seen her. I wouldn't recognize her on the street."

"You'll be shocked," Julie promised. "I pinned up the hem on her new dress since it needed to be shortened and she's sewing it while she learns how to take care of an infant. We know she is good with quite small children but infants are another matter."

"How is Timothy?" Charles asked.

"Very well." She winced. "Too well. Mrs. Herring wants more money. She says she needs beer allowance to rebuild her milk."

"He must be hungry." He mentally calculated his expenditures. He could pay more, though it would cut into his furniture budget soon. William needed to bring him good news from Hatfield. With any luck he'd have word of Timothy's family.

"Babies are always growing," Julie agreed. "But his face is already fuller, don't you think?" She pointed Charles away from the fire to a basket she'd acquired somewhere.

Baby Timothy dreamed, his eyes moving under his paper-thin eyelids. Julie had padded the basket with toweling and tucked a shawl he recognized snugly around him.

"I thought he was across the hall. I agree, his cheeks are fuller," Charles whispered.

"Look how he sucks with those little lips, even in his sleep," Julie said. "He'll wake soon and want more. I'll take him back over later on tonight."

Charles's fingers had thawed enough for him to remove his gloves. He set them by his hat. "Will Mrs. Herring be willing to take Timothy for another feeding now?"

"Not until she's done feeding her family," Julie whispered. "I'll have to make him more gruel. I'll make some for you, too, Charles."

"Don't you have anything else?"

"Not really. I'm hoping William will be home soon. I didn't want to take Timothy out in this cold."

Charles, feeling heroic, pulled his oysters from his pocket with a flourish.

Julie squealed when she saw them. "That will do very nicely. I do have some carrots and one potato put by. I'll make a quick stew. Can you put both of my pans on the hob?"

Charles set her soup pot and saucepan over the fire to heat, then poured some water from her can into the pot, figuring she'd need it for the stew.

Before Julie had returned with her shucked oysters, vegetables, and ground oatmeal, William came in. Charles shook his hand in the tiny hall and began firing questions about Hatfield.

William laughed and held up his hand in front of his merry face. "How many cups of tea did you drink today? Visiting our old ladies?"

Charles put a finger to his mouth. "Timothy's sleeping and Julie is working on our meal."

"Very good," William said in a lower voice. "I was hoping I didn't need to go outside again." He pulled a squashed packet from his pocket. "It's a ham sandwich, but the seller only had one left."

"We can cut it up and serve it with the oyster stew she's going to make. But you must remember you have Lucy to feed, too, now."

William rubbed his chin. "Mrs. Herring must have taken Timothy for long enough for Julie to go out for oysters?"

"No, I brought them. Mrs. Herring is being very demanding. In fact, I'd better go across the passage and give her a few more shillings to keep her happy." Charles clapped his friend on the shoulder and went out the door, leaving it ajar.

Across the way, a man who must be Mr. Herring was opening that door.

"I'm Mr. Dickens," Charles explained. He fished in his pocket and pulled out two half crowns. "For Mrs. Herring on account for Timothy?"

"Ah, yer tha father?" Mr. Herring said. A beefy man, he had an exceptionally well-victualed appearance. "I'm werry sorry to tell you, but ve can't keep that bastard child of yers."

"He's not mine," Charles said sharply. "I'm paying his way because his mother just perished in a terrible fire. We're looking for his father." He pushed back into his pocket and found another three shillings.

Mr. Herring took them with a grunt, then shut the door in Charles's face without another word.

"Extortionist," Charles muttered as he returned to the Agas' rooms. London was ever full of people trying to make a quick shilling.

Julie bustled back and forth, making the stew. William sat on the sofa, a silly grin on his face as he watched her. To be helpful, Charles took the water can to the roof cistern for a refill, regretting it as soon as the wind hit him. By the time he returned, William had Timothy cradled in his arms and their newest household member had returned.

"Why, look at you," Charles exclaimed. He wouldn't have known the mudlark without Julie's identification.

Lucy's white blond hair had been pinned back from a young, pale, saintly face. Her nose had a slight hook at the tip, pointing down to cherubic lips. She had a round jaw with a stubborn chin. Her eyes were dark and tumultuous under brows considerably darker than her hair.

She wore a simple black dress with a white shawl collar and a bodice with buttons up the front, none of which completely matched. Her fingers picked at the edges of her apron, and Charles realized he'd been staring.

"You must be older than I thought," he told her. "I'm Dickens. We've never met in daylight."

Her lips quirked. "I was born the year George the Fourth was crowned, I'm told, Mr. Dickens."

"That was eighteen-twenty-one," William called from his seat. "July, I believe. You are probably fourteen."

Charles nodded. "I believe it. It's past time for you to learn more skills than mudlarking."

"We did well enough," Lucy Fair said. She sat in an armchair pulled away from the fire, probably unused to this much warmth. "It was great fun until Lack and his gang came."

"I'll keep an eye on what's left of your little family," Charles promised.

"The stew is ready," Julie said as Lucy gave him a nod. "Lucy, can you pull chairs to the table?"

Lucy dutifully rearranged the room until four chairs were lined up around the deal table, then found bowls and spoons. They sat down with the pot of stew on a trivet and the ham sandwich cut into squares on a plate.

Julie ladled out her creation, muttering to herself about her need to visit the shops.

"Can't you just stand in the doorway downstairs? Plenty of street sellers pass by here," Charles said.

"Better prices down the road aways," Julie told him. "I like to go where I'm known."

"I can mind the baby tomorrow so you can go," Lucy said.

"Do you know what to do now?" William asked.

Lucy ticked off items on her fingers. "I just have to keep him warm, clean, and fed. It isn't so hard."

"It is when you're exhausted from the crying." Julie yawned.

She did look tired, Charles thought, but William clinked his wineglass against Charles's and began to talk about his political meeting. After that, Charles caught them up on the events in Mr. Screws's life.

Later on, the women left with the baby and went into another room to give him a bath. William poured the last of the bottle between their two glasses.

"Bad news, my friend," he said.

Charles's stomach lurched despite the excellent victuals. William had delayed relaying his Hatfield update. "No sign of a different Mr. Dickens?"

"No, you were publicly called Timothy's father at the Eight Bells Pub. That little maid is holding to her story."

"Did she claim to know me?"

"Not exactly. She said she saw you with her sister once, and the name was right."

"There are many variations of my name, some exceedingly common." Charles drained his glass as if it could bury his fears with the stew. "I appreciate you traveling for me. I am very concerned about the consequences of this folly. What if Kate finds out about Timothy before I have cleared up this matter?"

William drained his glass. "You might not."

Charles gritted his teeth. "I have something to show you. I picked it up from my desk earlier." He went to his coat and pulled out a notebook, then brought it back to the table.

"Let me do something about the fire." William rose and went to the coal hod. "It's cooling down in here."

Charles flipped through his notebook, looking for October 1834. When William came back, still holding his poker, Charles showed him the notations. "The *Chronicle* hired me in August, so I can't deny I was traveling. But in November, my father was arrested again for debt and I spent a great deal of time here in town raising money amongst our relatives and friends attempting to prevent disaster. See? I never went near Hatfield."

William sat down again, laid the poker against his knee, and flipped through the pages. "That's all very well, Charles, but do you have a twin?"

Charles laughed. "I don't look that unusual."

"I remember you complaining about this," William said, poking his finger at a page. He pulled a cigar from his pocket as he spoke. "You were sent to review a farce and discovered it was plagiarized from your own story."

"'The Bloomsbury Christening,'" Charles agreed. "How irritating that anyone who cares to can make use of our creative work and we are not paid."

"At least you aren't the most miserable man in the world," William joked.

"I will be if my fiancée discovers people believe I fathered a child."

"It would have been before you met her," William said.

"I am not sure that would matter very much, given my financial obligation to set up a household suitable for her. No, I need to find Timothy's father and get out from under the burden of his upkeep. The Herrings are going to bleed me dry."

"He won't need a wet nurse forever," William said.

"Can you afford to keep Lucy?"

"I can't afford not to have Lucy working for us." William stuck the cigar in his mouth and rose. "She's too beautiful to allow out and about. I'm worried about her future."

Charles chuckled. "Who'd have thought mudlarking a safe profession?"

"She's much too young to marry. We'll just have to do the best we can to train her as a maid of all work." He bent over the fire and lit his cigar.

"Maybe she can be a parlor maid after Julie trains her." Charles couldn't help the laughter that bubbled up.

"You eat Julie's dinners often enough," William groused. "No need to complain about her housekeeping skills now."

"That is true. She's become a good plain cook. Never burns anything these days. But the only reason your chambers are neat is because you move so often."

"Must you continue to hold a grudge, Charles?" William asked through a round puff of smoke. "My wife was your maid for only a few days almost a year ago."

Charles offered his friend a theatrical bow. "I am sorry, my good man, that the truth hurts. I am off to my own untidy chambers in a few moments to see if the laundress did her duties today. A dry shirt would be a luxury. But first, I should tell you about the Harley inquest, and share the tale of a missing corpse."

Back at Furnival's Inn, Charles found his brother drinking ale next to the dying fire. He had a copy of *The Pilgrim's Progress* open across his thighs. Charles glanced over Fred's shoulder and read aloud. "'Here is a poor burdened sinner. I come from the City of Destruction, but am going to Mount Zion, that I may be delivered from the Wrath to come; I would therefore, Sir, since I am informed that by this Gate is the Way thither, know if you are willing to let me in?'"

"Stirring stuff," Fred said drowsily.

"You sound more unstirred by your ale, young sir, than stirred by this literary classic." Charles yawned and went to pull the curtains as Fred set the book on the sofa arm.

Outside the fog had thickened until Charles could not even see the street lamps in front of the building. He heard the sounds of a carriage moving through the street, hooves muted by the fog. "I wonder if Bethlehem suffered from such darkness," he muttered.

Fred's only answer was a burp.

After he shooed Fred toward the bedroom, Charles went to the fire and added coal, then took his writing box and set it on the sofa. He cast himself down in the warm spot Fred had vacated and picked up his ale tankard, finding one mouthful left.

Thus minimally refreshed, he pulled the papers for his cornerstone sketch for his book, which was called "A Visit to Newgate" and was based on his research trip there a few weeks ago. The adventure had been everything he expected, and he didn't think his draft would need to be reconstructed too much to reach its final form. As difficult as visiting Coldbath Fields over the summer had been, Newgate was much worse.

He glanced over the first few paragraphs, troubled at the sight of his oblique reference to James Pratt and John Smith, who'd been executed for sodomy about ten days ago, weeks after he'd seen them at the prison. Seventeen men had been sentenced to die that fall, yet these two were the only men to actually be executed. In fact, they were the first public hangings at the prison for almost two years.

"Barbaric," Charles muttered, thinking uneasily of his friend Breese Gadfly. The songwriter did not always hide his romantic interest in other men well. These men had died because of the testimony of one sanctimonious landlord and his wife. How dangerous his friend Breese's life was. Mr. Screws, fragile as he was, would not last long in Newgate either, even though he would probably not hang at his age.

He stared at the pages for a few more minutes, then fetched himself a rum and water and went back to work. He finished revisions on that story, then moved on to the next, one of the sketches that had first run in the *Evening Chronicle*. The hour grew late, his candle burning down. His quill slipped from his fingers and his head settled back on the sofa.

Charles stirred. He heard a rapping at the door. The fire had died down and his candle had puddled, wickless, in its holder but the room had not yet gone cold. He felt his way to the mantelpiece and took a dip from a box, then held it into the coals until it caught fire. Ink dotted his fingers and shirt cuff from an accident with his pen. More work for the incompetent laundress. As he walked to the door, his fingers softened the tallow, which put off an unpleasant, sheepish scent. His flame danced along the walls.

When he opened the door, he saw nothing at first. Then he raised his candle. A thin, tall figure, shrouded by a dark cloak, stood in front of him. Fog, or perhaps smoke, swirled around his feet. Charles didn't recognize him but saw a hint of pale trousers when the man stepped forward.

"Charles Dickens?" moaned a sepulchral voice.

Charles, feeling a hint of unease, wished he had taken the time to find a candleholder. His hand was warm, and he was afraid the candle would bend and burn him. "Yes. Can you give me a moment?"

"Charles Dickens?" the man moaned, louder. Hands in fine white evening gloves pushed his hood back from his face.

Charles took a step back instinctively, holding his candle high. What fresh menace was this?

Chapter 7

In the candle's glow, Charles could now see a grave-white face burrowing inside the deep hood. He could not perceive any sign of a hairline, but the sunken cheeks and half-closed eyes reminded him of someone he'd seen recently. Did he look like Jacob Harley, or merely any corpse? Shifting in his doorway, he attempted to step closer to the figure, but the being held up his hands in warning.

"I bring you a message," the strange creature moaned.

"From whom?" Charles attempted to keep his tone skeptical, though his heartbeat rattled in his chest.

"The Beyond," intoned the voice.

"Beyond what?" snapped Charles, covering for his nervousness. Who was this creature?

"Leave the Screws household alone." His ghastly voice nonetheless held an air of menace.

Charles clutched his candle more tightly. It began to bend. "Who are you, sir?"

His visitor gave a spectral chuckle. His gums showed very gray, his teeth very brown, against the pale lips.

"Do not attempt to frighten me," Charles warned, switching his candle to his other hand. "Are you involved in the body snatching?" He took a quick step forward.

Before he could reach the cloaked figure, he heard a crash. A cacophony of sound resonated as the window at the end of the passage collapsed into a thousand shards. Charles covered his eyes and fell back against his lintel, trying to avoid the glass. The wind rushed through. He opened his eyes cautiously.

The hooded figure had disappeared in the commotion. An accomplice must have managed to smash the window from down below. As Charles righted himself, a door opened across the passage.

"Wot happened?" asked a young lawyer, rubbing sleep from his eyes. Named Alan Whitacre, he'd moved in the previous month. Charles didn't know him to speak to but the man dressed well and seemed a sober sort.

"The window," Charles said, holding up his candle again and stepping into the passage. His candle blew out. He swore and retreated, running his fingers along the wall to anchor himself.

By the time he had returned to his door with his relit wick, Mr. Whitacre had lit a lantern, his candle protected by the glass sides. Charles saw his sleeve twinkle in the candlelight. He brushed away tiny bits of glass that pricked at his fingers.

"Are you hurt?"

"No." Charles followed the lawyer down the passage.

"There ought to be a rock on the floor, something that broke the window." Mr. Whitacre, methodical, swept his lantern up and down the floor.

Shards of glass twinkled in the light, but Charles saw no sign of a projectile.

"God's teeth, but it's a bitter night," the lawyer muttered.

"The wind doesn't help. What broke the window? How did the specter manage it?" Charles's eyes darted everywhere the lantern's glow went. He refused to believe that a ghost had broken a window and disappeared. "Fiend."

"Calm down, Dickens. They'll board the window up in the morning. If you have a spare blanket, I'd suggest you lay it along the floorboards behind your door to keep the wind out."

"An excellent suggestion," Charles said, his mind whirling with ghost stories. One thing was certain. He'd be on Emmanuel Screws's doorstep at the top of the day, demanding to know who had attempted to haunt him. As much as he had initially detested the old man, he'd begun to suspect that greater forces were afoot than one cantankerous old soul who'd disliked the Dickens family.

Charles had not been to Finsbury Circus for three days. His first solo daylight visit the morning after the spectral call reminded him anew of how imposing the inner private park was, how solid and prosperous the inhabiters of the area were. His father had reached over-high in that attempt to get funds. Turning away from the sight of damp greenery over the fence, Charles's eyes skittered past the spot where Jacob Harley had lain. He took a double-sized step over it and went up the stairs.

Mrs. Dorset opened the door promptly after he rang. She wore unrelieved black, not uncommon for housekeepers, but on her it gave the air of one about to leave for the cemetery to pay respects. "Sir?"

"You'll remember me, Mrs. Dorset. I need to see your master."

"He is usually at the countinghouse at this hour."

"So early? I thought to catch him before he left." Charles pulled off his top hat and tilted it to the side to pour off the water he'd acquired on the walk over.

"He has not yet departed today." Mrs. Dorset sounded concerned. She stepped back to allow Charles to come inside. "If you will wait?"

He followed her to a room on the right of the entrance. She opened the door for him before walking toward the back of the house. Grateful not to have to return to the chilly parlor, he peered in to see a long, highly polished table, which would seat twelve. Only five chairs with carved backs were tucked in along each side. One ornate chair with armrests lined up at one end. The window side of the table had no chair. Two silver candelabras graced the table, ready with candles that definitely didn't smell of animal fat.

He went to the etagere behind the armchair to look at the painting over it, the only one in the room, passing by a pretty tiled stove that kept the room temperate. Mr. Screws must breakfast here as well as eat his evening meal.

Charles chuckled when he realized who featured in the painting. Mr. Screws had once allowed himself to be painted. There he was, large as life, graying hair sticking out in all directions, with, Charles assumed, his partner, Jacob Harley. Mr. Screws stood a little taller here than he did in life these days. Charles guessed the men might be in their midfifties or a bit younger, an idea borne out by the fact that they were dressed more in the style of the late Regency than this modern age of William IV.

Mr. Screws still had a pinched expression on his mouth, but Mr. Harley had a more jovial air. In that era, he'd already had a paunch, but also enjoyed rosy cheeks and a ready smile in the rounded face. Charles searched the painted face, looking for signs that matched his specter of the night before. Was the nose the same? The mouth? How could he say, given that these features were painted and the real-life creature may have decorated his face to give the appearance of the grave? For surely, the ghost had not been real, but some miscreant attempting to post as Harley returned from the grave?

He heard coughing outside the door. The door opened and

Mr. Screws tottered in. Charles went to take his arm. The man needed his cane for support this morning.

"Good morning, Mr. Dickens. Come to collect for your charity again?" Mr. Screws wheezed, ignoring Charles's outstretched hand. He fished a handkerchief from his pocket and coughed into it.

Charles saw that if nothing else, Mrs. Dorset kept the household linen very clean and white. "You had asked me to find Mr. Harley's, er, remains," he reminded the old man.

"I did not expect you to have any success, sir. No, he is on some doctor's table by now, being chopped up by students." Mr. Screws hacked. "I don't hold with it, sir."

Who would, except the men who profited from the body snatching? "I did trouble myself to hunt down Mr. Dawes's undertaking operation but the house was shut up tight. I could not think of what more to do on a winter's evening."

"I thought you were a man of ideas," rejoined Mr. Screws, his words punctuated by coughs. "I might as well have braved the police."

Charles ignored the man's lack of confidence in him. After all, he'd asked for help in the first place. He pulled out the chair closest to the stove. "Come and sit down, sir. Let the heat aid your lungs."

Screws pulled his arm away when Charles attempted to take it. He half sat, half fell into the chair.

"Why are you here?" the old man demanded. "What do you want from me?"

Had the old man's mind begun to wander? Why would he think Charles would not offer a report on the search for the undertaker? "The body might be missing, but the spirit is on the move." Charles pulled out the next chair and sat, his knees almost touching the bony Screwsian appendages.

Mrs. Dorset entered with a tray and took it to the opposite side of the table, then pushed it in between the two men. "Elderberry cordial and tea, sirs. Mr. Screws should have both for his cough."

Her master sneered. She stuck her nose in the air and walked out.

Charles poured cordial into the small glasses provided and slid one glass toward his host. "It might help prevent a chest cold developing."

"Pour the tea," the old man said. "Cordial is loathsome." Despite his words, he drained the glass, and it did seem to help his cough. After he had breathed deeply a couple of times, he spoke again, in a stronger voice. "What is this about Jacob's spirit?"

Charles slowed his voice to suit the tale. "I had a visitor last night, very late. A cloaked figure, deliberately trying to frighten me."

"Why do you say that?" He picked up his teacup.

Mrs. Dorset had put a honey pot on the tray, but no other accompaniments. Charles added honey to his tea.

"Helps with coughs," Mr. Screws said. "Did you add any to mine?" Charles nodded as he continued. "She is an efficient woman. I should have married someone like her, instead of chasing love and a pretty face."

"That sounds like a story," Charles said.

"But you were telling me one of yours." Screws gave him a long glance over his teacup.

"My visitor's face looked as if it had been dug up," Charles said. "Or at least been in a coffin for days. He told me to leave your household alone. Then, as I attempted to come close to him, to push the hood completely off his face and ascertain his identity, the window at the end of the corridor suddenly exploded. Glass everywhere, even on me. The creature disappeared." He pointed to the small nick on his cheek.

Mr. Screws laughed until he began to cough, all the wrinkles in his face collapsing in on themselves as if he were a spoiled apple. "He must have broken the glass in order to escape."

"No. The glass broke inward. I had glass on my sleeve and it littered the floor. One last thing." Charles leaned forward. "No projectile. We looked last night, my neighbor and I, with a lantern. Fred, my brother, and I looked again this morning. No one had cleaned up the glass but there was nothing else. No rock. No tree branch. Nothing."

Mr. Screws let out one last little giggle. "I almost hope it was Jacob. Such laughs we had when we were young. We were a jovial pair back in the days of Mr. Wintersea, where we apprenticed."

Charles saw his opportunity to learn more about the murdered man's past. Kate would appreciate the story, so he'd tuck it away for her. "Who was the pretty face you chased in those days?"

"Jacob had a sister," Mr. Screws said musingly. "Mary, she was. Mary Harley. She had—" his fingers gestured vaguely.

Charles couldn't tell if he was gesturing to a pretty face or a pretty form or something else entirely. "What happened?"

The man's lips trembled, but then he firmed them with a downturn of his flesh. "She rejected my suit, said yes to another apprentice, then died of cholera the next summer. Died unwed and much too young."

What a cold summation. His love had calcified into indifference with the passage of so many years. Charles hoped the same would never happen to his relationship with Kate. "Very sad."

"Yes. I never looked at another pretty girl after her betrayal." The old man sneered.

Charles could not help but remember his own unsuccessful three-year courtship of banker's daughter Maria Beadnell. If he hadn't had the heart to find another girl to love, would he have risked becoming such a man as Mr. Screws in the future? Thank

God for Kate, even if Maria's memory did still haunt him at times. "I am sorry you did not try again."

"She said I loved money too much." The old man stared into his cup as if the leaves could tell him a tale. "She must have been correct."

"I see."

Mr. Screws startled and glanced up. "But Jacob was a different character."

"Did he marry?"

"No, but he does have a son. A bastard, who was in fact at dinner that dreadful evening. Maybe he is the explanation for your visitor. Was he very like Jacob?"

Charles wondered why the son had not been at the inquest. Perhaps he had given his testimony before Charles arrived. "I thought so, but I never saw Jacob in life. I saw his body and his painted portrait." He indicated it on the wall.

"I have a more youthful miniature in my study. Come. I will show it to you." The old man put down his cup and rose. This time he took Charles's arm and they rocked out of the room together.

They went past one door in the hall. The space could not be sized for more than storage. Then they went into a room equally as large as the dining room and clearly set up for work. Mr. Screws released Charles and tottered behind his imposing desk. Behind that was a long table, nearly covered with papers. He picked up a small frame at one end and handed it across the desk.

Charles went to the window, which opened onto the back garden. He could see better once he'd opened the curtain. Jacob had been thirty or more years younger in this miniature. Maybe it had been painted for his mistress. He had dark hair and a ruddy face. Thick lips coarsened the face but the eyes were piercing, even in paint.

Given Mr. Screws's attachment to his business partner, perhaps the old man had arranged to have the body stolen himself. It had been so strange when he'd arrived today. Mr. Screws had not inquired into the investigation that he had ordered. Nor, did it seem, that he intended to go to the police. But where would Mr. Screws hide a decaying body?

Charles glanced through the window. Outside was a flagstone walkway around the back of the house, then a low hedge surrounded what might have been an herb garden. The space looked functional rather than designed for walking. He saw no sign of disturbance.

With a vague sense of unease, he remembered Mrs. Dorset's great bear of a son. Johnny Dorset could have dug a grave quickly enough, though no sign of one existed.

"Just herbs?" Charles inquired.

"In the garden?" Mr. Screws said from his chair. "No. We grow vegetables in the summer. Cabbages in the winter. Saves money. Better than we can get in the markets."

"I see. Ground is probably easily turned over."

"Yes, not yet frozen at this time of year. Johnny is good at the work."

Charles saw a small shed at the far end. Lots of shovels in there, he expected. Still, he didn't think a grave could be hidden in such a tidy space, not at this time of year in this cold. A coffin wouldn't fit in the shed.

He turned and handed the miniature back to Mr. Screws. "Are you well enough to introduce me to this bastard Harley?"

"Yes," Mr. Screws said with a quaver.

Primus Harley, the late Jacob Harley's bastard son, lived in a comfortable room on Steward Street in Spitalfields. The seventeenth-century house sported red brick and slightly tattered four-pane shutters over the windows. While an area with an extremely poor and sickly reputation, housing on the edge remained decent, despite the decline in the weaving industry. The younger Mr. Harley's chamber, probably once a parlor, had a large window overlooking the street.

From it, Charles watched Mr. Screws's coachman talking to his horses. Though only half a mile from Mr. Screws's mansion, the old gentleman had insisted on taking his carriage, and Charles did not blame him, given his unsteady gait.

Mr. Harley's fireplace dwarfed the room, but he made good use of it. He had a drying rack with a blanket over it, a good-sized hob, and presently poured water from the steaming kettle into a teapot. Despite all of these pleasing accoutrements, not least of all an open box of shortbread on the low table in front of a pair of armchairs, Charles could not like the man. He seemed to have no care for the common ties of family.

The good news had been that as soon as he had opened his door to them, Charles knew Mr. Harley had not been his ghostly visitor of the night before. He scarcely came to Charles's shoulder and he could not imagine the greasepaint it would have required to completely take the life out of his ruddy flesh.

Mr. Harley's mother must have been an Irishwoman, given the wild shock of orange hair on his head and the backs of his hands. Thick hands, too, which didn't match Charles's remembrance of the false shade's appendages.

He would not entertain the notion that his visitor had been an actual ghost, as the apparition had claimed.

Mr. Harley set down the teapot on the table and pulled a cane chair from his small dining table and brought it over to them.

"You know I never mind seeing you, Uncle Emmanuel," he said, perching on his chair. "But I have no interest in my father, his death or his funeral, nor his resting place."

"I thought you might care to know that his body has gone missing," Mr. Screws said. He coughed mightily and applied his handkerchief.

Mr. Harley's body finally stilled. "Are you well, sir? The tea will just be a couple of minutes."

Mr. Screws waved his concern away.

"Missing?" Mr. Harley continued. "No, I don't suppose I do care about that. Mother ended up in a pauper's grave, not even a resting spot of her own, thanks to my father refusing to marry her."

"He paid your way," Mr. Screws said. "You had a good education, Primus."

"But—"

"No," Mr. Screws said, with a hint of virile sharpness. "Your mother, who was nothing but a washerwoman when he met her, had a roof over her head and food every day of her life after she met Jacob. She could never have counted on that. He treated her better than her parents could have, or even some Irish husband."

"He should have married her," Mr. Harley protested. "She was devoted to him."

"In her way," the old man sneered.

"Nothing doing," Mr. Harley snapped. "She was an excellent woman. My father spent his life afraid of her popishness and petticoats, ridiculous things to fear. He preferred to hide in his countinghouse."

Charles's eyes widened. Mr. Screws's own instruments of vision bulged in their sockets. "I-I think the tea is ready," Charles stammered, hoping to reduce the tension.

"Very well," Mr. Harley muttered, wrapping his fingers around his pot and pouring thick tan liquid into coarse brown pottery cups.

Charles could smell that the leaves weren't fresh. He stood and went to the loom in the window. The silk on it appeared to be a half-finished garment, possibly a shawl, woven in a swirled pattern in light and dark creams. "Absolutely exquisite work," he said.

"It's for the Duchess of Beaufort," Mr. Harley said. "She has a large family and they keep me in work."

"Was your mother a weaver as well?"

"No, she died when I was ten. Then I was apprenticed in a trade suitable to her ancestry." Mr. Harley's eyes pierced into Charles's when he turned away from the loom. "I have naught of hers but a lock of her hair. My father let me keep nothing, calling sentiment womanish."

Why had a man so sentimental himself not taken a wife? Primus Harley must be around thirty. Perhaps he could not afford one. Or he had some unseen defect of personality such that would allow one to become a patricide.

"Are you satisfied, Mr. Dickens?" the old gentleman said. "As you can see, there is little chance that Mr. Harley was involved in either the theft of my partner's body, or his death, or your visitation last night."

"I believe you," Charles said. He trusted nothing.

"Truly, I do not understand why you dismiss the idea that it really was Jacob's shade," Mr. Screws said over his teacup. "If anyone could return from the grave it was him. He had an inextinguishable force of personality." He closed his eyes and sucked in the steam through his pursed lips.

Charles threw himself into the armchair and took a piece of shortbread, then bit into it savagely. He had so much work to do and the waste of time grated on his nerves.

"It is very good?" Mr. Harley asked, his gaze softening and anxious as Charles swallowed his bite.

His mouth warmed with the luscious velvet taste of butter mixed in an alchemy with flour and other ingredients. "Yes, I've never tasted better. What does it have in it?"

"Spices," Mr. Harley said with relish. "I don't like bland colors or food."

Mr. Screws broke into Charles's enjoyment. "You should take a look at Hugh Appleton next."

"Remind me who that is again?" Charles asked, taking another piece of shortbread as Mr. Harley lifted the box to his hand.

"The owner of the chain manufacturer who was about to be

ruined by Jacob," Mr. Screws said. "He had just mentioned at dinner that he was going to lower the axe, when he took ill and left the table."

"I'll speak to Mr. Appleton," Charles said.

"We shall leave you to your work, Primus," said Mr. Screws wearily. "I do wish you would remember your father in a better light."

Hugh Appleton's blacksmith enterprise perched on the south side of the river. Charles went across Blackfriars Bridge to Southwark to find it, craning his neck to see if he could spot any sign of mudlark activity on the foreshore, but in what passed for daylight at this time of year, visibility was too poor to spot anyone.

The smithy was an entirely different level of affair from the one he'd known behind his rooms on Selwood Terrace the previous summer. Here, you could tell that no families were eking out a threadbare existence in cottages behind the forge. The smithy was an enormous, busy operation, with men of all ages moving about self-importantly. Behind the main building was a solitary cottage, with a painted signboard announcing APPLETON CHAINWORKS to anyone visiting.

Charles walked through the yard to see if he could find the owner and understand why such a bustling enterprise had been about to be ruined by Jacob Harley.

He passed through the open front door of the cottage. Inside, three men, two in workman's clothes, were bent over a piece of paper spread over a table. None of them glanced up, but he heard heated conversation about specifications and tensile strength. The third man wore the clothing of a gentleman. While much younger than Emmanuel Screws, he had the leanness and the fidgety energy of the older man. He wore a dark suit, very plain, and when he pulled his hat off to scratch his head Charles saw he was bald except for wild dark brown tufts above his ears. The hat went up and down three times, and then the man cast it aside and pulled at those singular tufts of hair. His gaze wandered until he spotted Charles.

Charles inclined his head. "Charles Dickens, *Morning Chronicle*, sir."

"*Morning Chronicle*? What have we done to warrant the interest of such a publication?" the man asked. He nodded at the workmen, who rolled up the paper and departed with inquiring glances.

"I'm researching the demise of Jacob Harley," Charles said, leaving out the "why" he was doing such a thing.

The man's hands went to his hair again, then fell away. He folded his hands over his chest. His right eye twitched.

"What is the story of your involvement with Mr. Harley and Mr. Screws's countinghouse?" Charles asked. He looked closely at the man's hands. They belonged to a musician. He never could have trained those long, sensitive fingers at a forge. No scars, and his forearms looked too thin to work with metal.

"We supply chains to Fairbairn and Lillie. They've come down from Manchester to set up iron ship works here and we needed capital to start the work."

"Are you Hugh Appleton?"

"I am, yes. My father was a blacksmith, a successful one, and I expanded from his business."

"I see. An impressive smithy. I've seen what a two-man operation looks like."

Mr. Appleton's narrow chest puffed. "I have twelve senior blacksmiths. Expanded from eight after Mr. Fairbairn, the distinguished engineer, chose us for his chain work."

"You applied to Mr. Harley for a loan?"

"We've had the contract less than a year, you see. No time to earn enough to pay back the loan. When Mr. Harley visited and said he didn't trust my operation and he was canceling the loan, well you can imagine my distress."

Charles hardened his expression, imagining he was Sir Silas presiding over an inquest. "Did you murder him?"

The man's mouth dropped open. "Good heavens, no! I've never been to Mr. Screws's house, where he died. He wasn't a well man, but he managed to come here to speak to me."

"Do you have any theories?" Charles rasped.

Mr. Appleton emoted something between a laugh and a cry. "I haven't stopped praying since I had heard about the chain being involved in his death."

Charles shared, "I saw the death and testified at the inquest. The undertaker told me of evidence of interference by human hands before the chain ever went around his neck. I wonder that you weren't there."

The business owner sagged against the table. It took his weight as he dropped his head to his chest. After a moment, he linked his fingers together and bowed his head in obvious prayer. When he looked up, he said, "I wasn't called. Do you think Mr. Screws will finalize the cancellation of my loan?"

"I have no idea, but I will ask him to send you a letter," Charles said. He did not think this man had anything to do with the murder. That didn't mean some subordinate or family member wasn't involved.

"That would be very kind of you."

Charles sighed at Mr. Appleton's hopeful expression. He did not want this man's relatives to be guilty. "Do you have a second-in-command? A son?"

"My son is thirteen," Mr. Appleton said. "The oldest one. My brother worked with me until his death. I support his children with the business, but they are all girls."

"Then I very much hope that Mr. Screws makes a different decision," Charles said. The man could be hiding some other associate, but no suspect was obvious. He decided not to press on. He was due in Brompton for dinner and didn't want to miss spending time with Kate. "I will be in touch. Is there a hackney stand near here?"

"The nearest is some fifteen minutes' walk away, Mr. Dickens," Mr. Appleton said. "If you would permit me to walk with you, I would happily share my hopes for my business."

"That won't be necessary," Charles said hastily. "I am a reporter, not a partner in the countinghouse."

Chapter 8

For the Tuesday evening meal, Mrs. Hogarth and her kitchen girl had prepared a pork roast, cheese-covered sliced potatoes, and cabbage. A treacle tart came out after the meal, to squeals of delight from the children.

After the treacle tart pan was empty, the Hogarths sent the very youngest up to their cots with Mary to tuck them in. Mr. Hogarth lit his pipe and resettled himself in his armchair at the fireplace end of their dining table while Mrs. Hogarth poured tea. The girls took up needles and the boys, their books.

"Ye've been verra quiet tonight, Charles," he observed. "What's troubling ye?"

Charles changed seats to where Mary had sat next to her father, close to the fire. "Kate wanted me to help Mr. Screws so I've been chasing the story. I saw the chain manufacturer today, but I don't think he had anything to do with the death despite his business being threatened by the countinghouse. I met Primus Harley, who is Mr. Harley's illegitimate son."

Mrs. Hogarth put her hand to her chest. "I never."

"Yes, I agree that using a business's chains in a murder is

ghastly, but it doesn't mean that Mr. Appleton was involved in the nasty business," Charles explained.

"That is true," Mrs. Hogarth said, patting her dark curls back under her cap. "I meant that ye had to have dealings with the bastard son."

Charles forced a weary smile onto his face and took the cup of tea that she handed him. Taking into account Mrs. Hogarth's reaction, he knew he'd made the right decision not to tell the family about baby Timothy. "Given that a ghost popped up outside my chambers last night, I have to see everyone who might be involved."

"A ghost?" Kate exclaimed, wide eyed, from her spot in the rocking chair on the other side of the fireplace, away from the table. She dropped her knitting needles into her lap.

"I'm sure it wasn't really a ghost," he demurred. "But the situation was highly dramatic." He explained what had happened.

"You really didn't find a rock?" Kate asked. "Maybe it fell back out the window."

"The wind only went one direction," Charles said. "I'm certain Mr. Whitacre didn't kick anything out of the hole."

"I think it's a sign," Mrs. Hogarth said, as Mary came back into the room. "Mr. Harley must have been an appalling, unchristian man. Not worth wasting time on."

"What about Mr. Screws?" Kate said. "I still like him, and it's such an unusual sort of murder."

Charles smiled indulgently at Kate while Mrs. Hogarth passed a cup of tea to her oldest son, Robert, who passed it along to Mary. She sat next to her brother.

Mr. Hogarth chuckled. "Kate, my pet, ye need a better interest than murder. Flower pressing, perhaps?"

"Cooking?" Charles added helpfully.

Kate smirked at him. "I made the treacle tart myself, Mr. Dickens."

Charles brightened immediately. Visions of future tarts danced through his thoughts, quite eradicating all of the sketch revising he needed to do that night before he slept.

"I can make a better tart," Georgina said. "You should try my tart, Mr. Dickens. You'd like it ever so much."

Mrs. Hogarth spoke before he could reassure Kate's younger sister. "I don't want ye visiting this Mr. Screws again," she insisted, her nose pointing in Kate's direction as she picked up an embroidery hoop. "Finsbury Circus or not, he isnae our sort of gentleman."

Kate and Charles shared a glance. He cast about for a suitable topic, but before he could manage to open his mouth, Kate said, "I'm going to tell a ghost story. Mr. Dickens has already given us a very good one. Now it's my turn."

"Lovely," Mary said happily. She rose from the table and sat on a low stool in front of Kate.

Kate lifted her eyebrows and cleared her throat. "'Tis a tale of the Scots."

Charles noticed that her Edinburgh accent had made a dramatic reappearance. Normally, he heard only a faint trace of it.

"Gone five a.m.," Kate whispered menacingly, "and mist snaked around the boots of the men pawing through the rubble these past three hours, looking for the king and his men."

"Lord Darnley!" Mary called, shivering dramatically. "I love this one."

Robert set down his book and turned to face Kate. Charles and Mr. Hogarth exchanged amused glances.

"Aye," Kate said with a nod at her sister. "And the queen was up in Holyroodhouse, crying in her bed for her bairn's father. The purple velvet hangings hid her dark, dark shame."

Mrs. Hogarth grunted and bent her head over her stitches.

Kate winked at Charles. "Her head lifted as distant chatter drifted up the streets from Kirk o' Field. 'Let us go merrily to bed in singing . . .'"

Her voice lowered. "But it was gone morning, a February morning, and the whispers made no sense. They belonged to the night before, when the queen had left her sick lord to attend a party."

"On purpose," Robert interrupted. "For she wanted Lord Bothwell, not her husband."

"Dinna interrupt yer sister," Mr. Hogarth reproved.

Kate giggled, then went solemn again. "In the south field, under a pear tree, King Henry rose, his short white gown still despite the bitter wind.

"A yard away, poor William Taylor rose, too, a pale lute in his hands."

"Oooh," Georgina whispered, her darning forgotten in her lap.

"The king moved tae his fur robe, draped across the stubbled garden. He stared down at the spittle-encrusted garment, emotionless, and sang in a fine, clear tenor voice. 'Give ear to my words, O Lord. Hearken unto the voice of my cry . . .'

"The valet plucked dutifully at the lute as he drifted across the frost, behind the king.

"At Flodden Wall, the king stopped, his handsome young face distorting. The tendons in his neck stretched, his milky eyes unfocused, as his mouth opened tae an inhuman scream. 'Pity me, kinsmen, for the love of Him who had pity on all the world!'"

Charles shivered involuntarily at Kate's eerie cry. Georgina put her hand on his sleeve, clutching at him.

Kate's eyes opened wide. "The doomed men vanished as the garden gate opened. A harsh cry came up from a dust-soaked searcher. 'More bodies o'er here!'

"The searcher raced in, then doffed his cap as he realized he was in the presence of the king. His face went pale as he recognized the horrible truth. Darnley's body was faceup under the winter-branched tree, unmarked yet clearly dead."

Kate paused dramatically, then delivered another line. "Up in the castle, the queen clutched at her neck and coughed spasmodically, as if something had just cut intae the back of it."

"Ooooh," Mary crowed, then clapped her hands.

"She's headed for the block, that one," Robert said with relish as Charles clapped, too.

"Death stalks even the highest among us." Kate lifted her arm, her index finger focusing into a point. "No one is safe from his touch." She stood and poked her finger into Mary's side.

Mary giggled and stuck out her tongue as Kate dropped into a curtsey, then sat down again, face flushed with storytelling magic.

"You're such a good storyteller, Kate dear," Mary said, as her younger brothers hooted their approval. "How fun that was."

Kate schooled her expression and took up her knitting. "Maybe Father will give us a song now?"

The *Chronicle* office seemed extra chilly that morning when Charles walked in. He added coal to the stove before he took his coat off, then went to his desk. William slid his chair over and gave Charles a wide, charismatic smile after he sat in his desk chair. "Where have you been?"

"I went to the East End to see if Mr. Dawes had reappeared." Charles shivered. "Bloody cold it is outside."

William lost his smile. "The undertaker? Who died?"

Charles dropped his damp gloves on the corner of his desk. "Not died. Disappeared. Mr. Harley's body never made it to Kensal Green, remember?"

William yawned. "I'm not getting enough sleep with Baby Timothy about. The undertaker had it?"

"Yes, and I recognized him at the inquest when the coffin was picked up."

"So this isn't a case of a body remover masquerading as an undertaker," William mused.

"Someone must have paid him off," they said together. And smiled.

"Who would benefit from the body missing?" William asked.

"Who among the interested parties has a hiding place for a corpse?" Charles rejoined. "Not Mr. Screws. I checked."

"I saw Mr. Hogarth this morning, and he told me about your eerie visitor."

Charles leaned his mouth to his friend's ear. "Speaking of the Hogarths, say nothing to Mr. Hogarth about Timothy."

William quirked his lips. "I assumed as much. Nothing like the Scots for a dour interpretation of morality."

"Sometimes the man is the picture of reason, but his wife is not a fan of bastardy. I fear the consequences of her learning about the baby before I can prove I am not the father."

William leaned back in his chair and pulled a cigar out of his pocket. "Speaking of fatherhood?"

Charles lifted his brows as he realized William was smiling even more than usual. What was going on with his friend? "I detect a certain glow about you."

William grinned. "My wife is in an interesting condition."

Aha! Charles clapped him on the arm. "Such good news! And it explains the fainting."

William nodded. "She will have to rest. I don't want her losing another baby, like back in the spring."

"No, she was in a sorry shape for months," Charles agreed. Would she completely give up her acting career now? A pity, for she had been such a hit with her young supporters. She had traded fame for respectability. "I will cease my appearing for free meals."

"Oh, you can't stop that, with Timothy there."

"Do I need to remove him?" Charles said anxiously.

"No, no." William cut off the tip of his cigar. "Lucy is coming along. But when you do visit, bring food."

"Agreed," Charles said, putting out his hand for a shake.

"So back to this missing corpse—what is your plan?"

Charles told him about Primus Harley. In rooms, he couldn't

be hiding his father's remains. "Hugh Appleton has plenty of space at his smithy. Could even have burned up the body."

"But you can't imagine such a character haunting you."

"No," Charles agreed. "He did not seem like a killer and had no obvious partners who might have been so inspired. I will have to check the countinghouse property for hidey-holes."

"Have you been there?"

"No, but I met Mr. Screws's apprentice outside the inquest, an American called Fletcher. I'll write him a letter and he can show me around."

"It's a plan." William chewed on the end of his cigar.

"I'll send the note right now and head over after I write up an article." Charles rubbed his chin. "Visiting Appleton was Mr. Screws's idea. I'll have to get a list of enemies with deep pockets from him. Who could afford to pay a man to shut down a thriving concern? Who wants Appleton out of business?"

The countinghouse was in Lothbury, home to a number of banker and merchant offices. Screws and Harley occupied the ground level of an old soot-encrusted stone building. The sign had been freshly painted and the window and step scrubbed very clean, all the signs of prosperity.

When Charles walked in, he found a small entry with an unused coat tree. He soon discovered why. When he opened the inner door, he found an open room warmed to a degree above freezing by an old cast-iron stove. It had only one coal burning in the grate. The ornate detail above the door looked like a screaming man's face. The establishment welcomed people in, but then froze them right back out again.

Charles hunched into his overcoat and glanced at the three men at work on stools, quills clutched in gloved hands. Their bodies might have warmed the room somewhat, but all three were thin, weak, sickly specimens and would probably have been rejected if they tried to take the king's shilling.

The oldest of the three, perhaps thirty-five, set down his pen and slid off the stool, hand outstretched. "May I help you, sir? I am Robert Cratchit, the lead clerk."

Charles shook his hand, his gaze taking in three doors to the right. Mr. Screws's office, Mr. Harley's, and . . . a lumber room? If that were the case, he would have thought not quite so many chests, boxes, and ledgers would be strewn about the room, but perhaps the workers considered it a form of insulation. "I sent a note to Mr. Fletcher. Is he in?"

"Ah, I see. He is not here." Mr. Cratchit genially exposed a mouth of tan-colored teeth behind his thin, bloodless lips. "He has been forced to take on a number of Mr. Harley's responsibilities due to the unfortunate circumstances. I do not know if you are aware?"

Charles felt the drama of the moment. "I am Charles Dickens. I witnessed his demise."

"You don't say," the clerk exclaimed. "How very unpleasant, sir."

"Very much so, and as I'm sure you are aware, I've been taken into confidence."

"Indeed, sir," Mr. Cratchit agreed. "I have heard your name mentioned, sir."

Having had his fun, Charles returned to business. "No Mr. Fletcher, and no Mr. Screws, either?"

"They went across the river, sir, to see to the Appleton matter."

"Ah. Proceeding with the liquidation?"

Mr. Cratchit took Charles's arm and pulled him into the last office. He ducked out and took his candle from his desk, then joined Charles and shut the door.

"Mr. Screws considered Mr. Harley quite the equal of Wellington, sir. He would be sure to carry out any of his late partner's plans, no matter how petty."

"You disagree with that intention?" Charles looked around the space. Personal items still decorated the desk, an inkwell and a diary. A map of London, tattered around the nails, hung on one wall. The solitary window looked out over the mews.

The clerk clasped his hands over his nonexistent belly, his bulky mittens popping up over his knuckles. "I think Mr. Appleton's business is certain to do well. He just needs an extension on his loan."

"Why didn't Mr. Harley agree?"

"He was a tight-fisted, grasping sort," Mr. Cratchit said, then blanched. "Bless him, I shouldn't speak ill of the dead. It's not for me to judge."

"His body is missing," Charles said. "Any place here for a corpse?"

Mr. Cratchit giggled nervously. "Goodness me, no, Mr. Dickens!"

"What's the room next to this one? Storage?" Charles said coldly.

"Mr. Fletcher's office, sir. He's one of the Lees of Virginia, you know." Mr. Cratchit walked out of the deserted office and opened the door of the next room. Indeed, it was the office of a man of business, complete with a small desk, three chairs, and a sooty window that had a small green curtain to keep out the nonexistent sun in the tiny passage between this building and the next.

"I thought he was just an apprentice," Charles said, staring at the mound of files stacked along the wall.

"In our ways, sir, but he's a man of business. Learned the trade in Boston. He's stepped right into Mr. Harley's shoes, quite energetically so. Spent a year clerking with the rest of us before attaining his office, but we don't have his education."

"How long have you been with Screws and Harley?"

"Fourteen years," Mr. Cratchit said. "I've raised five daughters on my wages."

Charles imagined how low they must be, to dress in rags in a Lothbury office. Fifteen shillings a week? Yet he expected this man worked harder than anyone. "Any other hiding places?"

Mr. Cratchit made a come-hither gesture with his fingers next to his ear and they left the office. He pointed to an enormous blackened chest under a ledger-covered table against the far wall. "That's big enough, but last I checked, it was full of old rent books."

"It's thick enough, and cold enough in here, to hide the smell," Charles said. "Let's look."

Mr. Cratchit knelt down on the dusty floor and lifted the lid. The chest wasn't even locked. Charles peered in and saw that indeed rent books filled it.

"No bit of garden?" he asked.

"No, sir. What's happened, do you think?"

"Someone's paid the undertaker to hide it and close his business and run off."

"Or Mr. Harley is resurrected," said Mr. Cratchit nervously. "If he's sold his soul to the Devil, like."

The door to the clerk's room banged open. Mr. Screws stood in the doorway, weaving as he held the lintel with one hand and an old crooked cane with the other.

"Sold out his entire inventory," Mr. Screws quavered.

"What's that, sir?" Mr. Cratchit asked, bustling to his master as the other two clerks bent their bodies, vulture-like, over their ledgers. He helped Mr. Screws with his coat, then took his arm gently and trundled him into the first office.

Charles heard the click of flint against steel as Mr. Cratchit lit a candle and then laid a fire in the office stove. It must be the lead clerk's responsibility to be a nursemaid as well as maintain documents.

He followed them into the office. "You're saying Mr. Appleton is solvent again?"

"Again?" Mr. Screws said sourly, nodding at him. "For the

first time, more like. Someone wrote an article in one of the newspapers about the murder and the chains. The publicity led to one of the shipyards snatching up everything Appleton had in his warehouse. Needed a supply and Appleton had it."

"And?" Charles asked.

"He has paid everything due on his loan," said Mr. Fletcher, coming in behind him. "The cheek of the man. All our paperwork for nothing."

Charles glanced at the American and saw the twinkle in his eye.

"The police will hear about this," Mr. Screws squeaked. "A better motive for murder I could not offer."

"And at this time of the year, too," Charles said sarcastically, his loathing for the old miser renewed. Could he not be happy that the man had saved his business? What had happened to Christmas spirit in London? He turned to Mr. Fletcher, saw he was grinning, and felt relieved that one man in the operation had a heart.

"Why don't you come with me, Mr. Dickens?" said Mr. Fletcher. "Our employer will want Mr. Cratchit to catch him up on all the day's doings."

"Very well." Charles inclined his head to Mr. Screws, whose head was sunk rather low on his chest for that time of day, and followed the American into the middle office. He could still feel pity for the frail package that housed the unbending spirit.

Mr. Fletcher reached for his candlestick and vanished back out the door while Charles seated himself on the second chair in the room. He returned a moment later, candle lit. "I leave the door open since there is no stove," he explained. "But one must have some light."

"Indeed," Charles agreed. "I had better get to my own office. Did you have any advice for me about hiding places?"

"I did," Mr. Fletcher said. "Speak to Mrs. Dorset, since her employer is out of the house. I think you will find her conversation illuminating."

Charles's thoughts sharpened at that word *illuminating*. "Do you think she knows where the body is?"

"No." Mr. Fletcher colored slightly. "I meant that the dear lady would like to speak to you."

"I would like that as well," said Charles. "For no other reason than I want a second look at that large son of hers. Why does she want to speak to me?"

"The Dorsets are a formidable pair. She has the brains, and he, as is obvious, has the brawn," Mr. Fletcher said glibly. "I believe she has some history to relate to you."

Charles nodded. "Servants see all. Perhaps she can shed some desperately needed light on this situation."

"One other thing before you go," the American added.

"What is it?"

"The Royal Victoria tonight?" he asked. "I thought you and your lady might like to join me and my lady for *The Jewess*. It's supposed to be a marvelous piece. I've rented a box."

"How kind of you," Charles said. He looked at the narrow clock case across from the doorway and noted the time. "I'd have to get word to Miss Hogarth right away."

Mr. Fletcher pulled out a sheet of paper and pushed his inkwell to Charles. "Invite, invite," he suggested. "The postman will be by at any moment."

Charles did as suggested, then passed the letter back to the apprentice before leaving. Once on the pavement outside, he decided to go to Mr. Screws's mansion directly and avoid returning to the *Chronicle* for now.

Thankfully he didn't come across that many dead bodies. Sorting out who had created them took a great deal of time from his revisions.

A faint, gray winter light continued to break through the cloud cover. The fog had held off for now. Charles hoped the weather would stay that way as he didn't relish bringing Kate back to Brompton in heavy yellow muck. Horses could stumble or hit something just like a man alone.

At Finsbury Circus, Charles was astonished to see the greenery in the park opposite now matched by ivy woven through Mr. Screws's railing. A wreath of evergreens tied with what might have been a floppy red cravat. At any rate, it was much too thick to be a girl's ribbon.

He was so stunned that he even glanced up and down the street in case he'd gone to the wrong address. The mood felt so much lighter. The somber tone had gone along with the dark stain of Jacob Harley's life's blood on the pavement, scrubbed away by some good soul.

Some of the staff must have decorated for Christmas. Why? Had it been Mr. Harley who had brought darkness to Finsbury Circus, and not Mr. Screws? Was Kate right about the essential goodness of the man?

Chapter 9

Charles dropped the door hanger against the iron face. He'd become used to it now. It no longer seemed to reverberate with an unpleasant memory from his childhood, but, rather, times past and old age. After a few moments, Mrs. Dorset opened the door, still dressed in her usual black, but with a sprig of fresh-cut holly, three glossy leaves and three ruby berries, affixed like a brooch at her neckline.

Mrs. Dorset managed a thin smile. "Mr. Dickens?"

He nodded formally. "It is good to see you looking so sprightly, Mrs. Dorset. I understand you wanted to speak to me?"

She stepped back from the door and led him into the parlor, where the coffin had rested. "I think this will do. Mr. Screws will not be here for hours yet." She gestured him to a faded purple velvet armchair, then bent over the fireplace with a starter and dropped sparks onto newsprint under the coals until it caught fire.

Charles noted the scent of polish and the greenery nestled over the fireplace. Two red candles stood guard at either end on the mantelpiece. "Mr. Screws does not seem to be feeling cheerful, so I'm guessing all of this change is your doing?"

She played with the poker for a moment, settling the coals to her satisfaction, then seated herself on the stool next to the fire. Charles caught a hint of red petticoat under her skirt and averted his eyes.

"Mr. Harley were all but living here in recent months, Mr. Dickens, and ill at that." She sighed. "Then the coffin was here. I do like to keep a nice Christmas for Johnny but it weren't possible before."

"Mr. Screws won't interfere with your arrangements now?"

"He won't even notice." That tiny half smile was back. She seemed quite a different person now.

"I'm glad to hear he is an accommodating sort of master," Charles said. "My fiancée likes him rather a lot."

"He has grown as cold and hard as Mr. Harley in recent years, but maybe things will change now. We used to have music. He played the violin." She pointed to a case almost hidden in the corner, on the bottom of a shelf.

"You didn't like Mr. Harley."

She shook her head and pulled a handkerchief from a hidden pocket. "He were a bad man, sir."

"Bad to you, or your son?"

Her voice lowered. She didn't look at him. "Bad to me."

Charles saw the hunched shoulders. He matched his voice to hers. "He hurt you?"

She nodded quickly and dabbed at her eyes. "It were when Johnny was a baby. My husband died, he were a dockworker, and I needed work."

"How did you end up here?"

"Mr. Screws's mother was still alive then. She were a relative of mine, some sort of cousin. Mr. Screws hired me to take care of her. She were too far gone to mind about the babe being in the house."

"Were Screws and Harley already in business?"

"Yes. It's over twenty years ago now, but while Mrs. Screws

was alive, the gentlemen weren't close." She shuddered. "She were a fine lady and didn't like 'im, either."

"Were you badly injured by him?"

"I could have had another child," she whispered, then lost herself in a little sob before taking a deep breath.

Charles closed his eyes. Mr. Harley had been no gentleman.

Instead of regaining her composure, Mrs. Dorset began to sob in earnest. Charles rose from his seat and knelt next to her, patting her shoulder awkwardly. Had she ever told this story to anyone? He could not imagine Mr. Screws knew. If she had borne another child, she would have been punished, not Jacob Harley.

"Wot doing?"

Charles lifted his head. Johnny Dorset came through the doorway, barreling on his stocky legs toward his mother. His arms were at his side, enormous, sausage-like fingers splayed out next to his thighs.

He reached for Charles, looming over him. "Hit you," he threatened.

"No, Johnny!" Mrs. Dorset lifted her head. "He's a gentleman."

"Hurt you?" he asked in a plaintive voice.

"No, son," she said gently, then hiccupped. "Good man."

"Crying," her son whined, sounding like a young child.

Mrs. Dorset struggled to her feet. Charles rose with her to keep her steady. She went to her son and patted his cheek. "I'm fine."

Johnny's thick cheeks puffed out. "Hurt bad man."

"Not bad, good," his mother said.

Johnny growled in response and stared at Charles with pitted black eyes.

"I can explain," Charles said, his hands open.

"Bad," Johnny said again.

Johnny's speech and behavior told Charles the young man

suffered from limited understanding and a troublesome temperament. He felt pity for both him and the housekeeper, who only wanted a bit of peace and holiday spirit.

Would Mr. Screws want to find his dead friend's murderer if he knew the truth of his actions? Charles couldn't tell him the housekeeper's story, for fear that it would affect her position. Mr. Screws might not allow his friend to be maligned, whatever the truth. It sounded like, after his mother died, that he had cleaved to Mr. Harley as his only friend. Pity grew in Charles's breast. A large family gave so many opportunities for companionship and friendship. A small family isolated a man.

He nodded at Mrs. Dorset. "I'm going to leave so that you can comfort your son."

She nodded quickly, then tucked away her handkerchief and took Johnny by the arm.

Charles went into the front hallway. A maid scurried up the steps to the first floor as he walked by. He let himself out, then stopped on the pavement and looked up at the house.

Surely, he'd solved the murder. Johnny killed Mr. Harley. There must have been some incident with his mother that day, or he'd imagined one, and done the strangling and pushing out of the window himself. Charles went around the house to view the back garden in person. The small shed he'd seen wasn't locked. When he peered in, it held no coffin, no scent of death. Just unused canning jars and garden equipment. Where else might Johnny Dorset have a hidey-hole?

Charles and Kate met at the *Chronicle* that evening, then crossed the river together in a hired carriage on their way to the theater date with Mr. Screws's apprentice. They walked into the small entry hall of the theater and joined the throng milling around.

"It will be difficult to find our companions in this crowd." Charles had to shout over the crowd. "Look for a man who doesn't quite fit in."

"Is that them?" Kate called, lightly squeezing his arm.

He looked up and saw Mr. Fletcher on the first landing of the staircase to the left. Mr. Fletcher had dressed well in a brown coat with a velvet collar. Military braiding went down the front and sleeves. "Good eye," Charles told Kate.

The American smiled and gestured for them to come up. Charles waved in his direction. Next to him stood a neat, pretty, and decidedly younger-looking woman.

They threaded their way through the crowd until they could reach the steps. While traffic remained heavy, the other theater-goers allowed them to make their way to the landing with good cheer and many friendly greetings.

"Hello," Mr. Fletcher said jovially, lifting his voice over the noise of the crowd. "May I present Miss Osborne? My dear, this is Mr. Charles Dickens and his lovely fiancée."

"Catherine Hogarth," Charles supplied in a carrying voice at Mr. Fletcher's hesitation.

Miss Osborne wore a pink-and-white-striped silk dress. Charles watched Kate's gaze as it drifted from her wide picture hat and followed down the wide ribbons to where green scalloped details decorated the dress at the knee, not that he would think about another gentleman's fiancée's knees. But she dressed to great effect, as did Mr. Fletcher, though Charles thought her youthful air more legitimate.

Kate turned to him expectantly so he helped her with her cloak. "I'll just dispose of this," he called.

Charles bustled to the cloakroom while Kate climbed the steps on Mr. Fletcher's arm. By the time he made it back, all three of them were at the landing. Kate's green velvet, while not as wide as Miss Osborne's skirts, clung to her figure in a way Miss Osborne's did not. Charles preferred Kate's attire to the more expensive costume.

Miss Osborne applied her fan as he reached them. "What a crush!"

"You're English," Charles said as he recognized the local

accent. "How did you and Mr. Fletcher meet? Is the engagement new?"

"So many questions," she said with a tinkling laugh. "I met him in America when I traveled there."

"How delightful." Kate lifted her own fan to her neck. "I hope we can travel after we marry. Charles could report on American politics instead of British."

"Anything for you, my dear," Charles said gallantly.

"We should go up." Mr. Fletcher glanced at the crowd below them in the main lobby. "I ordered a couple of bottles of champagne and we don't want them to warm."

"No point in wasting cold champagne." Charles offered his arm to Miss Osborne at that agreeable thought. Mr. Fletcher followed suit with Kate and they climbed the steps together.

They spent ten minutes settling in, pouring champagne, and taking their first sips. Miss Osborne asked Kate about Edinburgh. Kate asked about the boarding school Miss Osborne had attended in Nottinghamshire. Mr. Fletcher described the delights of Virginia tobacco plantations and Boston social life.

Charles enjoyed the colorful anecdotes. He and Kate took turns telling the other couple about famed Holland House in Kensington, where they had been privileged to be guests. Mr. Fletcher effused about Ditchley House, once part of the Dividing Creek Plantation founded by Richard Lee.

Charles and Kate exchanged glances. He was impressed by these people. They weren't far off the mark and could almost fit in at a place like Lugoson House or even Holland House.

When Kate told her Lord Darnley ghost story, the two flushed pale with imagined terror. Just as Charles was about to tell them about his own spectral adventure, the curtains fluttered, indicating the actors were taking their positions.

Kate changed the subject from ghosts while there was still time. "What are your thoughts about Mr. Harley's death and disappearance, Mr. Fletcher? After all, you were in the house."

"No one in the house killed him. I can assure you of that," the American pronounced.

"What about the possibility of patricide? You think it was a suicide or an accident?" Charles asked.

"No," Mr. Fletcher said decisively.

Kate's eyes went wide. "How do you know that?"

"Are you aware that the kitchen door was found wide open the night of Mr. Harley's death?" Mr. Fletcher asked with an elegant flourish of his hand.

Indeed? Charles drained his first glass of champagne, then leaned forward eagerly. "Anyone could have entered into the house? Did you reveal that at the inquest?"

"Of course," Mr. Fletcher said.

Charles frowned. "Sir Silas didn't pursue the issue?"

Mr. Fletcher shook his head slightly. "He must not have thought it relevant."

"Isn't the garden fenced?" Kate asked. "Does it matter that the door was open?"

Mr. Fletcher lifted his glass to her. "Yes, but there is a gate leading to the mews," he explained. "As you know, Mr. Screws keeps a carriage. Johnny Dorset sleeps in the loft along with the coachman. Though the gate is kept locked both men have access to a key. Either of them could have entered the back garden through the gate, then accessed the house through the open door."

Satan's black teeth. Charles hadn't thought to venture into the mews and check the coach house. Multiple avenues of investigation opened with this news. Not only hints as to how the murder might have happened, but also a new location where a missing body might be hidden.

"Yes," Mr. Fletcher said, almost to himself. "Johnny Dorset came in and killed the old man."

Charles lowered his voice to match the other man's. "Why him and not the coachman?"

Mr. Fletcher smiled thinly. "The coachman isn't a lunatic."

"How can you be convinced it wasn't suicide?" Kate asked before Charles could respond to the American. "If Mr. Appleton had killed him, the chains made sense, but since Mr. Dickens is so convinced that the man is incapable of murder, surely suicide is more likely? A derangement of the mind brought upon by old age and weakness? He might have repented for his hard business ways."

"Men of business do not repent," Mr. Fletcher said in tones of utter assurance. "No, I keep my door locked at night out of fear of that overgrown monkey."

"He's frightful," Miss Osborne added, putting her hand on her fiancé's sleeve. "Dear Mr. Dickens, I suggest you acquaint yourself with Edward Pettingill, Mr. Screws's nephew, for corroboration on this point."

"He'll tell you we all fear for our lives where Johnny Dorset is concerned," Mr. Fletcher confirmed.

Charles understood that, but he remembered Mrs. Dorset's love for her damaged child, his love for her. Johnny Dorset was blessed to have his mother's love, but did none of his fellow creatures have pity for him? Was he really that dangerous, or was his appearance merely frightening? Had Mr. Harley attempted to attack the housekeeper again on that fateful night? "Wasn't Sir Silas interested in Johnny Dorset?"

"Given his obvious impairment, perhaps any death caused by that overgrown child would be considered accidental," Mr. Fletcher suggested.

"I wish our courts would be that kind." Charles brushed a curl out of his eyes, hoping to change the subject away from poor Johnny Dorset. "What about an inheritance? Is there anyone other than Mr. Screws with an interest in the business?"

"Not that I'm aware of," Mr. Fletcher said. "Mr. Pettingill might know more, since he is family."

"Is he part of the business?" *Or in the will.*

"No," Mr. Fletcher said, putting a finger to his lips as the lights dimmed. The conductor lifted his baton and a flute sounded over the rest of the orchestra.

Charles grinned as soon as the violinists started to play. They were very good. He knew they were in for a special performance. Kate's hand crept into his in the darkness and he clutched it as the music rose and fell. He forgot about the others in the box, or the champagne warming in the bucket, and simply enjoyed the sensual pleasure of the touch of fingers against his own, and Kate's shoulder pressing his.

The next afternoon, Charles went to see Edward Pettingill, Mr. Screws's nephew. He lived in a redbrick building on Cale Street, not far from the Hogarths.

Charles could see St. Luke's from the windows as he climbed up to the second story, where the Pettingills' chambers were. He couldn't help but note that the nephew did not live anywhere near the uncle. For that matter, he had no idea of Pettingill's parents, but assumed that Mr. Screws must have had a sister.

A very neat young woman in cap and apron opened the door. She didn't seem much older than Kate, and her brown dress, while not overadorned, had fashionable sleeves and didn't look like something a servant would wear. "Mrs. Pettingill?" he inquired, hoping there was such a person.

"Yes, sir?" she said uncertainly.

He handed her his card.

"The *Morning Chronicle*?" Her brow creased.

"Is your husband available, madam?" Charles asked. "Mr. Fletcher at Screws and Harley gave me this address."

"Has something happened to my husband's uncle?" she asked, confirming her identity. "He is very old."

Charles frowned. "When did you last see him?"

"My husband saw him on the last quarter day. Mr. Screws pays out on a family legacy those four times a year."

"On Michaelmas, then."

"Yes, and he will visit again at Christmas." She forced a pallid smile. "One moment please."

She closed the door. Charles still had no idea if the nephew had a profession. He hadn't asked Mr. Fletcher at the performance; his ears had rung from the glorious singing and Kate had been his focus.

The door opened again, widely this time. Mrs. Pettingill beckoned him in. "Right this way, Mr. Dickens."

Charles ventured into a short passage in between two rooms. She took him to the end of a dining table, where a fire blazed merrily.

"Please, take the best chair," she urged. "My husband is at his desk. I'll fetch him for you."

"He is a man of letters?"

"He writes scientific tracts about birds. His great love is tramping Hampstead Heath." She smiled self-importantly. "He is considered the leading expert in the migration patterns of birds of prey."

"Fascinating," Charles murmured. "One does like to meet an expert."

"What are you an expert in?" the woman asked.

"London life, I'm told." He gave a modest chuckle of self-deprecation. "I call myself 'Boz' when I write about it."

"Perhaps you can include my husband in one of your sketches, Mr. Dickens," she said, her cheeks brightening. "You see, it took me a moment, for my brain is never so quick as Mr. Pettingill's is, but I know who you are now."

He inclined his head and she trotted out of the room. While he expected preening and posturing in the upper-class salons he had occasional entry to, he had not expected it in a room with no decoration beyond a shelf of pewter cups and brown glazed stoneware jugs. Still, the woman had known of him, which spoke volumes.

A couple of minutes later, he heard a short burst of commotion in the passage, and then the door opened again. The man who entered was in his late twenties, despite the blue nightcap on his head. He had no hair, or rather, he had no eyebrows, so it might be assumed he suffered from some sort of condition that caused him to easily take a chill in these cold winter months.

"Mr. Dickens," the man said, coming forward and shaking his hand. "One does not expect a newspaperman in one's private chambers."

"I am visiting at your uncle's request," Charles explained. "Please see me as a private person."

The door opened yet again, and the lady of the house arrived with a tea tray. The towel over the surface sparkled white, though the pot and cups were of the same glazed stoneware as the jugs.

Mr. Pettingill saw him looking. "My father-in-law, dear man, is a potter, you see."

"Not a potter, my dear," the lady reproved. "He owns a pottery."

"My uncle, lovely man, helped him start it," Mr. Pettingill explained. "Elevates the family, you see."

"I do," Charles said, hoping Mrs. Pettingill's father could afford to pay off his loans. "Thriving, I daresay?"

"Oh yes," Mr. Pettingill assured him. "Excellent man, man of business."

Mrs. Pettingill gave a coarse little laugh and flounced from the room.

He put his hands to his cheeks. "My wife, excellent woman, does not see me as a man of business, you see."

"She seemed rightfully proud of your status in the bird community," Charles offered.

"Milk?" Mr. Pettingill asked. When Charles nodded, he prepared the tea. "No biscuits today, I'm afraid. I couldn't secure an invitation that she'd hoped for and I am not in her good graces. Sorry you have to be punished for it, poor man. Why did my uncle send you to me?"

"I'm afraid I misspoke," Charles admitted. "It was his apprentice, or rather, his fiancée, who suggested I speak to you."

"Whatever for?" Mr. Pettingill set down his tea strainer.

"To ask about Johnny Dorset." Charles, whose stomach was rumbling, pulled his handkerchief from his pocket and spilled chestnuts onto the table. He'd picked them on the way. "If you have a knife and a pan, we can roast these."

"A capital notion!" He went to a box on the mantelpiece and took out a knife, then took up a pan from its place on a lower shelf.

While he made X marks through each chestnut, Charles leaned back and considered the plain room. "Why don't you work at the countinghouse? They had to bring in an apprentice. Everyone there seems busy."

Mr. Pettingill's bitter chuckle was reminiscent of his wife's. "Uncle Emmanuel, dear man, doesn't want to employ relatives because he doesn't think we would work hard enough for him. Mind you, I'm his only close relative."

"That's unfortunate," Charles said, watching as his host put the nuts in the pan, drizzled them with water from a jug, and put it on the hob.

"Mrs. Pettingill prefers to cook in the other room, but I keep my things here as I do like a bit of toast in the wee hours."

"You must write in here," Charles said, observing the desk in the corner.

"It's the best room, in my opinion. But she has headaches, poor woman, and prefers the darker rooms."

Mrs. Pettingill reentered. She'd obviously been listening at the keyhole, because she announced, "Uncle Emmanuel would rather have a slave like that family man Mr. Cratchit than a young dandy like his nephew."

Charles looked at Mr. Pettingill, bent over the hob, the tassel at the end of his nightcap dangling over his shoulder, and did not see a dandy, though the young man seemed intelligent enough. Could he have first offed Mr. Harley, then planned to murder Mr. Screws, in order to inherit the business?

Or Mrs. Pettingill herself, who seemed like she had the ability to make strategic decisions.

She sniffed. "Chestnuts?"

"Mr. Dickens, excellent man, brought them," said her husband.

Her nostrils flared and she darted through the door again.

"Doesn't like me to spoil my tea," Mr. Pettingill explained.

Charles realized the time. "I had best not either. I have now remembered I am due in York Place for the meal."

"Oh, who do you know there?"

"The Hogarths. I am affianced to the oldest daughter, Catherine."

Mr. Pettingill tutted. "I do not know them."

"They are next door to Lugoson House. Musical people. They have fruit trees."

"Ah," he said. "Them. Beautiful house, but those Lugosons are dastardly people."

"I understand the late baron was as you described," Charles said. "But the current Lord Lugoson is but a lad of sixteen."

"His sister was murdered." Mr. Pettingill put his finger to his nose. "That is what comes of mixing into political matters. My uncle suggested I might become a member of Parliament. Implied he had connections. But I am a scientist, sir."

Charles nodded. "Before I go, is there any insight you might offer on Mr. Harley?"

"Not a godly man, Mr. Harley." He pulled the pan from the hob and set it on a trivet.

"His body is missing."

Mr. Pettingill poured the chestnuts into a cloth and covered them. "No shroud for the wicked?" he asked softly.

"Did you have any intelligence on Johnny Dorset before I go?" Charles asked.

"A lost lamb. He is attached to no soul but his mother. I understand a local baker was interested in courting Mrs. Dorset, but the son ran him off. Blackened his eye and scattered buns across the road. He's a peaceful, simple soul otherwise, works hard where he's directed."

"He'd attack someone he perceived as a threat to his mother, then."

"Yes, but old Harley was no threat. He was dying. I cannot imagine that old sinner having the strength to offer more wickedness than an unkind word or wheezed demand." Mr. Pettingill straightened his nightcap.

Charles smiled uneasily and said his good-byes, thinking it a very good thing that the Pettingills had their legacy. Though he could not cross them off his list. They seemed a bit mad.

The Hogarths provided him with a much better dinner than mere chestnuts. George, William, and James, the middle Hogarth boys, pelted Charles with questions about bird watching on Hampstead Heath after he explained about meeting Mr. Pettingill, but Charles had little to offer. George, though, had one of Mr. Pettingill's tracts and brought it to the table after dinner. The boys discussed buzzards and ospreys with alacrity, giving Charles rather more respect than usual because of his recent contact with their hero.

Kate pulled Charles into her father's study.

"Your mother," Charles warned.

Kate shut the door and, remaining mute, lifted her face to his.

"Darling," he murmured, and kissed her lips, still flavored with wine.

"My dear Mr. Dickens," she whispered, kissing him back. "I have missed you. How much longer?"

He cradled her cheek. "Spring, my sweet. The earliest spring day we can manage."

She rubbed against his palm like a cat. "I cannot wait until I am making you your own dinners, to your exact specifications. I know Mother put in way too much pepper for your liking."

"I am the smallest bit dyspeptic," he admitted. "But it is no matter." He bent to her and kissed her again, then startled away when the door behind him shook with bangs.

"Kate," called Georgina in a nasal whine.

Kate sighed loudly. "A moment, please."

"Mother needs you," she said loud enough for people to hear on the street.

Reverberating stomps told them she was walking away. Charles reached for Kate again but she pulled back.

"Duty must." She went to the door and put her hand on the handle. "Oh, I meant to ask you about Julie. I haven't seen her since her swoon at the caroling party. Do you think I should pay her a call? I have some time tomorrow."

Charles winced. "I'm to keep a secret."

Kate went still. "But I'm to be your wife."

Charles relented. "I never told you this."

"Very well."

Charles leaned into her ear. He could feel Kate shudder as his breath tickled her soft skin. "William told me she was in an interesting condition."

"How wonderful," Kate exclaimed, pulling back. "I must call on her."

"No!" His heart pounded in his chest for fear that she'd learn too much about Timothy. Julie did not tend to keep secrets, and the baby would likely be in her rooms when Kate called. Until he could prove the child was not his, he couldn't risk Kate finding out. The consequences would be dire. "She's fragile. She had that disappointment last year. We should let her rest. William's orders."

"It isn't good for a woman to be isolated," Kate said. "She's very young, you know."

"We'll let her husband make the decisions," Charles said. "Don't bother her, darling, not right now."

Kate drew herself up. "As if I'd be a bother. I simply thought I'd fix her a basket. Very well, Charles. I must go to my mother now."

Charles soon departed but was too restless to go straight home. Instead, he headed to the river and picked his way along the foreshore, stopping at a riverside tavern along the way for a hot rum and water.

He drank it quickly and walked out, as he was not dressed to blend into the rough crowd and no one knew him around the Regent Bridge area. Instead, he returned to his ramble, heading toward Blackfriars Bridge, where he could make the turn into the city and his chambers.

It was slow going among the rocks and debris. Clouds drifted across the waning gibbous moon, lighting his way in broad strokes. He enjoyed the rock of his feet against the surface, remembering the holes in his shoes just a year ago. He'd come a long way financially and his sturdy shoes were a visible reminder. His feet weren't even that chilled.

Shadowy people moved along the foreshore, but he didn't bother anyone and they didn't come near him. It took a sort of perfection of movement, a straight, sober back, head thrown at an arrogant angle, arms in such a position as to look ready to defend. A man might have anything in his pockets. A knife, a truncheon. No one ever bothered him because he didn't walk like a victim.

Without thinking, he headed into the shadows around the bridge, meaning to check on Lucy Fair's former gang, what little was left of it. He recognized the stocky forms of Brother Second and Cousin Arthur, seated against a support beam. Smoke wafted from a pipe clenched between the teeth of one of the older boys.

He whistled out a greeting. Then, without warning, his knees gave out as something hit him from behind. He went down on the rocks, catching himself painfully on his hands. Old shells cracked against his palms, biting into his flesh despite his gloves.

"'ey!" went up a cry from a familiar child's voice. "Wot you do that fer?"

Chapter 10

Charles felt rough hands reaching into his overcoat pockets. He flipped onto his back and kicked out with his legs, shoes scrabbling on the pebbled ground, then sprang to his feet, fists ready. But he was facing the wrong direction.

Lack, his attacker, gave a nasty laugh as he walked around Charles and pulled a pipe from his pocket. "Oi, it's you, is it?"

Charles dropped his fists as the youth tossed the pipe casually from hand to hand. *Bloody fool.* Breathing hard, he straightened his coat with aching, scraped hands, and walked toward the seated trio of boys with his attacker, never gladder that he and the Agas had rescued Lucy Fair from this mob. "I give what I collect for you freely but I won't be stolen from."

Lack snorted and reached into the ragged coat of the toothless boy, one of the boys hunched around a fire on flat bits of driftwood. Lack pulled out a pouch.

Charles looked over the younger boys. Brother Second was taking the punches now. He sported wounds similar to Poor John's wounds the night he'd given up mudlarking. But unlike John, Second had a hard, unfriendly expression on his face. He was already changing to suit the leader he'd chosen.

"How's doings, gentlemen?" Charles asked, forcing gaiety into his voice.

"We don't want yer blankets," said Lack, his bad eye rolling in its socket. "But you can hand over yer brass."

"That's not the kind of charity I offer," Charles said. "Buckets, blankets, clothing, boots. You can count on me for those if you behave yourselves. Food sometimes."

Lack swore like a sailor and spit in the fire.

"Oi!" Brother Second said, jumping to his feet with murder in his eye. Charles had no idea why. The toothless boy leapt up as well, and the two went at each other.

The melee distracted Charles, and it wasn't until he felt the hand at his elbow that he realized Cousin Arthur had come around the fire.

"I want to go to school," the boy whispered. "Am I too little?"

Charles took the measure of the boy, who was six. He'd joined the gang after his mother died last summer. Young, too young, but he couldn't be left here. "We'll find a place for you."

Cousin Arthur shuddered. "Can we leave now?"

"Do you have any belongings?"

"Not 'ere." He pulled Charles away from the fight.

Ignoring the others, they went up the ladder to the street. They weren't stopped.

"What about your little brother and sister? Does your grandmother still have them?" Charles asked.

Cousin Arthur nodded sadly. "I need a job. I can't go to school."

"We'll sort it out. For now, I'll take you to Lucy Fair."

The boy hopped and tugged at Charles's hand. How quickly he reverted to childhood when given a chance. Though Charles felt thoroughly dampened after his fall, he resolutely turned toward Cheapside and the Agas. He walked through the dark streets with the urchin at his side, feeling pleased with himself for taking another child from the rough gang.

Despite the hour, William opened his chamber door, holding a candle aloft.

"We're damp and dirty," Charles said cheerfully. "Let us in, will you?"

"What happened to your hands?"

Charles held them to the candle, then saw the rents in his gloves. "Must have cut them when Lack attacked me."

William sighed and stepped aside, then did a double take. "That's never Cousin Arthur?"

Lucy Fair stumbled into the main room, her hair in a braid over her shawl-covered shoulder. She rubbed her eyes, then spotted the little boy.

His expression went rapturous as he ran to her. She wrapped her arms, and the ends of her shawl, around him.

"I've missed you," she whispered. "It's only been four days, but how I've missed you."

"It's terrible now," the boy sobbed. "But I 'afta get brass!"

Lucy Fair looked up at William. "Could you change your charity?"

Charles and William shared glances. "The Charity for Boarding School Children with Siblings?" Charles suggested.

William shrugged. "Very well. Children should be in school."

Julie came out of the bedroom, still dressed but looking sleepy. She went to William. "Visitors?"

"I've brought you another responsibility," Charles said.

Her gaze shifted to Lucy Fair. "Is that Cousin Arthur?"

He turned in his friend's arms and waved shyly at Julie.

Julie went to him immediately and ruffled his hair. "Put the kettle on, Lucy. This boy needs a bath if he's to sleep here tonight."

"Will your father take him?" Charles asked William as the others went into the next room.

William put his hands on his hips. "We'll have to pay fees. My father can't run a charity school without a charity."

Charles pressed his fingertips to his eyes. *So much pressure.* "We need to keep funds coming for Cousin Arthur's siblings and the school?"

William nodded. "We can't let them down now. I'll speak to Lady Lugoson about an endowment for the school. That would take care of my father."

"I'll apply to Lady Holland," Charles added. "I'm meeting so many people, but they are mostly writers. And writers don't have money."

"They might spare a few shillings here and there," William said. "What about your friend Mr. Screws? With everything you are doing for him, he ought to be an easy touch."

Charles snorted. "He's no friend of mine. He is not the charitable sort, but I'll make sure to inquire before I pass out of his sphere."

"Might as well try to squeeze a few pence out of his fist. If you solve the murder he might pay you for your efforts," William suggested.

"I just wanted to make him pay," Charles said. "For turning my father down for a loan. I wanted him to be guilty and for a Dickens to send him to Newgate. It's all twisted now. I have to wish him innocent to try to get him to pay for some school fees?"

"Better than revenge," William pointed out. "Revenge isn't good for the soul."

"I wonder who wanted revenge on Jacob Harley," Charles muttered. "On Mr. Screws, too, for he is sadly diminished in his sorrow."

Julie bustled back into the room. "William, do you have anything we could dress Cousin Arthur in?"

"You know my wardrobe better than I do," William responded.

"There's that musty old trunk you keep hidden from me," she suggested.

William laughed. "It's full of love notes from my disappointed admirers."

"Julie?" Charles said as she shook her fist at her husband.

"What?" she asked, distracted.

He had remembered he must keep secrets. "I know you are much too busy to pay calls right now, but I wanted to ask you especially not to call on the Hogarths."

"Why not?"

He adopted his most serious expression. "They have strong opinions about illegitimate children, and any doubt as to my relationship with Timothy could cause serious problems for me."

"Very well." Julie patted his arm and pointed William toward his trunk.

"Couldn't you borrow something from your brothers?" William hesitated, gripping the key in his hand.

"You want me to go into Bloomsbury at this time of night and wake my mother?" Charles asked.

"No, I suppose not." William sighed. "I'll have to sacrifice the cloth I was giving to Julie for Christmas."

Julie squealed. "You keep presents in that trunk?"

William unlocked the trunk, which had been placed in a corner so unobtrusively that Charles had never really noticed it. "See?" He lifted out a thick bundle of soft dress fabric.

"It's perfect for an infant," Charles said, fingering the silky cloth as Julie hugged her husband. "But for Arthur?"

William winced. "For a shirt, at least."

"It's so soft," Julie said. "What was it for?"

"For the baby." William's ears went red.

Julie lifted the fabric and rubbed it against her cheek. After a moment, she sighed. "We'll sacrifice some of it for a shirt. I'll cut it out right now."

"I'll get Arthur's shirt from the kitchen." William went to fetch the small, ragged belongings as Julie spread the new fabric out on the table.

"What have you been up to, Charles?" she asked. "I thought you'd stay away from the mudlarks now."

"I will have to," Charles said. "Lack attacked me. Brother Second is turning very hard, and he's the only one left of our gang."

"Not everyone turns out right," Julie said, going for her sewing box. "Some boys are right little criminals."

"Let's hope neither of us have one of them."

"How is your Kate? Wedding plans coming along?"

"We've been too busy to talk about it. We went to the opera last night and tonight I dined with her family."

"The opera? That must have been nice."

"Yes. We went with Mr. Screws's apprentice and his fiancée. They are Mr. Powhatan Fletcher and Miss Amelia Osborne."

"What a name. He must be American. Or a savage?"

"No, a Virginian who claims to be descended from a native king."

Julie looked thoughtful as she pinned the edges of the fabric together. "Powhatan is a new sort of name to me, but I've heard the name Osborne before. I knew an actress by that name, but she must be American, too?"

"No, this lady is British. Apparently, she was visiting in America when she met Mr. Fletcher. Quite a bit younger than him, I'd say. Not much older than me."

William brought the dirty shirt. Julie clucked. "We can't put it over this lovely fabric. Can you gentlemen sort of hold it over the new cloth so I can cut a basic shape?"

Charles and William stretched the shirt over the table. Julie lopped off a piece of cloth that was roughly the right size and folded up the rest of it. After that, she eyed the shirt and cut into the fabric until she had four pieces. "I think that will do. Keep me company while I sew, will you, Charles?"

"We'll help," William said. "I don't want you up half the night."

"Very well. Pin up the sleeves, will you?"

William handed Charles pins and they both took a sleeve.

"Tell me more about this actress," Julie said. "Maybe she is the one I knew after all."

"She's very fashionable," Charles said, and described the dress she'd been wearing, thankful that his powers of deduction were up to Julie's very specific questions.

"I went to a party at my Miss Osborne's house, once," Julie said. "In Maiden Lane, above a dressmaker's shop. I thought her clothing rather flashy."

"I don't think flashy was the right word for my Miss Osborne," Charles reflected. "But fashionable."

"What else?" Julie demanded, threading a needle.

"I don't know. She has a round face, pointed chin, small mouth. Very pretty."

"My Miss Osborne had a thin face. She painted her mouth. I remember it as more of a slash." She stuck her needle into the cloth. "My, but this fabric is lovely to work with."

"Perfect for a baby," William said dreamily.

William had caught baby fever as intensely as any woman. Charles yawned. "Thread another needle so I can work on the seam, Julie."

"You can sew?"

"Some weeks ago, I had so much trouble with laundresses that Fred and I were forced to ask Mother for plain sewing lessons. Now I have an opportunity to put my new skills to use."

Julie chuckled and threaded him a needle. While they constructed the shirt, they listed every wealthy person they knew and debated how much money they might be able to gather for Cousin Arthur's school fees.

"We'll make it work," William said. "They are resourceful children."

"I agree." Charles lifted his gaze from his seam. "We'll help them with a better start in life. If we can give them expectations, no matter how grave their circumstances now, who knows what they can contribute to society in the future?"

Charles went to a political meeting on Friday morning and then spent the afternoon transcribing his notes for the *Chronicle*. The meeting required several columns. After work, he decided to return home and collect Fred. He'd take his brother to a chophouse and refresh himself on the possible murderers of Mr. Harley. He felt uneasy about Johnny Dorset and wondered if he should speak to Sir Silas. Should such a large, maybe lunatic be running free? What if he hurt Mr. Screws? The man didn't have much life left in him.

He went in his front door, pulling off his gloves. "Fred! Get your coat! Let's go out!" He didn't hear an answer so he went into the sitting room, where he found Fred sitting on the sofa with Kate. Charles was shocked to see her there unannounced. Her eyes were red and she twisted a handkerchief between her fingers, braiding a pattern through them.

Fred jumped to his feet, gave him a stare of pure death, and stomped into the bedroom. The door slammed.

Charles gave Kate a wide grin. "What was that all about, darling? Did something happen at his job?"

Kate's lips trembled.

Charles sat next to her and took her hand. "What is it? I've just left your father. Is it your mother? One of the children?"

She shook her head and pulled her hand away. Her full lower lip trembled against the sweet curve of the upper. "How could you?" she whispered.

"How could I what?" He tried to put his arm around her, but she tilted in the opposite direction. "I've been at work all day, darling. What has upset you? Allow me to fix it."

Her head snapped to him. "You have betrayed me, Charles. Allow me to end our engagement with dignity."

He laughed. He couldn't help himself. "End our engagement? Over what imagined betrayal?"

The cushion flattened under her hands as she pushed herself to her feet. "You know very well what betrayal. I called on Julie Aga today."

The words came instinctively. "I told you not to."

"I thought you misunderstood her needs. How could you know what a woman wants in such a situation?" Her face took on a mulish expression he'd never seen before as her voice rose. "It never occurred to me that you were hiding a bastard infant from me!"

"He isn't mine," Charles said calmly, attempting to take her hand again. Hers stayed at her sides. "There was a mix-up after the fire at Hatfield. Timothy belongs to a maid who died in the fire."

She stepped back. "You fathered a child on a maid?"

"Of course not, Kate. I'd never been to Hatfield House. I hadn't even been to the town of Hatfield until the fire. It's a mix-up."

"Julie said the baby's aunt identified you."

"She was in a sorry state," Charles said. "I must have looked trustworthy. I assure you, William is looking into it. We're supporting the baby between us until the father is found."

She sniffed emotionally. "You expect me to believe such a ridiculous story?"

"You can't possibly believe this of me. A bastard child?"

Tears dripped from Kate's eyes. "It was before we met, Charles. Just before we met."

"What was?"

"You did"—Kate worked her fingers—"that, before we met. And hid it from me. That is the worst thing, Charles. You hid it."

"I hid Timothy because I knew this would happen." Charles ground his teeth together. "I might have told you, but it was so obvious your parents would jump to the wrong conclusion. I promise you, I will prove he isn't my child."

She wiped at her tears. "You thought I'd believe anything you told me, despite the facts right in front of my nose?"

"We promised to believe in each other, Kate," Charles said. "I expect that. Because I will always tell you the truth."

She shook her head. "You told me to stay away from Julie Aga for the wrong reasons, Charles. I can't trust you."

For exactly the right reasons. Couldn't she see that? "I was trying to spare you pain. Please, don't end our engagement. Give me time to show you what the truth is."

She crossed her arms. Her slim body shook. Charles went to her, attempting to pull her closer to the fire, but instead, she called for Fred.

His brother came out of the bedroom, slamming the door behind him again so hard that the floorboards shook.

"Please take me home, Fred." Kate's voice trembled.

"I'm sorry I didn't confide in you, Fred," Charles said. "I'm helping a sad and confused girl take care of her nephew. Nothing more."

"You trust William Aga more than me, your own brother," he accused.

"That's another thing," Kate said. "After all the trouble we had with Julie Aga earlier this year, you still trust her more than you trust me."

"She's a married woman. You could not have cared for the infant. If you love me at all, Kate," Charles said to her back, "please don't tell your parents. I will make this right. Please say you'll marry me."

She lifted her hands into the air, then let them drop. Fred put her cloak around her shoulders, and they departed. Charles stared at the door after they were gone, then forced himself to his table to work. He had so much work to do that night, to earn money to keep Kate in comfort. If she didn't give up on him. At least she hadn't said the words, she hadn't ended their engagement in any final way. He pushed his fear to the side and picked up his pen.

Charles took Cousin Arthur to Mr. Aga's school on Saturday afternoon, since he was so young and had never been in a coach before. The boy had kept his new clothes very clean and his hair, displaying reddish highlights unseen on the foreshore, had been freshly cut by Julie. He appeared a proper, if nervous, new student.

Charles visited with Little Ollie and Poor John in the students' sitting room. They both seemed content and Little Ollie had gained enough weight that he needed a new nickname. Mr. Aga, so like his son William in appearance, if not dress or charming cityish personality, took custody of the latest mudlark with an air of gentle confusion, and didn't ask for funding, though Charles promised him he'd do what he could. He knew how hard it was to keep a school. His own parents had utterly failed at it, no thanks to Mr. Screws.

On the way back, inside the bumpy coach, he puzzled over Mr. Harley's death and disappearance, though his thoughts kept returning to Kate. She loved a mystery, and if he uncovered the truth, maybe she'd forgive him. As long as her parents didn't learn about Timothy, he still had time to repair her broken trust. After all, he hadn't fathered the baby. Kate's family might be above his on a social level, but she wouldn't find a better husband among her acquaintance, no matter her present upset.

When Charles arrived at 332 Strand on Monday morning, he found a note from Mr. Screws nestled in the pile of correspondence and assignments. After taking a quick look through his commitments and deciding they could be put off, he walked to the countinghouse.

"Good morning, Mr. Dickens," said Mr. Cratchit when Charles entered. He dropped off his high stool to shake hands.

"Added another lump of coal?" Charles asked. "It seems a degree or two warmer in here today."

Mr. Cratchit patted his cravat, not overlain by a thick comforter this morning. "Mr. Screws had some shipyard people in here this morning. Very prestigious." He leaned closer. "They stay longer if they remove their overcoats, so we warm up the place. Otherwise, Mr. Screws don't like it."

"Is that Mr. Dickens?" Mr. Screws's voice, coming from his office, pitched over his clerk's comments.

Charles patted the clerk's arm and went to the owner's office. "Good morning, sir. You wanted a word?"

"Come in, come in," Mr. Screws gestured. "Close the door, will you? No need for eavesdroppers."

"I don't have any news," Charles apologized. He would never take the old man into his confidence regarding the status of his engagement. "I was out of town."

"No worries, no worries. I am afraid we have a new problem." Mr. Screws poked a bony finger at his desk.

Charles bit back frustration. He had to take steps to find Timothy's father before it was too late. What else could be more important? "Did someone else die?"

Chapter 11

"Not yet," Mr. Screws said darkly. He fiddled with the lamp on his desk, causing it to flare. "In another age, sir, a bloodier age, you might have found a body across the doorway when you came in."

Charles held back a chuckle. He did agree with Kate, upon reflection, that the man seemed much too feeble to murder anyone. "A betrayal?"

"Perhaps, perhaps," Mr. Screws said. "I have paced, sir, until my feet hurt. Ever since the post came."

"Something in the mail." Charles nodded. "Bad news?"

"No news." Mr. Screws pushed a thin piece of paper in between his inkwell and a pile of files. "Take a look at this, my good man."

Charles soaked in the approving phrase as he glanced at the letter. Mr. Screws had come to believe in him, despite his dismissal of the Dickens family years ago.

The letter dated from late October. The correspondent was one James Dobbin from a firm in Boston, who seemed to be on excellent terms with Mr. Screws. The letter contained reminis-

cences of some forty years past and the doings of Mr. Wintersea's apprentices. This Dobbin must have worked with Screws
and Harley in his youth. He mentioned a new grandson being
born, the first male heir of the generation, and no doubt the
reason for the letter to be written. A paragraph unraveled some
shipping business in byzantine detail that Charles merely
skimmed. Then, Mr. Dobbin made a few rude remarks about
the American president Jackson before closing.

"Very well, sir, I've read it." Charles folded it and handed it
back. "What is the importance of this missive?"

Mr. Screws folded his hands over the letter. "I employed Mr.
Fletcher on the word of my old friend, James Dobbin, based on
a letter of introduction that Mr. Fletcher arrived with, here at
my office."

"Ah, that is how you came to take him on." Charles nodded
wisely.

"Yes, early this spring. But now, here is a new letter from
James Dobbin, transported all the way from America, dated
after the letter Mr. Fletcher arrived with, with no mention of
his protégé."

Charles grasped the problem. "You have not had a letter
from your old friend for months. Mr. Fletcher arrives with a
letter of introduction in when, the spring?"

"About April," he agreed.

"This letter is dated October. Why would he not check on
Mr. Fletcher's doings?"

"Suspicious," Mr. Screws declared.

Charles frowned. "Do you have the first letter?"

The old gentleman's hands shook as he went to a ledger box
and unlocked it. He poked through some piles until he pulled
out the letter. Charles came around the desk and they spread
the letters out side to side.

"Same letterhead," Charles said.

"Same handwriting?" Mr. Screws inquired. "Your eyes will be better than mine."

Charles scanned them, looking for any obvious mistakes. "I see nothing obvious. I can understand your concern, but how can you investigate it except by writing Mr. Dobbin again?"

"I will do that today," Mr. Screws vowed. "But I am glad to know that you don't see any sign of obvious forgery."

"He is a grandfather," Charles said carefully, taking a seat. "Perhaps he merely forgot Mr. Fletcher?"

"Perhaps, perhaps. But he was the sharpest of us apprentices. I'd hate to think his powers were slipping, sir."

A knock came on the door. Screws raised his voice and said, "Enter."

None other than Mr. Fletcher appeared. "I've just settled with Mr. Skye, sir. Two hundred profit on the loan."

"Very good, Mr. Fletcher," Mr. Screws said, then scratched the tip of his nose. "Tell me, how did you find Mr. Dobbin when you last saw him. Was he well?"

Mr. Fletcher leaned his head from side to side. "His vision is growing poor, Mr. Screws. Has to have letters written for him, ledgers read to him, and so forth. But still sharp, sharp as a needle."

"Tragic for a man to lose any of his powers of faculty," Charles murmured with a significant glance at Mr. Screws.

Mr. Screws nodded. "Very well. Mr. Cratchit will have a list of accounts for you to visit this afternoon."

Charles stood. "I'll walk out with you." He inclined his head to Mr. Screws and went back into the main room.

"Any word on Mr. Harley?" Mr. Fletcher asked, his mouth close to Charles's ear. "I know it's weighing on the old gentleman."

"Nothing." Charles coughed. "I really must get back to my own office. But we did enjoy the opera very much. Thank you so much for the invitation. Good day."

Mr. Fletcher offered his own salutation as Charles took his coat from Mr. Cratchit and went outside.

He started up Lothbury, dodging some people in front of a bank with signs, three beggars, and a hot potato seller as he contemplated how Mr. Screws might best manage Mr. Fletcher and the Dobbin situation. His fingers still felt warm after a pleasantly cozy visit in the counting office, but the heat had dried out his throat. He stopped at the corner to purchase a cup of saloop from a costermonger. Three ragged boys ran in his direction as he drank the hot, thick beverage. He knew the art of misdirection so he didn't flinch, put his hand over his purse to reveal its location, or stop casting his gaze around. Pickpockets could come at any direction and did their best when their mark was distracted.

He set the cup back on the costermonger's tray with his thanks, keeping his purse side facing toward the tray until the boys went past.

"No shoes," said the saloop seller with a frown. "In this cold."

Charles merely raised his eyebrows, just in case the costermonger was the misdirection, instead of glancing at the boys again. A street sweeper stepped off the pavement, setting his broom into the assorted muck in the road. Charles stepped into Princes Street after the boys, arms tight against his coat, during a break in the traffic.

He felt something against his left arm. Jerking, he turned and saw a youth darting away. He stepped into the middle of the street, not overly concerned. It wasn't possible for the boy to have reached under two layers of clothing to his inner waistcoat pocket in that brief of a moment. Then, he felt a sharp push on his back.

He stumbled forward into the filthy middle of the street. Glancing up, he saw the heaving bodies of high-stepping black horses. They were coming right at him. Without full control of his body, he went down on his knees heavily, squishing into the mud.

Sheer terror kept Charles in motion. His sore knee screamed

indignantly, but he could see the horses' eyes now, coming right at him. Shoving his hands into the muck until he reached the surface of the road, he struggled to push himself up. He could smell offal, feces, and mud all around him. Thoughts of Kate kept him moving. He couldn't end like this.

He fought against the sucking effluvia before it was too late. Above him, the carriage driver dropped his whip. His mouth dropped open in shock at the sight of Charles in his path.

"Oi!" someone shouted behind him.

Hands reached under Charles's armpits and hauled him upright and backward. The horses thundered past, their hooves only inches from his dangling feet. Confused and scared out of his wits, he allowed the hands to pull him onto the pavement. When he turned around, he saw a friendly face. He blinked and recognized the costermonger.

"Wot's wrong with you, then?" the man demanded, beating his fingerless mittens free of muck. "Don't you know how to move those plates of meat?"

Charles glanced down at his shoes, which were coated in stinking waste. "Did you see who pushed me?"

The costermonger shook his head.

"I saw a boy run off. Did you see him touch my arm? Was he wearing shoes?"

The man shrugged.

"Did you see anything?" Charles demanded. "I appreciate you saving my life, but I must know who was responsible."

The man looked over Charles's shoulder and smiled, holding up a cup. "Saloop, my fine sir? Best quality."

Charles gave up and stepped carefully back into the road, making it across this time on the flames of anger, if nothing else. Was his fall an accident or deliberately caused by those pickpockets? Or could it have been the mudlarks? Johnny Dorset? The hand that shoved him felt much larger than a boy's. And who did he know with overly large hands? Johnny Dorset.

The mere thought of Johnny Dorset made his blood boil. Not much he could do about ragged boys, but if Mr. Screws was supporting a violent murderer, he'd put a stop to it now.

Charles marched to Finsbury Circus, ignoring passersby who stared at the ruin of his fine clothes. It was one thing for a certain sort of man to walk around looking like this, but no one would doubt Mr. Dickens was a gentleman, especially not Mr. Screws. Under his topcoat, his frock coat, waistcoat, and silk cravat were spotless. Only his topcoat, shoes, and trousers had been ruined.

He stopped on the main road to have a boot boy scrape the mud off his shoes, but they were too wet to polish. He thanked the lad for his attempt and pressed on, limping.

When he rang the bell at Mr. Screws's abode, Mrs. Dorset answered promptly. She smiled; then her lips flattened when she saw his state. "What has happened?"

He pushed past her into the house, too angry for pleasantries. "Where is that son of yours?"

"What? Johnny? Why?"

"Do you know where he is?" Charles scanned the hallway, becoming acutely aware of the pain in his hands and knee. "Is he here? Can you account for his whereabouts?"

"No, Mr. Dickens," she said fretfully. "What do you think he's done?"

He ripped off his gloves and showed her his bloody palms. "Someone with large hands pushed me down in Princes Street. I could have died. I nearly did."

Her hands flew to her mouth, covering it. "He's not here, sir. But I swear he wouldn't hurt you."

"I find that hard to believe," Charles snarled. "Given his behavior when I last saw him. You remember he reached for me, and threatened to hit me. If you had not been there to stop him, I think he would have attacked me."

A key clicked in the door and it pushed open. Mr. Screws came in. "I'll take my lunch now, Mrs. Dorset." Then he caught sight of Charles. His face lengthened almost comically as he took in the pitiful sight.

"What has happened?" he asked.

"Pushed down in the street," Charles thundered. "I'm looking for Johnny Dorset."

Mr. Screws's jaw fixed in place. Mrs. Dorset burst into tears and ran from the room, her face covered by her apron.

The old man thundered, "He will leave my house this day if it is true, Mr. Dickens, I swear on it."

Charles nodded, gratified by the man's trust in his word.

"Let us go into the dining room," Mr. Screws suggested. "We'll ring for a maid to bring you slippers while your shoes dry."

Charles pulled off his coat, a difficult matter because the mud seemed to have molded the fabric to his body in the fashion of mummy wrappings, and left it in the hall. He followed his host into the room, where one setting had been laid out. Mr. Screws rang the bell.

By the time Charles had his stiff shoes removed, a small maid had dashed into the room. Mr. Screws gave his orders. She took the shoes, fixed the fire in the stove, and departed.

"Claret?" Mr. Screws suggested. "As a hedge against the day you are having?"

"Excellent, sir," Charles said, quite in charity with the old man for once. He used his handkerchief to bind up one palm and Mr. Screws sacrificed his white square for the other.

Mrs. Dorset came in five minutes later, holding a tray with two cold plates. Mr. Screws looked in disfavor upon the beef, cheese, and bread. "Where is the soup, madam?"

"In the kitchen, sir. I'll bring it presently. Cook was just adding a bit of fish." She sniffed. "My Johnny has come in, sir, and swears he was never near Princes Street this morning. He went to the market."

"Did he bring back anything?" Charles asked.

"No. He often wanders."

"Right," Charles muttered, as Mr. Screws's eyes shifted from him to his housekeeper and back again.

"My son did nothing but protect his mother from a situation he didn't understand," she insisted.

"What is that?" Mr. Screws asked, eyes narrowing. "You're now admitting he pushed Mr. Dickens?"

"No, sir." Mrs. Dorset straightened into military posture. "The other day, when my son wanted to attack Mr. Dickens. Johnny thought he'd been cruel to me. He misunderstood."

"It sounds like he might have thought he had a reason to attack this gentleman," Mr. Screws said.

"You've watched my boy grow from an infant, sir. Have pity. He has no evil in him."

"Yet he attacked that baker. He's becoming more violent. What if he decides John Coachman has done something to you? Or me? Are we safe?" Mr. Screws growled.

"How I miss your sainted mother. I've stayed for her memory, sir, but I won't have my boy insulted. I'll give my notice, sir, right away, and remove us both from this house." Mrs. Dorset pressed her lips together very tightly. She waited as if expecting protest. The old man said nothing. A spot of red circled her cheeks and she left the room after a short pause, as regal as old Queen Charlotte.

"What will happen next?" the old man muttered, staring blankly. "My business partner dead? My housekeeper fled with that great idiot son of hers?" He put a hand to his forehead. It trembled visibly.

Charles did not like to see Mrs. Dorset give notice, but he could not tell a man how to order his own servants. He hoped she had resources, such as other relatives. "These troubles seem to have no end, sir."

"In removing Johnny Dorset from the household, we may solve some of our concerns."

"Mr. Fletcher fears him," Charles said.

Mr. Screws nodded thoughtfully. "Then all the residents of the household are in agreement. The Dorsets have to go."

Chapter 12

Charles could see before him a man at his limit, despite the elderly man's bravado. He tried to think of someone to run Mr. Screws's house since he was responsible for removing Mrs. Dorset. His sisters were too busy and so was Julie Aga. He had no ideas for once in his life. "Do you have a housemaid you can promote?"

"There are two or three young idiots in the household. No one with any age, experience, or gravitas," Mr. Screws said.

"Is there a Mrs. Cratchit?" Charles suggested.

"Dead, I believe. His daughter keeps house for him."

Charles sneezed. The explosion set his forehead afire with pain. He drained his glass of claret.

"You had better remove yourself to your domicile and have your servants draw you a hot bath," Mr. Screws advised. "Otherwise, I do not credit you with the opportunity to stay in good health, sir."

Charles tried to blink and discovered his eyes ached. "I'll sweat it out over a steaming bowl of water when I return home."

Mr. Screws stood and limped to the cabinet that hulked against the wall. He rattled his keys and opened a locked door. A moment later he came back and set a bottle in front of Charles. "Glenturret whisky," he said with satisfaction. "That will cure you. Take it home and toast to my good health."

"That's very kind of you, sir," Charles said. How could he hate a man who gave him such a kind gift?

"The least I can do," Mr. Screws said gruffly. "Injured in the line of duty, only a cold lunch? What is the world coming to?"

"Mrs. Dorset seemed like a good housekeeper," Charles said, a shade of guilt at her fate coming now that he was calmer.

"Fair, fair, but I can't have her son about under the circumstances."

Charles sighed. "No, they have to go. A pity, excellent woman." He pushed himself to his feet and shook the old gentleman's hand. The slippers had never arrived so his feet were still frozen. However, an evening at home over a steaming bowl, whisky at his elbow, would suit him very fine.

Charles had to attend a political meeting out of town the next morning and found himself riding down Fulham Road early that afternoon, his palms aching whenever they jostled against the reins. His thoughts had not strayed far from Mr. Screws and baby Timothy as he recorded the accusations between politicians in shorthand. It seemed his Christian duty was to take responsibility for two souls, one on each end of life. The baby had excellent caregivers, unlike the old man. He feared Mr. Screws was not long for this world if he received indifferent care at home, and given Kate's fondness for the old sinner, he had best keep the man alive if he hoped to reunite with his beloved.

After leaving his rented horse at a stable, he walked over to Cale Street to see Edward Pettingill, in the hopes of persuading Mr. Screws's nephew to take on the problem of the old man. A bedraggled maid let him in, probably someone they hired weekly to do the heavy work.

He saw himself into the dining room, and found Mr. Pettingill, in a red nightcap this time, bent over some writings. The scientist dropped his quill into its stand and rose to greet Charles.

"I had not expected to see you again so soon, Mr. Dickens," he said, shaking hands. "Tea?"

"Thank you," Charles said. "It was a cold ride in from Wembley."

"I do not like to ride," Mr. Pettingill said as he took a tea chest from inside a cabinet.

"Is your wife out today?"

"Paying a call on her mother. She'll be back before dark. Until then I have Marla to watch over me. I'm hopeless without the tender ministrations of the fairer sex."

Charles wished he could say such a glib thing himself. How he wanted to come home to hot meals and warm embraces. But the urge to curse the little barmaid who had doomed him was not the impulse of a good Christian. "I have news," he said, abruptly getting to his business.

"Oh?"

"I was attacked yesterday in London. It might very well have been a pickpocket gang irritated at their inability to get to my purse, but, while a boy made the first move, I think I was pushed by a much larger person, and I had to tell Mr. Screws, because Johnny Dorset had threatened to attack me in his house once before."

Mr. Pettingill's hand paused, kettle over the teapot. "Did you have Johnny arrested?"

"No, but Mrs. Dorset removed herself and her son from your uncle's household, leaving him without a housekeeper."

The man resumed pouring. "I see."

He pressed forward. "Such an unfortunate business. I must

implore you to watch over your uncle despite your hard feelings. I think there is good in him, but he is old and not well."

"You like him?" Mr. Pettingill asked, his expression full of surprise.

Marla came in with a tray of ham sandwiches. "Your tea, sir?"

Pettingill clapped his hands together. "You are a miracle, my dear. Just in the nick of time."

Grateful, Charles took one of the thick sandwiches and a pickle.

"This will warm you up, sir," the man said. "After all these years, my tendency is to do nothing more than sneak into Finsbury Circus under the cover of darkness and check on things without interacting."

"Who would let you in?"

"I have a key to my uncle's house. I'm not considered untrustworthy, just beneath consideration."

Charles frowned. "Who was your mother?"

"She was four years older than my uncle. A close connection but my uncle did not like my father and was against the marriage. Long dead now, both of them." He bit into a pickle and poured weak tea for them.

Charles made his way through an even half of the food and drank most of the pot of tea while his host pointed out features of the birds he was sketching for a monograph by another scientist. "You are a paid illustrator?"

"Yes, I put myself out to hire for anything to do with birds. I have a good reputation. And, as you can see, my work is portable." He stared at the line drawing of a bird in flight. "I see that I shall have to cage myself into my uncle's world until new staff can be hired. My wife and I will pay a visit. After all, Mr. Harley's room is available."

"That does not trouble you?"

"I do not believe in ghosts." Mr. Pettingill smiled, a facial expression that confused the eye given his lack of eyebrows.

Charles remembered his recent spectral encounter, and told himself stoutly that he did not believe, either. After all, he had been in the presence of a few tragic deaths over the past year, and those unfortunates had not troubled to haunt him.

The door burst open and Mrs. Pettingill came in, pulling off her gloves. She wore a green wool dress that peeked out from under a purple cloak embroidered with black. An expensive ensemble. Had her family paid her dress bill, or had she hand-me-downs from someone who had married into wealth?

"Interesting tidings, Mrs. Pettingill," the scientist said as she walked over to him. "We are going to stay in Finsbury Circle for a time due to complications in my uncle's household."

She had parted her lips, ready to greet him, but now they compressed into a thin line. "Has he invited us to stay for the holidays?"

"We will be taking over his housekeeping."

"What?" gasped the lady of the house.

"Mrs. Dorset has been vanquished."

"Good heavens," she said. "But she was such an efficient woman."

"I found her rather likeable once Mr. Harley had gone to his reward," Charles admitted. "She seemed lighter."

"True, but that son is dangerous. Mrs. Dorset and I disagreed, rather loudly I admit, about the ingredients in mock turtle soup one day and I was afraid Johnny would strike me." She shivered. "Mrs. Dorset sent him from the room before anything happened. Is he gone as well?"

Charles nodded. The young man had violence in him, very possibly murder.

She perched herself on the edge of the chair closest to Mr. Pettingill. "I don't imagine we'll be able to hire new staff until after the first of the year. We will have to pack for a month."

"But you can do it, my dear?" her husband asked.

"Yes." She patted his hand. "It will be a relief, not having to pay the food bills for this time of year. I'll bring our pudding, since it is already prepared just the way you like it, but we will dine in style during the Twelve Days for once."

Mr. Pettingill's forehead wrinkled. "My uncle doesn't keep Christmas."

His wife's smile was much more wolf than human. "He will this year, or my name isn't Betsy Pettingill. Such roasts we will have, and good claret, and puddings. Roaring fires, hot cider, and iced cakes. We shall make the best of it."

As Charles left the Pettingill chambers and the calculating wife, he thought of who else might aid Mr. Screws. He decided to go to Spitalfields to see Primus Harley before meeting his sisters for an outing he'd promised. Mr. Harley seemed to have some regard for Mr. Screws, even if they disagreed vehemently over his mother.

He could hear the loom clacking as he went into the rooming house. Mr. Harley's door was open. He knocked and entered, immediately entranced by the work on the loom under the window. Blues shimmered and danced with creams and yellows.

"Very fine, no?" Mr. Harley said after he turned.

"No wonder the nobility commissions your work," Charles exclaimed.

"I'd rather be hired by the middle class. They pay their bills," Mr. Harley said sourly. "What brings you back, Mr. Dickens?"

At least some of them did. Charles thought of his father's perilously casual ways. "I am concerned about Mr. Screws's household and I wanted to make you aware of the situation, since you must stand in the place of a nephew to him."

"In a way," Mr. Harley agreed, setting down his shuttle. "What is wrong?"

"Mrs. Dorset has left, because I accused her son of attacking me in the street yesterday. If a costermonger hadn't rescued me, I'd have been struck by horses until I was dead."

Mr. Harley turned on his stool. "I congratulate you on ridding Mr. Screws of the Dorsets, sir."

He liked Mr. Harley better on this visit. "Are you aware that Mrs. Dorset accused your father of molesting her?"

"She was an attractive woman in her time, and a servant. My father would have seen nothing wrong with such an act," Mr. Harley admitted.

"I asked the Pettingills to keep an eye on Mr. Screws until a new housekeeper can be hired. I wanted you to keep an eye on things as well."

"Are you any closer to figuring out what happened to my father?" Mr. Harley asked.

"I wish I knew if Johnny had pushed me. If I did, I'd be certain he had done the same to your father." Charles paused. "Should I have any reason to suspect you?"

Mr. Harley scratched the back of his neck with those enormous, hairy hands. "I admit I had angry thoughts about my father but I didn't kill him. In fact, I want his murderer found."

He didn't see how anyone of Mr. Harley's short stature could have overpowered his larger-than-average father, unless the death had been to some degree an accident. "Should I give Johnny's name to the magistrate?"

Mr. Harley winced. "He can't defend himself. His understanding is poor, his facilities diminished. Without his mother to control him, I fear for his future. I have no doubt that his neck will see the inside of a noose someday, but my father was a crooked old sinner and anyone might have wanted him dead, assuming he didn't get tangled in those chains and fall all by himself."

"It does trouble me to accuse a man so clearly lacking in wits but he's also one with a violent temper." He took one last glance at the beautiful shawl on the loom. "I suppose I can't afford your wares."

Mr. Harley chuckled. "You couldn't even afford the silk. You dress well enough, but you aren't exactly a gentleman."

"I am a gentleman's son," Charles said coldly and turned on his heel.

Charles returned to the Strand. He had time to spare before he went to collect his sisters. But a few doors away from the *Chronicle*, he saw Kate. Though she wasn't close, he recognized her by the tilt of her head. She and her sister Mary must have been visiting Mr. Hogarth. Both young ladies wore bonnets trimmed with green, either new or freshly updated, and cloaks that he recognized.

His steps quickened instinctively. He went toward them, dodging a newsboy, a fellow reporter, and a flower girl, with a hand raised in greeting. But the coachman helped Kate into the carriage without noticing him, then reached to Mary while Charles was still two doors away.

"Mary!" he called, attempting to project his voice over the noise of the street. Too many carriages and hawkers and Londoners prevented his call from reaching her ears. Before he made it to the offices, the carriage was in motion, moving away from him.

In truth, he'd been lucky to miss them at the office. Mr. Hogarth would have asked questions if Kate had behaved strangely toward him. Thus far, she had continued to trust in him and keep her own counsel. What he'd give for the soft touch of her hand right now, for his beloved to tend his aches and pains.

Charles had seen theater notices for a stirring performance about the last days of Pompeii, along with acrobatic exhibitions, at the Victoria, so for a holiday treat he took his sisters Fanny and Leticia to the show.

In their box, the sisters were full of news about their loved ones.

"Mr. Burnett," dropped from Fanny's mellifluous voice. "Mr. Austin," came from Leticia's more strident tones.

"Kate," he sighed.

"What?" Fanny asked, her curls brushing his arm as he dropped a freshly purchased orange into her hands.

"Is something wrong?" asked Leticia.

He handed her an orange, then removed his gloves so he could peel his own. "I admit I'm in a rough spot with Kate."

"But no," Fanny protested. "The wedding is only a few months away."

Charles knew it well. "All couples have these moments. A wedding can be a great strain. There are familial obligations, expenses to consider . . ."

"Kate is such a delight. The wedding should be simple," Leticia said.

"Everyone loves Kate," Charles snapped.

"Doesn't she love us?" Leticia frowned.

He stared down his sister. "Of course she does."

"Then whatever is the trouble?"

"Holiday nerves," Charles muttered. He couldn't tell them how bad it was.

Fanny, always a good friend to him, patted his arm. "For some, Christmas is a sad time. Everything will be back to normal by Epiphany, you'll see."

Charles stared at the curtain, willing it to rise. As much as he loved his sisters, he wanted Kate.

"I pray I am up to the duty of a wife," Fanny whispered.

Charles patted her shoulder. "There could be no better wife than Frances Dickens, I am convinced."

"And no better husband than you, my dear," she said in return.

He hoped Kate still believed that.

The next morning, Mr. Hogarth called Charles into his office. "William is too ill to come in today."

Charles stiffened in his chair and fretted. Ill? Was Timothy ill as well? And what about Julie and her unborn child? "Th-thank you so much for telling me, s-sir," he stammered. "I shall attend upon them at once."

Mr. Hogarth's eyes narrowed. "Whatever for? The man has a head cold. The note he had a newsboy bring here was positively splattered with ink. Must have been sneezing."

Charles cleared this throat. "If that is not what you wanted?"

The editor sighed. "I need ye to take William's assignment. He was to attend an inquest at The Cooked Goose this morning."

"Oh? Who is the magistrate presiding?"

He consulted a paper on his desk. "Sir Silas Laurie."

"Our old friend," Charles said. "What is the case?"

"One Goodwin Golden, found dead in the river," Mr. Hogarth said.

The corners of Charles's mouth turned down. "That will be a delightful corpse."

Charles went to the now familiar public house. The case had not received much attention. A trio of newspapermen were on hand and were allowed stools since no family attended. The case open and shut with no trouble, due to the late Goodwin Golden having been in the company of a known cutpurse at a dockside tavern the night before he was found alongside the riverbed near London Bridge by a porter.

After the jury returned a verdict of manslaughter that afternoon and the corpse was nailed into its coffin and taken away, Charles asked Sir Silas for a moment of his time.

"It is Dickens, correct?" the baronet queried.

"Yes, sir," Charles said. "I wanted to ask you about the Jacob Harley situation."

"Yes?" Sir Silas pulled up his coat skirts and sat on one of the vacated stools next to Charles. "Have there been new developments? I think Mr. Kittle has the paperwork in our traveling file." He gestured to the man behind the makeshift desk, employing his quill rapidly over a piece of paper.

"This is the latest development," Charles said. He explained the attack on him in Princes Street.

"From what you say," Mr. Silas said thoughtfully, "there has been a new provocation from you since the death. Therefore, this potential attack may have no bearing on the Harley death. Which, as you recall, is currently designated an accidental death."

"I've been thinking about those marks on Mr. Harley," Charles said. "Johnny's hands are so absurdly large. Would he have made marks like that or would they have been larger?"

"We can experiment," Sir Silas said. He checked the watch on his waistcoat chain. "At this time of day there are probably a variety of workmen in the taproom downstairs. Are you game for a few bruises?"

Charles chuckled and nodded at the coroner. "As long as I can have a large rum and water afterward, I will tolerate some abuse. Why don't we go to the taproom?"

Chapter 13

Sir Silas slid off his stool and glanced at his assistant, Mr. Kittle. "I concur. You did sketch the bruises on the late Mr. Harley?"

Mr. Kittle flourished a sheet. "Of course, Sir Silas. Right here."

Sir Silas took the sheet. "Life size, you would agree, Mr. Dickens?"

Charles stared at the marks. "Yes, that looks right to me." He laid his fingers over the marks. "My hands are too small."

Sir Silas reproduced the motion. "As are mine. Mr. Kittle?"

The secretary obliged, displaying ink-stained hands. "Mine are about the same as yours, sir."

Sir Silas nodded. "Downstairs we go." When they reached the ground floor, he called to the barman for drinks and scanned the room.

Charles nodded at a trio by the fire. "A hulking bunch."

"I concur," Sir Silas agreed. "Into the breach."

Charles went up to the men. They had as hostile an air as a small mob, but when he told them he was a newspaper reporter doing an experiment to catch a murderer, they agreed to help for a fresh round of ale.

"None of them are as large as Johnny," Charles whispered.

"This gentleman closest to the fire isn't too far off," Sir Silas said, smiling at the mostly toothless dockworker in the corner. "May I borrow your hands, sir?"

The man pushed his chair against the wall. "Let's make this quick. My mouth is ready for that free drink," he growled.

"If I may?" Sir Silas pushed aside the empty tankard and set down the drawing in front of the man. "Put your forefinger and thumb thus," he said, demonstrating. "Do they fit in the marks?"

The man pressed down his digits then pulled away. Grease stains extended past the thumb marks on the paper.

"He's smaller than Johnny Dorset, yet the finger marks are larger than the killer's," Charles said.

"But what about the hands?"

Charles whipped out his notebook and set it over the secretary's drawing. "May we outline your hands, sir, for comparison?"

The man grunted once the barmaid approached with the tankards. Charles quickly drew around the man's hands, then went around the table reproducing the experiment.

"We should find a man with exactly the right fingers," Sir Silas said.

They had the attention of the taproom by then. Sir Silas wandered around the eight tables, looking down his nose. "Ah, here's a fellow," he called to Charles.

"Another ale if we can experiment on you," Charles told the man, who looked like a clerk in some kind of manufacturing office, because from the waist up he wore a good tailcoat, proper neckcloth, and waistcoat, but coarse breeches and boots below.

The man nodded.

"Success!" Sir Silas crowed when the man's fingers fit smoothly over the marks on the paper. "Trace his hands, my fine fellow!"

Charles did so, then paid for a meat pie for the clerk. He took a sip of his rum and water, feeling they'd accomplished a great deal. They might have ruled out Johnny Dorset as the murderer, even. But if not him, then who?

"Now for the bruising," Sir Silas announced.

"What?"

The clerk looked startled.

"I won't offend these fine men by asking you to disrobe, Mr. Dickens, but if you could remove your coat and roll your sleeve up to a fatty part of your forearm?"

Charles did as requested, choosing the arm he didn't write with. Sir Silas smiled with satisfaction. "Now, my good sir, could you please squeeze this gentleman's arm with your thumb and forefinger, very hard? We want to see the marks develop."

The clerk shrugged. "If you wasn't a gentleman, sir, I'd think you belonged in the madhouse."

Charles winced as the clerk squeezed his arm. Sir Silas ticked away seconds, rapping his toe on the wood floor of the taproom. "That should be enough," he said eventually. "Thank you, sir."

Charles rolled down his sleeve. The clerk muttered an apology but Charles brushed it away as unnecessary. Then he and Sir Silas went back upstairs with their cooling drinks, feeling very pleased.

Sir Silas had asked for food to be sent up. He, his secretary, and Charles ate soup and sandwiches while they waited for the bruises to bloom. After a few minutes, Sir Silas motioned to Charles's sleeve. He pushed it up, displaying angry red marks.

"Mr. Kittle, could you please trace and label these new marks?"

The secretary did so as gently as possible. Charles pretended he wasn't wincing at the feel of the quill scratching against the bruises. Then, Sir Silas compared them to the now rather dirty sheet with the original marks on Mr. Harley. "Very close." He showed them to his companions. "We have done good work."

"Do we know what the size of Mr. Harley's hands was?" Charles asked. "Could he have made the marks on his own flesh while fighting against the chains?"

"He could have, but it would be awkward," Sir Silas said after considering. "They would be higher up, I should think, if he was trying to remove the chains. None of this excludes Johnny Dorset from having attacked you."

"It's hard to know if Mrs. Dorset took him away because she thought he was guilty, or if she ran because she was insulted that I suggested it," Charles said.

"You would have to ask her," Sir Silas said lazily. "I find that simply asking questions is the best way to get answers. Mr. Kittle will make a tracing of the hand for you. Please let me know if Johnny Dorset's hands are the same size. This may be enough evidence to reopen the inquest."

"Thank you, Sir Silas," Charles said. "Wise advice."

Charles spent the rest of the afternoon writing up his shorthand notes on the inquest for the *Chronicle*. Mr. Hogarth came to his desk personally and told him William had sent a note saying he'd be in the next day. Charles thanked him, wondering if his editor even knew he and Kate hadn't spoken for almost a week. The family must be wondering where he had been, and the thought of their conversation on the matter, how the truth must soon come out, made his flesh prickle with nervous energy.

With that cheering thought, he went home by way of a cook shop, picking up Fred's favorite pork and potato pie, in the hopes of enticing his brother to speak to him again. He even purchased two plump little bundles of plum duff from a street seller near his rooms. Someone must be his friend again, even if it took a bribe.

When he opened his front door, he saw nothing but the back of his brother scurrying off. He set his bundles on the deal table in front of the fire. They still ate like bachelors, without an ordained dining table and chairs. God help him if he was living like this in six months.

He went and rapped on the door sharply. "Fred. I've bought your favorite dinner. Please come and speak to me."

Fred opened the door, a sneer on his face. "I've eaten."

"Really?" The scent of rich pastry, pork fat, and the pudding wafted past his nose.

His brother put his hand to his stomach. "I have every right to be angry with you. You haven't even introduced me to my nephew."

"Very funny." Charles kept his tone mild. "Don't you think I'd have told you the truth, one man to another, if I had fathered the child?"

Fred worked his lower lip between his teeth. "I honestly don't know, Charles. You do keep secrets."

"From Kate, maybe. Do you think her parents would have agreed to my suit if they knew about Warren's Blacking Factory and that I'd once been a grimy-faced, uneducated worker there?"

Fred sighed, looking older than his fifteen years. "Very possibly not, Charles. That's why you have to be careful."

Charles lifted his hands. "I couldn't take the child to the workhouse. He's so tiny. He would have died by now if I hadn't cared for him. Babies deserve better than that."

Fred nodded and gently touched Charles's shoulder. "I'm sorry, Charlie. But you should have told me."

"I forget you are a man, now." He smiled at Fred. "I need to do something about clearing my name, but I don't know what."

"I could go to Hatfield and see what I could learn," Fred offered.

"I appreciate that, but how would you know where to begin? The housekeeper at his mother's employment had no idea she'd had a baby. William has questioned people." Charles sighed.

"Have you placed an advertisement?"

"Yes, with no response."

Fred bit his lips. "Babies look very similar to one another. You can't take him from shop to shop and ask who he looks like. But maybe when he's older."

Charles chuckled. "Let's eat. While we do, we can discuss who else I might write. The local clergymen?" He walked past his brother and poured two cups of ale from their bottle, then set them down above the chairs.

"The other senior staff at her place of employment," Fred said. "Someone there must know of the mother's sweetheart."

Charles grabbed plates and utensils from their crate and set everything next to his food, then sliced into the pie, dividing it in two. This cook shop had layered the inside with good-quality bacon before filling it completely with generous cuts of pork shoulder, potatoes, and turnips.

"What's in the other bag?" Fred asked, pulling a chair to the table.

Charles sat on the sofa. "I brought an extra bribe."

Fred laughed. "Too bad pudding won't work on Kate."

"At least she hasn't told her father." Charles took a big bite, feeling famished. He'd forgotten to eat a midday meal.

"She's a good girl and she loves you." Fred matched his bite, just as a knock came at the door.

"I'll get it," Charles said, wiping the greasy corners of his mouth with the back of his hand.

He opened the door, never expecting to see the sight of one tall, slight man in a massive cream comforter and a blue sleeping cap. "Mr. Pettingill!" he exclaimed. "What has you out and about this evening?"

The man rubbed bloodless, gloveless hands together. "You must-t-t wonder how I had your address." His teeth were chattering.

"Never mind that, come to the fire," Charles said, pulling him in. "You aren't dressed for the night air."

"I never g-g-go out at night, generally," said the man.

Fred had leapt up and was adding coal to the fire.

Charles felt the ends of the comforter and found it damp. He unwound Mr. Screws's nephew from it and draped it over the back of the armchair William had given him when he left Furnival's Inn. Fred went to the kettle and poured some hot water into a cup, then doctored it with the bottle of rum that rested on the mantelpiece.

"Thank you," their visitor said. "Your brother?"

"Yes, this is Fred Dickens," Charles said. "Would you like to join us for our meal? We have scarcely tucked into our pie."

Mr. Pettingill took a deep drink. Color came back into his face, though he coughed as the rum hit the back of his throat. "I cannot stay, Mr. Dickens. I've come to fetch you."

"Why?" Charles asked, sitting down and setting his fork into his pie. He shoved a large bite into his mouth.

"Mr. Screws, poor man, has collapsed, I am afraid. Your warning to me was well timed. My uncle is not well."

Charles stared at him, speechless. "I suppose I should have expected this, given the state of his appearance. Do you have a carriage waiting?"

"No, but I saw the stand in front of your building."

Charles nodded. He glanced up and down Mr. Pettingill's thin form, noting his knobby hands. Were they the size of the killer's? "Fred, go and see if you can find a pair of mittens that will fit this gentleman."

Fred glanced over. "Leticia made me an oversized pair two years ago. They itch, so they are still in my trunk. I'll get them."

"Too kind," Mr. Pettingill said, wrapping his hands around his cup and drinking again. When he was finished, he said, "You must wonder why my uncle wants you."

"Do you know the reason?" Charles cut off another piece, thick with bacon and turnip, then gestured to his guest.

"No, thank you. I will have another drink, though."

Charles rose, mouth full, and fetched the kettle and the rum bottle. By the time he'd satisfied his guest, Fred was back, waving a massive knobby pair of white knitted mittens.

"Excellent, good man," Mr. Pettingill said. "Very obliged to you, young sir."

"I'll lend you a cloak as well. I'll bring it back with me later on."

"My uncle, old gentleman, never explains himself," said the nephew, "but something has him most alarmed."

"Then we'll be off." Charles took one last bite of pie and left the puddings for his brother. They'd have to write letters another time.

The hackney pulled up in front of the now familiar house. Mrs. Dorset's decorations still survived. In fact, Mrs. Pettingill seemed to have woven holly complete with berries into the ivy that had already been wound around the iron railings.

Mrs. Pettingill opened the door. Her husband smiled at her. "I've brought our Mr. Dickens, dear man."

"Good evening, sir," she said.

"I am sorry to see you again under such troubling circumstances," Charles said as he entered. "Has there been any change?"

"He is conscious," she replied. "I feel as if we have come just in time. I'll take you upstairs to his private chamber."

Charles climbed the steps behind her. When the stairs turned, outside the view of any casual visitor, the good carpet vanished, replaced by some elderly, stained stuff. The passage was bare.

"That's the room we've taken," Mrs. Pettingill said, pointing to the room where Mr. Harley had fallen from. She turned away from it and marched down the hall, then knocked on a cracked-open door. "Uncle Emmanuel, here is your Mr. Dickens."

Charles pushed open the door despite the lack of response. He went in, noting the washstand and wardrobe. All had the musty scent of an older person. The hangings were very fine, some kind of patterned red velvet that hung on thick iron rings from a plain wood bed frame.

One side was open to a fire in a tiled stove similar to the one downstairs. Between the open curtains, Charles saw Mr. Screws arranged on a heap of pillows, his face gray. When he opened his mouth, however, Charles observed that his tongue had a pink and healthy appearance, despite his skin.

Mr. Screws lifted a hand, which trembled weakly. Charles took it and sat on the edge of the bed. "I am sorry Miss Hogarth isn't with me, sir. She's very good in a health crisis."

"I have suffered too much in these past days," the old man whispered. "I must rest."

"That is exceedingly sensible, sir, but what about the counting-house? You have employees. Is Mr. Fletcher trained well enough to take on your duties and Mr. Harley's?"

"I am giving my business to my nephew and retiring." He clutched a book to his breast and closed his eyes.

Charles stared at the old man, resting on his pillows.

With that new piece of information, Charles couldn't help but reconsider Mr. Screws's nephew. Was he behind everything? He knew what he had to do. Get imprints of the man's fingers.

Chapter 14

Charles felt a wave of sympathy for Mr. Screws, gray faced on his pillow. "You may change your mind once you recover your health."

"I will not." Mr. Screws patted his book.

Charles sighed. "Please do not sign any papers regarding the business until we are certain who killed Mr. Harley. I don't suppose his ghost has visited you with anything helpful? Young Primus seemed to think his shade was about."

Mr. Screws laughed, or coughed, Charles wasn't certain. "No. I have not seen him."

"I am glad you still have a sense of humor, sir." He paused. "Are you certain Mr. Pettingill wants the business? He is a man of science."

"He is the only close family I have."

"And Primus Harley was trained as a weaver," Charles said. "At least I assume Mr. Pettingill is an educated man."

"He is." Mr. Screws squeezed Charles's hand. "Mr. Fletcher will help him until he returns to America."

"When will that be?"

"I do not know." Mr. Screws yawned. "I must rest."

Charles patted Mr. Screws's hand with his free one, then removed himself from the old man's grip. "Rest well. I will speak to you again soon."

He walked out of the room. The Pettingills huddled in the passage.

"What did he say?" Mrs. Pettingill asked.

"That Mr. Fletcher will help your husband run the business."

Mr. Pettingill licked his lips. "I never thought he'd relinquish it. I have no training."

Charles judged the man to be nervous, not triumphant. "Why don't we go to dinner?" he suggested. "Somewhere with a good roast? We can discuss the matter." If he could find somewhere with napkins and get the man to wipe greasy fingers on the cloth, he might be able to compare it to his sketch of the killer's hands.

But the nephew shook his head. "My place is here, though it is very kind of you. But I am sure you do not know the business, either."

"I'll go to dinner with you, Charles." Mr. Fletcher had come up the stairs without anyone noticing. "How is Mr. Screws?"

"Weak," Charles said. "But still in possession of his wits." *He hoped.*

Charles followed Mr. Fletcher into a chophouse in the banking district, not far from the Screws and Harley establishment. Inside, the customers presented as well fed and prosperous, a sign of an expensive but good-quality meal.

"Do you come here often?" Charles asked, setting his gloves on the bench beside him and taking off his hat.

Mr. Fletcher did the same. "If I can put it on my expense account with the firm. It's very good meat and not too many vegetables."

A fug of yellow cigar smoke rose from the table in front of them. Mr. Fletcher took an appreciative sniff. "Smells like back home. My family, the Lees, you know, still have a number of tobacco plantations in Virginia."

As they ordered their food and had it served, the American prosed on with Richard Lee this, and Paradise that, as well as Ditchley and various other place names. Charles found it difficult to straighten it all out. "How long did this Richard Lee live?" he inquired.

"Oh, I'm talking about the founder, and the son, and the offspring," Mr. Fletcher said. "All staunch royalists despite what happened later."

He was off again. Utterly self-absorbed with the glory of his ancestors, rather like the British nobility. Did all Americans who knew how to trace their roots back to William the Conqueror obsess over their ancestors like this? And didn't Mr. Fletcher see the irony in revering the Lees when his most distinguished family line was through a family called Corbin? Shouldn't that be the name that dripped so reverently from his lips?

The more Charles listened, the more he realized he couldn't discern how exactly Mr. Fletcher was related to any of these people. That might have been the fault of the wine, which was excellent. Charles's glass kept filling, and he kept drinking.

Eventually, his eyes were at half mast. He could see snow falling outside. "Excellent," he said, speaking over Mr. Fletcher's story about some medical man in the Lee family. "We had better find our beds before all the horses in London are stabled due to the weather."

Mr. Fletcher broke off and turned to the window. "When did that begin?" he exclaimed.

"Indeed," Charles said. "My point is made in snow."

His companion threw coins down on the table and rose. "Winter is not my favorite season. Sometimes I fancy taking my chances in a place like New Orleans, or even sailing out to be a bookkeeper for some plantation in the Caribbean. Always fortunes to be made there, if you can survive the fevers."

"I like London," Charles said, weaving behind Mr. Fletcher as they went through the tables to the coatrack.

Mr. Fletcher threw on his outerwear, then pulled something out of his pocket. He thrust it at Charles, who reached for it.

Somehow, their hands did not connect. The item thudded to the ground. Mr. Fletcher, holding his wine better than Charles, snatched it up again and handed it over, careful to ensure that the binding fell into Charles's palm that time, instead of merely touching his fingers.

"Miss Osborne remembered that Miss Hogarth wanted to read *Lodore*," he explained.

"The first volume," Charles said, glancing at the tome. "I had heard that the author of *Frankenstein* had penned a new novel. Thank you, but it looks very new."

"I purchased it the next afternoon after our theater night. I found it interesting, so I'm passing the first volume along while I read the second."

"That is most kind," Charles said. What a gracious gesture. He pulled on his coat, and carefully tucked the volume inside. "I am afraid I do not collect many books. I am so busy with my own writings at the moment."

"I do not ask for repayment," Mr. Fletcher said with a gallant swirl of his muffler as he wound it around his neck.

"I can give you a word of, well, warning, I suppose, in return," Charles said.

"What is that?"

"A friend of mine, a retired actress, tells me there is an actress operating with your fiancée's name."

Mr. Fletcher's eyes widened over his encompassing muffler. Then Charles heard his chuckle from behind the dampening wool. "It is probably a stage name, chosen because it is so pretty."

"I am sure you are right," Charles said. "I didn't mean to

imply, of course. I know very well how the denizens of the theater are regarded. I once fancied becoming an actor myself."

"Oh?"

As they went on to the street, Charles regaled Mr. Fletcher with his abortive attempt to audition for the theater, thwarted by a severe cold.

"I think that illness was heaven sent," Mr. Fletcher said. "For you have clearly found your gift in another sphere, that of storytelling."

Charles blinked stinging snowflakes from his eyes. "Thank you. I will return your favor by presenting you with the first volume of my sketches when it is printed."

"I look forward to it," Mr. Fletcher said. "I hope it makes you a very rich man."

Charles's feet felt frozen to his shoes by the time he entered his chambers. The snow had briefly turned to rain, then back again, leaving parts of his clothing icy and snowy altogether.

"Charles!" Fred leapt up from the sofa, rosy cheeked from a generous helping of coal freshly popping on the fire. "I am so glad you are home."

"Are you?" Charles said acerbically. Though grateful that his brother loved him again, he felt sick from the cold and the wine. He went into the bedroom, shedding his coat, muffler, and hat behind him. Once inside, he pushed up the window sash and breathed. In his acidic state, he even worried about the fate of those poor clerks in the countinghouse. Would it stay open under the management of Mr. Pettingill? He had not the feral instincts of a Screws or Harley.

Fred came up behind him. Charles hit his head on the sash and reeled back. The explosion of pain was the last straw to his injured stomach. He leaned forward again and cast up his accounts over the pavement below.

"Satan's teeth, Charles," Fred exclaimed. "What is the matter with you?"

Charles turned and leaned the back of his head against the cold window. "Too much wine, that is all. Too much misery in the world, and at Christmas, too. It's not right."

"I'm sorry you knocked your head. I was only going to suggest you get dressed again so we could go coin hunting. Haven't you missed the excitement of last winter, grubbing in the dirt for hidden treasure?"

"Whatever for?" Charles's brain and belly sloshed with wine.

"To sell, to purchase Christmas gifts for the girls," Fred said. "You know they've been busy all month making us new mittens and socks. I don't have any talent with which to make things."

"No?" Charles said blearily.

"I tried to make a little toy theater for the boys but it collapsed," his brother said. "I want to buy some penny candy at least."

"I don't need the money from found coins," Charles said. He had a good income these days. The only benefit in life left to him, it seemed.

"Maybe Julie would go with me?" Fred suggested.

"William would never allow it given her condition," Charles said. "The very idea."

"You want to go to bed?"

"I didn't drink that much," Charles muttered. "It's just that I hit my head."

"I believe you," Fred assured him. "You can still form sentences."

Charles put his hand to his forehead and considered his brother, who was eagerly shifting from side to side in his bid for attention. At least he hadn't been deserted. He found a thread of his own cheer and forced his eyebrows to rise. "I bet you a penny that you can't balance a spoon on your nose for five seconds."

Fred grinned. "I bet you the penny I'm going to win off you that you can't balance on one foot for ten seconds."

"In my shoes or without them?"

"Without, blockhead. Your shoes are soaked."

The next morning, Charles felt ill when he sat up. The room spun and his stomach felt like he'd swallowed rocks. He remembered the wine and the gambling and let his head drop back on the pillow, closing his eyes until he felt he'd achieved equilibrium again.

"Water," he croaked, hoping Fred was in their rooms somewhere, but no one came. He must have gone to work.

Charles pushed the covers back and pulled the chamber pot out from under the bed using his sock-covered toes. Then he went to the window and leaned his head against the cold.

Outside, the yellow fog had descended again. Only a certain lightness above indicated daytime. He'd have to wait for church bells to even know the hour. A yawn told him his body required more sleep, but he had an endless pile of work to do both on his book and at the *Chronicle*.

He went to his diary to see where he was promised for the day. The words swam in front of his eyes but he eventually read his own notation. He was meant to be at the Lesser Hall for speeches that morning. While he wanted to check on Mr. Screws, it would have to wait for now.

Swearing, he pushed his hands through his unruly hair. He made himself ready and sped out the door, stomach churning, for what was left of the parliamentary buildings after last year's fire.

Come afternoon, he made his way up the Strand toward the offices. He still hadn't been able to eat but had ducked into a public house near the Lesser Hall for a tankard of ale, which had reduced his headache somewhat. His brain told him he should be churning over the question of possible war between

France and America, but his thoughts kept turning to Kate. Only a week remained until Christmas and he felt farther away from her and their marital prospects than ever.

When Charles walked into the reporter's chamber at the newspaper, something seemed to be very wrong. Thomas Pillar, the under-editor, scuttled away just before he would have met Charles's eyes. No office boys were present, dashing about with messages. Worst of all, William stood at his desk. He faced Charles, his face ashen.

Charles's mouth formed the name *Julie* and William shook his head in the negative.

"Charles?"

He turned to see Mr. Black, the editor, crook a finger at him. Having no choice but to follow, he walked out of the chamber after one last glance at his sorrowful friend.

Instead of taking him to his own office, Mr. Black opened Mr. Hogarth's door. He ushered Charles inside, then shut them both into the room with the coeditor. Neither of the men offered him a chair.

Instead, Mr. Hogarth set his pipe in an ashtray and stood, tucking his hands under his tailcoat behind him. "I'm afraid we won't be requiring your services any longer, Charles."

Chapter 15

"What? Why?" Charles demanded. "I haven't missed any meetings, or any deadlines." How could they think of sacking the best parliamentary reporter they had?

What had Kate done? He pulled his notebook from his coat and faced off with the other two standing men. "I have my shorthand notes from Lesser Hall this morning. I know I'm very busy with my book but my work here hasn't suffered."

"It's not that," Mr. Black said with a sigh. He sagged against Mr. Hogarth's desk, his body language making it clear that he wasn't pleased with these proceedings.

The coeditor shook his head.

"Then what?" Charles asked, knowing what was coming from the expression on Mr. Hogarth's face.

"I am not willing to work with ye any longer," Mr. Hogarth said. His hand shook as he picked up his pipe again.

"I have great respect for you, sir," Charles said earnestly. "If you've heard otherwise, I assure you it isn't true. It's an honor to write for you."

"What ye have done to my daughter shows anything but respect." Mr. Hogarth shoved the stem into his mouth.

Charles squeezed his eyes shut. Kate must have decided to formally break their engagement without any further contact with him. "I'm going to win her back, sir. It's all a misunderstanding. We love each other. We'll sort it out."

Mr. Hogarth's lip curled. "I will not employ a man who fathers a bastard child while courting my daughter."

"I didn't," Charles insisted, forcing his temper *down*. Theatrics would only hurt him. "The infant, Timothy, is not mine, in the first place. I'm trying to find his father."

Mr. Hogarth continued to stare at him, a skeptical look creasing his brow.

Charles blurted, "And secondly, even if he were, he was conceived before I met Kate."

"How do you know that?" Mr. Black asked as Mr. Hogarth's eyes narrowed further.

Charles thrust his hands under his coat skirts, wiping sweat off his hands. "Because his aunt, young and distraught over the loss of her sister in the Hatfield fire, told me the circumstances of his birth. The babe wasn't a foundling. He had a mother."

"But not a father," Mr. Hogarth said, acid around the pipe stem.

"That she knew of, sir. I'm sure her dead sister knew." Charles swallowed. "It's not me, sir. I promise you."

"You're a man of the world, Charles. You have every right to be," Mr. Black said. "I don't judge you, but obviously Mr. Hogarth feels differently, as he has the right to. Miss Hogarth is his daughter."

Charles wouldn't fall for the obvious attempt to get him to admit something. He straightened his shoulders and touched the bow on his neckerchief to make sure it was straight. "I didn't wrong Miss Hogarth, but I also didn't father the child. The mother was a maid at Hatfield House. The father came from much closer than Furnival's Inn."

"How do you know that?" Mr. Black asked.

"She worked directly for the old noblewoman. If she had more than a half day to herself a month I'd be surprised. No, the father must be someone employed on the estate."

Mr. Hogarth bit down on his pipe stem until Charles could hear it cracking under his teeth. "Ye should have confessed all. Instead, ye wrapped William into yer lies."

Charles's heart rate sped. How had he never recognized how stubborn his fiancée's father could be? "No lies, just men of honor attempting to save a baby from a Christmas of dying in the workhouse. The young aunt might yet come to her senses and care for her nephew."

"Unacceptable," Mr. Hogarth muttered around his pipe.

"You cannot want the child to die?" Charles clutched his curls on either side of his head. He felt tiny pops along his scalp as tender hair pulled out. "We've gone to a great deal of trouble and expense to save him. Here I am, risking my very career on the matter."

"At the expense of your good relationship with my daughter. She deserves a respectable man."

Charles fixed his gaze on Mr. Hogarth with an impertinence he'd never before dared. "In this season of the Christ child, how can I not save a defenseless infant from the censure and cruelty of the world? I've done nothing wrong." He lowered his hands, holding the man's eyes.

After a long pause, Mr. Black's gaze went to the other editor's unsoftening gaze, then returned to Charles's. "You need to clear out your desk, Mr. Dickens. I am sorry, and I wish you luck."

Mr. Hogarth dropped back into his chair, saying nothing. Charles walked out, knowing that he did not take good wishes from his mentor.

William stood again when Charles came to his desk but Charles shook his head. They could talk later.

He emptied his wastebasket into William's, ignoring the sidelong glances from other reporters, and piled his belongings into his own. When he pulled an old damaged coin from its spot in the drawer, one he'd never sold because no one had been able to figure out what it was, he realized he should have gone coin hunting with Fred after all. There had been times last winter when the old coins they'd found around the law courts had paid for things they needed to keep their nascent household going.

His body went cold as he stopped moving for a moment. He felt faint. How could Kate be so vindictive as to share her feelings about the baby with her parents, especially after having kept Timothy a secret for a full week? He had trusted in her good sense. What changed? Surely she hadn't stopped loving him.

"I'm missing something, William," he said in a weak voice as he securely stoppered his ink pot. "Not just about what sweet Kate has done to me, but everything. The baby, Mr. Harley, everything."

"I can see what has happened and it is not right. However"—William turned in his chair—"you scarcely sleep. You've taken on an indomitable amount of work. It's no wonder you are having problems."

"I have to manage everything." Charles slid his fingers around his desk drawer, gathering the last few things as he tried to find his strength. Three shillings lingered, tucked into a corner behind a bit of paper. Attempting to show manly levity, he tossed them into the air and juggled them. "My life is like this."

One of them dropped to the floor as he fumbled. He went to his knees and crawled under his desk, looking for it. After the events of the summer, he'd promised himself to manage his finances more carefully, so that he'd never be caught out by a charlatan again. Hating himself for caring about one measly shilling, he snatched it from a dark, cobweb-infested corner and shoved it into his pocket, dust and all.

"After you've finished your revisions, maybe you can finally find time to have that career on the stage after all." William grinned at him.

Charles shook his head. "I'll apply at the rival papers. Someone will want me. I'm the best, indomitable." He warmed to his theme. "I'm the Inimitable One." He liked the sound of William's word. But inimitable described him perfectly.

"That's it, Charles. Leave with your head held high. Another paper might pay you even more."

Charles winced at that, though he kept his face calm. He knew Mr. Hogarth paid him better than he perhaps deserved, because of Kate. He'd promised more than he'd delivered where his sketches were concerned, but he'd been pelted with opportunities like his book, and he hadn't thought anyone minded, as his reputation grew. Without Kate, his prospects could diminish.

He locked his hands around his wastebasket and stood soldier straight. "Onward, always onward."

"I'll see you very soon," William promised. "Little Timothy had a fever this morning so don't come over tonight, though."

Charles nodded and marched out of the reporters' chamber. The baby's fever was another worry to add to his litany of troubles. He must have income to pay for the child's care. No one turned away, exactly, but no one met his eye or wished him well, either.

It didn't matter. He'd neglected his relationships at the newspaper of late, spending his free time with Ainsworth and other literary types. He'd make up for all of it when his book revisions were done.

Charles had a lonely night bent over his deal table in front of his fire. Fred had dashed in long enough to use up all of their water to wash his hands and face before departing for some seasonal spectacle or other with his friends. Charles could not blame him. When he'd first been out in the world he'd gone to the theater almost every night, too.

Eventually, when his throat grew dry from the coal smoke, he took their water can outside. The night air beckoned him as soon as his feet hit the stairs, so after he returned with his can, he bundled up more warmly for a long walk.

He decided to avoid the river after recent events. After all, they couldn't offer any more charity in that direction as they had to pay for Brother Second's siblings and help with school fees. His feet took him toward Brompton without him realizing it; he'd made the journey on foot so many times.

On one of the more dilapidated thoroughfares, a woman stepped from the mouth of a dark court, her hair covered with a shawl.

For a moment, Charles thought Julie was stalking him as she had last winter, in order to get away from her abusive mother. But the woman dropped her shawl and he saw she was a good fifteen years older, her face lined with care.

She held out her hand, beckoning him, a smile exposing broken front teeth.

He shook his head. "Not tonight, lovey. Stay warm."

She tilted her head and he considered giving her a coin to make her go away, but he had to be careful with money, now. He moved away. She didn't protest, abuse him in strident tones like sometimes happened. Maybe she wasn't a lightskirt at all, but the lookout for a gang of thugs, ready to fall upon him and steal his possessions when he went with her to the wall, where the likes of her usually did their work.

His stomach turned over, and Kate's face came to mind. Hers was the only hand he wanted to take, the only form he wanted to embrace. His entire being was settled on her, despite her betrayal.

He walked on, tallying up her faults, but knowing his fault was greatest, for not trusting her with the truth from the first. Why hadn't he brought Timothy to Mrs. Hogarth at the start? Even if she'd only kept him for a night, he'd have established his innocence.

Or at least as close to innocent as he could have made it. The character of the Scots was a more judgmental one, with their long history of Calvinist leanings. He might have wound up in hot water right then and there, without Kate and a hungry babe in his arms.

But he never should have chosen Julie as his confidante over Kate. What a fool he'd been.

He reached his old territory, footsore after a long week, wishing he still lived here so he could sit for a while. At Selwood Terrace, he peered in the windows of Breese Gadfly's lodgings, a fine apartment on the main floor, but the chamber was dark and he had no idea where his songwriter friend was on a Friday night.

Strolling on, he buried his exhaustion in contemplating the previous summer, until he found himself alongside the orchards on Fulham Road. Behind him, a gust of wind shook the apple trees and then what had been a relatively pleasant night vanished in a pelting of hail. He pulled his muffler over his mouth and nose and tried to protect the back of his neck with his coat collar. Shards of ice coated his arms in an instant. He couldn't stay outdoors.

Across the street lay the comfort he'd been denied, the Hogarths' hearth and home. But Lugoson House next door was all lit up. He could claim sanctuary there. It appealed to him more than going to a tavern.

He crossed the road, keeping his gaze resolutely away from the Hogarths' gate, his eyes filling with tears from the biting wind and no other reason. Trotting, he went past the orchard on the side of the Hogarth property and along the formal garden, then rang the bell at Lugoson House.

He huddled in the colonnade, waiting for the door to open. By the time it did, he felt half frozen. Still, he was taken by a ferocious sneeze when the door opened and warm air tickled his nostrils.

When he blinked away moisture, he saw Panch looking down at him, his head held at the habitually strange angle from his stalk-like neck. The butler opened his mouth as slowly as a snail, so it seemed to Charles.

"Mr. Dickens," he said in lugubrious tones.

"Panch!" Charles showed his teeth to the butler. "Would Lady or Lord Lugoson be so kind as to receive a half-frozen writer this evening?"

"Hoping to spend some time in the library?"

"I would indeed," Charles said. He enjoyed escaping there and used the privilege shamelessly when encouraged by William.

Panch stepped back. "The Agas are not here this evening."

"I know," Charles said. "I was out for a walk, but as you can see, the weather worked its foul magic on me."

"Better hail than the yellow fog," the butler opined, waiting politely for Charles to work his frozen fingers over his clothing.

He handed his coat to the butler. "There you are."

Panch held the dripping garments away from himself as he turned. "You know the way, sir. I will alert the household and send in a tray."

"You are a king, Panch," Charles exclaimed.

The butler sniffed but said nothing as he left the foyer. Charles went to the library, finding the remains of a fire and an old paper theater on one of the tables. Perhaps young Lord Lugoson had resumed the hobby he once shared with his sister.

Charles glanced at the decorations and the paper players, recognizing a Mozart opera. He hummed under his breath as he perused the shelves, looking for something to occupy his time.

The first tome to catch his eye was *Childe Harold's Pilgrimage*. He opened the leather-bound volume, his gaze lighting on the frontispiece. An uncouth creature with a spear and wings stood manfully on a rock, master of all he surveyed. It had only been a week since Charles had felt the same way, before he lost Kate. But he couldn't lose his confidence now.

No, he needed to find Timothy's father in order to fix everything with the Hogarths, instead of waiting for the information to come to him. He shut Byron's work and went to a writing table, not even bothering to stoke the fire before he put quill to ink, writing letters that he left unaddressed to the steward at Hatfield House and the local vicar there. He'd learn their names later.

What else? He needed to figure out who had killed Mr. Harley so that Mr. Screws could recover his health and release his hold on Charles's life. He decided to methodically list out the suspects in Mr. Harley's death and rule out as many as he could.

Before he could do more than write in the general listings of Dorset, Appleton, Harley, and Pettingill, the door opened. He looked up, expecting his tray, but instead, a vision of beauty presented herself, like something out of Byron's poetry.

Lady Lugoson, a mere decade older than Charles, glided into the room. Out of mourning for her daughter now, she wore a navy gown that set off her golden beauty in a vision of severity. At moments, she had a tendency to overindulge, but this evening she looked clear eyed and steady on her feet.

Charles stood, ready to pay his respects, but instead of looking happy to see him, she shook her head at him.

"Mr. Dickens, what are you doing here so late?"

"Hailstorm, my lady," he said, taking her hand in playful fashion. "It's nothing I haven't done before. Panch didn't seem to mind."

"He's the butler, not the master of my son's home," she murmured.

He stared into her eyes, sensing a distance that had never been there before. "What is wrong, ma'am?"

"I have happy news," she said, pulling away and clasping her hands in front of her.

"Oh?" He didn't sense happiness from her.

Her lips turned up. "You may congratulate me. I am to be wed."

"I had expected it long since," Charles said. And indeed, he had, for she was a beautiful woman. Despite what she'd suffered at the hands of her first husband, she was made to wed again. He wouldn't allow himself to feel the pain of another loss of safe harbor again, not tonight.

"Yes. Do you know Sir Silas Laurie?" she asked.

"Indeed I do. I've even been to his home," Charles said, surprised. "What a brilliant choice! Excellent man. You'll be very happy, I'm sure."

She nodded. "I am used to busy men. My son has decided to attend Oxford next year, and so, c'est le temps pour un change."

"You are well matched in every way," Charles promised. "Title, fortune, industry." He winked. "Even looks."

She blushed prettily. It took a decade off her age, hiding the fine lines around her eyes.

Charles nodded, warming to his theme. "I am gratified to have my friends find a life together." At least he hoped the coroner regarded him warmly. He hoped Lady Lugoson would find some happiness in what had been a difficult life.

"You can be my son's guest for tonight, but then you must leave for propriety's sake first thing tomorrow," Lady Lugoson said.

"I hadn't thought to spend the night," he protested.

"You must," she announced. "It's too ghastly to walk and I can't send the horses out either, not in this hail. I could hear it pounding outside the windows in my little parlor. The windows are thicker here."

Charles listened for a moment. The sounds outside were muted by glass and curtains, but he did hear the clatter of the hailstones. "Very well. I'm surprised you don't think I should go over to the Hogarths'."

"I know you and Miss Hogarth are having problems," she said delicately. "I know about your position as well, dear Mr. Dickens. I can't offer you work in my household, I'm afraid, not with my son leaving, but I will buy ten copies of your book as soon as it is available."

This was unwelcome news in the extreme. Aghast, he asked, "How did the news travel so quickly?"

Her mouth screwed up, as sour as if she'd bit into a lemon. "The Hogarths' maid and my son's valet have become friends."

"Oh, dear," Charles said.

"Yes." She curled her upper lip. "We'll break up the romance if my son takes him to Oxford. I have to decide what to do about that. I didn't want to interfere in Mrs. Hogarth's domestic matters, but given what that family has done to you, well, perhaps I should not mind."

"You are a good friend to me," he reinforced.

Flustered, she busied herself with the coal hod, casually dropping a shovel of coal onto the fire as if she often played tweenie. "You have been a very good one to me, Mr. Dickens. I do hope we will always be friends, but you will have to be careful. Mr. Hogarth is well respected in your field."

"You don't think he'll prevent me from gaining work elsewhere?" Charles asked.

He heard the lady sigh. "Perhaps Sir Silas can help you after we are wed."

Charles closed his eyes, afraid he would not be able to find work if even Lady Lugoson couldn't help him. He had solved her daughter's murder less than a year before. Would the break with the Hogarths destroy his standing in the world? He'd thought his own natural ability could conquer any difficulty, but if Mr. Hogarth destroyed his character, what did he have left?

Charles woke abruptly the next morning when he heard a clink in the room. He pushed himself to a sitting position on an unusually soft bed, a curtained bed. Pulling open the edge of the fabric, he saw a tea tray on a table. The window curtains had been drawn back and he smelled a fire.

He leaned back, smiling. This was how the upper classes lived. He'd been so deeply asleep that he'd forgotten Panch had shown him into a bedroom at Lugoson House after an hour or so. After he struggled free of the feather bed, he washed his face and hands in the basin and poured tea, then took it to the fire. He rocked in the rocking chair, utterly lost despite the comfortable surroundings. Who was he without his position? How should he balance looking for another against his book responsibilities? He supposed he should be happy he didn't have to factor setting up his household with Kate into this twisted bargain. No more did he need to save for furnishings or improved chambers at Furnival's Inn. And Fred had his own income now. Charles did sums, made calculations, still saw his money running out by the end of winter if he didn't take other employment. He had Timothy to support until they found the boy's father, if William couldn't be persuaded to pay all the bills. How long before he could be weaned?

Giddy with frustration and loss, he shoved his arms into his frock coat, then went to search out one of Panch's deputies so he could retrieve the rest of his possessions.

Half an hour later, he'd resisted accepting an invitation to breakfast with the Lugoson family and left the house. What he did not resist was walking across the apple orchard in between the houses. When he reached the edge of the Hogarths' herb and vegetable garden he stopped and sighed.

The jumbled rows and tangling herbs reminded him of the Hogarths' untidy home. While he'd meant to break Kate of her mother's habits, now he just wanted her again, messiness and all.

The kitchen door opened while he stood, contemplating. He looked up, heart leaping in his chest, but instead of his darling, her sister Mary appeared. As he watched, she pulled her shawl tightly around herself and after shoving her feet into clogs dashed through the garden until she met him.

Though smaller and darker than her older sister, he delighted in Mary's wit and appreciation of himself. He forced a smile through his dreary mood and bowed his head to her.

"What are you doing out here?" she asked.

"I stayed next door last night. I was caught in the hailstorm."

"I heard that. Father is fretting about the state of the roof." She paused and blushed. "But I don't imagine you want to hear about him right now."

"He has hurt me both personally and professionally," Charles responded.

Mary let out a breath and pulled up her shawl to protect her head. Charles felt the first raindrop fall on his arm and hoped more hail did not follow. Even for him, an inveterate walker, the weather was displeasing.

"My dear Mr. Dickens," Mary said formally.

Charles felt something lodge in his chest, like a bubble of air keeping the inner workings of his body stretched beyond endurance. "Not you, too, Mary," he whispered.

She shook her head sharply. "I believe you aren't the baby's father." She patted his arm. "I'm a true friend to you."

"If you believe me, why doesn't Kate? She knows my heart."

Mary took a step closer, until he could feel her breath on his chin. "Kate did not tell our parents about the baby."

Charles put his hand on her shoulder, steadying himself. Kate hadn't betrayed him. "Then who?"

Chapter 16

Charles could scarcely believe the evidence of his ears. His feet insisted on a little jig. They slid in the mud outside the Hogarths' kitchen door and he had to put out his arms to balance himself. "Kate didn't betray me to your parents?"

"Georgina did it," Mary said, looking amused at his exuberance.

Charles, so elated that he couldn't trust his hearing, had to ask again. "Kate hasn't played me false?"

She smiled up at him and drew her shawl closer against the cold. "No, Charles. Georgina overheard Kate telling me what she knew. Kate told me how much she loved you, dear sir, and awaited proof that could stand up in society about this baby."

He gritted his teeth. "But Georgina tattled."

Mary nodded and reached into the pocket of her apron. She pulled out a piece of paper. "Here, it's a letter from Kate."

Charles stared at the small slip like it held the words of a Catholic saint. Reverently, he took it from Mary, fingers unsteady in his thick mittens, and unfolded the paper. His gaze went over it so fast that he only caught snatches. Kate, his dear

Kate, expressed her confusion and begged him to resolve the matter quickly. "Of course I will, as quickly as I can," he exclaimed.

Mary peered out from her shawl, her cheeks pink. "What?"

"Sort this out," Charles said. He lifted the paper to his eyes and read more carefully. Toward the end, she begged him to keep helping poor Mr. Screws as she was afraid the mystery of Mr. Harley's death would affect his health terribly. "She can't help thinking of others despite her own cares."

"You can fix this, can't you?" Mary asked.

"I must have little Timothy's aunt recant her accusation," Charles said. "I may not be able to find the father, so the aunt is my best bet. But to take her from her employment, bring her to London? So she can appear in front of your father and tell the truth?"

"It would terrify her," Mary said. "Maybe a letter?"

"I could forge that." Charles sighed. "No, I must prove my innocence with a great show of integrity. Mary, I need my job back."

As she shook her head soberly, Charles heard a window bang above their heads. He glanced up to the upper story of the Hogarths' house and saw Kate.

She had drawn back the curtain. Behind the window, he could see her hands under her chin and thought he detected tears on her cheeks despite the distance. He craned his neck to get the best glimpse of her, but, after a quick twitch of her lips, she turned away. He lost sight of her.

"I feel like Romeo," he told Mary. "If only you had a balcony under the window."

"With Father in the house it isn't safe. There is no cover of night." She touched his arm. "You'd better not be seen here right now, my dear. Go to Hatfield and force a confession out of that girl."

"Do I do that or help our Mr. Screws?" Charles asked. "Kate wants me to deal with him as well."

"Be selfish," Mary urged him. "Do not let this cancer spread."

"I have thought that someone at Hatfield House might confess the truth. Surely someone knows who the dead maid's lover was." He cupped Mary's chin with his mitten, grateful he still had her at his back. "You are always a good friend to me, Mary. Keep my dear girl strong."

He tucked the letter into his pocket and watched her run back into the house, sliding on her clogs through the mud. Another raindrop hit his arm and he moved on to the road, deciding to stop in at Mr. Screws's abode before deciding what to do about Hatfield and Timothy's aunt.

It had wanted only a week to Christmas the day before, and now, despite the general absence of holiday spirit in the land, Charles noticed evergreens and holly woven into the rails on the better houses everywhere. The butchers and bake shops had a higher volume of customers than usual.

In Finsbury Circus, Mr. Screws's home continued to fit in with all the rest, despite the change of staff. Mrs. Pettingill was keeping up the high standards of Mrs. Dorset. The steps were scrubbed free of mud and the evergreens still looked fresh.

When the door opened, Charles did not recognize the very young maid. Her cap didn't fit on her undersized head. It slipped over one ear as she grandly gestured her approval of his entrance into her master's house. She still lisped like a child as well, but her "Mithster Thcrews" sounded charming enough that Charles might have tipped her on a more prosperous day.

He was sorry to hear that the man sat in his best parlor today, where the coffin had waited the inquest. In fact, Mr. Screws, fully dressed but also wearing a nightcap, sat on a low stool in the alcove where his partner's sarcophagus had rested.

"What are you doing, sir?" Charles asked. "This does not appear to be a happy contemplation."

"It was a sad day in this house when Jacob Harley died," Mr. Screws said in a quivering voice. "But it brought me you, dear boy, and I am grateful for it."

"I thank you," Charles agreed, warming under the praise. "But meditating on your friend's death is not good for your health." He went to the wall and leaned against it. The cold room did not please his health, either. Only slightly warmer than the air outdoors, it made his nose drip.

"Have you any report to make?"

"Before we talk, why don't we go into the dining room? You have that tidy stove in there, and that will get us warm."

"You require warmth, young man?" Mr. Screws's voice rattled in his throat. "Human kindness, perhaps? It is a rare thing to find in this house."

"Sir," Charles said, holding out his hand. "I offer it to you."

The old man grasped his hand. Charles managed to lift Mr. Screws to his feet. He supported the icy figure across the hall. The dining room had an occupant, Mrs. Pettingill, who was knitting in Mr. Screws's chair, her neatly shod feet very close to the stove.

She jumped up. "Oh, sirs, you gave me such a fright."

"Ma'am," Charles said. "Mr. Screws needs his stove, I am afraid."

She nodded briskly and gave a little smile as she edged toward the door. "I am very glad you take such tender care of our uncle, Mr. Dickens. I hope he will take a little broth now. I will speak to Cook." She scurried out, a hank of yarn bobbing behind her.

"Broth," Mr. Screws muttered as Charles helped him into his seat. "A waste of good beef, I tell you."

Charles nodded and sat in the next closest chair to the stove. Mrs. Pettingill had not stinted on coal for her own comfort. "I prefer a good pie, myself."

"Ah, yes. Is your soon-to-be little wife a good cook?"

"She is coming along," Charles said. "She is the eldest daughter of a large family. They have kitchen help."

"Good. Knows all about self-sacrifice, then." Mr. Screws cracked his bony knuckles. "Now, as to the matter at hand. What have you learned?"

"I am sorry to say I've made poor progress, but I have time for sorting out the suspects now, as I do not need to do any more reporting before Christmas."

Mr. Screws lifted white-threaded brows. "Taken a holiday, have you?"

Avoiding the question, Charles thought quickly. "If this were a play, who would the murderer be?"

"A play? Eh. Haven't seen one in years. One of those versions of *Frankenstein*." He pushed back his sleeping cap on his forehead. "Now that was a tale."

Charles's eyes widened at the aside, at the way Mr. Screws smacked his lips. Possibly he wanted to burn down the countryside in pursuit of the one who had murdered his friend. "A lover, probably," he said, answering his own question. "That would be the choice of a playwright."

Mr. Screws rubbed his hook-like nose. "I don't know if Jacob had a mistress in recent months. You know he was unwell."

Charles pushed his feet closer to the stove, hoping his toes would dry. "If he'd had a mistress, would she have come here?"

"No, not to here or the office. He'd have gone to her, and since no strumpet has asked for money at either location, I suspect you seek a phantom, Mr. Dickens."

Charles heard the note of humor in the old man's voice. "Very well, then. At least we know the culprit has some money, as he has paid the undertaker to shut down his business for a good long time. Any sign of theft in the countinghouse?"

"No, sir, there is not." Mr. Screws sucked at his teeth. "However, I would like you to return tomorrow since I am waiting for a letter that might be of use to us."

Charles assented just as the door opened and the tiny maid came through with a cup on a tray. Just the one. He took the singular cup as a sign and departed. Kate couldn't accuse him of ill serving Mr. Screws.

A trip to the British Museum Reading Room netted him the names of useful Hatfield-area contacts at St. Ethelreda's Church as well as St. Luke's, the other local parish. He wrote to the marquess and enclosed the letter he'd written to the Hatfield House steward as well. Maybe someone would be willing to speak to Lizzie Porter's fellow maids.

Once home, he picked up his pile of papers and went to the Royal Oak in Leather Lane, a pleasant old public house that always had freshly scrubbed walls and a good fire going. He spent the afternoon there, ignoring the customers as they came in and out, putting his sketches in order for his publisher.

When Charles arrived home after dark he found Breese Gadfly waiting for him, playing dreidel with Fred. His friend's black hair lay tousled over his forehead, and his sideburns scooped under his cheeks, highlighting their leonine perfection. Fred looked like a grubby child next to the elegant songwriter, his fingernails half mooned with ink and a day's worth of beard on his cheeks. He'd only recently needed to shave every day.

"You look lower than a match girl in the rain, my dear," Breese observed, lounging back on Charles's best armchair.

Charles attempted to smile as he crossed to his writing box to stow his papers inside, but his eyes were gritty and red from too many hours hunched over his writing next to the fire. Once the sky outside had darkened, there had not been enough light to work. He'd called for a candle but the barman had run out.

Fred leapt up from his stool to stoke the fire. "Hot rum and water?" he asked.

"No." Charles shook his head. "I've had enough spiced wine to drown my sorrows."

Breese spun one of the dreidels. It landed on the "nun" side. "I forfeit my turn. What are the sorrows of the day?"

"Better than forfeiting your position." Charles caught him up to date on his estrangement with Kate and what had led to him losing his post.

After Fred took in the words, he drained a rum and water of his own. "Will I have to support you now?" his younger brother asked.

"Indeed not," Charles said. "I'll sort it out, find something to do until the truth is revealed. Kate has remained true to me."

"That is all that matters," Breese said soberly. "I might be able to help. It's too late to sell anything to the panto market, but there are always people needing songs. Why don't you write with me tonight?"

"Happy to," Charles said. "There is also my operetta-in-progress. I'd love to hear your opinion on what I have planned."

"You always have something brewing."

Charles nodded. "I need to remember that is the wise thing to do. Always juggle, never settle in to just one occupation."

They spent the evening crafting sad lyrics about a maiden who drowned herself over a misunderstanding. Charles gave in to the rum once his eyes started to feel better, but their heavy drinking made him melancholy, not merry as he wanted. With Christmas only a few days away, would he be able to spend the twelve days with Kate or remain in exile? He wanted to feel pride for his defense of the innocent baby Timothy, but mostly, he just missed his love.

The next morning, Charles went to see Mr. Screws as requested. The old man had dressed more carefully than usual, and even had a sprig of holly pinned to his tailcoat.

"You look like a man who slept well," Charles said, feeling quite the opposite. His thick head ached.

Mr. Screws's thin lips twitched. "This new cook our Betsy

hired has cured my indigestion." However, his hands shook as Charles helped him with his coat.

They took the Screws carriage to a coffeehouse called Cigar Divan, which had an entrance fee, and therefore had a better class of clientele than the usual workman's morning visitation. Charles had never been there, though its Strand location meant he'd passed by any number of times.

Inside, a fug of cigar smoke hung under the ceiling, casting the room in a yellowish haze. Mr. Screws knew what he was doing, confidently walking past the main room and into a smaller chamber, where sober men of business chatted over their newspapers and morning libations.

A man stood as they reached the far wall. He had a bald head and a deeply lined forehead, but no age spots, putting his time on earth at around forty years. His clothing looked foreign. Too many checks in the fabric, the cut of the breeches a little too tight, the coat somewhat too loose.

"This is Congressman Edward Winthrop," Mr. Screws said. "From Massachusetts. Congressman, may I introduce the distinguished journalist Mr. Charles Dickens?"

"Very pleased to meet you, sir," the congressman said. "Have a seat."

Charles recognized none of the soft lilt that Mr. Fletcher had in his voice as he and Mr. Screws sat. Either he had a head cold or a very different accent. "What an honor, sir. Very pleased. I have sat in the gallery here for years, taking down the words of British politicians, but I've never met one of the American breed."

"I'm here to discuss insurance," the congressman said briskly. "In our American state of Rhode Island, a company recently sold a fire insurance policy. I'm researching what is being done here in England so I can bring the information back to my state of Massachusetts."

"I hope you are able to attend a few holiday gatherings at the same time," Charles said politely. A waiter came and brought them cups of coffee, apparently preordered.

"I have good connections here," Congressman Winthrop said with the careless assurance of class. "An aunt married an Englishman, and it's good to see her again after so many years. She was a favorite visitor in my childhood home in Boston."

"How do you know Mr. Screws?" Charles inquired. "Have you done business together?"

"Mr. Dobbin is one of my dear friends and supporters," the congressman explained. "I've been aware of his dealings with Mr. Screws's establishment for many years."

"How nice that you can finally meet." Charles glanced at Mr. Screws. "I take it that you have some intelligence from Mr. Dobbin regarding our concerns?"

"The thing is, Mr. Dickens, Boston and Virginia don't mix well. It's a matter of the original American settlers, Virginia aristocrats versus Massachusetts Puritans."

"You're suggesting our Tidewater Virginia aristocrat, Mr. Fletcher, would be unlikely to have a position in Boston?" Charles suggested.

"Let me put it this way." Congressman Winthrop leaned forward. "I doubt Mr. Dobbin would employ a braggart like this Mr. Fletcher in his business. He'd know that it wouldn't go over well with his clients."

Charles considered. "Mr. Fletcher is very family proud. He told me that a Mayflower descendant married into the Lee family. Let me see. An Allerton, I believe?"

The congressman smiled thinly. "While I believe that Mrs. Lee was a most excellent woman, her ancestor was a more controversial character. He lost his position in the colony due to some ill dealings. It may be that Mrs. Lee was more pleased with the family she married into than her own."

"Well, well," Charles murmured. He had nothing to add to that theory. "But for all his pride, Mr. Fletcher has done his job well, and is trusted."

Mr. Screws coughed in pronounced fashion. The other two men waited until he cleared his throat. "Mr. Dickens, I now believe the original Dobbin letter was a fake."

"Then Mr. Fletcher will lose his position with you?"

Mr. Screws stared into his coffee cup, as if it held answers. "I must admit, sirs, that Mr. Fletcher does excellent work and is a true gentleman. With the loss of Mr. Harley, I can ill afford to do without his assistance."

"He bears watching," the congressman said, lifting his cup to his lips. "Excellent brew."

"It's considered the best in London," Mr. Screws said. "As is my countinghouse."

The congressman lifted his thin brows. "Yet you are trusting a charlatan."

"We are the best," Mr. Screws repeated. "The dear boy likely forged the letter simply to get us to take him on as an apprentice."

Dear boy? Had the old man latched on to Mr. Fletcher simply because he had no one else? Or rather he did, in his nephew, if only he could see that. Hopefully, proximity would bring the two men to rapprochement.

On Monday, Charles was shaken awake by Fred. "What?" he mumbled.

"Charles, you're going to be late for work. Don't you have a meeting you need to turn up to?"

Charles blinked at his brother. "Lost my position, remember?"

"I think you should give it another try," Fred urged. "Remember, Kate didn't betray you. Mr. Hogarth has had a couple of days to calm down."

Charles pushed himself up. "I thought I'd spend the day with Mother. It's her birthday, you know. I meant to take her on a walk. Maybe to *Othello* tonight at Covent Garden."

"That's fine, Charles, but go to work first, all right? I don't want a repeat of the summer."

Charles glared at him, alert now. "I have never let you down or allowed you to be homeless or hungry, which is more than I can say for our parents. We are going to be fine."

Fred nodded dolefully. "I just thought you needed a boost, is all. You are normally so cheerful, but that has not been the case lately."

"Romantic troubles are depressing," Charles said, forcing a smile. "But I know Kate loves me, so there is nothing to fear."

Charles entered the *Chronicle*'s offices late that morning, dressed in his best frock coat with the velvet collar, his most freshly pressed neckerchief, and shined shoes. He passed back into the offices as if he still worked there.

Mr. Hogarth's door was open when he peered in. Charles drew himself up and rapped on the door.

"Mr. Hogarth, sir? Might I implore you to give me a moment of your time?"

Kate's father had a pencil in his hand and was drawing lines on a piece of paper at his desk. His head was wreathed with smoke as he puffed on his pipe. He glanced up and grimaced at Charles. "What is it?"

Charles immediately felt the futility of his mission, but remained calm. He had right on his side. Pushing the door closed, he stood at Mr. Hogarth's desk. "Kate is wrong about the baby. I'd like to see her and address the situation. I know she isn't indifferent to me and I don't want to lose her."

"I am aware that she isnae indifferent tae ye, Charles," the editor said in his most pronounced Scottish brogue. "That is why I want ye to stay away."

Charles waited to be condemned for speaking to Mary, but the reprimand didn't come. Which meant he couldn't admit knowing that Georgina had betrayed him. "Then let me stay here, and do my job. It's Christmas, sir, and my brother is very alarmed about my loss of position."

"No, Charles. This situation has made me question your judgment in any version of the truth."

"What was I supposed to do, let the baby die?"

Mr. Hogarth didn't answer that. He set his pipe on its plate. Charles saw his jaw work. "I warned ye long ago to stay away from Julie Aga, and this is exactly the sort of trouble I'd foreseen. That actress is trouble."

"Kate has long since accepted her," Charles said. "Mrs. Aga is expecting a child. William Aga's child, not mine. She's respectable now, married, not an actress."

"She has a mad mother," Mr. Hogarth said. "Blood will tell."

Charles fought to keep from clenching his fists. If his blood told, he'd end up in debtor's prison, just like his father. Was that what Fred feared? "It does not, Mr. Hogarth. Blood does not tell. You are greater than your father. I am greater than mine. Mrs. Aga has chosen a quiet life."

Mr. Hogarth picked up his tobacco tin. "My answer is no."

Footsteps pelted along the passage outside the office.

"Mr. Dickens, Mr. Dickens!" called a thin voice.

Charles pushed the door open and peered out. "I'm Dickens, what is it?"

"I've been sent to fetch you," a ragged boy said. He had a fresh cut on his forehead that looked infected. Charles hadn't seen him before, but he wore shoes, so probably a street child and not someone from the mudlarks.

"To where?" Charles asked.

"Mr. Screws's house," the boy said before coughing hard. "Bloody soot. Sorry. You're wanted."

Charles nodded and turned back to Mr. Hogarth.

"We're done here," said Kate's father stiffly.

"For now," Charles said quietly. Then he stepped out, flipped the boy a coin, and went back to the street, feeling half a decade older and more desperate than before. What was he going to do now? Charles Dickens was not a failure. He was still needed, by Mr. Screws if no one else. How ironic, that the man of business who had rejected his father had begun to rely on him when no one else would do.

In the street, Charles dodged street hawkers and carts, carriages, and a great abundance of women, doing a bit of holiday trading in better weather than had been seen in London of late. He passed by a girl with bunches of mistletoe wrapped in red ribbon and a cart heaped high with evergreen bows. Steam rose from an urn full of spiced wine. He pressed on, though he could not think of why Mr. Screws needed him yet again. Perhaps he ought to go to Spitalfields first and see if the undertaker had turned up yet. At some point the bribe would cease to pay Mr. Dawes's expenses and he would return to his profession.

Instead, he kept going on. At least someone thought him worth a conversation.

When he reached Finsbury Circus, he found John Coachman lounging at the front door. Charles climbed up the steps after searching the street for the carriage itself and not finding it. "What's going on?"

The coachman shook his head. "Bad news, Mr. Dickens."

"Is it Mr. Screws?"

"No, sir. 'e's all right."

"You seem to be on guard."

"I vas asked to be." He turned and opened the door, then saluted Charles. "There you go, sir."

Charles walked in. The ground floor seemed deserted as far as the front of the house went. He wouldn't be able to hear anything in the servants' part of the house, hidden as it was behind a thick baize-covered door. Above him, though, he heard footsteps, so he went up to the family rooms.

He found the small maid sitting on a bench at the top of the stairs, wiping at her eyes with her apron. Charles wished he had learned her name on his last visit. At his approach, she looked up and sniffed, then mutely pointed him toward the room where Mr. Harley had met his height-challenged demise.

Charles turned left, then peered into the open door of the room. Mrs. Pettingill sat on the edge of a four-poster bed, clutching a handkerchief. A rocking chair faced away from Charles, toward the window. A table had been pushed underneath it. It hadn't been there during Mr. Harley's day, but it was heaped with books and papers now.

"Mr. Dickens," Mr. Screws said, coming from the space in between the table and the bed. Charles hadn't seen him because of the bed curtains. Pale, except for high circles of red on his cheek, he could have been an elderly, painted doll.

"What has happened?" Charles felt his chin compressing into his muffler, as if he could hide like a turtle. He forced himself to stop it and hold his head high, despite the forbidding sense of menace in the room.

"Come here." Mr. Screws gestured him forward with a shaking index finger.

Reluctantly, Charles obeyed. Mr. Screws pointed at the rocking chair. Charles went all the way to the window, glancing through the half foot of space where the curtains were open to the park in the center of the circus, then turned back again.

To see death.

Chapter 17

Edward Pettingill slumped in the rocking chair in his bed-chamber, once Jacob Harley's. Charles saw no sign of the in-and-out mechanics of breathing in the thin, winter's afternoon sunlight.

"No sign of life," he whispered, glancing up at Mr. Screws, who made futile washing gestures with his hands in the doorway. Had the old man meant to escape the death chamber?

The tassel of the dead man's red sleeping cap rested on his forehead. He still wore his dressing gown over his shirt and trousers, as if he'd started his morning routine and never had a chance to complete it. The shirt lay open, exposing a neck that had been draped in something extremely odd.

Against his better judgment, Charles leaned forward, and saw a long white length of silk wrapped around the dead man's neck, along with a strand of pearls. Judging from the color of his skin, Mr. Pettingill had been strangled to death, though the cloth hid the marks on his neck.

"It's a dreadful business," Mrs. Pettingill choked. "My poor Mr. Pettingill."

"This must be the work of Primus Harley," Mr. Screws quavered. "He has the strength to do this. An intimate death, Mr. Dickens."

Charles walked around the rocker, eager to get away from the staring eyes of the dead man, the expression of confusion. "The slats in the chair were used." He bent down. "I can see where the wood was rubbed. I see what you mean about intimacy. He would have been close enough to smell Mr. Pettingill, but still, he wouldn't have had to look him in the eyes."

"So debasing," Mrs. Pettingill said, looking very unfuneral-like in an aged pink silk dress. "Clearly the work of a degenerate member of the lower classes."

Meaning Primus, son of an Irishwoman, Charles supposed. Was the widow too cold, too unfeeling? Where were the tears, the screams? "I understand this took some strength, but why do you suspect Mr. Harley's illegitimate son specifically?"

The widow snorted and dabbed at dry eyes with her handkerchief. "He has done it to get control of the business. He is killing us all, one by one."

Charles remembered Mr. Screws had not suspected Primus Harley. "Was he his father's heir? I hadn't thought so."

The old man squeezed his fingers into fists. "A solicitor came to the countinghouse this morning. I knew the man. Jacob had used him before. He had a will with him. I hadn't known it existed, but Jacob had left his estate to his son."

"But not the business?"

"No, that was mine, due to old contracts from the formation." He stepped forward to look at his nephew again.

"Then Mr. Harley never would have received ownership of the countinghouse. He isn't named in your will, correct?"

"I don't have one," Mr. Screws said. "If I die, I suspect Primus could make his case for taking control."

Mrs. Pettingill gave a little scream, then fell silent.

Mr. Screws stared defiantly at the widow. "There was no one

else. We were two men quite separate from society. Who did we have, but his son and my nephew?"

"You didn't name my Edward in a will?" Mrs. Pettingill whispered. "Oh, Mr. Screws, we all die. We must taste eternity in the end."

"If I'd known Jacob had made one, I'd have done the same," Mr. Screws said in weary tones. "How the years pass." He swayed on his feet.

Charles took his arm. "Come, I'll take you to your private chamber." He supported the elderly man through the narrow space between the bed, Mrs. Pettingill's lower appendages, and the rocking chair, not breathing until they had reached the passage.

"It must be a recent death," Charles ventured. "I smelled nothing more than what I thought were the contents of a missed chamber pot."

"That is why I posted the coachman at the front," Mr. Screws said. "I was afraid the killer was still here. But the kitchen maid searched the house and no one is in the house except myself, the widow, the two maids, and the cook."

"Mr. Fletcher?"

"At the countinghouse. He was there when I returned home for a hot meal."

"Mrs. Pettingill seemed quite a resentful person," Charles ventured.

Mr. Screws shook his finger. "I won't hear of her being suspected."

"Why not? We aren't killers. Maybe it didn't take as much strength as we thought."

"She is my dependent now. It would be unchristian to mistreat her," Mr. Screws said in a lecturing tone. He took a key from his pocket and unlocked his bedroom door.

"Is that a new measure of safety?"

Mr. Screws nodded. "Since the night Jacob died. No one is allowed in here, except to clean."

Charles sighed. If a maid had the key, the lock probably gave no more than a dangerous, false sense of security.

Mr. Screws sat down in an armchair by another stove, not decorated this time. It was the only chair in the room, so Charles leaned against the wall.

Mr. Screws sighed. "If Mr. Harley didn't do it, then Mr. Appleton probably did, because it was Mr. Pettingill who told us about his business in the first place and talked Mr. Appleton into accepting the loan that he almost defaulted on."

"I didn't know that. If only Mr. Appleton didn't appear to be such a meek and respectable sort." Charles didn't think him any more likely than Mrs. Pettingill. He understood now why Primus Harley seemed the better candidate. But why had Mr. Pettingill been showing an interest in the countinghouse when he'd been kept out of it? It didn't sound like very Pettingillian behavior.

"What do we do now?" Mr. Screws asked.

Charles rubbed his nose. "I'll need to go for a constable, unless you want the coachman to do it."

"You go please, Mr. Dickens. You're used to speaking to the police."

Charles scratched his annoying itch again. His finger came away black with soot. How long had it been since the windows in this room were opened? "I'll have the kitchen maid bring you up something hot to drink." Before he closed the door, he said, "You might want to lock yourself in until the police come."

He went downstairs, gave the maid instructions, and left by the front door in search of help. After fifteen minutes of searching on the main road in the cold, he heard the telltale rattle and headed in that direction. He didn't recognize the constable, but appreciated the calm way the graying policeman pulled coin purses from inside a youth's shirt as a soberly dressed, tubby man some twenty years his senior berated both the thief and the officer of the law, with his bulbous index finger flashing back and forth between their two faces.

Another constable arrived. They conferred and the original one took the lad by the collar and marched him down the road, probably heading for the police station. It wouldn't end well for the child, whose toes poked out from his ripped shoes. How could he learn ethics when he clearly led a life of want?

The victim continued his tirade, holding his recovered purse, raining down epithets on the new officer's head, but the second constable seemed less calm than the first.

When Charles approached, the constable seemed eager for distraction.

"Sir?" he asked with a hint of desperation widening his shadowed eyes.

"There's been a murder at Finsbury Circus," Charles said, instinctively pointing in that direction. "Inside one of the houses."

The constable adjusted his heavy, reinforced hat as the gentleman suspended his tirade.

"A murder?" the gentleman said, regaining himself. "Pish posh, sir. Finsbury Circus does not have murder."

"That's wrong," the constable insisted. "Why there was a murderous death there just about three weeks ago."

"I am glad you think so, Constable," Charles said. "For I agree with you, though the inquest did not declare it such."

"Didn't it?" The constable's brow creased. "I hadn't heard. Well then, who's dead now?"

"Another man, in the same house."

"The other old gentleman? They were talking about him down at the pub. Never gives a penny when people collect for charities," the constable said.

Charles knew they were both speaking about Emmanuel Screws. "No. I'm afraid it's his young nephew, and no one could deny it is murder this time."

"We'll have to send for the coroner. What a mess." The constable went into the street and circled his rattle over his head, the whirring sound calling for reinforcements.

The robbed gentleman turned up his nose. "I'm so glad we moved into Myddelton Square, despite the construction."

Charles listened to the man prattle on about the advantages of living in Clerkenwell with half an ear. Had he not enough troubles without another death? He needed employment; he needed his reputation restored; he needed vindication.

He covered his mouth with his hands and breathed into them to restore the feeling in his nose with his somewhat warm breath. When another constable passed within hearing of the rattle, the second constable, who by then had revealed his name was Thornton, left with Charles for Finsbury Circus.

"This is no way to manage a murder," Constable Thornton said mournfully as they walked through the noontime streets. "With the ever-increasing number of people in London, we have to do something about the policing situation."

"The Metropolitan Police is only a few years old," Charles said.

"It's insufficient," Thornton snapped. "We are miserably overworked. Drunkenness is a plague."

"I sense you are more educated than the average constable," Charles said. "You have the speech of a gentleman."

"My mother educated me. Better born than my father, she is now forty-five and utterly worn out by life. There was no money for school." He cleared his throat. "My hope is that I do not meet my future bride until I am at least forty and she is over thirty. I wish to break the curse of a large family."

Charles thought of Kate, just twenty. But she was a perfect little miss to his mister, and he did not want to lose her. If he could not regain her family's trust, she'd be married to someone else within the next couple of years, too tempting a fruit to be left on the tree. "I believe there are plenty of governesses, schoolteachers, and the like moldering away in their twenties with educations and no families to take them out in the world."

The constable winked at him. "Exactly. There is a vast army of women that age desperate for a good home. I intend to make something of myself, and I have many years in which to do it."

"Don't you get lonely?"

"I board with a married brother. I share a bedroom with my nephew and pay very little."

Charles had thought the constable a couple of years older than he at least, but he worked outdoors, aging his face. At twenty-three, he could not imagine his life comprising half a bedroom with a child. He had too much ambition to accept such humble surroundings now.

When they reached Mr. Screws's house, Charles saw a small man at the door, his top hat at least the length of his arm. Primus Harley.

"I can't believe it. One of the suspects is at the door," Charles told Constable Thornton.

"Oi!" the constable said.

Primus Harley turned and waved at Charles, then awkwardly made his way down the stairs. "I can't rouse the house. Why isn't anyone answering?"

"Where have you been these past hours?" Charles demanded.

Primus frowned and held up a box. "Visiting a friend. She made more of that shortbread you liked so much. I thought it might cheer Uncle Emmanuel."

"Would she testify to that?" the constable said in a domineering manner.

Primus's face went very red. "I was with her all night until I walked here."

"Mr. Pettingill is dead," Charles said, taking pity on the man. He might very well be innocent. "Murdered."

"Murdered? I thought you had banished the Dorsets!" Primus exclaimed.

"I would not say this murder seemed to be the work of Johnny Dorset," Charles said. "Your father's death had something of blunt force about it. This death was more intimate."

"I hope we shall have more help here within the hour," said Thornton. "I want this friend of yours spoken to before you see her."

Primus screwed up his face mulishly. "I won't leave this house until you do. I don't wish any stain upon my character."

The constable pushed past him and banged on the door until footsteps could be heard.

Mrs. Pettingill opened the door to them. "I wondered if we would ever see you again, Mr. Dickens," she chided, ignoring the other two men.

She had changed into a black dress. The fashion of it dated to so many years ago that Charles thought it must have adorned a long-dead Screws. Fold lines had whitened some of the dye, but the fabric was good silk.

"This is Mr. Pettingill's widow," Charles said to Thornton. "How is Mr. Screws?"

"He wouldn't let me into his chamber," said the new widow. "Whatever did you say to him?"

"I advised caution," Charles said. "He didn't look well."

"He could have some kind of fit," said the exasperated lady. "I've just lost my husband. I don't want to lose his uncle as well."

"I'll check on him," Charles said. "You take Constable Thornton upstairs. We'll put Mr. Harley in the parlor." When she visibly hesitated, he coaxed, "We will do everything we can to put your mind at ease."

"But Mr. Harley might have killed my husband," she said.

Charles smiled reassuringly at her. "He says he didn't. The police will check his story and will have an answer soon."

She dabbed at her dry eyes again. "This way, Constable." She gracefully tilted her head toward the staircase.

Charles took Primus to the parlor, where his father's body had once laid in state. "I'm going to lock you in."

The weaver grunted and took off his hat. "Will you at least take the shortbread to Uncle Emmanuel?"

Charles shook his head. "You can do it when you're exonerated." He left the room and turned the key in the parlor door lock, then pocketed it. Then he went up and knocked on Mr. Screws's door. When he heard no response, he called for Mr. Screws. "It's Dickens, sir."

A minute later, he heard shuffling footsteps, then the key in the lock. Mr. Screws peered out, then gestured Charles in.

"I thought you trusted Mrs. Pettingill," Charles said.

"I thought about what you said after you left," said the old man, sitting down heavily on the chair by his stove. "And locked myself in."

"Oh?" Charles leaned against the wall.

"My nephew was not a grasping sort of fellow, but his wife could be ambitious. No." He shook his head sadly. "I may not be able to trust her. Or anyone else in this house."

"I understand." Anyone could take advantage of an ill old soul. He told Mr. Screws about Primus Harley and gave him the parlor door key.

"Regardless of Mrs. Pettingill's honesty or lack thereof, I cannot expect her to take messages back and forth between here and the countinghouse," Mr. Screws added.

"You have Mr. Fletcher for that."

"He will need to run the place, I am sorry to say. I do not think I can make it up and down my own steps." Mr. Screws coughed weakly and sighed. "No, sir, for the first time in my life, I need a confidential secretary."

"I can place an advertisement for you," Charles offered.

"Why not take the position yourself?" the old man suggested. "You are on leave from the newspaper."

Charles closed his eyes, pride warring with reality. He hated to be idle, and he needed funds in order to have any hope of a future with Kate. Also, Mr. Screws might be the only person willing to hire him. Still, he demurred. "I have my book to finish."

Mr. Screws wrinkled his nose and opened his jaw, suppressing a sneeze. "I understand, but I can trust you, Charles. You were outside when Jacob died, and at your newspaper office when my nephew was murdered."

"Very well," said Charles, surprising himself. But how could he say otherwise, with pride in the Dickens name thoroughly redeemed? A position of trust with a man who had once rejected his father for a loan? "Temporarily."

After Charles left, he went to visit his mother at last. She opened the door of the Dickenses' Bloomsbury chambers with an expression of delight.

"Many happy returns, Mother," he said with a kiss on her cheek, his smile easy now that his fortunes were looking up.

"Such a pleasure to see you today, darling," she cooed and ushered him in, the lace on her sleeves fluttering.

His mother settled herself comfortably in the second-best chair. Letitia sat on the stool at her feet, winding yarn. His father was already in the best chair, the day's newspapers in his lap.

Charles pulled fruit from his overcoat pocket and dropped it into his mother's lap, on top of her knitting. "I've just been by the orange girl. Happy birthday."

"Very nice," she exclaimed.

"Nothing better on a winter's eve," his father added. "The best portion of a good man's life: his little, nameless, unremembered acts of kindness and love."

"I agree." Charles recognized the Wordsworth quotation.

"It may not be much, but"—he pulled a package from his other pocket—"sausages from my favorite butcher, an even dozen."

"Oh, Charles, how can you afford it?"

His father frowned, dampening his mother's enthusiasm. "You must count your shillings, boy, under the circumstances. Do not be profligate."

Charles frowned. "You have heard about what happened at the *Chronicle*?"

"I am in shock over your career fall, my boy."

"We both are," his mother added.

Charles stiffened. Blood left his extremities and heated his face. But he could not lash out. He could not dishonor his father by pointing out that he was more successful than his father ever was, and his father threw away a prosperous career, which Charles did not do.

He would show them, his parents whom he had supported through numerous disasters brought on by their own profligacy. He would apply for new newspaper positions the second Mr. Screws was safe to die in peace. He knew he was the best shorthand reporter in the business. Someone would want him. Even if he was declared guilty of fathering a bastard, the business was full of men with irregular lifestyles. "Mr. Hogarth never would have cared about a possible illegitimate child if it hadn't been for my engagement to Kate. This is personal."

"Oh, Charles!" his mother exclaimed.

Letitia put her hand to her mouth.

"Oh, you can't believe it," Charles snapped at his sister. "I was never anywhere near the mother of the infant in question."

A sneer crossed his father's normally jovial face. "And yet, sir, my son is the laughingstock of the newspaper business due to your pride over being engaged to your editor's daughter while consorting with a mere inn maid."

"How can you possibly think the story is true given how ridiculous it is?" Charles demanded.

"Young men have to sow their oats." His father smirked and took a sip of wine from his ever-present cup. His mother bent her head over her knitting.

Letitia gave him a wild glance and went back into the kitchen.

Had his father even bothered to defend him to his cronies? Charles schooled his expression and did not rise to the bait, for his mother's sake. "I have a new position, as a private secretary to Emmanuel Screws, the owner of a countinghouse."

"My stars," his mother gasped excitedly. "How wonderful."

"I start tomorrow," Charles said, gathering enthusiasm from hers. "It's a new trade to learn, but I have hopes that it will be temporary."

"Giving up journalism for business?" his father said, snapping his top newspaper. "Not a terribly sound notion."

"At least, sir, he trusts me, which is more than can be said for—"

Letitia reentered with a jangling tray before Charles could finish his retort. He was the better for it. Knowing the truth himself was more important than reminding his father of his failure with Screws and Harley more than a decade before.

Letitia set the tray on the little table in between the two armchairs. Her mother snatched the bit of lace decorating the table out from under the tray just in time.

"Letitia," she snapped.

"Sorry, Mother."

The lady of the house sighed noisily and tucked her lace out of sight on the mantelpiece, behind three pine cones, a sprig of holly, and a pewter candlestick.

"Are the boys at school?" Charles asked, remembering how his parents had allowed him to roam London without any thought of educating him when he'd first come here from Kent after being thought a gifted student there.

"Yes, dear," his mother said blandly.

He bit back a grimace. But Letitia picked up on his irritation and quickly poured the tea. The two of them took their cups to the dining room table, where they pored over a scrapbook Henry Austin, Charles's old friend as well as Letitia's betrothed, had made for her.

He stayed for dinner, wishing his father could be as grateful for his company as Mr. Screws was, and then left after. The streets were slick with moisture and his breath fogged the air. The moon scarcely cut a sliver into the night sky and he had to rely on the street lamps for light. Even so, he felt restless and decided to talk William into a walk.

When he turned up on Cheapside, Julie was busy with baby Timothy.

"Can William come and play?" he asked, pulling a comical face.

"He's in the bedroom, working on some bit of writing. I'll ask him." Distracted, she handed the baby to Charles. "Jiggle him around. I think he has a tooth coming in. He cries when I stop moving."

Charles took him, bouncing gently from side to side while Julie conferred with William and took a couple of minutes for herself in her bedroom.

"What brings you to our humble chambers?" William asked. He wore an old coat Charles hadn't seen in a year and had circles under his eyes.

"I thought you might like a walk."

William peered at him. "You look positively jumpy. Another visitation from your specter?"

"Worse," Charles said. "Another murder."

"Oh, no." Julie rushed back into the room and took Timothy from Charles's arms, as if he might be contaminated with death.

"Who?" William asked, walking into the small area by the front door and plucking a comforter sprawled across the boot bench.

"Edward Pettingill."

"Wasn't he staying with Mr. Screws?" William asked.

"In the same room Jacob Harley fell from," Charles said grimly. "Same room, two deaths."

"What a puzzle." William abruptly shifted focus. "Shouldn't you be looking for a position?"

"I've one with Mr. Screws for now. He thinks I'm merely on leave from the newspaper to finish my book."

"I prefer to think of it that way myself," Julie said stoutly. "Every day Timothy looks less like you. See how narrowly spaced his tiny eyes are? Not like yours at all. Your eyebrows are much more widely separated."

"Could be from the mother," William said with a ghost of a smile on his tired face.

"Maybe I shouldn't take you out," Charles said.

"Just to the pub," William said, heading for his hat. "Let Julie have some peace. She's already had to send Lucy to bed."

Charles followed on his friend's heels as he walked into the outer passage. "What's wrong with Lucy?"

"Feeling closed in. Not used to all this time indoors."

"Is Julie taking her to do the marketing?"

"No, because Timothy isn't feeling well. She and Julie even had a very small spat." William jumped the last two steps to the ground floor, where the chophouse was, the windows darkened now.

Charles guessed he felt pleased to be out of doors himself. "Do you want to hear all the details?"

"Wait until I have a glass of something hot in front of me. Julie and Lucy have been too busy to take care of me."

They walked in companionable silence until they came to an elderly pub next to a church. Inside, the fire smoked and the taproom was half empty, but the drinks were a penny less than elsewhere so they decided to stay.

When William had his boots stretched out toward the fire and a hot glass of punch in his hand, he smiled easily for the first time that night. "Tell me all."

"Mr. Pettingill was strangled," Charles said, explaining the scene.

"A woman could have done it with the tools used," William mused.

"But the fingerprints on Mr. Harley's arms were male sized."

"Mr. Pettingill didn't have the same marks from what you saw. Could there be two killers?" William drank deeply and raised his hand to get the barmaid's attention.

"Why would there be? Mr. Screws had just decided to give Mr. Pettingill the countinghouse. Surely these men are dead because of the business."

"Why wasn't Mr. Screws offed?"

"He's probably at severe risk," Charles said. He set down his almost untasted cup as acid soured his belly. The old man liked him, trusted him. No, he wasn't a kindly old fellow, but Charles appreciated his tough spirit. Mr. Pettingill, on the other hand, had seemed to be kindly. A lot of schoolboys would be devastated to hear of the death of their hero, gone tragically too soon. It seemed the countinghouse was a curse cast upon these two men. Who would be the next to fall foul of this evil?

"You really shouldn't be so involved. Taking the position as his secretary is beneath you. It's a step backward, especially with such a skinflint as Screws. What kind of wage did he offer?"

"It's tolerable," Charles muttered into his glass. He hadn't even asked about the pay. "Not a junior wage."

"Ri-ight," William said, then flashed his old grin at the serving maid as his drink arrived.

Charles ordered a bowl of stew. "The position won't last long. Mr. Screws is a dying man with a palsy."

"At least he can't be the murderer," William said. "He could have helped someone out a window, I suppose, but he couldn't have strangled anyone."

"At least not Mr. Pettingill," Charles agreed. He had set that theory aside some time ago without even realizing it. Mr. Screws had loved Jacob Harley too well to kill him. Mr. Fletcher or Mrs. Dorset would have told him if the men had been fighting.

"A conspiracy between the old man and Mrs. Pettingill?" William suggested.

The waiter delivered Charles's stew. "Why would they want Mr. Screws's nephew dead?" Charles picked up his spoon. "He was a great man, you know. Boy's own hero, with his birding expertise."

William drained his second glass. "Did he become too familiar with the housekeeper?"

"She's gone," Charles said. He put his head into his hands. The cold metal of the utensil branded his cheek. "I don't know. She didn't mention it."

"I wish I could return to Hatfield and deal with the infant situation but I need to stay with Julie," William confided. "She's becoming terribly attached to Timothy. I want his future resolved before our own child comes."

Charles coughed and took a bite of the stew. It tasted flavorless. "I think the fireplace is irritating my lungs. Are you warm enough to walk now?"

"Very well."

Both dogged by their own thoughts, they made their way through remembered thoroughfares, retracing the streets they both had so often journeyed the summer before, when they had rooms at Selwood Terrace.

"Strange to walk this now," William mused. "I have become soft, with Lady Lugoson sending her carriage to us."

"Did you ever think you would call such a woman aunt?"

"I never really thought about marriage at all," William admitted. "I wasn't like you, with your dream of being a proper paterfamilias, the man your father never was."

"You think that's why?"

"I know it is. You were already trying to get married at eighteen. I didn't know you then but I've heard the Maria Beadnell story often enough."

They walked on, stopping in front of the Hogarths' house.

"They aren't abed," William said, pulling Charles into the side garden when he saw the lights were still on.

"How do you know Kate's room?"

William reached down and gathered a handful of gravel from the pathway through the herb garden. "I'm next door all the time, Charles. Really, it's a wonder Julie has learned to cook so well." He shot the gravel in an arc so that it rattled down Kate's windowpane.

Charles was frozen. What if Kate saw them and waved? What if she refused to speak to them? He agonized, staring at the wavering flame of light behind the window.

Chapter 18

A moment later, Charles and William saw the light of a candle move to the side of the upper window and a dark shape come up next to it. The window pushed outward and Kate stuck her head out, whispering, "Julie?"

Charles's eyebrows rose. "Julie?"

William grinned and rubbed gravel off his mittens, whispering, "Now we know how they have come to be better friends." He raised his voice. "It's William and Charles! Come downstairs."

Charles pulled him back. "I can't see her. She doesn't want to see me."

"Nonsense," William said firmly. "It's her sister who is the problem, not her."

They waited outside, shifting from side to side to stay warm. Charles made Os with his frosty breath. William patted his pocket as if thinking of a cigar but Charles shook his head, not wanting the scent to attract any other Hogarths.

Eventually Kate opened the kitchen door and stepped out, sliding her feet into pattens. She wore her navy cape with the velvet collar, and Charles could only imagine, with an unsettling feeling at the base of his spine, the nightdress she wore underneath.

"We need your counsel, sweet Kate," William said.

"You shouldn't be here," she whispered, lifting her candle, staring only at Charles. "If my father saw you I'd be in a great deal of trouble."

Charles lifted his hand, wanting to take her in his arms and ban the cold, but he saw her warning glance and kept his distance. "There's been another death, darling girl."

Her gaze sharpened. "What? Who?"

"Poor Pettingill, Mr. Screws's nephew. Strangled in the same room Mr. Harley fell from."

"What do you think?" William asked. "Two killers?"

Kate frowned. "Of course not. Just one killer."

"I've been puzzling over the notion that perhaps Mrs. Pettingill killed her husband," Charles said. "She's a strong personality and an unhappy woman at that."

"Never," Kate insisted. "A wife would never be so unnatural toward her husband."

"Yet a fiancée would be," Charles countered.

"A fiancée is still ruled by her family, until she joins in holy matrimony," Kate snapped.

William chuckled and put his arm in front of Charles as if to hold him back. "This isn't getting us anywhere. Come, Kate, give us something to work on."

"Why was he in that room?" she asked.

"They moved in to care for Mr. Screws," Charles said.

Kate tapped her lower lip with her fingers. "What had Mr. Pettingill learned that caused his death?"

Charles answered promptly. "He'd learned that Mr. Screws was going to give him the business to run."

"That's the reason then. Who didn't want him to run the business?"

"Birding enthusiasts?" Charles answered.

She stepped closer. "Be serious, Charles. Two men have died. An old man lost his dearest companion. A woman has been widowed. You need to stop this. Whoever Mr. Screws appoints next will be marked for death."

Charles saw the bleakness in her eyes. She was so close now. He could smell the rose oil in her uncovered hair. His hand went out to touch hers.

She recoiled, her eyes going glassy with tears. Without another word, she turned and dashed back into the house. The wind caught her candle flame and extinguished it.

"It's like she vanished," Charles whispered after the door closed.

"She'll reappear when you need her." William slapped him on the shoulder. "She still loves you, you nob-head."

The next morning, Charles appeared early at Finsbury Circus, spurred on by Fred's enthusiasm for his new position.

Mr. Screws, at his dining room table, grunted when Mrs. Pettingill, wreathed in black, ushered him into his dining room. All signs of Christmastime had been removed from the outside due to the mourning period. Who had taken the time to gather the trimmings?

"I understand how Jacob felt in his last days, confined to these quarters," Mr. Screws said, his shaking hand setting down his teacup. He had dressed but still wore carpet slippers instead of shoes. His feet were turned toward the stove but Charles thought he detected a continuing shiver.

"The weather is so unwholesome. I'm sure you'll feel much better by April."

"If I live that long. But if I do not, who will take the business?" he fretted.

"I have pondered that very question, sir. Who is your heir now? For surely, that person is in danger."

"It must be Primus, for there is no one else," Mr. Screws said wearily. "The business put into trust, for lawyers to pick over, and him to receive the proceeds."

Having been in Primus's home, Charles knew the man had no security. He would welcome anyone, in order to sell his wares. "He must be protected. I am assuming that his lady friend agreed that he couldn't have been here to kill your nephew?"

"Yes," Mr. Screws said. "The police assure me that he was seen by half a dozen people at the time. He could not have been in my house then. Mrs. Pettingill sent him home."

Mr. Fletcher poked his head through the half-open doorway, his top hat and gloves ready for the outdoors. "I am off to the countinghouse now, sir."

"Send Mr. Cratchit directly here," Mr. Screws ordered. "He'll know what ledgers to bring."

Mr. Fletcher nodded and winked at Charles, then vanished.

Mr. Screws opened his writing desk and wrote a quick note before handing it to Charles. "Take this to my solicitor. He'll need to come and make me a will. You can witness it."

Charles took the note. He still felt like he had icicles in his nose, but back into the busy streets he would go. "Should I go to see Mr. Harley?"

"No. Let us not draw attention to him. Pray return with my solicitor or one of his clerks."

Charles nodded and followed in Mr. Fletcher's wake. His errand didn't take terribly long. He returned with the solicitor, a fellow even older than Mr. Screws, in a hired coach, then waited in the hall while the men talked, since the solicitor asked for privacy. Luckily, he'd brought part of his book folded into his pocket and he worked on his edits while he waited.

Eventually the solicitor left. Mr. Screws instructed Charles to wait in the hall for Mr. Cratchit to arrive, leaving him to feel like some sort of bodyguard instead of a secretary. He edited on, jumping up when he heard the knocker, happy for a distraction since he'd nearly made it through the pages he'd brought with him.

"At work? With Mr. Screws?" Mr. Cratchit asked. His nose gleamed red with cold and he had a hole exposing skin in his left mitten.

"Confidential secretary. For a couple of weeks."

Mr. Cratchit frowned. "I daresay he needs the help, poor man. Mr. Fletcher scarcely leaves the countinghouse. He's trying to do the work of Screws and Harley along with his own."

"It's unfortunate that young Mr. Harley wasn't trained for the business."

"Some high sticklers as clients. I don't think Mr. Harley could have brought in a bastard son without damaging the trade." Mr. Cratchit sneezed. The mighty wind he created sent the stack of ledgers he carried crashing to the ground.

Charles knelt to pick them up as the clerk pulled a grimy, hole-pocked handkerchief from his sleeve and blew.

"Goodness me, such a sneeze! Careful not to bend the edges, good sir. Mr. Screws has very high standards, you know."

Charles carefully slid each loose paper back where it belonged and handed the ledgers to Mr. Cratchit. "I wonder about the state of your shoes, sir, now that I know what care is taken with the ledgers."

Mr. Cratchit stared down at the mud caking his old, stained brown shoes. "Very muddy in the Dials today. Rained hard overnight. Expect the good folks on the top floor, Irish, you know, found a goodly dose of clean water leaking through the roof early this morn."

If Mr. Cratchit lived in the Dials with the poverty-stricken Irish immigrants, he must be poor indeed. What kind of wages did Mr. Screws pay? Had he been a fool to take the position? There had yet to be a mention of his pay.

Mr. Screws had considerable wealth but everyone around

him seemed impoverished, except Mr. Fletcher, who would have his own resources.

Mr. Cratchit gave him a creaky little bow and went to the dining room to deliver the ledgers. Charles sat back on his chair, rather dazed. He'd bring more work with him tomorrow, telling himself that it didn't matter if he was paid little if he spent most of the time cast on his own work. He spent a good twenty minutes thinking up a new sketch about clerks and their shoes, but then remembered he probably had nowhere to send it. Had Mr. Hogarth begun to slander him across London yet? This was hard times, indeed.

As he leaned against the wall, musing, Mrs. Pettingill came down from the stairs, a couple of stuffed flour sacks dangling from each hand. He rushed forward to help her.

"May I ask a kindness of you, Mr. Dickens?" she asked, her eyes downcast, very unlike the Mrs. Pettingill he was used to seeing.

"My time is your uncle's, madam, but with his permission I will aid you."

She held out the sacks to him. "Will you please take my husband's clothing to a secondhand dealer for me? I cannot bear the commission myself."

"If that will help." No widow would want to see her husband's intimate possessions sprawled across a table, much less hung on lines around a used clothing stall. But why would she want to be rid of everything so soon? He stared at her more intimately than ever before.

As she blushed at his frank perusal, he saw the repaired lace at her collar, and the practical strip of black muslin sewn around the hem. She must need the money the clothes could bring. Had the old miser not offered her an allowance?

He nodded and took the bags from her, gently settling them against the wall. "I will interrupt Mr. Screws and beg permission."

"Oh." She put her hand to her throat. "Do wait until his meeting is over. Is it with someone important?"

"His clerk." They shared a glance. Poor Robert Cratchit was no one important.

"I will make dear Uncle Emmanuel a fresh pot of tea and bring it in. Then you can come in behind me and ask," she decided, and went down the passage toward the kitchen.

Why couldn't she ask Mr. Screws himself, since it was her commission? His suspicion renewed. Had she wanted the clothing out of the house because seeing it would remind her of something very bad she had done, like killing the gentle man she had wed?

Mrs. Pettingill was no fainting, flyaway slip of a girl, but a sturdy woman of more than middling height. She probably stretched wider than her late husband across the middle. Yes, she might have overpowered him from behind.

Charles winced as his fertile imagination saw the possible scene unfolding. He should tell Mr. Screws to ensure that she didn't leave the house, in case she went after Primus Harley. No new widow should be seen out of doors anyway, especially a genteel one.

Once again, he found himself regretting the loss of the competent Mrs. Dorset. She'd have been a better gatekeeper than the old gentleman.

When the widow reappeared, he followed her into the dining room, where Mr. Screws was berating Mr. Cratchit about some fault of one of the lesser clerks. He paused long enough for his niece to gesture Charles forward and gave permission for Charles to go to the shops for her.

Upon exiting the house, Charles sucked in the smoky air outside like it was spring again and he was walking through country hedgerows. He was far too active a person to sit doing nothing in a front hall for hours. Given the time of day, he didn't need to return to Finsbury Circus again until morning.

He decided to see Reuben Solomon in Middlesex Street. The old clothes man, known to Charles from last summer's lack of financial liquidity, radiated kindness and honesty. The man had taken in some items he'd purchased, and offered good advice as well.

Mr. Solomon, seated on a bench in front of his table, had bundled into his winter costume. Though hidden under a canvas roof and behind a line of hanging clothing, he still worked outdoors. To his habitual top hat, the long beard of red streaked with white, and the heavy coat, he'd added mittens, a muffler, and a blanket. Instead of a cup of wine at his elbow he had a pottery mug of coffee. Charles recognized the two women huddled against the wall of the building at the back of the stall from previous visits, sharing a wool blanket while they sewed.

"Mr. Dickens." The old man nodded. "I never forget a face, you see."

Charles grinned and stepped up to his table, ducking under a pair of secondhand winter coats upgraded with shiny buttons. "It has been a few months."

"You look the same," the man responded, fingering his beard. "Sit down." He waved to the women to bring another cup.

One of them took a pot off of a brazier and poured steaming liquid into another pottery mug. Charles took it with thanks and breathed in the dark brew.

"What is in those sacks? Have you had another turn of fortune?"

"It is a long story, Mr. Solomon, but I am carrying out a commission for a new widow. She wished to have the price of her late husband's clothing and I knew you would give me an honest deal."

The dealer grunted and pushed the breeches he'd been piecing together to the side. He called out in Hebrew to the older woman, who scuttled forward to pick it up, leaving the table clean. "I have time for a story while I look through these sacks."

Charles hefted his sacks and set them on the table, then undid the strings at the top of each. "Let us make sure nothing is hiding in these garments."

"Like jewelry? We will check each pocket." Mr. Solomon took off his gloves, exposing long fingers reddened with cold. While he loved his walks, Charles could not imagine spending the day outside without being in motion. He took the stool opposite the dealer and drank his coffee.

"Well?" The dealer looked at him expectantly.

Charles's sip of the nearly boiling coffee went down the wrong way. He coughed, tears springing to his eyes. "I've lost her."

"Who? The sleepy-eyed young lady with a love of ribbons?"

Charles nodded and wiped his eyes with his mitten. He sipped more cautiously, feeling the warmth move down his chest. "I rescued a baby from a silly maid who thought I was the infant's father."

"Are you?"

"Absolutely no chance of it, but the mother died and I was a handy fool. I brought the babe to London and my Kate found out about it. I think she believes me, but someone overheard a conversation about the baby and told her parents. I've lost Kate, and my position, and my reputation."

"Why doesn't anyone else believe you?"

Charles shrugged. "I think it's easier to believe a lie than the truth. As successful as I've been over the past year, I've had my rough spots, as you know. I had to put the wedding off a few months. We should have been married by now. Her father might have thought I was a bad bargain, even though I've continued to make progress in my career. I even have a book coming out next year."

Mr. Solomon nodded wisely, his fingers still moving through the clothes. Charles recognized the blue nightcap and felt a pang for the lost bird expert.

"If your Kate truly loves you, you will have her back in the end. If not," his watery eyes twinkling, he added, "I have a lovely granddaughter, Hannah, who would make you a good wife."

Charles tried to smile but couldn't find the expression. "I am honored, sir, but I love Kate. I am resolved to have her and she has not entirely given up on me. I do not think I will become the man I was meant to be without her."

"Then don't doubt her. You'll find a path to the truth."

"Of course," Charles added, "in the midst of all this personal disaster, people have been dying again. Including the man whose clothes you hold."

"Oh?" Mr. Solomon's fingers stilled. "How did this man die?"

"Strangled," Charles said succinctly. "In the same room where another man died some weeks ago. We think they are dying over a business the first man co-owned and the second man was going to manage and inherit."

"Who do you think killed them?"

"I would like to point a finger at the widow, but I have to trust my Kate, don't I?"

"She doesn't think the widow killed her husband, despite her desire to rid herself of his clothing?"

"No, she thinks the murders are business related. I must say the clothing being sold so soon surprised me. The widow is not hungry, or cold, or in any kind of danger, even if she might be poor. Her husband's uncle has been very protective of her."

"Could he have other kinds of feelings for the widow?"

"He's very ill. I don't think so. I think he's holding close what little family he has left." Charles drained the last of his mug. "Kate said it would be unnatural for a woman to kill her husband, but I must say there are definitely unnatural aspects to this situation. A ghost, a missing body . . . it is all a tangle."

Mr. Solomon arched an eyebrow at the word "ghost" but asked the obvious question. "Who benefits from these deaths?"

Charles had a flash of memory. "The widow wore a mended dress today, but I'd seen her in an expensive dress before."

"Where did it come from?"

"I don't know anything about her wardrobe." Charles thought through the possibilities. The Hogarth girls had plenty of fine clothes they couldn't have afforded thanks to the generosity of Lady Lugoson. Did Mrs. Pettingill have a similar benefactor? Or was there a more sinister story behind the differing quality of her wardrobe?

"Then you will have to investigate."

"Isn't a widow better off with her husband alive?" Charles said. "I think so, based on what I know. He seemed to be a very nice man, distinguished even. His uncle trusted him."

Mr. Solomon nodded. "Then you have to agree with your Kate for now. Who inherits the business?"

"A Mr. Harley, but he is a dwarf. I don't think he could have killed the victims. There is another wrinkle to the situation."

"What is that?"

"A damaged creature whose mother was employed in the house. Johnny Dorset might have sneaked in and done it, but he had no reason to kill the second victim."

"Reason for the first?"

"Oh, yes." Charles saddened at the thought. "Johnny is unlikely to plan to kill. He is capable of rage, but not forethought."

"Perhaps he's decided he enjoys killing, if he is mad."

Charles sighed. "Or there are two killers. There is also a man, a manufacturer who had a loan, who has every reason to be angry at this business but I've met with him and he did not seem like a killer."

"Who else is on the scene?"

Charles shrugged. "Servants of the household, people who work for the business."

"Could any of them have done it?"

"None of them would benefit. Other than the business, the two victims have nothing in common."

Mr. Solomon fished a yellow nightcap from a coat pocket. "It is a puzzle. A wise scholar of my people once said, 'Before a thief steals, he has learned to lie.'"

Charles thought about the saying. "You are saying that someone may not be who I think they are?"

"Indeed." Mr. Solomon stroked his beard. "I agree with you that this widow is unlikely to be impoverished. This is good fabric, nothing more than two years old. She feels guilt, this person. She does not want to look on her husband's possessions."

"Will you buy them?"

"Yes." The dealer spread his long, chilblained fingers. "It is good cloth. It will sell, and quickly. There is nothing hidden in the fabric."

They agreed on a price and Charles securely pocketed the money before departing for home, none the wiser. Still, he had plenty to do with his time. He wanted to get his book edits home and another stack under way.

On Wednesday, Charles went to Finsbury Circus prepared with triple the amount of papers to edit in his coat pocket. He asked Mr. Screws about his salary and they set a very respectable renumeration for his efforts, much relieving him. Then, Mr. Screws sent him to the countinghouse with a load of ledgers early in the afternoon, once he had worked through what Mr. Cratchit had brought him midmorning. After that, Charles needed to escort Mr. Screws to the inquest for Mr. Pettingill.

He switched out the ledgers with the aid of Mr. Cratchit and was turning to leave when Mr. Fletcher stuck his head out of his office door.

The hair over his ears had started to grow, highlighting the gray parts. He looked frantic and overworked, perhaps unready to have moved from apprentice to principal so quickly. Despite that, his voice was cheery as he suggested, "Fancy the theater tonight?"

"The theater?" Charles said, juggling the ledgers.

"Yes, a musical performance, a benefit I believe, with myself and my fiancée, and you and yours?"

Charles cleared his throat. "It pains me to admit, but I am not able to see my Kate in public at the moment."

Mr. Fletcher's eyebrows rose. "What a calamity! What happened with dear Miss Hogarth? Miss Osborne had so looked forward to deepening the friendship."

Charles kept his expression blank. "Yes, it is very sad, but I have not yet lost hope, nor has she. It's an issue with her father."

"I see." Mr. Fletcher patted him awkwardly. "Fathers can be trouble. My Miss Osborne is an orphan. Her parents raised her and then conveniently died before I met her."

"I see," Charles murmured, not sure of how to respond. While his parents could be troublesome, he did not wish death to befall them.

Mr. Fletcher's very being electrified, as if he'd been transported by some great idea. "My dear sir, you must go with us," he insisted. "Just the thing. Music for the shattered soul. We will take care of you."

"Mr. Screws might need me," he temporized.

"Not in the evening. He is not that sort of master. Where will you be? We shall fetch you in a hired carriage."

Charles gave in. Who knew what he might learn from Mr.

Fletcher? An evening spent with Fred glaring at him did not sound soothing. Especially after the ordeal of another inquest.

Several hours later, Charles's head ached as he stood on the mezzanine level of the sumptuous theater, a glass of champagne in his hand. The gas lamps smelled. His shirt felt too tight, courtesy of sitting too much lately, instead of walking.

He'd spent hours seated at the inquest. The coffin had been open, though at least they had not left Mr. Pettingill's body in situ for the jurors. The sight of that placid face, never again to speak enthusiastically about birds, made Charles's stomach ache. This time they had brought back a verdict of "sudden wrongful death by the hand of another where the offender is not known." Sir Silas had nodded significantly at Charles after the verdict was read, making him think that Mr. Harley's death might be reconsidered now.

"Are you well, Mr. Dickens?" Miss Osborne inquired as she ran her fingers down the gold-tasseled edge of a curtain. "You have a greenish cast to your skin."

"I think that light is defective," Charles said, pointing to the sconce on the wall. "Would you mind if we moved away from it?"

"As long as Mr. Fletcher can find us, I have no objection. The poor man suffers from a weak stomach at times, and even I agree that the cockles were off. I hope our drinks will counter-act them." She smiled and emptied the contents of their champagne bottle between their glasses, then walked with him away from the milling music enthusiasts.

That had been part of the problem, too. The sopranos screeched and the basses rumbled, none of them very good. Charles had been raised in a musical family, as had Kate. His standards had become too high to appreciate such a ruckus.

He grinned to himself.

"What is amusing you, sir?"

"Ruckus," he said, trying out the word on his tongue. "I just thought of that word. Your fiancé must be rubbing off on me, for me to think of such an Americanism."

She put her hand through the crook of his elbow and drew him farther down toward the subscription boxes. "I think it is absolutely perfect that you are working for Mr. Screws. Just think of it. You and Mr. Fletcher can run the business together for the poor old dear."

"Why is it that women like him so?" Charles asked. "My Miss Hogarth sees him as a dear old thing, too."

"Men return to infancy in their great old age," Miss Osborne said complacently. "We think of them like we do babies. Don't you agree?"

He started to demur, but she asked after his family then, and his childhood, before moving on to his career to date. His head pounded, Mr. Fletcher did not return, and he began to have the uncomfortable feeling that he was being grilled for information about himself and his friendships.

Perhaps it was simply that his head ached so. He had enjoyed his share of exciting adventures, bowling his way through the country, even up to Scotland, in search of stories. Any woman with a love of exciting tales would find what he had to offer satisfying.

"You must—" Miss Osborne stopped and blushed prettily.

He put his glass to his mouth and discovered it empty. "What, my dear? You must ask me." His voice had developed a thick quality.

She put a hand to her décolletage, drawing his attention to the soft curve of her breasts. He blinked. His vision swam. He'd become a little drunk. Had he eaten dinner?

"You must allow me to acquire an autographed copy of your book when it is released. I will treasure it always, as a sign of our special friendship."

He wanted to protest that he scarcely knew her, but her finger fluttered distractingly at the slopes of her breasts, first touching one side, then the other, like a pendulum.

"There you are." A hearty American voice reached Charles's ears.

He drew back and attempted to smile at Mr. Fletcher. "I apologize. The light where we were waiting was not working."

"I could smell the gas." Mr. Fletcher peered at him. "Are you well? You are flushed."

Miss Osborne touched his forehead with cool fingers. "He's warm, my love."

Charles handed Mr. Fletcher his glass. "I beg your indulgence but I think I must go home."

He nodded. "You must be well for tomorrow."

"Thank you." He could only sketch a wave and dart down the hall to where he knew a back staircase hid in the darkness.

Once outside, he felt immediately better. His eyes cleared. Cigar smoke had been as thick in the theater as gas fumes.

No wonder theaters burned down so often. He made his way home with bleary inattention. The air, though not clean or clear, was an improvement from indoors. He went into his rooms reluctantly, hoping his brother had gone out.

Instead, Fred sprawled across the sofa, the fire blazing merrily in front of him, their stoneware ale jug on the rug at his feet.

"No outing?"

"I haven't wanted to spend the coin, given the unsteady state of your career," Fred fretted.

Charles let his body fold into the couch in rag-doll fashion. "I still have my book deal and my temporary position."

"For how long?" Fred asked, draining his glass.

"Until Mr. Screws dies, I imagine. He does not keep me busy but it is enough that I know he needs me."

"People die at this time of year."

"Yes, the weather is unforgiving," Charles agreed. "But I assure you, I am not our father. Mr. Screws offered me a generous number of shillings a week."

"You are awfully passive about the baby," Fred argued. "It is not like you."

"I have written letters that I hope will bring new information to light. I should go to Hatfield again myself and sort out the situation," Charles admitted. "I have relied too much on William."

"I'm worried," Fred stated. "I know you. These murders weigh too much on you, and you haven't Kate to provide comfort now."

"That's not true. When I see her I know she still loves me." Charles's tone sounded bleak even to himself. "It is something."

"Something," Fred muttered, staring at the fire. "We all need something."

Charles had just resolved on going to bed when a knock came on the outer door.

Chapter 19

Charles forced his resistant body to rise in response to the door knock. He missed those days when the person at his Furnival's Inn door was usually William, ready with a cheerful plan for the evening. These nights he didn't know what to expect.

He took a deep breath of the evergreen boughs Fred had piled in the tiny entry, no doubt prefatory to decorating their rooms. The sharp scent lent a little energy to him, but his shoulders still stiffened when he opened the door.

"Yes?" he asked cautiously.

The black-cloaked figure did not have the height of his previous ghostly visitor. This one also had a lacy veil over her face. Though it obscured her features, he preferred it to sepulchral makeup.

Her hands indicated a desire to move into his chambers. He blocked his door with his arm. "What mischief is this, madam? What do you plan?"

"Mr. Dickens, it is I."

Charles frowned. The voice had some air of familiarity, but he couldn't quite place it. "I, madam?"

"Betsy Pettingill." She had an air of exasperation.

His eyes widened. "How do you know where I live?"

"Mr. Screws had it in his papers."

Charles sighed and let his arm drop. "Very well. You may enter. My brother is here to chaperone." As a widow she might not need a chaperone, but he felt the need for one himself.

She brushed past him. He could smell the dye in her veil as she passed. It must have been a white veil before today, reminding him of her recent loss. He also remembered that she might be a killer. Was she not surprisingly eager to remove to Finsbury Circus when he'd announced Mr. Screws's household distress? Far more than her husband, and he suspected her to be an intelligent woman.

Once he had the door closed and locked, he very deliberately helped her with her cloak and veil, to remove any hint of the ghost from her person.

Fred stood and bowed.

"Fred, this is Mrs. Pettingill," he explained. "She runs my employer's household."

Fred nodded. "Do you want me to stay?"

"I couldn't ask you to take the trouble," the lady said sweetly, ignoring the evidence that Fred had been very much at home in front of the fire. "Really, my dear, you must run along."

Fred's gaze slid past Charles and he moved fluidly until he'd vanished into the bedroom. At least his brother would be safe if Mrs. Pettingill wanted to do him harm.

But he began to get the feeling the new widow had other ideas. When she turned, he discovered she'd blackened her eyelashes. He noticed because she blinked at him several times, a coquettish gesture that didn't match her forthright personality.

Then, she twisted her hands together and seemed to shrink. "I beg an audience of you, my dear Mr. Dickens."

"Would you like to be seated?" He gestured to the sofa, only then noticing Fred must have spilled his ale, given the wet spot in the center.

Instead of replying, she threw herself into a huddle at his feet. Her skirts rustled against the carpet and she clutched at his shoes. "I will be a good wife to you!" she howled.

"What?" Charles, too shocked to process her words, stepped back.

She oozed forward and grabbed his ankles. "Please do me the honor of proposing marriage!" Looking up at him, her eyes transformed into slits by the heavy cosmetics, she blinked rapidly. "I'll be a good, true wife to you."

He swallowed hard but realized he wasn't truly affected. She'd set them both up as characters in a play. In real life, no woman would behave this way. "Compose yourself. You cannot possibly be so desperate, madam."

"It is not desperation, but desire, Mr. Dickens. A desire to be your wife."

"Won't Mr. Screws leave you something in his will? You're Mr. Pettingill's heir and you are still living in Mr. Screws's abode. Dedicate yourself to him." He attempted to lift his foot, but she held tightly above his shoes.

"I cannot."

"You are but freshly a widow. Cease this panicking and allow yourself to mourn, as surely any wife of such an excellent man as Mr. Pettingill should."

"Oh, my dear Edward." She gasped, choked, bent her head and coughed.

Charles waited, paralyzed by her clutching hands. They inched up his thick wool socks. Did she mean to find his bare flesh?

"I admit I have no faith in my uncle-in-law, but, Charles, by marrying me, you are gambling that you are marrying an heiress."

"I did not give you permission to be so familiar." Kate called him Charles often now, a process that had come on gradually after their engagement. It was special, his name an endearment from her lips. He didn't want to hear it from anyone else.

She lifted her head and howled again. "I apologize. You are so dear to me that 'Charles' is my own heart's name for you."

He felt acutely uncomfortable at this turn of events. What was wrong with the widow's behavior? He rapidly calculated the possibilities. Could she be trying to cover up some kind of relationship with Mr. Harley or Mr. Appleton? That expensive gown he'd seen her wear in a previous encounter might have been a gift. He'd heard of impoverished widows remarrying quickly, but this was downright insanity. The body had not yet been buried. In fact, he wasn't sure where it had gone after the inquest.

"I implore you, madam, to think of your Edward, so tender in his grave, though I do not know if he even has one."

"He does," she sobbed. "A private family vault. He is already there, poor soul."

"You had him taken there directly after the inquest?"

"Yes. The Pettingill cousins took him. I couldn't trust anyone else after what happened to poor Mr. Harley."

Poor Mr. Harley? Now here was the first time he had heard that man spoken of with any tenderness.

"Poor Mr. Harley indeed," he muttered. "How can you speak of leaving dear Edward's elderly relative for another man? I am sure both your husband and Mr. Harley would want you to watch over Mr. Screws."

"Who will watch over me?" she cried, clutching at him again. "Am I not my husband's heir?"

The skin around Charles's neck tingled. Why were women continually throwing themselves at him? This never happened before he met Kate. "I cannot stay with you. I have a young brother to watch over. You must be strong and vigilant for both you and Mr. Screws."

She sniffled. She let go of him and wobbled to her knees. "I see I have come to the wrong man for help."

He stiffened. "I am promised to another, but I assure you that as long as I am Mr. Screws's secretary, I will be in his house or about the duties he assigned as faithfully as anyone could. I also promise you I will learn who murdered these men and bring them to justice."

He helped lift her to her feet, while making sure to touch her as little as possible. "What can you do that the coroner could not?" she asked.

"I have solved murders before," he said darkly. "I can do it again." And set his world back to rights.

On Christmas Eve morning, Charles pushed his brother out the door early, for the fog lay thick outside their windows and he knew Fred would have a slow walk to work. He made sure Fred wore gloves under his mittens and dressed very warmly. They would attend church services tonight after the workday was done. Tomorrow would be a feast with their family. Charles could already taste the Christmas pudding, presently hanging in his mother's pantry.

After that, he thought he'd take a coach to Hatfield, assuming Mr. Screws didn't need him on Saturday. People who'd left the area might return for Christmas, and he hoped to gain new insight as to who Timothy's father was. He might also find the little maid had an older relative in town who might be able to take the child in, or at least be made aware the Agas had him.

He hummed a merry tune as he gathered his clothes and notes. While he sat in Mr. Screws's hall waiting for orders, he planned to draft a story, originally meant for the *Evening Chronicle*. It would go in his book now. The revisions were almost done.

He heard a knock on his outer door. A message from Mr. Screws perhaps, to send him on an errand? He opened it and received a delivery boy along with a blast of frigid air. The boy's muffler sat so high over his face that Charles could see nothing but a pair of bright blue eyes.

He thanked the boy and shut the door, then took the note

over to his teacup and opened the missive. He took in the words, but not the meaning, so he read it again.

> *Mr. John Macrone presents his compliments to Mr. Charles Dickens, and, in returning the enclosed manuscript, begs to express his regret that the controversy in which the author is involved is not one that he can hopefully or usefully enter into. If the concerns about the author's moral turpitude are positively resolved in the future, perhaps this excellent work will be able to return to our publishing calendar.*

Charles's vision washed with red. The letter had not actually come with his text, but alone. Macrone was playing chess with him, by placing his book on hold. The publisher had concerns about his moral turpitude? How dare he? Now he couldn't afford to go to Hatfield himself and make another attempt to learn the truth about the baby.

He drained his teacup and groaned. Fred did not need to hear of this financial blow. He was nervous enough, and little though he remembered of his father's early adventure in debtor's prison, he knew all too well the drama of over a year ago, when his father went to a sponging house while Charles tore around the city gathering loans from everyone he knew. They'd ended up here at Furnival's Inn as a result.

He'd have to trek to Pall Mall and give his publisher a piece of his mind immediately. After fighting the hold, he'd then go to Mr. Screws's home to commence his workday. After all, ever since his novelist friend William Ainsworth had introduced him to John Macrone, he'd considered the man a friend. The publisher had been depressed since losing his first-born child in November, but he couldn't lose faith in the *Sketches*. They both needed to make money on the project.

Charles marched into the offices after a damp walk, hoping to find one of his friends about. Macrone published many wonderful authors and had the clout to persuade the well-respected mad genius George Cruikshank to do his illustrations.

His publisher, only a few years older than he, usually greeted Charles with a ready smile and a warm handshake, but today, the charisma had vanished from his face and his hair stood up in tufts. He was alone, standing in front of the fireplace in his inner chamber.

"What are you doing here?" he demanded. "Didn't you receive my note?"

Charles pulled off his gloves and held his hands to the crackling fire. "I will swear on the holy Bible that I do not have an illegitimate child," he promised. "Will that satisfy Mr. Hogarth and his cronies who are bent on doing me ill?"

Macrone collapsed into a desk chair. "It does not seem likely. I can't afford to publish the book now, Charles. It won't get any notices, thanks to Mr. Hogarth."

Charles sat next to him, knowing he fought for his professional life. "I can provide proof of never being in Hatfield before last month," he said. "There are no articles, no travels, nothing. Even Miss Hogarth doesn't believe this slander."

"How did her father find out?"

"One of his other children overheard a conversation and repeated it."

Macrone sighed. "I must take the respected Mr. Hogarth's word that you are a degenerate."

"You know me better than that." Charles touched his publisher's shoulder. "Who wept with you when little Frederick died? Me, not Mr. Hogarth. Who vouched for me? Ainsworth, not Hogarth. He's rigidly against bastard children and rushed to judgment, but it was a false judgment."

"Charles," Macrone began.

Charles shook his head. "It is Christmas Eve. I saved a four-month-old infant from certain death. I brought that child to London because his distraught aunt was confused and upset due to her sister's death in the Hatfield fire."

"But," Macrone interjected, his handsome, intelligent face marred with deep emotion.

"I acted on Christian charity, not degeneracy. Quite the opposite." Charles set his hand on his publisher's arm. "You were a father, John. You would have done anything to save Frederick's life if it had been possible. How can you imagine that I, having seen what you went through, would have done anything less for fatherless Timothy than I did?"

"But Mr. Hogarth?"

"You must believe me. I demand it, John, I really do. I am not little Timothy's father, but I am his guardian, his angel if you will."

Macrone's jaw worked. His eyes went glassy. Charles almost felt bad at his manipulation, but Timothy's future was at stake as well as his.

Macrone took a deep breath. "I am very glad my little Frederick brought some good into the world. I am glad you saved the child, Charles. You are a good man."

"Thank you." Charles smiled at him. "Will you resume preparations for my book to be released?"

Macrone nodded. "Though it may destroy me."

Charles pulled his latest revisions from his pocket with a flourish. "I am almost done. Here are the latest edited sketches."

Macrone took them with sober intent. "I'll give Cruikshank the next set of instructions for his illustrations."

Charles stood and shook his publisher's hand. "Thank you. You won't be sorry. Please wish Mrs. Macrone a very happy Christmas for me."

He walked back to the street, feeling pleased with himself, though his stomach felt greasy and queasy with nervous energy. Every orphan should have a protector like Timothy had.

* * *

"Where have you been?" Mr. Screws said irritably from the parlor as Charles entered the house. Dressed for the outdoors, he was seated, but with his cane between his knees, ready to help him rise.

He had noted Mrs. Pettingill had not opened the door as he'd been used to her doing; rather, she'd allowed a maid to do so. Likely she'd kept out of sight due to her embarrassment over her behavior the night before.

"I apologize. I had an urgent matter to take care of regarding my book. As you know I had planned to devote my time entirely to the project."

"Yes, of course," Mr. Screws said, the side of his mouth turning up in a sneer.

"You are not working in the dining room today?" Charles asked.

"I am quite restored," the old man snapped. "Congressman Winthrop has requested a meeting with me this morning and I wanted you along."

"Ah," Charles said. "Some more intelligence about Mr. Fletcher?"

"I would imagine so." Mr. Screws scratched at his hook of a nose, then stood. "I really cannot afford to lose Mr. Fletcher, you know. I had hoped he would remain in London until I died."

He brushed past Charles and walked out the door. Charles followed in his employer's wake as he carefully stepped down to the street, one hand clutching the stark railing, the other, his cane. The Screws carriage came up the street and they climbed aboard.

"Are your hopes dashed over Mr. Fletcher?"

Mr. Screws clicked his false teeth. "It is likely. I knew I'd have to increase his salary since his workload has increased, which irritated me, but his loss is unimaginable."

"Is there anyone else? Anyone you've missed?"

"I have cast about for whom to leave the business other than Primus. I did have a cousin, Mehetabel Screws, who lived in Kent. He and his wife, a woman of some private fortune, have died but Mr. Pettingill still corresponded with his son. They would have been related through my father."

"Perhaps Mrs. Pettingill has the address?"

"Indeed. She is the one who reminded me. Just this morning we wrote a letter to inquire as to the son's circumstances. My cousin was trained for the church. I have to assume his son has an education, as well as some sort of interest in science, or my nephew would never have bothered to correspond."

Charles wished for some sort of novelistic ending to the story, finding out that baby Timothy was related to Mr. Screws somehow, and that he would inherit a fortune. Alas, that was not how real life worked. But he had a thought. "It sounds promising. One wonders if you'll discover that he's been in London all this time?"

Chapter 20

The coach rattled, bouncing the two men up and down. It had run over something in the road. On the pavement, boys stared at Charles curiously as he passed. He wondered what had gone underneath the wheels.

"No, Mrs. Pettingill said the address on my cousin's letters had always been from Kent," Mr. Screws said in answer to his question. "Mehetabel's wife had a lifetime interest in a fine house."

Charles knew his point had gone entirely over the old man's head. If this cousin knew he was in line to inherit a fortune, he might be the previous heir's killer. But it sounded like he might have money. "It would be good to know more about your young cousin."

"Mrs. Pettingill will know more. Mehetabel and his wife were in close communication with Mr. and Mrs. Pettingill. I believe Mrs. Pettingill received all of Mrs. Mehetabel's personal effects after her death."

"That must account for why Mrs. Pettingill has such an unusual wardrobe."

"What do you mean, sir?" The old man thumped his cane between his legs against the floor of the coach.

"She has both fine gowns and mended ones."

Mr. Screws lifted his chin. "I do not pay attention to such things. She is a woman of clean habits, which is enough for me."

Charles decided to stop pressing the subject. "Is Mr. Fletcher in the countinghouse today?"

"Early this morning, I sent him across the river to investigate a business that has asked for a large loan. He should be back by now."

They went slowly through the fog-cloaked streets but soon Charles was helping Mr. Screws onto the pavement in front of the Screws and Harley countinghouse. Just behind them another coachman called to his horses and pulled to the side of the road behind the Screws carriage.

Mr. Screws waited, shivering, while the second carriage discharged two men. Congressman Winthrop had on a brand-new overcoat, though it would not remain perfect for long, given the casual way he held a cigar with a long ash at the tip. The second man appeared to be about the same age, but of a more continental appearance.

Charles recognized him. "That's Aaron Vail, the American chargé d'affaires."

"I wonder what he's got to do with Mr. Fletcher," Mr. Screws said in a low voice.

The congressman held out his hand for a hearty shake before he had even reached them. He quickly made introductions.

"Do you have some helpful information for us, Mr. Vail?" Charles asked.

"Based on the provided description," Mr. Vail said with a surprising French accent, "I would like to see this Powhatan Fletcher."

"Is the name familiar to you, sir?" Mr. Screws asked.

The new man nodded.

Mr. Screws let out a long, pitying breath and brought them inside. One of the clerks, warming his hands in front of the stove, squealed when he saw his employer and raced, rat-like, back to his desk.

"That's him," Charles said into Mr. Vail's ear. "The man who is standing next to the seated clerk." He nodded at Mr. Cratchit's desk, where he and Mr. Fletcher were looking at a ledger.

"*Escroc*," Mr. Vail said to himself. "Where can we speak in private, Mr. Screws?"

"My office, right this way." Mr. Screws led them through the clerk's room and into his office. Four men were a tight squeeze, as there were only three chairs.

Charles gestured the visitors to take the seats. "I believe you recognized him, Mr. Vail?"

The man's long face looked even more mournful. "I am afraid so. This Mr. Fletcher is a ne'er-do-well who disappeared with a British actress from a troupe visiting the District of Columbia."

"Go on," Mr. Screws said, steepling his fingers in front of his chin.

Mr. Vail crossed his legs. "They left after fleecing a wealthy American widow."

The congressman shook his head angrily and pulled another cigar from his pocket. Charles wasn't sure where the first one had gone. "Do you know his name?"

"I believe he told you the truth about that," Mr. Vail said. "While he is indeed the descendant of Tidewater Virginia aristocracy, his parents died bankrupt, having lost their plantation when he was a boy."

"So he never worked for my friend," Mr. Screws said.

"As far as I know his only career was that of a waiter in a

chophouse." Mr. Vail glanced at the newly lit cigar with distaste.

"You brought him in as an apprentice. You taught him the business," Charles said, feeling the need to defend Mr. Screws's instincts. "He might be doing his work here properly. For now."

"He did seem to have some basic knowledge," Mr. Screws said, considering. "It could have come from books."

"I would not trust him," Mr. Vail said, seeing, as Charles did, that Mr. Screws wanted to justify keeping the man. "If he stole from a widow, as a confidence man, he might be playing the same game with you."

"What would you expect will happen?" the congressman asked.

"Fletcher might ask Mr. Screws here to invest in a business of his own. Or simply suggest an investment in a business that only exists on paper, and pocket the funds." Mr. Vail gestured in Gallic fashion. "He will learn enough to gain your confidence and decide how best to remove a great deal of money from you. Meanwhile, he is living a comfortable life. He is in no rush."

Charles remembered what Julie Aga had said about another woman named Osborne. "Was Amelia Osborne the name of the actress? From what you are saying, it sounds like the same woman."

"I do not know," Vail admitted.

Charles's heart rate increased. He knew they'd uncovered a new suspect. "Could he be a killer? Mr. Screws's partner died recently, though whether by accident or murder we don't know. However, just a few days ago, Mr. Screws's nephew was slain."

"Have you made him a partner? An heir?" Mr. Vail asked.

"No," Mr. Screws said.

"Then it seems unlikely. He is after the money," Mr. Vail said.

"What if Mr. Harley discovered the truth?" Charles asked. Outside of the office, he heard the sounds of doors opening and closing, then muffled greetings.

"He would have told me immediately," Mr. Screws said. "Given how ill he'd been, that scenario is most unlikely."

Charles ran a finger around the edge of his neckerchief. It seemed to be tightening around his neck. "The money is enough of a motive to stay in the countinghouse."

Mr. Screws nodded suddenly, his cheeks wobbling. "I shall have to make an end to it then, and hope my young cousin can come into the business."

"Hadn't you better move slowly?" Charles asked. "For the sake of the business?"

"Very little will be accomplished in the next two weeks," Mr. Screws said. "People say that no one celebrates Christmas anymore, but they assuredly do not trouble themselves with much industry at this time of the year."

The Americans nodded and rose. Mr. Screws struggled out of his seat. "Thank you very much, sirs."

"I am glad to have helped," Mr. Vail said.

The congressman waved his cigar and they left.

"Send Mr. Fletcher in to me," Mr. Screws said, his face freezing into a mask. "Stay out of my office, but within earshot, while I deal with him."

"Yes, sir," Charles said quickly, seeing a hardness in the man he scarcely recognized, or at least had forgotten. Kate would not like this version of Mr. Screws.

He went to Mr. Fletcher's office. The American glanced up with a smile. "What is it, Dickens? I have to leave for the St. Katherine Docks in a minute."

"What are you going to do there?"

"Meet with a wine merchant. Wants a loan to get his product out of the warehouses down there." He tapped a file. "I need to bring him this paperwork."

Charles picked up the file. "Come with me."

Mr. Fletcher frowned but stood up from his desk and buttoned his coat. Charles handed the file to Mr. Cratchit and told him to take it to the merchant, then led Mr. Fletcher to Mr. Screws's office.

The American showed no sign of fear. Either he had no idea what was coming or he was playing his role until the bitter end. He might very well not have seen the other men.

Charles passed Mr. Fletcher into the office and leaned the door closed but didn't shut it, so that he could hear and assist if needed.

"Mr. Fletcher," Mr. Screws said in a biting tone, "it has come to my attention that you are not a man of business, but a waiter."

"Excuse me?" Mr. Fletcher asked.

"Have you even met James Dobbin? For I assure you, he does not seem to be aware of your existence."

Mr. Fletcher tucked his fingers around his coat lapels and thrust out his chest. "Oh, sir, I can explain, you see, I admired your business so much and wanted to be a part of it."

"All the way from America? Where you made a business out of fleecing widows?"

The American deflated slightly. "I'm a reformed man, due to the education I experienced here, sir."

"You don't say."

His hands went in front of him, open palmed. "I'm respectable now. I'm to marry soon. I'm in an honest trade."

"You are in a trade where you gain a great deal of intimate information and trust," Mr. Screws snapped. "I have no doubt that you were here to set up some of my unfortunate customers, or even myself, for the biggest confidence game of your career. To think I let you stay in my home."

Charles heard a chair squeak back. He peeked into the doorway and saw Mr. Fletcher go nimbly to his knees at the side of the desk.

"I beg of you, sir," Mr. Fletcher said, tears choking his voice. "At your hand, and Mr. Harley's, I have learned an honest trade for the first time in my life. I was cursed with intelligence and no education. I had the breeding for a better life but no opportunity. You have given me all that."

"How dare you say his blessed name, late in our memory?" Mr. Screws thundered in the tones of a much younger man. "You will leave my business and my home this very day, sir. Charles!"

Charles put his head through the doorway. "Yes, sir?"

"Escort Mr. Fletcher to my home and pack his bags, if you please. I do not want to see him again."

"B-but my wages, sir," Mr. Fletcher stammered.

"I will pay you nothing," Mr. Screws said with a snarl. "I am sure your week's wage will be but a drop in the bucket compared to what you have cost me in thievery."

Mr. Fletcher's injury seemed so genuine that as he put his hand over his heart, Charles could feel the hair on the back of his neck rise. "I have stolen nothing. I have been honest every second of my time in this great city."

"Bah, humbug," Mr. Screws spat. "Take him to fetch his coat and nothing else. Not a pencil. Not a scrap of paper."

"Does he have keys that I need to confiscate?" Charles asked.

With a great show of weariness, Mr. Fletcher pulled a ring of keys from his waistcoat pocket. Charles snatched them away.

"And the other one," Mr. Screws demanded.

Mr. Fletcher pulled one house key from his other pocket. He dropped it onto Mr. Screws's desk.

Charles inclined his head and removed Mr. Fletcher to his office. He saw the clear signs of the great man Mr. Screws had once been, but knew the exertion would cost him, and he had too much pride in the old man to let Mr. Fletcher see any sign of weakness now.

"You believe me, don't you, Dickens?" Mr. Fletcher said in tones of utmost honesty when they were in his office, clutching at Charles's hand.

Charles glared at him and pulled his hand away. "I believe the congressman and the ambassador who made testimony against you. Now fetch your coat. We need to leave."

He did not like to play the role of the heavy, but Mr. Fletcher was still so sunk in his role of good employee that he did not misbehave, manipulate, or change his persona.

Back in Finsbury Circus, Charles helped empty the bed-chamber wardrobe into Mr. Fletcher's carpetbag.

"Where will you go now?" Charles asked, watching care-fully as Mr. Fletcher packed the miniature of Miss Osborne that waited next to a Bible on the bedside table.

"To confess all to my dear one." Mr. Fletcher's voice caught with emotion. "She may want to call off the wedding now."

Charles was unsure of the wisdom of letting Mr. Fletcher flee into the winds, as it were. He wasn't entirely sure they even knew his real name. "What will your exact address be?"

"I shall have to return to America, as I am sure Mr. Screws will not provide a character for me," Mr. Fletcher said with such a lack of understanding that Charles could see the actor in him.

"He had so much respect for you," Charles said. "You are a man of great talent. Why not find honest employment when you return home?"

Mr. Fletcher lifted an eyebrow but said nothing.

"What did you hope to gain from me?" Charles asked. "You made such an effort to gain my friendship."

Mr. Fletcher's mouth crooked up on one side. "You are not the most honest of men, Dickens, but you do have talents. I might have brought you in on my pursuits if I had continued to flourish."

Chapter 21

Taken aback by Mr. Fletcher's assertion of his dishonest character, Charles led him downstairs from the bedroom to Mr. Screws's front door without another word. He had admittedly been dishonest of late, but only because he was guilty of wanting things to be as they ought to, and would be in the future, rather than what they were at the moment. The falsehood perpetuated on him, that of being Timothy's father, was the real injustice.

Charles saw the disgraced man of business to the pavement, reflecting that this was a dreadful way to spend the day before Christmas. He then returned to the house and summoned Mrs. Pettingill to inform her of Mr. Fletcher's banishment.

The widow said almost nothing to him, still visibly embarrassed by her proposal of marriage to him. After she promised to notify all the servants that Mr. Fletcher wasn't allowed on the premises, he walked to the countinghouse, worried about the proprietor's health after such a dreadful scene.

Along the way, he purchased a cup of potato soup from a street vendor and drank it down, and debated the possibility that he would be asked to take over Mr. Fletcher's position when he returned. Did he want to take on the responsibility of a countinghouse? He didn't want to start over in a new business after becoming the best in his former career. Also, if he didn't prove himself to Mr. Hogarth in such a way that led to his job being returned to him, he'd never have Kate, either.

He had to find Timothy's father, even if it meant leaving his temporary employment with Mr. Screws. He went inside, nodding at the leaderless clerks who glanced up as he entered, then went to Mr. Screws's open door, thinking to terminate this situation. The business owner had his chair turned and Charles couldn't see him. He stepped quickly into the room, afraid.

His palms tingled. "Mr. Screws?"

Slowly, the chair swiveled around, revealing the old man in the same state as before. Charles's heart began to beat again.

"Have you taken care of the situation?" Mr. Screws asked.

"Assuming he doesn't have spare keys. With Johnny Dorset gone, you might want to hire some stout manservant for a time."

"It is Christmas tomorrow, Mr. Dickens," the older man said wearily. "No one will want to work."

Charles sighed. "I understand. For myself, I have the responsibility of a younger brother."

Mr. Screws waved him away like an irritating bug. "I do not request it of you, sir. I want your brain, not your form. I'd like you to spend the day categorizing the papers in Mr. Fletcher's office. I'll need to get a new man in as soon as possible. Take this down, will you?"

Thank goodness. Mr. Screws planned to hire someone else. With relief, Charles snatched a quill and a notebook from the end of the table and sat down. "Yes?"

"Wanted, a confidential clerk who thoroughly understands the routine of a merchant's countinghouse. He must be about thirty years of age, possess an enterprising disposition. Excellent testimonials required." Mr. Screws cleared his throat. "Our address and so forth. You know the thing. Take it over to the *Morning Chronicle*, will you?"

Charles's hand froze on the page. "Why don't we have a clerk take it to the newspaper? It would be best for me to inventory Mr. Fletcher's office quickly, in case there is any trouble coming, or any meetings we might miss."

"Yes, a good idea." Mr. Screws waved his hand. "Send Smith. He moves more quickly than the others."

"Anything else, sir?" Charles asked, quickly finishing the advertisement.

Mr. Screws licked his lips. "There is something I had better confess, for the good of Mrs. Pettingill if nothing else."

"Yes?"

"I buried a good amount of money in my back garden, and I cannot believe I was so foolish as to allow Mr. Fletcher to live on the premises." The words had flowed out of Mr. Screws in a rush. Once they had passed out of him, he leaned back in his chair.

"Where?" Charles asked, appalled.

"Under the herb garden." He smiled fondly. "Jacob and I buried the first box one summer night three years ago, when Mrs. Dorset was off visiting her sister."

"Very well," Charles said softly. "I assume you mean it to be her inheritance."

Mr. Screws nodded.

Charles felt very sober. "Very good, sir. Perhaps you should inform your solicitor of this information. May I also add an advertisement for a male servant?"

"Make him young, too young to interfere with Mrs. Pettingill," Mr. Screws said. "She's a pretty one, isn't she?"

Charles bent his head and wrote rapidly. He did not agree.

Charles and Fred went to Bloomsbury for Christmas Eve services with their family. A few snowflakes fell as they entered the hushed church, lit by softly glowing candles. A choir matched the tone of the night with gentle carols, celebrating the birth of the Christ child. Charles tried hard to embrace the beauty and hope of the night, promising himself that he and Kate would be side by side at services next year. In fact, he told himself to be nostalgic, that this would be his last Christmas as a bachelor. He prayed for Mr. Screws's health, and Mr. Cratchit's. Closer to home, he prayed for baby Timothy, and Julie's unborn child as well. If he might be so bold, he even prayed for a solution to the murders to come to him, for a killer to be brought to justice.

Fred was garrulous as they walked home through the crowds on the street, enjoying the cleaner air the snow brought, and the joy of the season. Carolers warbled every few blocks, reminding Charles of the night Jacob Harley died. He resolved to put death out of his mind for the holiday, and looked forward to a Christmas Day visit to the Agas, with the gift of a small wooden rattle for Timothy, his very own Christmas child.

They stopped at a chestnut seller, then ducked into a public house for a pint, and finally made their way home when the air became so bitingly cold that Charles felt like his nose might snap off.

In the passage in front of their door, Charles could just barely make out a small shape in the near darkness. Mrs. Pettingill again? Another ghostly visitation? He struck a lucifer against the wall and held it up.

A small woman struggled to her feet, using his door to push herself up. Fred rushed forward and helped her stand.

"She's half frozen," he reported. "Do you know her?"

She wasn't a Hogarth, or a Dickens, or Julie or Mrs. Pettingill. "Let's get her inside," Charles said, mindful that angels could be passing through on this holy night.

He unlocked their door and went in to light the fire they had waiting. As soon as the coals had caught, he struck another lucifer and lit the lamp.

Fred was busy trying to help the stranger out of the various shawls she'd bundled around herself. "Help me with these knots. My hands are frozen."

"Come to the fire," Charles said gently, and led the woman deeper into their chambers. The fibers of her clothing were damp, but eventually he had the ribbons untied. The fire was warm enough for Fred to break the ice in their water jug and start making tea.

Charles lifted the lamp to the mute woman's face. Her poor skin had suffered terrible damage. One cheek had been badly burned and the wounds were only starting to heal. "Are you a friend of Lizzie Porter?"

"Who is that?" Fred asked.

"The maid who died. Timothy's mother."

"I am Lizzie Porter," she said in a hoarse voice.

"What?" Charles gasped. His hands went as cold as the maid's. The poor, broken soul in front of him was Timothy's mother? "Not dead?"

"Lord Salisbury's steward told me where to find you. You sent a letter? They took up a collection at Hatfield House to send me here, the servants, that is. I'd lose my position if the master knew about my Timmy."

Charles's teeth chattered, either from nerves or from the cold. Gratitude that one of his letters about Timothy had hit the mark made him want to sag in relief. "How did you survive? I was told you had died."

"Those who found me didn't know who I was at first. I was unconscious. Some rescuers took me to the charity hospital nearby, but they weren't any who knew me, see? I just left two days ago. Is my boy here? Is he—" She put her fist to her face.

Charles could see more burns on her wrist. He reassured her quickly. "He is fine, Miss Porter. You needn't worry. I had a rough time with him that first day but I found him a good home and an excellent wet nurse."

Her lips trembled. Charles helped her to sit while Fred poured boiling water into their teapot. He handed her a handkerchief, not wanting her tears to touch that burned cheek. "You are a miracle, a real miracle."

"I've been livin' a nightmare," she sobbed. "I thought he might be dead. What a little fool Madge is."

"Why was she so sure I was Timothy's father?" Charles asked, clearly, so his brother would hear.

Fred paused with his hand still holding the rag-handled kettle.

"My man's name were Dickinson," she said with a sniff. "Oh, he's dead, run over by a cart in Hertford. He was a delivery man, see."

"Did your sister know him?"

"She saw him once, on her half day. She were invited up to the house. Yer a bit like him, sir, slight with dark curly hair."

Charles sighed. "I'm sorry he died."

"Never even saw the baby," she sniffed. "Dead three months before he came. He'd promised to marry me, soon as 'e could afford his own cart."

Charles nodded, then glanced up at Fred. His brother inclined his head. At least he had Fred back on his side.

"Can you afford to take care of him?" he asked, blowing on his icy hands. "Your mistress died in the fire."

"I'm a good worker. The master told the housekeeper I could train in the kitchen. Maybe be a cook someday." She paused. "Since I took good care of his mother."

"You have a safe home for Timothy? He's thriving in his current placement."

"I have to have him close to me," she said, tears welling again. "You talked to the family who had him to foster before, at the stable yard? They didn't know you so they didn't tell you the truth. They'll take him back. I can afford it, coz they're cousins o' mine."

Charles nodded. He'd suspected as much, though the family had been closemouthed at the time. Would Julie accept the loss of the baby she'd cared for during these past weeks? He hoped her own child would be born safely, to ease empty arms.

"Drink your tea," he suggested, "and we'll bundle you up again and take you to him."

Charles didn't even have to ask Fred to assist when the tea was gone. He helped Lizzie with her shawls and even suggested she take off her boots so he could insulate them with fresh newspaper for warmth.

They walked through more merriment on the streets. Charles, feeling better about everything, bought sprigs of holly from his match girl. She pinned them to the lapels of his and Fred's coats, and on the side of Lizzie's bonnet. The young mother smiled for the first time at the little gift.

Outside the Cheapside building, parishioners streamed in and out of the church opposite, while the air smelled of smoke and meat from the chophouse, doing a brisk business in bachelor meals. Charles and Fred pulled Lizzie up the stairs between them, careful to touch nothing but her hands, since neither of them knew the extent of her wounds. Charles had asked enough questions of Hatfield's local doctors when he was writing his article on the fire to know she hadn't suffered the worst kind of burns, since she had somewhat recovered in a little less than a month.

He knocked on the Agas' door. No one responded right away and he was about to try across the passage when William opened up.

"Happy Christmas!" he said with surprise. "Is this another mudlark?"

Charles shook his head, but Fred spoke before he could. "It's Timothy's mother! Charles isn't his father, she said so."

William sagged against the door. "You are Miss Lizzie Porter, returned to life?"

She gave William a little curtsey. "Yes, sir. May I see my baby?"

William smiled at her, but Charles could see the sorrow in his friend. He led them to the fire and insisted Lizzie take one of the good armchairs. After, he went into the bedroom. Julie came out, followed by Lucy, carrying the baby, wide eyed despite the hour.

"Five months now," Charles said with a flourish of his hand as the baby was presented.

"He's changed so much," Lizzie whispered reverently.

Julie seemed to understand at once who this visitor was. She gestured to Lucy, who placed Timothy in Lizzie's arms. The young mother winced a bit, as he must have been put down on a burn, but she rearranged him and smiled tenderly at her son. Baby Timothy freed a hand from his wrappings and waved it in the air. Lizzie kissed the little fingers. A tear rolled down the scarred cheek.

"It's Dickinson, not Dickens," Fred announced. "The sister had it wrong."

"Oh," William breathed.

"She's likely related to half the village," Charles said. "They didn't want to tell secrets, and poor Mr. Dickinson has been dead these eight months, and was from another town besides."

"You've got to tell Mr. Hogarth," William said. "Right now, tonight. Don't spoil Kate's Christmas."

Fred nodded effusively. "It's ever so important to know Charles was telling the truth."

Charles hesitated. He'd have to take this poor girl and the babe into the cold again.

"I have bricks heating," Julie said with an intensity he hadn't seen in her for quite some time. "William will get a carriage or you won't go, but I agree. Kate deserves to have the truth told to her parents."

Charles looked at her, really looked. She squared her shoulders and proudly put her hand on her own stomach. Was it rounded? He wasn't entirely sure, given the heaviness of her winter gown. Nodding, he mouthed his thanks as William agreed to see if a carriage could be found on Christmas Eve.

"I don't like the odds," William said, as he layered on gloves and comforters. "All of London is visiting or churching on a night like this."

"Go to Mr. Screws," Charles said. "Tell him it's an emergency. He keeps his own coach and he owes me an errand of mercy."

They settled in to wait for William's return, drinking hot apple cider. Fred darted around like a housefly, checking windows, while Lizzie sat in the center of it all, placid with the baby.

"How will she feed the child on the road?" Julie asked Charles in a low voice. "Her milk will be gone by now. Or will you bring her back here tonight?"

"It will depend on what Mr. Screws gives William permission to do," Charles responded. "If we can have use of his carriage for a day, we can get them home without additional cost."

"He'll need milk," Lucy said. "I know someone who keeps a goat, just about ten minutes' walk from here."

Charles gave her the money. The girl took a jug and ran out the door. She returned just as Fred called that William had stepped down from a coach in front of the chophouse.

Charles took the jug and a bundle that Julie handed him, complete with food, hot bricks, and a drinking cup. Fred pulled on his coat and helped Lizzie with her shawls while Julie and Lucy took turns whispering good-bye to the now sleeping infant.

"He was fed just before you came," Julie told Charles. "He needs milk again in about five hours."

"It will be tricky, but she'll have to manage," he responded.

"I could go with her," Lucy cried. "To help, and come back to London on the coach."

No one had considered the girl's feelings, or the fact that Timothy was her employment. "Lizzie?" Charles asked. "Would you like a helper on the way to Hatfield?"

"If she wants to come I'd be 'appy," Lizzie said. "But I don't 'ave the money for another fare."

"There won't be a fare at all," Julie said. "Go downstairs with them, Lucy, and do what William says."

She nodded and everyone streamed out of the door, leaving her in their wake. Charles glanced back but Julie seemed at peace, her hand back on her stomach. He shook his head and found himself grinning as he followed everyone down to the coach.

By the time they arrived in Brompton the hour had grown late. Both of the girls yawned and the baby woke. Charles told Mr. Screws's coachman he'd bring him food and drink before he had to drive to Hatfield and they'd only be a little while. He could see that the upstairs lights were already out.

Resolutely, and followed by everyone, he opened the gate and walked up the front walk, hoping someone would wake upstairs and then lights would go on with the commotion.

Instead, when he rapped on the door, it opened right away. Mr. Hogarth stood with a lamp, still in his clothes. He looked exhausted, even the hair of his muttonchops fluffed out.

"It's ye, is it?" the editor said, "the cause of our holiday disfavor, come to life?"

"I am sorry for it, sir, but I told you the truth, and I can prove it."

Mr. Hogarth stepped back, sighing, and let them enter. His gaze moved over Fred, who grinned merrily, and Lizzie, resting on her burned cheek, then to the baby and Lucy.

"Could Kate come down?" Charles asked.

"No, Charles. She's gone to bed after crying her way through services. I won't wake her."

He took them into the dining room. "Fred, can you stir up the fire?"

A sleepy maid peered out of the kitchen. Charles asked her to provide a hot drink and sandwiches for the coachman outside. She nodded and shut the baize door.

"Are you going to Hatfield?" Mr. Hogarth asked.

"Miss Porter is taking her son home. Lucy is going along to help her," Charles said. He made the introductions.

"He's a precious bairn," Mr. Hogarth said roughly after taking a longer look at Timothy. "Dark hair like yers, Charles."

"'is father were called John Dickinson," Lizzie said. "We were to be married but 'e was kilt afore we could. I never saw this man, Mr. Dickens, until tonight. My sister told me what she'd done. She's a bit touched, my Madge. I'm very sorry for the trouble."

"We thought ye died," Mr. Hogarth said, a gentler tone now.

"I were in the 'ospital. No one knew because the man who took me were from another village, and I didn't come 'ome for almost a month. I didn't even know 'er ladyship 'ad died." She sniffed and wiped her eyes on Timothy's blanket.

"Is this the truth, Charles?" Mr. Hogarth asked.

"As I know it." He looked the man right in the eye. "I have told you the rest, how I'd never been to Hatfield until the paper sent me there."

Mr. Hogarth pulled out his pipe, his gaze going to the stem. "Very well. Ye can return to work after the first of the year."

Charles wished he were in a position to turn the offer down after what he'd suffered. He knew Mr. Screws didn't expect him to stay on, though, and he wasn't suited for the counting-house life. His head was too full of stories, and if his book sold well, an entirely new world could open for him. One with novels and plays and every form of writing. "Thank you. And Kate?"

"I will speak to her in the morning." Mr. Hogarth clenched his teeth around his pipe stem.

Charles nodded. The kitchen maid brought out a jug and a wrapped package. "Then I will say good night. Miss Porter and Lucy have a long journey tonight." He handed the items to Lucy and she gently propelled her charges out of the room.

Mr. Hogarth hesitated, then said, "What about you?"

"Fred and I will walk as far as we have to, and hopefully find a conveyance. I need to see Mr. Screws and tell him when he can expect to see his carriage again." Fred stepped next to Charles and squared his shoulders in line with his older brother's.

"Very well. I'll have my daughter write ye." Mr. Hogarth lit his pipe.

"Are you sure you don't want to wake her?" Fred asked. "It's such good news. They can be married now."

Mr. Hogarth patted Fred on the arm. "Nae, not at this hour."

Charles wanted to turn away, but he much preferred to be in Mr. Hogarth's good graces. Recent events had taught him how much power the man retained over his life. He took a deep breath and said, "I look forward to resuming our pleasant personal and professional relationship. I am sorry if this situation gave you any personal embarrassment, but I had to do what was right for this poor child."

Mr. Hogarth sighed. "Ye should have brought the child to us that night."

"What would you have done with him if I had?" Charles asked. "He was in a fragile state. You have no wet nurse across the hall here, nor sympathy for an illegitimate child. The baby is not at fault for the misfortune of his parents."

Flames licked tobacco as Mr. Hogarth lit his pipe. "Ye are right far too often, Charles." He smiled around his pipe. "Yet look at all the trouble caused."

"We had better go." Charles took Mr. Hogarth's proffered

hand in a firm grip, then gestured to his brother. When they went outside, Lizzie and Timothy were already in the carriage.

"What will I do now, Charles?" Lucy asked in a whisper. Her words flew from her mouth like smoke on the biting air.

"I'm sure Julie will continue to need you. For now, enjoy the adventure. A Christmas trip to Hatfield and back." Charles reached into his pocket and gave her his last two shillings.

She smiled and waved shyly at Fred, then climbed up. The coachman called to the horses. In his high-crowned beaver hat and red coat, he looked a lot like Father Christmas. The old team had been with the old driver for so long that he didn't even need his whip to get them moving.

Charles smiled at his fanciful thoughts and turned away.

"Let me guess, you gave her all your money, didn't you?" Fred asked.

Charles wiggled his fingers in his gloves. "She might need it during her travels. We can walk and think about Mary and Joseph's journey to Bethlehem. This is nothing." He hesitated, wanting to go to the side of the house and throw pebbles at Kate's window, but he didn't want Mr. Hogarth to catch him.

Fred followed him past the Jewish burying ground next door to the Hogarths' house. Few people were out walking here and fog brushed at them as they walked toward London.

"We'd better find a hackney before we lose visibility," Fred said.

"No money," Charles sang.

"I have enough." Fred broke into a rousing rendition of "God Rest Ye Merry Gentlemen" that had a passerby step back in surprise.

Charles reached for his brother's arm and pulled him on. "Not next to a graveyard. It's in poor taste."

"Look, isn't that a hackney?" Fred asked, ceasing his warbling and pointing into the swirling fog.

"A phantom hackney or a real one?" Charles pushed his curls out of his eyes and back under his hat so he could see.

Fred blinked. "I think I imagined it. Let's walk more quickly, shall we?"

"I thought Lizzie Porter might have been a phantom tonight," Charles mused aloud as they trotted. He slowed down. "I cannot keep up this pace."

"Too many mince pies," Fred snorted, but he slowed down, too.

"I have to tell you about the curious case of Mr. Fletcher today." He beguiled them both with the story of the American confidence man.

"Zooks," Fred exclaimed. "Is he the murderer?"

Charles shrugged. "No one seemed to think so. The Americans seemed to know about confidence men." The gears of his mind worked, a water wheel seeming to sluice facts for his perusal. "What if he was the ghost that night? A confidence man might know the sort of tricks that could break a window like that."

"He could have had an accomplice," Fred suggested.

Charles squinted. A public house, windows bright with light, the shadowy figures of men hoisting glasses, and the sounds of carol singing tempted him, but he pressed on with feet and thoughts. "I do believe his height matched that of the ghost."

"A confidence man might have a kit of disguises, I suppose," Fred added.

"Why not?" Charles asked, pulling his brother to the street. A hackney cab had just pulled up to the public house and disgorged a couple of drunken young fools, holly sprigs in their caps. "Hold up," he called to the bundled driver, and climbed into the open cab, followed by Fred. It would be a chilly ride, but at least they would reach Mr. Screws more quickly.

The driver whistled to his horse. "Bit of a slow ride tonight, sirs, what with the fog."

The rocking of the carriage soothed the brothers into a daze. Charles and Fred both pulled their mufflers over their mouths and noses and burrowed as deeply into their hats and coats as they could. The driver amused himself by nipping from a flask and singing bits of old country carols. After he ran out of holiday tunes, he began to sing drinking songs, after begging their pardon. A couple of songs in, he started one about a Covent Garden actress.

"Wait a minute," Charles exclaimed, half a verse in. He had remembered something. "Driver, take us to Maiden Lane, first."

"Very good, sir. We aren't past it yet," the driver said, taking another swig from his flask.

Chapter 22

Fred stirred next to Charles. His brother had been half asleep on the coach's seat despite the bitter Christmas Eve chill, rocked by the motion of the moving vehicle. "Why do you want to go to Covent Garden?"

"I remembered Julie told me about the actress Amelia Osborne. What if Mr. Fletcher's fiancée really is that same woman? Julie told me where she lived. She'd been there for a party."

"An actress could play a ghost," Fred agreed, sitting up. "If either she or the American played the specter, wouldn't that mean they were the killers?"

"No." Charles's brain churned. "I was warned to leave the Screws household alone. No confidence man would want me prying."

"He has a good reason to kill, though, at least he might," Fred said. "What if Mr. Harley discovered what Mr. Fletcher was up to?"

"We still don't know what that was," Charles pointed out as the cab turned onto Maiden Lane. "Presumably he was learning enough of the business in England to know how to fleece people, though there is no sign of him having done anything yet."

"Except two men are dead," Fred said. "And he was practically running the place as a result. He didn't even need to be the heir."

"You're right," Charles said slowly. "He just needed to have authority. People who loan money have a great deal of power. It is an excellent way to gain wealth. It is a confidence game if you lend money to people who will never be able to do more than pay off the interest."

Fred sucked on his teeth loudly as the horse stopped in front of a dilapidated building. "The actress must not be wealthy."

"There is a chance we have the wrong woman," Charles said, glancing up at the stone façade. A lamppost stood in front, emanating enough gaslight for him to see cracked windows with rags stuffed through in an attempt to keep winter out.

"It is a boardinghouse, not a fine address," Fred said. Light glinted off a sign before the fog swirled and obscured it.

"Let's go in," Charles said. "Pay the driver, please."

They both hopped down as a crowd passed by, staggering a bit as they sang "I Saw Three Ships." One of the girls was dancing and grabbed Charles's hands, attempting to spin him around. He spun her into one of her friends. They both giggled and danced away.

When Charles glanced at the building, he noticed a face in the window above the dressmaker's shop Julie had mentioned, an old woman in a lace cap. He waved at her and she opened her window.

"Wot?" she demanded.

"I hope you are having an excellent Christmas, madam," he said. "I wonder do you have a Miss Osborne in residence?"

"I might," she said suspiciously.

"She's about my age, very slim and pretty, with dark hair. Dresses in quite a flashy style, like her fiancé, who is an American?"

The old woman sniffed. "She's not at home this evening."

Charles nodded. "Thank you."

He pulled Fred down the street. "Let's go into the mews and see if we can find a way in, out of prying eyes."

"What are you hoping to find?"

"Maybe we can find the cloak the specter wore that night," Charles suggested. "I helped Mr. Fletcher pack up his room at Mr. Screws's house, but it wasn't there."

They went around to the back of the buildings. The mews held none of the delightful scents or sounds of the holiday. Despite the cold, it reeked of decaying garbage. Charles counted the buildings. Miss Osborne's had been the third.

"Do we know which rooms we are looking for?" Fred asked, as Charles pulled open the back door.

"Julie told me where the party was."

The door led immediately to the back steps. This had probably been a single-family home in some century past and these had been the servants' stairs. He went up to the second floor and pushed open the door that led to the main passage. "The party was in the front," he whispered.

Fred lit a lucifer. "Four doors. Was she on the left or right?"

"Above the dressmaker's shop," Charles said. "Top of the house."

"It ran the length of the building."

Charles bit off a curse. "You're right. Let's try the rooms on the left, because the ones on the right are above the old woman and she might hear our footsteps." He went to the door and rattled the knob. It twisted under his fingers.

Holding a finger to his lips, he pushed open the door. Behind him, the match went out. He blinked, his eyes not sure what was in front of him. Eventually, he could discern a little light from the windows in the front of the room. He stood very still and listened for breathing, but heard none.

Gesturing Fred in, he lit a lucifer of his own. "How many rooms?"

Fred pointed to a cavernous darkness. "Must be at least one more."

Charles crept into the darkness, illuminating a little more with each step. A fainting couch, upholstered in faded velvet; a table piled with scripts; a cracked vase, pretty but empty.

"Scripts," Fred said. "We must be in the right place."

Charles put his finger to his lips again as his lucifer burned down. He held it in the open doorway and saw a bed, empty and neatly made. Quickly, he went to the plain candleholder next to a washbasin and lit the stub of candle.

"No one's here," Fred said.

Charles circled the room. The only other piece of furniture was a wardrobe. He opened it and recognized the dress Miss Osborne had worn the night he'd met her.

The evidence was clear. Mr. Fletcher's fine miss and Julie Aga's actress were one and the same. He grabbed a box at the bottom of the wardrobe and opened it up, holding the candle high. It appeared to be letters.

He pulled out the box and brought it to the bed. "Fred, come and help me look through these."

He and Fred stood shoulder to shoulder. Holding the candle between them, they flipped through the letters.

"Actress," Fred confirmed, setting a letter on the yellowed coverlet. "This is from a theater just near here, confirming a part last year."

"Mr. Vail was correct," Charles said, finding a folded notice from an American theater. He set it in the box. "I don't see Mr. Fletcher's possessions here. But what about that ghostly cloak?"

Fred went back to the wardrobe and hunted around. "Just women's clothing."

Charles went to the doorway and stood, looking for hiding places. The floor, just tired wood boards, seemed nailed down and there was only minimal furniture. With a sigh, he went down on his still sore knees and crawled under the bed.

"Blasted woman!" he cried, coming out with a wadded lump of dark wool.

When Fred spread it out on the bed, they both could see the greasepaint marks in the hood.

"Mr. Fletcher's begging for a second chance was a total act. He was in cahoots with Miss Osborne all along. They are confidence men," Charles declared.

"But are they murderers?" Fred asked, wiping the greasepaint smeared on his gloves back onto the wool.

"Or simply thieves?" Charles added.

"Just thieves."

The Dickenses whipped around at the sound of the seductive female voice. They'd been discovered.

Chapter 23

Amelia Osborne stood in the doorway of her bedroom. As Charles and Fred watched, she let her blood-red hood slide off her glossy hair. Her cloak fell down her bare shoulders and puddled on the floor. She unpinned her hair as they watched, open mouthed. Long tendrils of curling chestnut flowed over her creamy skin, caressing her breasts, scarcely contained in the V-necked evening bodice of bronze lace she wore.

"Y-y-you aren't a k-k-killer?" Fred stammered, peeking a little from behind Charles.

She smiled. Red lip paint made her mouth the most visible feature on her face.

Charles held the candle stub high, trying to keep it steady. "Why did you haunt me? How did you break that window?"

"You are a cool customer, Mr. Dickens." Miss Osborne put a hand on her hip. Her yellow silk skirt swished as her legs shifted invisibly underneath. "I like that in a man."

She took a couple of steps closer.

Brave, given that she didn't know if they had weapons. "The ghost was taller," Charles said.

"I know all the tricks of the trade, my dear," she cooed.

"Did Mr. Fletcher destroy the window from below?" he asked.

"I know all about your lost position at the newspaper." She reached out a hand and ran a manicured finger down Charles's shirt. "I like a younger man. How about I give up on Mr. Fletcher and teach you? I bet you wouldn't get caught."

Fred opened his mouth, but Charles quickly held up his hand.

She continued. "Together, we can still take over Mr. Screws's countinghouse. Charles, you are already working for the old man."

"I didn't give you permission to be so familiar," he snapped.

"Oh, Mr. Dickens," she cooed, reaching up and running her long fingernail over his sensitive ear. "You poor dear. I can teach you so much."

His entire body seemed to seize at the intimate gesture. He put up a fist and snarled, "You're a day late. I've been proven innocent and I have my old job back. Besides, I'm an honest man."

Her lips curved. She slid her finger down the side of his face. "There is such violence in you. I like that in a man."

He shoved the candle at Fred. "I may not be a perfect gentleman but I'm not a murderer. Did you kill Mr. Harley and Mr. Pettingill?"

"Of course not, you silly man," she said, soft voiced but cold eyed. "I have an alibi for Mr. Harley's death. Mr. Screws himself was at the dinner table with me that night."

"Who did you and Fletcher pay to do it, then?" Charles demanded. "Johnny Dorset?"

"Don't be silly. I had no need to kill anyone. I had an inside man. We'd have taken over soon enough, with nothing more than doddering old men in charge, or that fool Pettingill."

"When would you ever have met Mr. Screws's nephew?" Charles asked with narrowed eyes.

"Mr. Fletcher had worked there long enough to meet him at various gatherings, with me on his arm, of course."

"He was no fool," Charles said. "A sad loss, I assure you."

"How droll that you want to educate me." She smirked.

"Did Mr. Fletcher kill those men?" Fred asked.

"No." Her eyes went flinty. "He worked hard for those old men. He'd come up in the world under my tutelage, you see. From chophouses to a countinghouse. He fancied he'd be like one of those ancient Lees with their trader businesses in London."

Charles frowned. "I thought they were plantation owners in America."

Miss Osborne lengthened her face and let the tiniest tip of her tongue poke out. "There were a lot of Lees. I could write a book about that ghastly family by now."

Charles's brain rattled through possibilities. She'd admitted she desired to be a criminal, but what had she actually done if she wasn't a killer? She had conspired, but had she achieved anything? "Forgery."

"What?"

"Did you forge those letters to Mr. Screws?" he asked.

Her eyes narrowed into slivers. "We are at an impasse, Mr. Dickens. I could call the night watch and have you arrested for stealing."

He spread his hands. "I've stolen nothing and we are old friends. Also, you are not a respectable person, while I am. No, no one would believe I was guilty of anything." He hardened his voice. "When will Mr. Fletcher be here?"

"I have no idea," she said calmly.

"H-he isn't dead, is he?" Fred asked nervously.

She tittered. "No, silly boy." She leaned closer to him. "Boo!"

Fred jumped back. Charles grabbed her by the arm and shoved her onto the bed. He meant to seat her there, tower over her given that they were about the same height, but instead she relaxed until her torso and head were against the coverlet, her glorious hair spread like Medusa's snakes over the yellowed fabric.

Charles thought of Kate, and Christmas, and Mr. Screws's safety. "We'll leave," he said. "For now."

He grabbed Fred's arm and marched him out.

"Candle?" Fred asked, lifting it.

"Keep it. I wouldn't put it past Mr. Fletcher to ambush us in the dark passage."

They went back to the mews. Charles could see Fred's huge yawn. Around them, bells pealed as the clocks in the churches of London hit midnight.

"Happy Christmas, brother," he said, squeezing Fred's arm.

Fred grinned sleepily at him. "Happy Christmas. What do we do now?"

"Warn Mr. Screws. He won't trust Mr. Fletcher again, but he doesn't know Miss Osborne was the mastermind."

"Won't he be asleep?"

"Elderly people don't sleep well. And Mrs. Pettingill needs to be warned."

"She might be the killer," Fred pointed out. "We can't trust her."

"You were right," Fred said when they arrived at Finsbury Circus. He blew out the candle. "There's a light on."

"Dining room," Charles explained. "Warmest room on the ground floor." He stepped in between bushes in front of the window and knocked at it.

A minute later, Mr. Screws's face appeared at the window. He looked pale and his mouth rounded with fright. Charles waved and the old gentleman pointed to the left, looking annoyed.

They went to the front of the house. A minute later, Mrs. Pettingill opened the door.

"You aren't abed?" Charles asked, then blushed to have asked such an inappropriate question.

"I prefer to stay up and meditate on the Christ Child," she said piously.

"This is my brother, Fred," Charles said.

His brother inclined his head and then they followed the widow into the dining room.

"You must have news," Mr. Screws said, rising wearily to his feet. He wore carpet slippers but otherwise had remained dressed.

"Has something happened, Mr. Screws?" Charles asked. "You look as if you've had a dreadful shock."

"I fell asleep in my chair here, but I woke when the fire died down. And then I saw it, along the wall." The old man trembled.

"Saw what?"

"I saw Jacob Harley's ghost," Mr. Screws whispered, spittle appearing at the edges of his mouth.

Charles drew back instinctively. It couldn't have been Miss Osborne. She'd been with them. No drafts swept through the room. No windows had been broken this time. "In a cloak, like I saw?"

"No, he was a mere shadow in the corner." Mr. Screws pointed his shaking finger again. "But he spoke to me."

"What did he say?"

"That it is time for me to reflect on all I have done in life, before it is too late."

"Anything else?"

"Isn't that enough?" the old man said with a hint of petulance. "I do not wish to meet Our Lord with stains upon my soul. I shall spend the rest of what life is left to me in prayer. I will be like Christian and learn from my mistakes." He lifted a leather-bound volume of *The Pilgrim's Progress* that had been on the table next to him.

"What stains are on your soul, sir?" Charles asked.

"I must make things right with Mrs. Dorset," said Mr. Screws, pushing one hand heavily against the table. "I have done that dear woman a terrible wrong."

"If you write her a letter, I will take it to her," Charles promised. "But that is for another moment, during daylight. I have something important to relate."

He coughed wetly. "What?"

"Sit," Charles insisted. "You must sit first."

Mr. Screws did as he asked.

"Thank you. We found Mr. Fletcher's fiancée this evening and discovered she was an actress, not a lady of quality. She, or possibly Mr. Fletcher himself, played the ghost who warned me to stay away from this house."

"They broke your window," Mrs. Pettingill said. "Surely they were in cahoots."

"My thoughts exactly," Charles confirmed.

"Did he kill Jacob?" Mr. Screws asked with a wheeze.

"You yourself gave them an alibi," Charles pointed out. He poured tea into Mr. Screws's cup and pushed it toward him. "Can you break it?"

Mr. Screws picked up his cup and closed his eyes. After a long, pregnant pause, he said, "I admit that Mr. Fletcher did leave the dining table for an extended period of time the night of Jacob's death."

Fred let out a loud "huh" but Charles shushed him, knowing Mr. Screws had more to impart.

"He claimed some stomach trouble had kept him away."

"He could have killed Mr. Harley?" Mrs. Pettingill asked. "How I wish I had been there that night, Uncle."

Mr. Screws wheezed again and shook his head regretfully. "It was a good twenty minutes before Mr. Harley fell from the window."

"Some misdirection," Charles said. "Could he have started a sort of slow strangulation that led to Mr. Harley falling twenty minutes later?" That must have been what happened. Mr. Fletcher had done it somehow.

Mr. Screws bowed his head. "I know not, but your brother's head is nodding."

Fred sat up abruptly, then let out an enormous yawn. "We won't leave you, sir, not with these confidence people on the loose."

"I should hunt down Mr. Fletcher now," Charles said. "I'm sure he killed your friend and nephew, Mr. Screws."

"Sleep first," Mr. Screws said. "You can't bring back our lost ones. No need to make yourself ill."

Charles nodded. "We'll stay downstairs. Mrs. Pettingill, if we light a fire in the drawing room we can sleep in there."

She stood. "A blessed idea. I will light the fire if you take Uncle upstairs."

Charles helped Mr. Screws to his feet and together they tottered up the stairs. When he had the old man in bed with his curtains drawn against the cold, he went back downstairs and spread himself out across the sofa while Fred stole all the chair cushions and made himself a nest in front of the fire.

Charles smiled to himself as he fell asleep. He'd find Mr. Fletcher in the morning, and then once that was sorted, he'd see Kate.

Charles woke early Christmas morning with a light heart and a sore back. The fire had gone out, so he stepped over Fred, who was wrapped in his coat, and did his best to get a blaze going again, then left the drawing room in search of the kitchen.

A kitchen maid still slept in front of the fire there. She stirred when Charles entered and sleepily went to fetch water to start tea for the household. Charles lit the hanging lamps since only a watery winter light came in through the windows even after he opened the curtains. He found a wrapped loaf of bread and cut a slice for himself.

Outside, he heard the ring of metal against something. Was the fog carrying carriage noises across the mews? He went back to the window.

In the garden, he saw the shadowy shape of a man and a shovel. Charles's senses heightened. He sincerely doubted any gardener worked on December twenty-fifth. Grabbing a long roller meant for pastry work, he unlatched the back door and went out onto the paved area between the house and the garden.

Squinting through the gloom, he could only see the back of the man. He continued forward, holding his rolling stick in both hands. The man looked up as he approached.

Despite the cap and thick gray muffler, he recognized Mr. Fletcher. The murderer had come to call. What was he after?

The American recognized him, too. He yelled something, maybe a Virginia war cry, and rushed at Charles with the shovel.

Charles feinted back, lifting his stick. "What are you doing here?"

"Looking for the money, you fool!" Mr. Fletcher came at him again, ululating something that sounded right out of the Welsh Marches this time.

Charles lifted his stick with a two-handed grip, clashing it against the wood above the shovel bowl. The old shovel wood splintered. Calling his stagecraft into memory, what he'd learned during his brief attempt to train as an actor, he jabbed with his stick as if it were a sword, placing his other arm in a fencing posture, and broke the shovel handle in two.

Mr. Fletcher, still light on his feet, threw the shovel handle directly at Charles's head. The metal hit him with a glancing blow. He stumbled back, dazed. Mr. Fletcher ran toward the shed.

Behind him, a female shrieked.

"Get the police!" Charles called to the maid, holding his head, then took off after the American. He didn't have his coat on, and his shoes slid through the muddy paths as he careened around them. Realizing he was being a fool, he took off across the grass. If Mr. Fletcher found more weapons, who knew how much longer his rolling stick would last?

Mr. Fletcher rattled the lock on the shed, then kicked at the door with his foot. Charles, acting with instinct, threw the rolling stick at the man's back. It stunned him and he fell to his knees.

Charles raced forward and grabbed the rolling stick before Mr. Fletcher could. He tugged the man's coat down to his elbows, imprisoning his arms.

"Charles!" Fred yelled behind him. He came pell-mell across the yard.

"Check him for weapons," Charles wheezed, holding Mr. Fletcher against the door.

Fred checked coat pockets in three layers of clothes. "Nothing."

"Check his boots," Charles suggested.

Fred came up with a knife holstered in a boot top.

"Be reasonable, Charles," their prisoner said. "I was looking for money, not trying to kill anyone."

"I know you were the ghost," Charles said in Mr. Fletcher's ear. "Miss Osborne offered to cut you out of your scheme after you were thrown out and take me on, instead."

"What?" Mr. Fletcher shrieked and bucked. One arm came out of his imprisoning sleeve and he flailed widely. Charles wasn't prepared and he fell back, still dizzy from the blow earlier. Fred held him up.

"Yes," Charles pressed. "You've lost. You're a failure. Your puppet master is done with you." He grabbed Mr. Fletcher's free arm and spun him around. His head hit the wooden shed door hard. Charles watched his teeth crunch into his lower lip.

That had to hurt. He took the knife from Fred and brandished it at the American.

Fred crossed his arms over his scrawny chest and glared in tandem with Charles.

The other man swore and pulled his coat back up over his other arm, blood trickling from his cut lip. "After everything I've done!" he growled. "I left America for that bitch."

"And your beloved Lee plantations," Charles mocked.

"She was happy." Mr. Fletcher's voice rose. "She said she was happy!"

"No woman likes a man who has lost his position," Charles pointed out.

"I killed for her," Mr. Fletcher said. "Killed. For. Her."

"I know," Charles said, vindicated by the confession. He wanted to dance around, but stayed in control. "Your greed made finding you easy. Thank you for that. We can enjoy our Christmas."

"Why did you kill Mr. Harley?" Fred asked.

"He was a drain on the business." The man's voice rose again. "Then Screws had the audacity to bring in his weakling of a nephew."

"Did Miss Osborne order the murders?" Fred asked.

"She was willing for me to do anything to make her rich. He's rich, you know, Screws. A miser. He buries chests in the garden here, then gloats over the map of his burials late at night. I couldn't kill him or I'd lose access to this treasure trove." He lifted his coatless arm in a sweep over the landscape.

Charles understood why the plantings were so underdeveloped. Their roots didn't have a place to spread. He didn't know how much money waited under the soil, but Mr. Fletcher's words matched what Mr. Screws had said.

Mr. Fletcher's eyes moved in their sockets. Charles could see he was looking for a way to run. Unfortunately, he didn't know how many constables were walking their beats today. He held up the knife again, the threat obvious.

"We can't let him get away," Charles whispered to Fred. He spoke louder. "Out of curiosity, how did you break my window that night?"

"She did it," Mr. Fletcher said, drawing himself up. "From

outside. If you think to have me thrown in prison, I assure you she is just as guilty. I expect her to hang at my side."

"Such tattered dignity," Charles mocked, more alert to danger than he'd ever been in his life. "As if I don't know you are going to try to escape, and if you don't, you'll be attempting to take the guards into your confidence. I almost saw through you so many times, and then you'd pull me in again with your games."

"Do you know Amelia tried to kill you, Charles?" the American said with a sneer.

Fred's mouth dropped open. "When?"

He shifted from side to side. "She followed Charles and was the one to push him into the path of the carriage, afraid that he was going to reveal our plans." He turned his head to Charles. "You aren't as intelligent as you think you are, blaming that half-wit Dorset boy."

Chapter 24

Charles bristled at Mr. Fletcher's insult. "I certainly am exactly as intelligent as I think I am." *A genius, really.* Bending his knees, he picked up a rock he'd spotted and handed it to Fred as a weapon.

"Amelia Osborne is the truly evil one," Mr. Fletcher opined, his eyes still fixed on the knife Charles held. "My life in America didn't have much future because of my father's bad reputation, and when I met Miss Osborne, she shared her dream of becoming a fine London lady. Bit by bit, she put me on the path to destruction."

"It's not the act of a gentleman to blame a lady for his sins," Charles said.

The American snorted. "After we came to London together, I was working as a waiter in a London club when I heard Mr. Harley and Mr. Screws discussing the need to bring in a younger partner.

"She forged the letter giving me the credentials I'd heard the men discussing so I could go to the countinghouse. Mr. Screws gave me the position and Miss Osborne began to plot how I could take over the entire valuable business."

Charles felt rain drip on his bare head. He shivered. "How did Mr. Harley die?"

Mr. Fletcher smirked. "Will you let me go if I tell you?"

Charles shrugged. "That's not to say we won't send the police after you."

Fred went wide eyed, but Charles hadn't offered to release the man. In fact, he picked up another rock just to make his point clear.

The American licked his bloody lips, staining his teeth. "I wrapped the chains around a chair. I killed Mr. Harley by strangling him with the chains when I was away from the dinner table."

"But he fell out of the window," Fred exclaimed.

He tried to pull his coat over his shoulders. "The chair tipped over at some point after I'd returned to the dinner table. Mr. Harley fell out the window in front of you. I'd opened it because of the smell of the dead man, hoping to keep the odor from coming down the stairs. Just my bad luck that you were outside at the wrong moment."

"Did you pay the undertaker to hide the body?"

"What is going on?!" Mrs. Pettingill shrieked from the kitchen door.

"Send for a constable," Charles called. "We've caught our killer."

"But you said you wouldn't," Mr. Fletcher protested.

"You imagined that," Charles said. "Where is the body?"

The door slammed behind them as Mr. Fletcher said, "Mr. Harley's body is in a crypt under the church across the street. We stole it in the hopes of keeping Mr. Screws off-kilter." He giggled. "We won't see that undertaker again anytime soon. Paid him from Mr. Harley's own cashbox."

Disgusting. While Mr. Fletcher may have been the charm and muscle of the con operation, Miss Osborne must have been the brain. "Help me get Mr. Fletcher into the house. We all need to get out of the rain."

Fred was bare headed as well, and rain dripped into his face. Together, they reached for Mr. Fletcher's arms and dragged him into the house. He fought, attempting to head-butt Charles and kick Fred, but between the two of them they managed to get him into the kitchen, where Mrs. Pettingill had rope ready to tie him up.

They were both huffing and puffing by the time the deed was done. Charles had never noticed how large the man's hands were, or how strong his arms. No wonder it had not been difficult for Fletcher to overpower an ill and elderly man.

"The kitchen girl has gone to fetch the police," she said, making expert knots around Mr. Fletcher's arms and a ladder-backed chair after the Dickenses coiled the rope in all the most strategic places.

"I'd like some coffee," Mr. Fletcher said pitiably, but he was ignored.

"I hope the constable comes soon," Charles said. "We have much to tell him about Mr. Fletcher and Miss Osborne. After that, we need to change and go to our parents' home."

"You'd be home much sooner if you let me go," Mr. Fletcher offered with a dazzling grin.

He looked much older and smaller when soaking wet and tied to a chair. Charles no longer enjoyed the man's jests. "Do you have a handkerchief you could stuff into his mouth?" he asked Mrs. Pettingill in his most pleasant tone.

Before Charles left the Screws household, he obtained Mrs. Dorset's address from the cook. He and Fred went home and changed as soon as they had explained to the constable and Mr. Screws what had happened in the back garden, what Mr. Fletcher had said, and where to find Mr. Harley's corpse, if not the undertaker who had gone missing.

After a calm holiday with the Dickens clan, wherein Charles thrilled his family with the story of Mr. Fletcher's dastardly plan to take over the lucrative countinghouse, and delighted them with the news that he'd proven himself to be an honest man and had his position at the newspaper back, he went out again, alone this time.

He found Mrs. Dorset at her sister's home in Camden Town, near the canal. Her sister's husband worked on a boat, and the small two-story house had a briny scent to it. The former housekeeper received him in the small parlor in the front, a fire being especially lit for the occasion.

"I have a letter for you, ma'am, from Mr. Screws," he told her, after her sister, a shrinking woman with Johnny Dorset's protruding eyes, brought in a tea tray, nearly dropped it after tripping over Charles's foot, apologized, and ran out again.

"Why are you in charge of Mr. Screws's business?" she asked acidly, her hands remaining in her black-clad lap.

"Come, Mrs. Dorset. Weren't we friends once? It was your son who threatened me," he coaxed.

She took the letter when he offered it again.

"There we are," Charles said. "I have been acting as Mr. Screws's private secretary over the holidays."

Mrs. Dorset glanced at him before returning her spectacled eyes to the letter. An expression of delight grew on her careworn face, but then, worry wiped out the happiness. "Mr. Screws is offering me my position back. What has changed?"

"Mr. Fletcher killed Mr. Harley and Mr. Pettingill. He killed the old man by strangling him with the chains during the dinner. He had opened the window, and somehow Mr. Harley's body fell out while we were caroling. We were all fooled by the belief that he had died when he fell from the window, instead of somewhat earlier."

Mrs. Dorset looked to the plain cross over the fireplace and murmured a prayer. "Mr. Pettingill?"

"Everyone thought Mr. Fletcher was so busy at work, but all he had to do was close his door and climb out the window to return to Finsbury Circus."

"Will Johnny be able to return to the house, too?"

"Don't you think you should send him to the country? To work on a farm, maybe?" Charles asked.

Mrs. Dorset poured tea with a shaking hand. "I could not be apart from my boy, Mr. Dickens. I love him and he loves me."

"I think Mr. Screws might be able to love you himself, if you gave him your attention."

She set down the teapot so abruptly that the table rattled. "I want no man. After what's been done to me by men, I'd be just as happy to retire if I had the slightest infirmity. But the Lord has blessed me with strength, you see, so I had best return to work, if my Johnny can stay in the carriage house like before."

"He can," Charles verified. "I am sorry for any way in which I pointed the finger at him."

Mrs. Dorset inclined her head. "Mr. Fletcher is a slippery one. I didn't suspect him myself. I still don't see why he did it."

"He wanted control of the countinghouse." Charles explained the man's history. "Now, I must go, but I hope you accept Mr. Screws's offer. He needs you."

"I will write him today, Mr. Dickens. You needn't wait for my reply."

"His coachman drove me here. I'm sure Mr. Screws wanted me to return with your response."

"Very well. Drink your tea while I write." Mrs. Dorset rose and took the letter to a small writing case.

"May I borrow a sheet of paper?" Charles asked.

She handed him a sheet. He wrote on it in pencil while she scribbled a few words on the back of Mr. Screws's letter and handed it to Charles after she had sealed it into the envelope.

"Will you return immediately?" Charles asked.

"Yes." She forced a smile. "Johnny is eating my sister and her husband out of their home. I will see you in Finsbury Circus soon."

Charles returned to the coach outside with the letters.

"Back to Mr. Screws?" the man asked.

"No. I want you to take me to York Place in Brompton first, and then you can return us to the mews." Charles sealed his letter while the coachman coaxed his horses south, and then he dozed in the comfortable carriage until they were on Fulham Road.

He had the coachman stop at the Hogarths' house and jumped down. "I'll just be a minute."

No word had come from Kate, but there had been no time for any. He thought he'd preempt her joyous resurrection of their engagement with his own note.

When he knocked on the door, hoping his love would answer it, or at least friendly Mary, his own sweet supporter, Mrs. Hogarth answered it, still clad in her navy going-to-church best.

"Good afternoon, Charles," she said.

He greeted her. "I'm sure Mr. Hogarth has told you about the baby, and that it isn't mine," he said. "Does Kate know? Can I see her?"

Mrs. Hogarth shook her head. "This is a sacred day. We've had no talk of such things."

"You obviously know."

"Mr. Hogarth told me," she said calmly.

He thrust his note at her. "Would you please give this to Kate? After she's told the truth? I just want to assure her that my love is still true."

She took the note without saying anything. He hesitated, but he could hardly push past her and shout that he'd solved the murder. Kate might not even be pleased, since she had missed so much of the excitement. Finally, he wished Mrs. Hogarth a happy holiday and returned to the carriage, feeling less like a conquering hero and more like a man who'd been hit on the head with a shovel handle and had to sleep in his clothing without so much as a blanket.

He woke up when the coachman turned into the mews. When he went into the house, he found Mrs. Pettingill reading to Mr. Screws in the parlor from a book of sermons, and they both had peaceful looks upon their faces.

"What are you doing here?" Mr. Screws asked.

"Your voice sounds stronger," Charles said.

"The danger is passed, my boy," Mr. Screws said. "Now that I know the truth. Thank you. Why don't you return to your family for the rest of the day?"

Charles smiled and wished them a peaceful evening. Hopefully, Mr. Screws would live long enough to put Mrs. Pettingill in his will. And Mrs. Dorset as well as the counting-house clerks, like the long-suffering Mr. Cratchit.

He had just reached the front hall when the door opened again and Mrs. Pettingill slipped out. "What is it?"

Mrs. Pettingill smiled uneasily at him. "I want to thank you especially."

"For what?"

She laced her fingers together. "Mr. Fletcher was kind to me and I am very grateful you uncovered the terrible truth before I fell into his clutches."

"Good heavens, I am so glad as well." He shook his head. "Especially since Miss Osborne controlled him."

She nodded. "Women of evil nature are simply the worst. You see it in the Bible. You seem happier, Mr. Dickens."

He smiled broadly. "Never better. It has been a very good Christmas."

"We will see you tomorrow. Come early, mind, because Mr. Screws believes employees should work all the earlier on December twenty-sixth after having a holiday on Christmas."

Charles nodded and opened the front door. Then he remembered and turned. "Tomorrow is Sunday, so I will not be in early tomorrow. But I will be here Monday." He walked outside and stood on the top step, feeling like the mood of Finsbury Circus had changed. Though he'd never be able to come here without seeing that body drop through the upstairs window.

"Mr. Dickens!"

He glanced down and saw the constable on the pavement. Stopping the door from shutting, he told Mrs. Pettingill to look out. "Happy Christmas, Constable Thornton," he said, recognizing the man.

"I just wanted to tell you that we picked up that Osborne woman at her rooms," the constable said. "There shouldn't be any more danger to the household, ma'am."

Mrs. Pettingill clutched her shawl. "Mr. Screws will be so relieved, Constable. Thank you."

She and Charles smiled at each other, and then she went back inside and shut the door.

Whistling, Charles walked to Bloomsbury to join his family for charades. On the street, the mood remained a happy one, even if there were drops of rain instead of cleansing snow. He bought a kissing ball from one girl, and more lucifers from another, then a pie from a third. By the time he arrived in Bloomsbury, his arms were happily burdened with several little gifts for his family.

The next day, after another round of church services, Charles visited the Agas, concerned about what Lucy Fair would do without an infant to tend. He wanted to make sure she had seen her charges safely to Hatfield and that William had agreed to keep her employed.

"Charles!" Julie said when she opened the door. "It has been ever so quiet here these past few days." She had ivy wound into her red hair and her color was very bright.

He smiled at her and handed her a package of fruitcake that his mother had insisted would be good for an expectant mother.

"How kind," she said when Charles had explained. "Your mother is a delightful woman. Did you have a nice Christmas?"

"I solved the murders," Charles said proudly.

"You what?" William came around the corner as Charles took off his coat.

"Make me a hot toddy and I will reveal all," Charles declared as Julie led him close to their fire.

William and Julie sat, enraptured, while Charles dramatized his and Fred's Christmas morning adventure.

"I wish I had been there," Julie fretted. "I have so little amusement these days."

William scoffed. "Training a mudlark to be a maid?" he asked. "Caring for an unexpected foundling?"

She glared at her husband. "It wasn't so long ago that I walked these streets in the night, having my own adventures."

"I am glad those days are over," William said sourly. "Another drink, Charles?"

"Lucy will have a home?" Charles asked.

"We sent her up to my father's school as a special treat for the boys for the week, but Julie will continue to train her as a maid of all work, and she will stay to care for our baby when it is born in May."

Charles exhaled. "I am glad to hear it." Though Julie knew only a little about practical housekeeping, her heart was true and he felt reassured that Lucy Fair had a long-term home.

Charles went home after eating dinner with the Agas, feeling the Boxing Day letdown. He sat in front of his fire that night, working on edits and thinking about writing a novel. He had no use for this much solitude. When would Fred return home? When he heard a knock on the door, his pulse jumped. Then he remembered that all danger had gone. He'd gone out for the evening newspapers and had seen a report that Mr. Harley's body had been recovered.

Thinking maybe it was Aga, or Ainsworth, or even his publisher, he jumped up to open the door.

Instead, it was a smaller form, dainty in an expensive cloak.

"I'd recognize those eyes anywhere, Miss Hogarth," he said gravely.

"Oh, Charles." Kate pushed back her hood and fell into his arms, laughing.

Across the hall the doorway opened and Mr. Whitacre glanced out.

"No phantoms this time. I hope you had a lovely Christmas," Charles called out.

The lawyer looked at him, confused, and shut the door again.

Charles laughed and returned his gaze to Kate. "How did you get here?"

"I used my Christmas money to hire a carriage."

"No chaperone?"

She blushed and shook her head. "I'm your daring girl again, my love."

He pulled her inside and wrapped an arm around her shoulders, speaking into her pink shell of an ear. "I was afraid you were the mere phantom of my hopes and dreams."

She turned until her lips were just a breath apart from his. "No, your goodness has brought me back. My father told us about poor Timothy Dickinson's mother. What a tragic tale."

"Very," he agreed.

"I suggest we marry very soon, so that any further misunderstandings cannot tear us apart," she said, her eyes very bright.

"I will do my best to put my finances in order," he said, leaving unsaid the problems her father had cost him. "But you must promise me something."

"Anything, Charles."

"You must promise you will cleave to me in the future and trust me, not your parents."

"I did trust you, Charles, but I am under their control."

"Not for much longer." He kissed her cheek. "Why don't you make us some tea, and I'll open the tin of fruitcake my mother sent home with me?"

"Very well," she agreed. "But let us spend our private time better than this. It is so rare." She shivered delightfully. "And forbidden."

He winked at her and quoted Shakespeare. "Why, there's a wench! Come on, and kiss me, Kate."

She laughed and dropped her cloak on the ground, then returned to his arms. He rained kisses down on her forehead and cheeks, until he dared to find her soft, rather chilly mouth.

"Oh, Kate," he whispered against her lips. "I was afraid I'd lost my bonny lass."

"Never," she promised. "But wed me quick, before anyone else dies at our feet."

Acknowledgments

I want to thank you, dear reader, for picking up this third book in the A Dickens of a Crime mystery series. If you haven't read the first book, *A Tale of Two Murders*, and the second, *Grave Expectations*, yet, I hope you take the opportunity to enjoy more Dickensian adventures through 1830s London. I am so grateful for the book reviews you wrote and please keep them coming.

Thank you to my beta readers Judy DiCanio, Dianne Freeman, Walter McKnight, Mike Flynn, Eilis Flynn, Cheryl Schy, and Mary Keliikoa on this project. I also thank my writing group for their support: Delle Jacobs, Marilyn Hull, and Melania Tolan. Also, thank you so much to my agent, Laurie McLean, at Fuse Literary, and my Kensington editor, Elizabeth May, for your work on the series, along with many unsung heroes at Kensington.

I have continued to respect the life of Charles Dickens and kept him doing the work and walking the streets that he did during the timeline of my book to the best of my knowledge. Not that I think he was ever an amateur sleuth or worked briefly as a private secretary. My plot is entirely fictitious, as is most everyone in the book.

BOOK CLUB READING GUIDE for

A Christmas Carol Murder

1. Charles Dickens's novella *A Christmas Carol* inspired aspects of this novel. What themes did you recognize? Does reading this book make you want to read or reread Dickens's work?

2. *A Christmas Carol* has been filmed in many ways many times. Which is your favorite version? Do you like it when the comedic aspects are emphasized or the macabre?

3. *A Christmas Carol* is a paranormal tale. Do you expect otherworldly elements to be part of any work that refers back to *A Christmas Carol*?

4. Did you know that Dickens is considered to have brought back the celebration of Christmas to England? What is it about his fiction that stimulated this change?

5. What did you think the addition of the infant Timothy character added to the story? Did Charles do the right thing where he was concerned?

6. How did you react to the Hogarths' behavior around the Timothy rumors? Were you on their side or Charles's?

7. Discuss the Charles/Kate relationship in this book. How did you feel they both handled themselves given the stresses they were under?

8. Usually in fiction of this kind, you'd see characters like the mudlarks appearing to gather information the sleuth could not. Instead, this series has been breaking up the mudlark team and moving them off the foreshore. Why do you think the author approached the mudlark story in this fashion?

9. What do you think the relationship of Mr. Screws and Mrs. Pettingill will be in the future?

10. Did Charles treat Johnny Dorset appropriately? Given the times he lived in, is there anything he could have done differently?
11. Lady Lugoson found herself a new husband in this book. Were you surprised by the person she chose?
12. Which character would you say has changed the most in the series over these three titles? Do you like what has happened to them?

THE PICKWICK MURDERS

Heather Redmond
A Dickens of a Crime

In this latest reimagining of Dickens as an amateur sleuth, Charles is tossed into Newgate Prison on a murder charge, and his fiancée Kate Hogarth must clear his name . . .

London, January 1836: Just weeks before the release of his first book, Charles is intrigued by an invitation to join the exclusive Lightning Club. But his initiation in a basement maze takes a wicked turn when he stumbles upon the corpse of Samuel Pickwick, the club's president. With the victim's blood literally on his hands, Charles is locked away in notorious Newgate Prison.

Now it's up to Kate to keep her framed fiancé from the hangman's noose. To solve this labyrinthine mystery, she is forced to puzzle her way through a fiendish series of baffling riddles sent to her in anonymous poison pen letters. With the help of family and friends, she must keep her wits about her to corner the real killer—before time runs out and Charles Dickens meets a dead end . . .

Look for **The Pickwick Murders** *on sale in November 2021!*

Chapter 1

Eatanswill, somewhere in Essex, January 5, 1836

A bugle blared in Charles Dickens's ear, coming from a raggedy band of marchers passing him on the way to the hustings set up in Eatanswill's market square. Yellow-brown cockades pinned to the lapels of old-fashioned tailcoats and ladies' capes demonstrated that these were the followers of the local Brown party, allied to the Whigs. Charles tipped his hat at a particularly pretty daughter of the voters. She went pink and put her hand in front of her mouth, then dashed to her mother's side. Behind her straggled a couple of young boys, beating drums out of time.

To the right, another group marched between a coal distributer and a cloth merchant's place of business, also routed to the hustings. A streaky royal purple banner attached to a bakery's awning flapped in the bitter January wind. The cloth already shone white at the top, where a light rain had loosened the dye. This must be the Purples, allied to the Tories.

He surveyed the scene from a two-foot rock embedded next

to a public house door. It gave him enough height to see across the Election Day crowd. Would the vote be for Sir Augustus Smirke, the favorite son of the Purples, or go to Vernon Cecil, the darling of the Browns? One or the other would become a Member of Parliament for the first time.

Charles, parliamentary reporter for the liberal *Morning Chronicle* newspaper, hoped Cecil would carry the day. With any luck, a clear majority would offer its voice and the local sheriff could call the election instead of having to schedule a poll some few days in the future, in which case Charles would not be able to go back to London that night. He'd have to write his story and send it on the express mail coach back to the *Chronicle* offices in London.

Resounding "huzzahs" blazed into the air as another phalanx of men appeared between the buildings. He recognized William Whitaker Maitland, the new High Sheriff of Essex, leading the parliamentary candidates, who were followed by their most prominent supporters. Sir Augustus towered over Sheriff Maitland, a man well above average height, with a majestic belly to match. Mr. Cecil did not have the height, though the profusion of gray-streaked reddish curls poofing out from underneath his top hat gave him at least one measure of distinction. Charles knew him to be the son of an important local landowner, but felt unease for his prospects as age and experience were not on the Brown candidate's side.

Shouts came from the left, displaying real alarm this time, instead of pride. A small group of horsemen galloped into the square, coattails fanned out behind them. The first man had a shotgun across his arm and the other half dozen held rakes or hoes as if they were jousters of old, ready to go head to head in battle with other knights. In their workworn attire, they looked like they belonged to the logging or hunting trades in Epping Forest, rather than professions here in town.

The horsemen pressed forward through the crowd of locals. People jumped back or fell in their wake, moving like the wind-blown brown and purple banners that hung on posts jutting from some of the houses. A horse and rider knocked over a boy. The boy screamed, his foot at an odd angle. A man hurried to his side, grabbed him, and hoisted him into the air, settling him on his shoulders.

While Charles had been watching the intruders, the high sheriff and candidates climbed onto the hustings. The tempo-rary stage had bunting in the parties' colors decorating the wooden railing. A lectern, probably borrowed from St. Mary's, a venerable medieval church on the edge of the square, was set up for speeches.

Sheriff Maitland pointed his finger at the gunman as he thun-dered up to the very edge of the husting. "I see you, Wilfred Poor. You and your men are welcome to vote, but not until you hand over that shotgun."

Wilfred Poor lifted the gun and, for a moment, Charles stiff-ened, afraid he would fire at the high sheriff. Instead, Poor fired into the air. The crowd ducked instinctively, including Charles. Initially, pandemonium reigned. But just as quickly as the crowd reacted with screams, they subsided, until the only nearby sound was a dog barking in one of the houses near the church.

Poor lowered the muzzle of his gun until it was pointing into the belly of that giant, Sir Augustus. "Where is my daughter?" he screamed.

Sir Augustus's lips curled, but he said nothing. A trio of his men pushed forward, as if to provoke a reaction, but Sir Au-gustus's long arms spread out, holding them back.

Poor repeated his anguished query, the tendons of his neck in high relief.

"What's wrong, Wilfred?" Sir Augustus mocked. "Can't keep control of your own women folk?"

One of the horsemen chuckled and glanced at the man next to him, his expression changing at the anger in his neighbor's face.

"You aren't much of a man," Sir Augustus said in a teasing lilt.

"Come now, Sir Augustus," one of the horsemen said in a rough country drawl. "Amy's been missing these past three days."

"No one's forgotten she's your maid," added another.

The shotgun, which Charles had not taken his glance from, shook in Poor's hand. The horseman closest to the upset father patted Poor's arm.

"We know you took her," another horseman said to Sir Augustus. "Just give her back and we can get about this business of the election."

"Speech," called a brave soul in the crowd.

The horseman closest to the speaker threw his hoe in that direction. A man fell. Charles craned his neck, looking for blood spill. The high sheriff called for his men, a few local constables hovering around the edges of the bunting, to arrest the rider, but he wheeled his horse around and galloped off before they gathered their wits. One of the constables broke away for crowd control, pushing a couple of women who were attempting to climb the buntings to escape the horsemen. Another knelt next to the fallen man. The last constable raced out of the square in pursuit of the villain on the horse.

Charles whipped his head around when he heard the sheriff call out an order. Charles's brand-new hat caught in a gust, which sent it flying past the window of the public house and down the shadowy street. He leapt off the rock to chase the expensive felted beaver cut in the Regent style. He loathed having to replace it so soon, and in a crowd like this, some light-fingered thief would grab it if he took his eyes off it for even a moment.

He reached out, his fingers just touching the brim before the hat flew again. Stumbling, he put on a burst of speed in front of the open door of a tobacconist and snatched his hat before it tumbled off the pavement and into the dirt road in front of the square.

He glanced up, grinning with his success, and saw a young man, hat lowered over his brows. The lean form and rather worn clothing caught Charles's eye with a note of familiarity. The youth jerked. He straightened, then vanished around the side of the tobacconist's shop, black curls fluttering around his neck.

Charles's thoughts flew back to last summer, and a vegetable plot not far from London's Eaton Square. Curls like that had spilled out from a straw hat worn by the young farmer Prince Moss, so enamored of the cold, beautiful, and amoral Evelina Jaggers.

Charles followed the pavement to an alley passing behind the shop. He stepped in, figuring this was a small town and violent criminals were unlikely to be lurking in alleyways in daylight. The young man had vanished.

Charles surveyed the collection of barrels and rubbish. He heard the crackling of a fire, probably coming from the smithy that backed up against the alley. A couple of warehouses boxed in the smithy. The youth could have gone anywhere.

He turned away. His job was to follow the election, not chase men who had a clear right to go wherever they wanted. If it had been Prince Moss, he had reason not to greet Charles after the events of last summer. Charles and his friends had hoped that Miss Jaggers and her swain had left England entirely, but they were not wanted for any crimes.

He returned to his stone perch. Two local voters were carrying the fallen man from the crowd into one of the houses on the left side of the square, probably a doctor's office. The constables were standing next to the horsemen who had remained in the square, keeping a vigilant eye on them.

Wilfred Poor had surrendered his gun into the high sheriff's hand. He gave an anguished cry, that of a wounded animal, then swayed in his saddle, shaking.

"Why don't you go home, Wilfred," said Sheriff Maitland, not unkindly.

"I'll stay for the vote," the broken man said. "I want to make sure that blackguard doesn't win."

"Speech!" called a man from the crowd.

"Let's get onto business!" cried another.

The high sheriff cleared his throat and introduced the Brown candidate. Charles took rapid notes in his best-in-class shorthand, but the speech was nothing out of the ordinary. Protect the working man, keep trade free, expand the franchise. All the usual sort of things, customized to the town's interests.

The less than enthusiastic reception made Charles concerned for Mr. Cecil's success. Then Sir Augustus was introduced as the Purple candidate. He spoke about protecting the town and the country from liberal encroachment, calling out several men in a humiliating sing-song, like a local schoolteacher he called a trumped-up peasant, and similar insults. The better dressed men in the crowd shouted "hear, hear" several times and Charles had the impression of a vicar speaking to his faithful, despite the insults.

His gaze drifted to Wilfred Poor, but despite the gun he'd arrived with, his temperament seemed far more even than that of Sir Augustus, who, as he came to the end of his speech, was red in the face, spittle flying. He finished with his fists in the air, the crowd shouting "Protect Eatanswill!" along with him.

The mayor walked to the center of the hustings and called for a vote. The back of Charles's neck prickled as Mr. Cecil's name was called. He glanced around, feeling like he was being watched by unseen eyes, but saw no one.

As expected, Mr. Cecil only received a faint round of applause. Mr. Poor wheeled his horse around, the dark circles under his eyes deepening as he saw how limited the support was for the liberal candidate. One of the other horsemen still present took his arm. Mr. Poor stared at his shotgun, but obviously decided he'd never have it returned now. The horsemen left the square at a sedate walk while the high sheriff called Sir Augustus's name.

Charles winced in disgust as the crowd of men surrounding the platform called their support. No need for this election to move to the polls. Sir Augustus had won easily, returning a Whig to Parliament for 1836.

Charles walked into the tobacconist's shop to buy a cigar as soon as the proprietor entered from the square. He asked the man for a brief history of Wilfred Poor, and soon had an earful of his family's mistreatment by the Smirkes. Dead wife, missing daughter, hand-wringing old mother who had quite lost her senses in despair.

Not twenty minutes later, Charles walked to the coaching inn at the edge of the main road, so he could catch the stage back to London to file his report. His editors would be pleased by his article, if not by the election's outcome.

"Well done. It's so pretty, Kate," said Mary Hogarth, admiring the blond lace decorating the neckline of her sister's new evening gown. "I can't believe this silk was second-hand."

Kate spread out the skirt made of spotless, unsnagged silk. "It's lucky we visited Reuben Solomon's stall that day. I'll bet you this dress was only worn once. A wine stain down the front and havers, off it goes to the old clothes man."

"It must be pleasant to be so wealthy." Mary pinched her cheeks to bring color into them.

Kate followed suit. "Wealth comes with its own burdens. I shall like keeping our little suite of rooms with just you to help me." Charles had agreed they would add Mary to his household after they wed, assuming Mother could spare her, which would make up a foursome then, since his brother Fred lived with him, too.

"It will be a treat," Mary agreed.

The sisters talked about their neighbors while they dressed for the party. It wasn't often they were invited to an evening at a titled lady's home. In fact, they had only become acquainted with their neighbor at Lugoson House across the orchard one year before, when they had heard screams during their Epiphany Night party.

That had been the night Kate met Charles, then a new parliamentary reporter working for John Black and her father at the *Morning* and *Evening Chronicle* respectively. Little had she realized as they stood vigil in the room of dying Christiana Lugoson that she would fall so deeply in love with him less than two months later.

Both of Kate's parents and their parents before them had traveled in distinguished literary circles, first in Edinburgh and now in London, but with someone like Charles joining the family, they had acquired new status and important friends. Charles had a brilliant future ahead of him and Kate could scarcely believe she was the wife he had chosen. He had promised they would wed in the spring. In a few weeks, they would ask for the banns to be called at St. Luke's down the street. Soon, she would be his and he, hers.

The door rattled, then opened. Georgina, eight years old and bursting with self-importance, announced, "Charles is down-stairs and everyone is ready to leave." They followed Georgina out of the room the sisters shared, excepting little Helen, and went down to the dining room where the family always gathered.

When Kate walked into the dining room and saw the thick dark locks, bright hazel eyes, and full lips of her fiancé, her face went so hot that her cheeks reddened of their own accord. She drank in the sight of him.

He spotted her and sketched a bow. She curtsied with a laugh, and then he touched her hand. A tremor went through her at the press of his flesh to hers. She could scarcely wait for spring.

Her mother sorted the older from the younger children with a no-nonsense air, then her father led the way to the front door and down to the street. Kate held Charles's arm on the pavement, even though she was in no danger of slipping. The rain had held off, though the air was bitter cold. Conveyances rolled by on the street, out of sight, holding other revelers.

Mary, on the other hand, stayed close to her mother. Kate knew she feared giving Fred, a year younger, too much attention. Fred had tender feelings for her sister, but she considered the young man a child, even though he had a position at a law firm now.

A liveried footman had the door of the renovated Elizabethan mansion open when they came up the steps, as another party was ahead of them. Kate recognized Lord and Lady Holland, quite the grandest personage she had had occasion to know.

The Hogarth and Dickens party passed through the doors behind the Hollands. The old-fashioned front hallway still had wood paneling, though Lady Lugoson was slowly modernizing the premises now that she'd committed to staying in England. Any visitor's eye went immediately to a double staircase directly ahead of them, but Lady Lugoson did much of her entertaining in the long drawing room that looked out over her formal garden.

After they left cloaks behind and the ladies changed shoes, the footman took them to the room's entrance and Panch, the venerable butler, announced each party in turn. Few paid attention as the room held quite a crush of people.

Still, Lord Lugoson, just sixteen and home from school, dashed up to greet them and seemed happy to meet Fred Dickens for the first time. He took the lad off to meet other youths.

Kate spotted Charles's fellow reporter, William Aga, standing next to the closer of the two fireplaces heating the room. Charles tilted his head at Kate and they disengaged from her family to greet the Agas.

Kate's father did not like Julie Aga, William's wife, who had once trod the boards and tended to create complications. But Kate and Julie were often thrown into each other's company and had come to terms.

"Excellent reporting," William exclaimed, thumping Charles on the back as soon as he was close. William, tall and athletic, had a ready smile that everyone responded to. His reporting focused on crime for the *Chronicle*. Julie, red-haired and lovely, scarcely showing her pregnancy yet, took Kate's hand and squeezed, her eyes dancing merrily as she took in the new gown.

"Part of your trousseau?"

"No," Kate said, blushing. "But I am working on that."

Lady Lugoson, an ethereal blonde, approached them on the arm of her baronet fiancé, the coroner Sir Silas Laurie. Her gown was cut much lower on the bosom than Kate's, and had few decorations. The beauty lay in the perfection of the best black silk, with a white silk and lace underskirt. Kate saw Charles's gaze dart over the gown, then he inclined his head.

"I read your latest article, Charles," Sir Silas said. "Very dynamic. I wonder that your Mr. Poor did not assassinate Sir Augustus right at the hustings, given the fervor of your descriptions."

"Sir Augustus is dreadful," Lady Lugoson interjected with a toss of her head. She had been a political hostess while her first husband had been alive. "How unfortunate it is that he won the election."

"Do you know him well?" Charles asked. "He is a conservative."

"Sadly, he was a friend of my late husband." Lady Lugoson's soft mouth turned down. "They were at school together and remained close."

Kate winced. Everyone knew the late Lord Lugoson had been an evil seducer, with just enough charisma to charm the families of his victims. The future sounded bleak for that Mr. Poor's daughter. The shotgun-wielding assailant might be correct in his assumption that Sir Augustus had taken her. "Such dangers you find yourself in," she murmured to Charles.

"Have done," Charles said with a chuckle. "There were hundreds of men in the square, and not a few women and children. I was nowhere near the gun."

As her father came alongside Kate, William said, "I should report on the missing girl for the newspaper. Maybe I can find her."

Her father cleared his throat. "We couldnae print the story. We may be a liberal paper, but that is reaching too far even for us."

Julie frowned. "What can be done to help the unfortunate girl?"

"Nothing until she is located," Kate rejoined. "I wonder if Sir Augustus will bring her to London?"

Charles's head felt a bit dim the next morning, the possible consequence of too much cigar smoke and rum punch at the

Epiphany party. It had been a jolly night, however, and unlike the previous year, no one had died.

He arrived at the *Morning Chronicle* newsroom at 332 Strand almost on time the next morning. After greeting his fellow reporters, he found a messy pile of correspondence on his desk. The letters included an offer of work at an inferior newspaper, a letter from a Member of Parliament thanking Charles for quoting his speech properly, and a note from William Harrison Ainsworth, inviting him around for dinner that night.

He ignored the rest of the pile and dipped his pen into his ink pot to scrawl a note at the bottom of the note, expressing his regret that he could not attend dinner with the popular novelist. He suggested he reschedule for some time next week. That night, he and Kate were promised to a Member of Parliament's dinner party.

Charles blotted the note and sealed it up, then set it aside for one of the office boys to send. Tom Beard, who had helped him procure this job two autumns ago, winked at Charles as he passed by. Charles watched his friend until he was half turned around.

"Hate mail," William Aga remarked, tossing down a letter and pushing his chair backward until it bumped against Charles's chair.

"From who?" Charles asked, extricating his legs from the position they'd become tangled in.

"Newgate Prison," William said with a shake of his head. "You would think a prisoner would better spend his money on lawyers than complaining to members of the press."

"I have nothing so exciting," Charles said, reorienting his chair before flipping through the rest of his pile. He spotted a very fine piece of linen note paper, addressed to Charles Dickens, Esq. The seal was so large it might have covered a gold guinea, as some people did to send funds to relatives. "I may have spoken too quickly."

William leaned over the letter, exposing Charles's olfactory senses to the pomade separating his friend's tawny curls. He poked his ink-stained finger on an emblem centered on the seal. "This is from the Lightning Club."

Charles sat back, then bent forward again. He didn't know what to do with his hands. His fingers danced nervously on his thighs. "The Lightning Club? You don't think I'm being offered a membership, do you?"

Connect with U s

Visit us online at
KensingtonBooks.com
to read more from your favorite authors, see books
by series, view reading group guides, and more.

for sneak peeks, chances to win books and prize packs,
and to share your thoughts with other readers.

f **𝕏**

facebook.com/kensingtonpublishing
twitter.com/kensingtonbooks

Tell us what you think!

To share your thoughts, submit a review,
or sign up for our eNewsletters, please visit:
KensingtonBooks.com/TellUs.